Before the
FULL MOON
Rises

Book 1 of the Chronicles of the Secret Prince

M.J. Bell

Cover art by Aria Keehn

Interior format by The Killion Group
http://thekilliongroupinc.com

Thank you.

Dedication

For Daniel, my inspiration, my guide

And for Connor, Brendan, Benjamin, Samuel, Sofia.
Ethan, and Joseph, the lights of my life

Prologue

September

Yellow and blue flames danced in the fire pit at the center of the cave, silhouetting the dark grotesque shape hunched in the corner and casting an unearthly shadow on the wall as the creature drew with a stick in the dirt. After several minutes the stick stilled and the beast squinted at his work. With a low growl, he threw the stick to the ground and swiped a portion of the scribble away with his huge hairy arm. No matter how he shuffled things around, the results continued to weigh heavily on one factor. That concerned him.

He unfolded his legs and stood, his head coming within inches of touching the high ceiling. *Where is the fool?* he thought, expecting to have received news by now.

At that very moment, as if summoned by his thoughts, a gigantic black wolf appeared in the cave entrance.

"Master Grossard," Rellik, the wolf, said in a gravelly voice as he respectfully bowed his head.

The beast turned and focused his black eyes in the dim firelight.

Rellik remained at the entrance; his senses heightened as he tried to decipher his master's mood. Sniffing the air, the wolf took a few cautious steps forward. He had made a significant discovery in the lower realm—an unexpected development that could affect the plan—and he knew Grossard was not one for surprises.

Sensing Rellik's hesitation, Grossard vanished from his spot with a small pop and instantaneously reappeared in front of the wolf.

Grabbing Rellik by the throat, he lifted the wolf off the ground until they were nose to nose.

"Is it done? Did you secure the woman?" asked Grossard, exposing his sharp, saw-like teeth as he spoke.

"Y-yes, Master, j-just as you asked," Rellik replied between gasps for breath.

Grossard looked into Rellik's eyes and a semblance of a smile spread across his grotesque features. "Finally!" he exclaimed. "Everything is in place. Nothing can stop me now."

"Ye-yes, Ma-master," Rellik croaked, struggling to escape the steel grip.

Grossard grunted and released the wolf, his smile remaining in place as he walked back to the fire pit. Rellik scrambled backward as swiftly as possible, putting as much distance as he could between himself and the monster before broaching the subject of his discovery.

"Master, there is one more thing."

Grossard's head snapped around at Rellik's tone, his eyes, black as onyx, glowing through the smoke of the fire.

"The woman ... has a son," Rellik stammered, the last words coming out in a mere whisper.

Grossard glared at Rellik for a moment, letting the words sink in before he walked around to the other side of the pit. Reaching into the flames, he picked up a burning branch and carefully studied it, showing no sign of pain as the flames licked at his hand.

"A boy, you say?" he asked in a surprisingly calm tone.

"Yes," Rellik replied, "... a young boy. I was unaware of his existence until I took the woman."

"Humph. A child from the lower realm is of no concern to me. Why are you bothering me with this now?"

"The ... er ... boy is ... he is the king's son," Rellik said, taking another step backward.

Grossard appeared calm. It was only a small twitch in his jaw that gave evidence to his simmering anger. "I've heard no news of Oseron being a father."

"No, Master, no one knows. The woman left the realm without

telling anyone she was with child and she's had no communication with Them since. The king himself wasn't even aware of the birth."

"And what makes you think this boy is Oseron's?"

"When I sensed the woman was hiding something, I used the charm you provided. She had no choice but to tell me the truth."

"I see." Grossard thought for a moment. "But you say They have no knowledge of this child?"

Rellik nodded, but when he saw Grossard's brow rise in question he realized his error and hurriedly added, "No... no knowledge."

Grossard's lips curled into a grotesque smile once again. "Ha! What I would have given to see Oseron's face when you delivered his son to the tower." When Rellik didn't join in and laugh along with him, Grossard's smile faded. "You *did* put the boy in the cell along with the others, did you not?"

Rellik cleared his throat. "Um, no ... not exactly, Master. I was unable to get to the boy. He wasn't with the woman when I found her. By the time I learned of him there was no time left. The gateway was about to close."

Grossard visibly tensed and Rellik recoiled and hurried on. "But I ... um ... the boy was not brought up in the ways of the Ancients. The woman vowed he was never told of his father or anything of our world, and she was under the effect of the charm so she couldn't have lied. The boy knows nothing of Them, and They know nothing of him."

Grossard's fiery gaze bored into Rellik. "So let me see if I understand you correctly. You say this boy is still free in the new country?"

Rellik nodded his head. "Yes, Master."

"You left him there? Oseron's son?"

"I had no choice," Rellik replied in defense.

Grossard's brow drew together in concentration as he paced back and forth, studying the burning branch he still held in his hand. "If the boy truly knows nothing of the high realm, he'll not understand why his mother was taken, or by whom for that matter," Grossard voiced his thoughts out loud after a lengthy pause. "*If* that is the case, there's no possible way he could help Them, as long as he remains unaware and in the lower realm." His words trailed off.

The room grew silent again as Grossard mulled over his thoughts.

"It's also highly unlikely he would be able to discover the location of the gateway on his own. Even if he did, he wouldn't be able to pass through from the new world until the eve of the equinox. By then it will be too late," Grossard continued.

"Yes, yes … that was my thinking too," Rellik agreed.

Grossard stared at the burning branch, his brow knitted in deep thought as Rellik stood motionless by the entrance, nervous sweat running into his eyes. Then without warning, Grossard turned and heaved the branch. It whizzed through the air and barely missed Rellik's head before it smacked into the wall behind in an explosion of burning embers that rained down onto the wolf's back. With a loud yelp, Rellik shook fiercely to dislodge the tiny particles that were quickly burning through to his skin.

"Let me make myself perfectly clear, and make no mistake about it," Grossard ground out through bared teeth. "I have waited too long for this moment. If your incompetence costs me the crown, I guarantee you will regret the day you were born, and so will your family."

Rellik's muscles quivered, but his eyes didn't drop from Grossard's intense glare.

"You say the boy knows nothing of Their world. I'm not willing to risk the chance you're wrong," Grossard added. "Go and keep watch on the old woman's house. She is Their link. If the child does arrive, bring him to me immediately before They discover who he is."

Grossard's eyes drilled into Rellik to reinforce his point. "Have you told anyone else about this boy?"

"No one, Master."

"Well, at least you did something right. Make sure you keep it that way and you might still live."

"Of course, Master."

Grossard turned back to the fire, contemplating how the boy's appearance might impede his plans. After several minutes, he heard a shuffling sound at the entrance and looked over his shoulder to find Rellik still standing there.

"What are you standing there for? Did I not just tell you to *go!*" Grossard growled, making a threatening move toward the wolf.

Rellik jumped and nearly backed into the wall in his haste to retreat. As he cleared the doorway of the cave, Grossard yelled after him.

"You know what will happen if you fail me, Rellik!"

Bowing his head once more, Rellik turned and ran into the fog that was hanging low over the shoreline outside the cave. Smoke rose from a lingering ember stuck in his coat as he climbed onto the rocks and started his ascent up the side of the cliff.

Chapter 1

May

Deston Lespérance held his breath and lifted the window up another inch, raising it ever so slowly to keep it from squeaking. In all the time he had spent devising his plan to run away he never once thought about the window. He cursed under his breath for his stupidity. If anyone in the house heard the noise, he'd be caught for sure.

Checking his watch for the tenth time, he pushed the window up once more, finally getting it open enough to squeeze through. After sucking in a big gulp of air and blowing it out through his mouth, he shoved his backpack through the opening. He threw one last glance over his shoulder, then ducked under the windowsill and climbed out onto the roof of the back room addition. Time was running out, but this was one part of the escape plan he couldn't rush.

He warily scooted a few inches away from the window and braved a glance at the lawn below. The dried, yellow grass wavered before his eyes and his stomach pitched violently. He hurriedly scrambled backward to the safety of the window ledge, his face drained of all color.

Deston hated heights. He had for as long as he could remember. It was one of many things he'd been teased about over the course of his life. Even back in grade school he was the only one who couldn't climb to the top of the jungle gym without getting woozy. But that was then and this was now, and he wasn't going to let his fear take over. This was too important.

With white knuckles clutching the window frame, he dared another glance at the ground below. Sweat beaded on his forehead and an unwelcome picture of Jeff lying in a heap on the grass flashed through his mind. Jeff, another foster child at the Motleys' foster home, was Deston's only ally—mostly because he disliked the Motleys as much as Deston did. Many a night he and Jeff would stay up late, planning how to sneak out of the house and run away. But in a single stroke of bad luck, Jeff broke his foot jumping off the roof in a test run, putting an end to his hopes of escaping the *detention camp*—a term they both used for the foster home.

Deston pressed his lips together and squeezed his eyes shut, pushing the image of Jeff aside. *I'm not going to break anything. I'm going to make it out and disappear. They'll never find me.*

He'd been repeating this same affirmation for days, but he meant it now more than ever, because this was it—his last chance. If he didn't get away now, by tonight he would be on his way to France. He couldn't let that happen. His mother was somewhere in Pennsylvania and if he left before he found her, there would be no one out there looking for her.

Deston wiped the sweat from his forehead with the sleeve of his T-shirt and carefully felt his way to the edge of the roof, keeping his eyes focused on the neighbor's roofline instead of the ground below. He threw his backpack over the side and rolled onto his stomach, inching his body down until his legs dangled off the edge. As his fingertips gripped the eave, he closed his eyes and pictured his mom's face. Then he held his breath, counted to three, and let go.

His feet hit the ground first, then his butt, and in the next instant he was flat on his back, staring up at the blue sky. He blinked into the sun as the realization he survived sank in. Cautiously, he lifted his right arm, then his left, and then each leg to assess the damage. Again, to his utter amazement, all his limbs moved as they should.

"Yes," he whispered, holding back the loud cheer he wanted to scream out. Once he was free and clear of the detention camp, then he would celebrate.

He sat up slowly and reached for his ball cap, still in a bit of a daze. His hand trembled as he placed the cap on his head, but he felt better than he had in a long time. The hardest part was over, and just thinking about being free sent another rush of adrenaline surging into his veins.

Deston gingerly pushed himself to his feet and winced as a twinge of pain shot through his left ankle. He lifted his foot and rotated it in the air to assess the damage before setting it back down. It was definitely tender and could possibly be a sprain, but he'd come too far to let it stop him.

He gritted his teeth as he grabbed his backpack, bent low—the way he'd seen commandos do in the movies—and limped up the side of the house. When he reached the front, he paused and peeked around the corner. The yard was empty and there was a clear shot over to the neighbor's unruly junipers. A smile spread across his face, followed by a soft chuckle as he imagined Mrs. Storm, his caseworker from the Welfare Department, receiving the news he was gone. It would almost be worth sticking around to see that—almost.

Deston was not a fan of Mrs. Storm. She had come into his life shortly after his mother, Joliet, mysteriously disappeared, and she immediately took charge like a bull running through the streets of Pamplona. Her first order of business had been to yank him out of Mark's house, his one and only friend, where he'd been staying since he had no one else to turn to. She had insisted it would be much better for him if he lived with the Motley's—a real foster family. She couldn't have been more wrong.

If that wasn't enough, she continued to meddle in his life until she dug up some so-called relative, Nicolette Jolicoeur. Deston had never heard his mother mention the name before, but this Nicolette was supposedly Joliet's cousin. Mrs. Storm then wasted no time making arrangements to ship him off to France to live with this relative he didn't know. And being he was only fourteen, he had no say whatsoever in the decision. As far as Deston was concerned, Mrs. Storm had single-handedly ruined his life, which was why he didn't mind her suffering a little grief of her own.

Deston glanced behind him to make sure he was still in the clear. He then darted out from behind the corner of the house. With his eyes fixed on his target he didn't see the dark figure appear out of nowhere. The next thing he knew, something hit him hard and knocked him off his feet.

"What the ff…" The rest of Deston's words faded out as he pushed his ball cap back and looked up into the acne-covered face of Larry Motley, who had his hands on his hips and a triumphant smirk on his face.

"Where do you think you're going, butthead?" Larry jeered.

Deston gawked in disbelief. Of all the people to run into, why did it have to be Larry? As the Motleys' only biological child, and self-appointed lord and master of the household, Larry took delight in torturing any foster child who had the misfortune of being placed in their home. He was a bully just like the ones Deston had endured for years at school before he learned kung fu. Deston's life changed after that, because it seemed he had a natural ability for the sport and earned the first of his three black belts in record time. But even with all the training, Deston never lost his animosity for bullies, and for Larry in particular, who took an immediate aversion to Deston.

For eight months, Larry had done everything in his power to make Deston's life a living hell, but now as the bully stood between him and freedom, Deston's loathing of him peaked to a whole new level.

"You know the next time you want to sneak out of the house, I suggest you not go and tromp all over the roof," Larry snickered.

A thousand thoughts of how he could hurt Larry plowed through Deston's mind, but time was precious and he knew he could outrun him just as easily as fight him. However, as he scrambled to his feet, Mrs. Motley and Mrs. Storm came out the front door.

"Here he is, Mommy!" Larry beamed, grabbing hold of Deston's arm before he could make a move.

Mrs. Motley's pinched face puckered even more than usual as she turned her head. "Oh my, Deston, I thought you were up in your room." Realizing that might sound as if she didn't know what was going on with her foster child, she quickly added. "I'm glad you're here. It's time for you to go. Time does fly by, you know, and we certainly must keep to our schedule, now mustn't we?"

Mrs. Motley's gaze moved to Larry and her face lit up as if she were in the presence of an angel. "Cupcake, would you run up and get Deston's other bags, while we say our goodbyes? Pwetty pwease?" she said in the baby voice she always used when talking to her only child—the voice that made Deston want to gag every time he heard it.

Any other time Larry would have passed the task off to one of the other foster kids, but not this time. A wide grin nearly split his face in two at the look of defeat on Deston's face and he gleefully pushed by Deston, giving Deston's arm one last extra hard pinch to make sure there would be a nice bruise to remember him by.

Mrs. Motley, oblivious as always, continued jabbering away at Mrs. Storm, as she picked up Deston's backpack and ushered him toward the waiting car. Mrs. Storm, huffing along behind, tried to keep up, bobbing her head instead of answering, to conserve her breath.

At the car, Mrs. Motley stood back all prim and proper, her hands folded in front of her—a perfect imitation of the saint she imagined herself to be. Her sharp, pointed face and puckered lips made the attempt to smile, but it was forced and never reached her eyes.

"It's been so nice having you stay with us, Deston, dear," she said for Mrs. Storm's benefit. "You're such a fine, young man. But I'm sure you're anxious to reconnect with your own family." She shook her head and rolled her eyes to the heavens. "I must say, I still can't believe you're going to France ... how exciting!" She let out a squeak of feigned excitement, then heaved a heavy sigh. "If only I were so lucky. I have always dreamed of going across the pond, you know."

She beamed again as Larry appeared in the doorway, but Larry's eyes were on Deston, making sure Deston was watching his bags being dragged through the mud.

"Maybe someday Larry and I can come visit you. We could have our own little family reunion. Won't that be wonderful, dear?" she said, putting her arm around Larry's shoulders as he stepped up beside her.

Deston tuned her out in self-defense minutes after she

started talking, as her voice had the same effect on him as fingernails scraping across a blackboard. His thoughts turned to his mother and he wondered how she would ever find him when she came back. He couldn't imagine her thinking to look for him in France. That thought brought back his previous misgivings about the timing of this so-called cousin's appearance. For his whole life there had been just him and his mother, and Joliet had told him more than once that they were all alone in this world. So why would this relative wait until now to show up?

"Deston, did you hear me?" Mrs. Storm said, breaking into his thoughts. "Tell Mrs. Motley thank you for all that she has done for you."

Deston rolled his eyes. All Mrs. Motley and Larry had ever done was make his life miserable. An uncomfortable pause followed before Mrs. Storm squeezed his arm, making it clear she expected him to reply accordingly. He jerked his arm away in response and glanced up at the determined frown on her face. With a defeated sigh, he grudgingly mumbled, "Thanks," and climbed into the backseat of the car, without looking at the Motleys again.

Mrs. Storm flushed with embarrassment and gave Mrs. Motley an apologetic smile before turning and stuffing her bulk into the passenger's side, as the driver loaded Deston's bags into the trunk. Grabbing hold of the back of the seat, she heaved herself around and gave Deston a stern look.

"That was very rude, young man, but I will overlook it this time because I know you're upset. I understand it's hard for you to accept your mother is gone forever, but you have to realize facts are facts and no amount of wishing is going to bring her back."

Deston had had this same conversation with Mrs. Storm and the police many times over the past months. Squaring his jaw, he glared at her, but it had little effect and she prattled on.

"Her car went into the creek, for heaven's sake. Teams of men and women searched for days and found no traces of her exiting the water. The authorities have done all they can and I'm sorry to say, but you're going to have to accept that sometimes bad things happen to good people." She paused for him to reply, but he remained silent. "You've made it perfectly clear you don't want to go to France, but as I've already explained multiple times, your cousin is the only living relative I could find. And this really is for the best." Her eyes softened. "I'm sure it won't be as bad as you think ... you'll see."

Deston lowered his eyes and stared at his lap, wishing they would all just leave him alone and let him live his own life. But she went on and he realized his bad luck wasn't going to end any time soon.

"I almost forget to tell you, I received a lovely letter from your cousin a few days ago. She sounds very nice and extremely anxious for you to arrive," she said, trying unsuccessfully to ease his misery. When he didn't respond she shook her head. "I'm sorry, but your options are limited. You're old enough to understand the State can't continue to care for you once we find a relative who is willing to do so. I would think you'd be a little more grateful. At least you have someone who wants you. Many children don't, you know."

Deston scrunched farther down into the seat. He didn't care about other children at the moment. He didn't care about his cousin, either. The only thing he cared about was going home, but he knew there was no chance of that happening.

"Oh, come on. It's not so bad. Think of it as a great adventure—an adventure into an unknown foreign land just like the first explorers," Mrs. Storm added in one last attempt to cheer him up. But Deston had already shut her out.

With a sigh, she turned back to the front and signaled for the driver to go. He started the car and threw it into reverse. As the car started to back out, another car pulled up in front of the house and a tall, skinny boy with shaggy, black hair jumped out. It was Mark.

"I asked Mom to drive me over so I could say goodbye," Mark said in a rush, skidding to a stop beside Deston's window.

Deston looked up at Mrs. Storm with pleading eyes, hoping she would let him get out and talk with his friend one last time.

She checked her watch and nodded her head. "Keep it short. We don't want you to miss your plane."

Without hesitating, Deston threw the door open and scrambled out of the car. Together the two boys walked away in silence.

"So I guess you didn't make it out, huh?" Mark asked when they were safely out of the hearing range of the adults.

"Larry caught me," Deston sighed.

"Ah man, I had a feeling he would find some way to screw with you again. He's such an a-hole. I wonder how he figured out what was going on? I didn't think he had enough brains," Mark added in a weak attempt at humor, but neither he nor Deston thought the situation very funny.

Not knowing what else to say, Mark exclaimed, "This sucks!"

"Yeah, it does."

They walked to the end of the sidewalk.

"So listen dude, I promise I'll get him back for you. Actually, I've already got it planned out. You 'member those pictures we took of him—the ones where he's practicing his kissing on the mirror?" Sure of the answer he hurried on. "I've already made a couple dozen copies of them, and Matt knows this kid who goes to Larry's school. He said he'd hang them around for us. Can you just imagine? I wish I could be there. He's never going to live it down."

The thought of the humiliation the pictures would cause Larry brought a brief smile to each of the boys' faces, but it didn't last.

"So you really have to go, huh?" said Mark.

"Yeah, it looks that way." Deston hung his head.

"Is there anything I can do?"

"Nah, it's too late."

They stood in silence a few seconds more until Mrs. Storm stuck her head out the window and cleared her throat loudly to signal it was time to go. Deston looked over his shoulder and back at Mark.

"Well, I—"

"Oh, wait!" Mark cut him off. "I almost forgot. Here, this is for you." He shoved a wad of tissue paper tied with string into Deston's hand.

As Deston tore into the paper, his eyes grew wide. "Dude, your pocketknife? No way!"

Mark had received the pocketknife for his birthday a month earlier and Deston had thought it was the coolest thing he'd ever seen. The knife was loaded with an array of special attachments, such as a penlight, a magnifying glass, a compass, and even an extra saw blade. Deston had been saving his allowance to get one, but time had run out before he had the chance to accumulate enough cash.

Deston looked up, his face showing his shock. "I … I can't take this. It's too much."

"Nah, go ahead. It's okay. I can always get another one. Besides, they probably don't have anything like that over there in France. And you need it more than me … 'cause, well you know, the compass can help you find your way home."

Deston felt a lump building in his throat. This was for real. He was going to France, and there was nothing he or Mark could do about it. For all intents and purposes, his life was over.

"Thanks," he whispered.

In response, Mark punched him in the shoulder and they bumped knuckles one last time before heading back to the car.

As Deston approached, Mark's mom stepped up and pulled him into a hug.

"It's going to be all right. France is a beautiful place. I'm sure you aren't going to mind it as much as you think. And you know where we are if you need us," she said, tears welling in her eyes as she kissed his forehead.

Deston nodded his head and climbed into the backseat, afraid if he said anything the tears he'd been holding back would begin to flow for real.

Mrs. Storm signaled the driver to go and Deston looked up at the ceiling, fighting the urge to jump out of the car.

"Hey," Mark yelled, running after the car as it started down the street. "I'll keep looking for your mom. So will Matt and Jeff. We'll find her. You'll see."

Deston turned to wave goodbye through the back window, but his gaze landed on Mrs. Motley and Larry. Seeing the victorious grin spread across Larry's face filled Deston with renewed loathing. He flipped back to the front as a bitter taste filled his mouth and a sinking feeling grew in the pit of his stomach.

Chapter 2

Ten and a half hours later, the wheels of US Air flight 758 touched down at Charles de Gaulle Airport in Paris, France. Deston pressed his face to the window, watching the ground crew scurry out of the way as the plane taxied to the gate. He had never flown before, but not even the thrill of his first flight could improve his mood. Throughout the long hours while everyone else on the plane slept, his mind continued to spin, rehashing every event that had taken place since the day Joliet vanished.

It was hard for him to believe it had only been eight months since he last saw her. She disappeared on September 10th, a day that was burned into his memory forever. She called him from work that morning before he left for school in a panic and told him not to leave the house or open the door for anyone. She was acting very bizarre and her voice trembled, which wasn't like her at all. Even weirder were the words she said to him right before her phone went dead.

"Deston, I love you so much. Nothing in this world or any other can ever break our bond. Don't ever forget that. You're my hero and I know you're strong. Don't let anyone tell you different. Just follow your dreams and your heart— they'll give you the answers."

She had never talked that way before and her strange words had haunted him ever since. The authorities believed she was dead, but he knew different. He was also sure her last words were some kind of clue to her whereabouts. But he couldn't follow the clues and find her if he was thousands of miles away. A feeling of hopelessness pressed down on him and the old resentment of not having a father emerged. He wouldn't be in this mess if he had one.

He knew, of course, he had a father somewhere. It was just that he had never met the man and knew nothing about him, except for his father's name and that Joliet had met him in France. Only once had Joliet ever talked about him and that was because Deston had found his birth certificate hidden between the pages of an old book and had asked her. The question had caught Joliet off guard and fear sprang to her eyes before she could look away. That reaction both surprised and alarmed Deston. Then, before he had a chance to tell her it didn't matter, she began to relate how she'd met his father in the forest by her childhood home. There was a definite strain in her voice when she talked about how much they loved each other, and to his horror, she broke down in the midst of the story and started to cry. It was the first time she had ever cried in front of him, and to this day, he could still remember the feeling of utter helplessness. Each of her tears was like a stab to his heart and he vowed right then to never ask about his father again.

Though Deston never asked about his father, it didn't stop him from thinking about him. At times when he stood in front of a mirror, he would play a game and try to imagine what his father looked like. In his musings, he decided he must look like the man, because he certainly didn't look anything like his mother.

Joliet Lespérance was tall and thin, with a perfect chiseled nose, high cheekbones, beautiful straight, black hair, and the most incredible violet eyes. More than once Deston wished he looked like her, but other than inheriting her eyes, there wasn't much resemblance between the two of them.

He'd give anything to have hair as straight and shiny as hers, instead of the straw-colored, unmanageable curls he was cursed with. He also wished he didn't have so many freckles or the stupid dimple that appeared in his right cheek every time he smiled. His ears also had an odd shape to them and kind of stuck out from his head, but at least he could hide them under his hair. He could not hide the thing he hated most about himself, however, and that was his height. Joliet kept telling him he needn't worry so much because tall genes were in his lineage.

"You'll eventually catch up, and on that day, I'll get to say I told you so," she used to say. But that was little consolation to him at the time since he stood a head shorter than everyone else in school.

Those words once again drifted through his head during the flight across the ocean and his heart felt like a lead weight in his chest. He was never going to get to hear her say "I told you so," and she would never get to see him grow taller. What had he done to deserve this?

As the plane crawled to a stop, Deston looked over at Barry Hill, sleeping in the seat beside him. Barry was the welfare worker assigned to escort him to France since Mrs. Storm didn't like to fly—although Deston guessed the real reason was because she couldn't fit into the seats.

He gently shook Barry's arm to wake him. Barry yawned, smacked his lips together, and snuggled deeper into the pillow, falling back to sleep while the other passengers filed out. As the last passenger walked up the aisle, Deston tapped him on the arm again.

"Sir, I think we need to get off."

Barry opened his eyes and looked around, momentarily disoriented. Then he bolted upright in his seat. "Where are we?" he grumbled.

"We're in Paris."

"We are?" Barry said, looking around in shock at the sight of the empty plane. "Why didn't you wake me sooner?"

As one of the flight attendants came down the aisle toward them, Barry jumped up, the crease of the pillow still marking his cheek.

"Is anything wrong, sir?" the woman asked, flashing her flight-attendant smile.

"No, no. I was just waiting for everyone to depart is all. Crowds, you know," Barry replied, shaking his head and rolling his eyes.

The attendant nodded her head knowingly, and continued to the back of the plane, as Barry pushed Deston in the opposite direction toward the exit. After claiming their luggage and making it through customs, they stepped through a set of double doors and into the terminal where a small crowd of people had congregated and were holding up signs with passenger's names neatly printed across them.

Deston came to an abrupt halt as the sea of signs waggled in front of his face, but Barry pushed the placards aside and stretched tall, searching for the right name. He'd volunteered for the assignment only to take advantage of a free vacation and the quicker he got rid of Deston, the more time he'd have to enjoy it.

As Deston perused the crowd, his attention was drawn to a torn piece of cardboard with the name, "Lespérance," scribbled across it in barely legible handwriting. "Mr. Hill," he said, tugging on Barry's jacket. Barry shook him off. "Mr. Hill?" Deston pulled on his jacket again.

Brushing Deston's hand aside, Barry snapped, "Just a minute! I'm trying..." His words stopped short as he too spotted the little old man holding the makeshift sign. He signaled the man with a quick wave and shouldered his way through the crowd, dragging Deston along with him.

Upon approaching the old man, Barry immediately lapsed into an animated, one-way conversation in French, as Deston hung back scrutinizing the stranger. His eyes traveled from the holes in the man's pants, to the dirty jacket at least three sizes too big, up to the old, tattered beret on the man's head. The same sinking feeling he had when he left the Motleys returned and he wondered what kind of place he was being sent to.

After several minutes, Barry seemed satisfied he'd found the right person and pulled a stack of forms from his bag that would release him from any further responsibility. He handed them to the old man to sign and turned back to Deston.

"Deston, this is Monsieur Bellew, who wishes to be called Peter. He'll be escorting you the rest of the way to Lieu de Merveille and to your cousin. I'm sure you won't give him any trouble," he said with an "if you know what's good for you" kind of look.

Once Peter handed the signed papers back, Barry briefly scanned them, gave a nod and stuffed them into his bag.

"Well then, I shall leave you in the hands of this very capable gentleman," he said to Deston. "Don't forget to write Mrs. Storm and let her know how you're getting along. She'll want to hear, I'm sure."

Peter stepped up, and without saying a word to Deston, took one of his bags and headed toward the exit, leaving Deston with his largest bag and backpack standing next to Barry. Barry didn't notice Peter had left, for at that moment two tall, leggy French girls in miniskirts and tight-fitting sweaters brushed by his arm. A slight leer lifted the corner of his mouth as he watched the girls walk into one of the terminal shops. He adjusted his tie, ran his hand through his hair, and looked down his nose at Deston.

"All right then, I'm sure you'll be very happy here with your new family. Good luck to you," he said, giving Deston a push toward the exit. Then without another word, he turned and hastily walked away in the direction the girls had gone.

Deston had no emotion on his face as he watched the last of his American ties blend into the sea of people. Then with a heavy sigh, he put the strap of his backpack over his shoulder, picked up his other bag, and walked through the exit doors.

As he stepped out into the exhaust fumes of the heavy traffic rushing back and forth in front of the terminal, he stopped dead in his tracks and squinted into the sun. Hundreds of people were scurrying every which way, pushing past one another to get to the lines of taxis and buses waiting at the curbs. It took him a long moment to locate Peter, who was trudging on without looking back. With a soft curse, he jogged to catch up.

Peter stopped next to a car that was so small Deston wasn't sure it even was an actual car. It looked more like a toy, and not much bigger than Mark's little sister's Barbie Jeep. He let out a short laugh, but quickly sobered as he realized the toy car, which didn't look at all safe, was what was going to take him to his cousin's.

The knot in his stomach tightened as he stood back and watched Peter tie his bag onto the roof. Once the bag was secure, Peter snatched the other out of Deston's hand and stuffed it into the small slot behind the seats. As Peter plodded around the car, he motioned for Deston to get into the passenger side, again without saying a word.

Tentatively, Deston bent and looked in the window. The seat was pushed way forward to accommodate the bag in the back, leaving very little leg room. As Peter slipped behind the wheel, Deston heaved another heavy sigh, opened the door and wedged himself into the seat. For the first time in his life, he was glad he was short, but even his small frame didn't help. His knees still touched the dashboard, and his backpack in his lap pressed uncomfortably into his chest.

Peter took no notice of Deston's discomfort, and offered no words of solace. He started the car and pulled out into traffic, ignoring the blasts of horns from other drivers. Deston gritted his teeth and stared straight ahead through the bug-splattered wind-shield, as cars darted in and out in front of them and horns blared on all sides.

Within a few kilometers, Deston was numb all over, and not just from the cramped quarters. The strain and long hours of the trip was taking a toll, and it was a blessing Peter was unsociable.

There was a time when Deston spoke fluent French, but that was long ago when he was a toddler and first learning to speak. French was, in fact, his first language. However, once he started school and the other children teased him about his heavy accent, that was the end of his French. Looking back, he realized it was a pretty stupid move on his part. However, at that time he had no way of knowing he would be living in France one day.

Stealing a sidelong glance at Peter, Deston again wondered who this strange little man was. Peter didn't have the same last name as Nicolette, but that didn't mean a thing. He could still be her husband. As Deston thought back, trying to recall what he had heard about Nicolette, it suddenly occurred to him he had no idea if she was married or if she had a family. He hadn't taken the time to learn anything about her, as he was planning to run away and didn't think he would ever meet her.

Deston pulled the bill of his cap down low over his brow so he could study Peter better without being obvious about it. Peter looked old—like in his eighties old. Deston frowned. He had assumed Nicolette would be around the same age as Joliet, in her early thirties, seeing as how they were cousins and all, but if Peter truly was her husband, then she must be older than he thought. As he looked at Peter, he wondered again if Nicolette was even his relative.

Deston's gaze moved down to Peter's dirty, tattered clothes and his nose wrinkled in distaste. *Maybe he looks like this because they don't have running water in their house.* He winced at the thought and rolled his eyes in misery. But there wasn't anything he could do about it, so he slumped against the door and turned his attention to the passing scenery to take his mind off his troubles.

The city of Paris was well behind them and the car was traveling along a tree lined highway. The monotony of the view was hypnotic. As he watched one fence post after another fly by, his eyes became gritty and his eyelids felt as if they were filled with lead weights. He hadn't slept one second on the flight over, which meant he had been up nearly twenty-four hours straight. He fought to stay awake, but there was no contest and within a few kilometers the battle was lost. As he slipped into a deep, sound sleep, the dream that had haunted him every night since Joliet's disappearance began to play.

Deston stood in a small, circular room with stone walls and no windows. The only light was coming from one flickering candle sitting next to a bowl of water on a table at the head of a cot that was pushed up against the wall. A man was lying on the cot, his face hidden by the shadows, and was so still it was hard to tell if he was dead or alive. There was also a woman in the room, dressed in a thin white robe with a hood pulled up over her bowed head. She sat slumped in a chair next to the cot, her fingers entwined with the man's. The man suddenly stirred and the woman's head jerked up. She reached for the cloth in the bowl, wrung it out, and laid it across his forehead as she muttered sweet words of love to him. He stilled at her touch, and she leaned down and gently kissed his lips.

Deston sensed the woman's sorrow, and for some unknown reason, he felt it was his fault. He had done something to cause her enormous pain, although he didn't understand how that could be. He didn't know either the man or woman and he had no reason to feel guilty.

As he tried to make sense of what was happening, the door to the room burst open. As a huge, dark shadow spread across the threshold, the air was sucked out and the room turned into a vacuum chamber. At that moment, Deston went from being an onlooker to a participant in the horror. He gasped and his hand went to his throat as he fell to his knees and struggled to fill his lungs. He looked up to see the cause of his dilemma, but the light from the hall distorted the doorway and all he could make out was a dark, bulky shadow. An overwhelming sense of evil and hatred, thick as soured milk, penetrated the room and Deston's fear paralyzed him.

Minutes go by and Deston's lungs were burning from the lack of air. He looked to the woman for help. To his surprise, she sat in the same position and calmly talked to the man just as she was before. The shadow didn't seem to have an effect on her, which confused Deston all the more.

As the shadow grew and creeped across the floor like a sinister, black fog, Deston opened his mouth to warn the woman, but nothing came out. He could neither speak nor move. All he could do was watch in horror as the shadow closed in on the couple. Then, right before it overtook them, the woman pushed back her hood and looked up. At the sight of his mother's violet eyes, Deston reared back. Joliet smiled sadly in return, seemingly not at all surprised to see him. Then her eyes filled with tears and she softly called out his name.

Chapter 3

Deston woke with a start at the sound of a slamming door. His heart raced and he was drenched in a cold sweat, as he was each time he awoke from the dream. He rubbed the sleep from his eyes and looked up to see an old woman hobbling down the front steps of a small stone cottage. Neatly trimmed bushes and tiny, white and yellow flowers formed a wide border along the foundation of the house. More multicolored flowers edged the walkway down to a small gate and wire fence that separated the house from a gravel driveway.

The old woman herself looked like a gypsy, complete with a stereotypical puff-sleeved, scooped-neck blouse tucked into a long, print skirt with an apron tied over it. Her round, wrinkled face was framed by a scarf, which covered her hair, except for a long gray braid that dangled over her shoulder almost to her waist. She wore two large gold hoops in each ear, and the sun reflected off the cluster of medallions around her neck.

The woman stopped to talk with Peter for a moment, pointing to a window in the upper level of the house, before making her way around to Deston's side of the car. As she approached, Deston unfolded his legs and stepped out, bracing himself with the door, as his legs were tingling and buzzing from the long ride in the cramped quarters.

He stood face to face with the woman, who was no more than a few inches taller than him. She was not at all what he expected and looked to be as old as Peter. But how she could be that old and be Joliet's cousin didn't make sense.

As Deston scrutinized Nicolette, she looked him over as well. She reached out, gently placing a hand on his cheek and smiled into his eyes. It wasn't just a surface smile like Mrs. Motley's, though. Her smile lit up her whole face, causing her wrinkles to fade and she instantly looked decades younger. Her violet eyes, just like his and Joliet's, sparkled with a youthful intensity, and her cheeks plumped out like two rosy balls.

"I have waited a long time to meet you, *mon garcon*. I was so afraid I would pass over before I had the chance," Nicolette spoke in a thick accent and her eyes were glassy with unshed tears. "You have the Lespérance eyes. Did you know that?"

Deston had never met anyone quite like this woman before. Her gaze hypnotized him and he couldn't move or think. And there was the strangest sensation inside his head as if she was dissecting all his thoughts and secrets. Her spell kept him completely captured until she blinked and stepped back an arm's length to look him over.

Disoriented and confused, Deston took hold of the car door with both hands to keep from falling. The silence pounded loudly in his ears, and his palms grew sweaty. He knew it was rude not to respond, but his mind was so scrambled he couldn't come up with anything to say. As the seconds ticked off and the pressure to say something rose, he finally blurted out the first thing that popped into his head. "You look like a gypsy."

As an amused look flashed across Nicolette's face, Deston's cheeks turned a bright pink and he dropped his eyes to the ground.

Nicolette laughed a loud, hearty laugh. "Pfew, so you think I look like a gypsy, eh? Did you know here in this country, calling someone a gypsy is considered an insult?" Waving the comment away with her hand, she continued, "But I know you did not mean it as such. *Non*, Deston, I am not a gypsy. I am Nicolette Jolicoeur, your *maman's* cousin. But I want you to call me NiNi, like all my friends do. *Oui?*"

Deston's cheeks were still hot as he looked up through his eyelashes. "Mom's never mentioned you. She told me her family was gone and only her and I were left."

"Ooooo, you poor *bébé*," NiNi said, a sad expression replacing her smile. "Such a shame you grew up not knowing your family. But as you see," she spread her arms wide, "I am here and very much alive. And there, you see?" She pointed over her shoulder at the cottage. "That house is where your maman grew up. We used to play together right out there in that meadow."

Her brow creased. "I do not know why Jolie would tell you such things as that, but ... well, it has been fifteen years. I guess she may have thought—" NiNi paused and shook the thought away. Looking back at Deston, her smile returned. "Did you know your maman wrote to me once, right before you were born? I still have the letter somewhere in the house. I will show it to you later. I never heard from her again after that one time." NiNi cocked her head, a pensive look in her eye. "So much time has passed," she sighed. "So much time wasted. I can see how she might think I was gone."

Deston stood up straighter, a belligerent look suddenly hardening his face. "My mom's not dead," he blurted out.

A soft light came to NiNi's eyes. "Oui, I know."

"Huh? You do? How?" Before she could answer, he hurried on, "If you really believe that, then you know I shouldn't be here. When Mom comes back she won't know where to find me."

"Non, you are wrong in that, Deston," NiNi said, shaking her head. "Jolie will know exactly where you are. Trust me. And there is no other place she would want you to be right now, but here with me. I am all that is left of your maman's family. This is the safest place for you."

Deston stared into her smiling eyes. This woman was a perfect stranger, yet in an odd way he felt she understood him better than anyone else had in months. The fact she also believed his mother was still alive was an added bonus. He finally had someone on his side— someone who would listen. Maybe together they could find out what really happened. He smiled for the first time in weeks and as she smiled back, it suddenly occurred to him she was speaking English.

"Hey, you know English?"

"Oui, I do. Just between you and me, most French people speak English, although they do not always admit they do. I, on the other hand, am proud of my second language. My husband, Jean Pierre, God rest his soul, lived in the new country for over ten years. It was he who taught me much of the English, which has been very useful when the American tourists who come to visit the forest happen upon my little farm. I enjoy visiting with them. It helps make the days not so lonely."

NiNi brushed her hand over his cheek again, a sentimental look flickering across her face. She wanted so badly to throw her arms around him and never let go, but she was afraid he would think her a crazy old woman. As she stood there smiling into his eyes, the hairs on the back of her neck suddenly stood on end. Her body tensed and she wrenched her head around over her shoulder as if expecting to find someone behind her, but there was no one there.

"Come," NiNi said with a sudden urgency in her voice. "Let us go inside to talk." Taking hold of Deston's arm, she practically dragged him toward the house. "I made a special apple tart for you. I know growing boys are always hungry. And from what I hear, those flying contraptions have horrible food. Though I have never been on one myself, so I cannot say from experience," she added with a nervous laugh. "And let me tell you this, you will never get me on anything that flies through the air. These old bones require solid ground beneath them."

Deston looked up at the cottage as NiNi hustled him through the gate. It was a quaint two-story with a bright, purple door and green shutters on the windows. Some of the cement between the stones of the wall was dark and crumbling, showing its age, but mostly it looked well cared for and homey.

"Did you say Mom used to live here?"

"Oui. She was born right here in this house. My family and I lived on the other side of the meadow," NiNi said, pointing over her shoulder to the green field behind her.

"I moved into this house after your *grand-mère* crossed over. There was no one else to care for the place and I always did love this old house. After I married Jean Pierre we had many happy years here together and made many wonderful memories. For the last two years now, I have been all alone." She waved her hand in the air. "I cannot complain, though. My life has been full. I have only one disappointment in that I was never blessed with a child of my own. So you must see what a joy it is for me to find you. You are a godsend."

NiNi pulled Deston through the purple door and glanced hurriedly over her shoulder once more before slamming it shut and turning the key in the lock. With a relieved sigh, she proceeded down a long, narrow hall to a wide archway at the back of the house, towing Deston along with her.

As Deston walked through the archway into the mammoth kitchen that took up more than half of the house, he came to an abrupt halt. It was almost like stepping back several centuries in time. There was an electric light hanging down from the ceiling, but there were no electrical appliances, just a gigantic fireplace that was big enough for a full-grown man to walk into and not bump his head. A large iron pot hung over the fire grate and a square was cut out of the back wall for a baking oven. Next to the fireplace was a wood-burning cook stove. Next to it was a metal box on legs that looked like one of the old-fashioned iceboxes.

Deston's eyes traveled around the room, stopping at the long counter along the back wall and the hand-operated water pump attached at the end. NiNi saw him eyeing the pump and pointed to a large, stainless steel sink and faucet hidden in the corner at the other end of the counter.

"Jean Pierre put that in for me some five years ago. He was always trying to bring me into the twenty-first century," she chuckled. "I went along with some of it, but I would never let him take out my pump. I am an old woman after all, and what is that saying you Americans have? "A new dog does not learn old tricks?""

"You can't teach an old dog new tricks," Deston corrected, having heard Mark's grandmother use the same saying many times.

"Oui, oui! That is what I am, an old dog," she cackled. "But this," she gave the pump a loving pat, "this is part of the soul of the house. The kitchen would be sad without it, and so would I."

She hobbled over to the stove, motioning with her hand toward the large, oak plank table. "Sit," she instructed.

Deston, still extremely tired from the flight, happily obliged and scooted in on the bench while NiNi cut into the tart.

"I remember when your maman had to stand on a stool to reach the handle of that old pump," NiNi said as she joined him at the table and set a steaming slice of tart in front of him.

"Did you say you played with Mom when she was little?" Deston asked before shoveling a big bite into his mouth.

"Oui, our Jolie was a petite thing and the favorite of everyone in the family. But *mon dieu* was she full of mischief. She occasionally let me tag along with her, but mostly she preferred to wander the forest alone. I tried to follow her many times, but she was faster than a sprite, that one was, and she could lose me in the blink of an eye. One minute she was right there in front of me and the next ... poof, she was gone," NiNi laughed. "I admit I was somewhat of a pest back in those days, but I could not help myself. I adored her and wanted to be just like her."

Deston's eyes glazed over as he listened and tried to keep up. Clearly, his brain was not functioning, or else he was misunderstanding her accent, for NiNi would have already been a grown woman when his mother was a little girl.

NiNi laughed again, "Do you know she convinced me once she had found Merlyn's secret hideaway in the forest? She even told me she learned some of his magic. I remember one time when she was extra annoyed with me for something I had done, she warned me if I did not stop she would turn me into a duck!"

"Merlyn?" Deston's eyebrows shot up. He turned to look through the back screen door at the trees across the drive. "In that forest?"

NiNi waved her hand in dismissal, "Ack, that was our Jolie. She had a great imagination and even greater stories."

As Deston stared at the trees and thought about his mother growing up in this place, it occurred to him that if NiNi had been around when his mother was young, she had to know about his father. His father could even still be around these parts.

His eyes shined with hope as he turned back to NiNi. "Sooo ... um, you must have known my dad? Oseron LaForester?" he asked, trying hard to sound nonchalant.

NiNi's eyes opened wide in shock, but she instantly recovered. "Oseron? Where did you hear that name?"

"I found my birth certificate. That was the name listed on it. Mom told me she'd met him here in France, but that was all she ever said about him."

"Hmmm," NiNi nodded in understanding, the worry lines on

her forehead relaxing a bit. "Let me see. I ... er ... I do not recollect that name. I do not believe he is from around here," she added much too swiftly. Then, just as quickly, she changed the subject. "I can tell you this, it was a sad day for all of us when Jolie left for America. She was such a pretty thing. None of the rest of us girls stood a chance when Jolie was around. And truth be known, we were all a little jealous of her."

She stared across the room with a long-ago memory in her eyes and a strained smile frozen on her lips. After a moment she shook herself back and went on to tell him about the time a carnival came into town.

Deston listened the best he could, but with food in his stomach, his mind drifted into a cloud once again and his eyes began to droop. He wanted to hear everything about Joliet's younger days, but things were making less and less sense as NiNi went on with her story. Soon his head lulled to the side and his eyes closed without permission.

NiNi suddenly halted her rambling in mid-sentence as if someone had yelled at her to shut up. She looked over at Deston and with a knowing smile, patted his arm lovingly. "Ack, well, enough for today. There will be many days for us to talk and reminisce. Right now I think you need to rest. Come ... I will show you to your room. Oui?"

Deston gratefully followed her up a narrow flight of stairs to a small attic room, which was meticulously cleaned and arranged for him. The room's high ceiling came to a point in the middle and sloped down from there, following the roofline until there was no more than six feet between it and the floor at the sidewalls. A narrow box bed had been built into the short wall.

As soon as Deston saw the bed, he forgot about everything else and stumbled over to it like a zombie. He flung himself down without even taking off his shoes and was out before his head hit the pillow.

NiNi's heart ached as she lifted Deston's legs onto the bed and slipped his shoes off. "You poor bébé," she said, pulling the soft quilt over him. "I wondered how much Jolie would tell you of her life here. It does not surprise me she kept the truth from you. You are so young and innocent—too young to know of some things, and much too young to have to deal with them." She shook her head sadly. "But we do not always get to choose the timing of when our destiny calls."

NiNi brushed Deston's hair back and leaned down, planting a kiss on his forehead. She knew Joliet had given up much to protect him. She could only hope that sacrifice was not in vain. And now it was her turn to protect him, and only the Universe knew for sure if she was brave enough and strong enough to handle such an important job.

NiNi stood silently and watched Deston sleep for some time before turning and retracing her steps to the kitchen. She hobbled up to an old chest in the corner of the room and retrieved a worn, tattered bible from the drawer. It flipped open in her hand and she took a faded letter from between the yellowed pages. She didn't have to read it, for she knew the words by heart. She held it to her chest as a tear ran down her cheek and dripped off her chin.

Chapter 4

Deston opened his eyes and stared up at the familiar sight above his head—a midnight blue ceiling painted with the white stars and planets of the night sky in perfect astronomical order. His mom had painted it shortly after they moved into the house. For as long as he could remember, it was the last thing he saw at night before going to sleep and the first thing he saw in the morning upon awakening.

With a big yawn, he stretched and rolled to his side in contentment, pulling the quilt up under his chin.

Thank God it was only a bad dream.

He shivered as the disturbing images of the dream danced at the edge of his mind. As they lingered, he suddenly had an urge to see his mother. "Mom!" he said under his breath, rearing up and swinging his legs over the side of the bed. As soon as his feet touched the rough wooden floor instead of the braided rug of his room, his heart seized. It hadn't been a dream after all. It was all real.

Squeezing his eyes shut, Deston moaned and fell back on the bed. Tears clogged his throat and eyes, and despite his effort to hold them back, one escaped and ran down his cheek. He pressed the heels of his hands into his eyes as the events of the past few days slowly replayed in his head: Larry catching him before he could run away, the long flight to Paris, meeting Peter and NiNi—it all came back.

With the thought of NiNi, their conversation of the night before came to the forefront of his mind. Most of what had been said was still somewhat of a blur, and the bits and pieces he could remember were just as confusing as when he first heard them. He had obviously missed quite a lot, but as he tried to sort it out, his head began to throb.

Deston rubbed his temples to ease the ache and listened to NiNi humming and bustling about the kitchen below. All at once it occurred to him that it was highly unlikely he'd ever go home again. With that thought, his heart began to ache just as bad as his head. He blew a puff of breath to move the hair out of his eyes and let his gaze roam around the room. It was a small, but cheery space with no door, only stairs leading straight down to the kitchen.

He really wasn't ready to face NiNi again, but he knew he couldn't stay up in the room forever, and the building pressure in his bladder made it clear he wasn't going to be able to hold out much longer. With a groan, he pushed off the bed and silently tip-toed down the stairs, hoping to be inconspicuous enough to get by NiNi without her noticing him.

Even though he didn't make a sound, and NiNi was standing at the sink with her back to him, she called out before he was halfway down the stairs. "Well, if it isn't Rip Van Winkle! I was just about to go up and make sure you were still there and had not been carted off by one of Brocéliande's hungry wolves." She chuckled as she turned to face him. "You know, I do not believe I have ever known anyone who could sleep fourteen hours straight."

"Fourteen … no way!"

"The toilette is right through there," NiNi pointed to a small doorway behind the staircase as she moved to the stove.

Deston cast a questioning glance at her as he hurried to the door. It seemed she had once again read his mind and that was more than a little disconcerting.

As soon as Deston disappeared behind the door, NiNi set about preparing a plate of roasted chicken and a glass of milk for him. She was just placing them on the table when he emerged from the bathroom, his hair wet from trying to get it to lay flat. The heavenly aroma of food immediately hit him and his stomach answered angrily in protest. Until that moment he hadn't realized how hungry he was.

He made a mad dash for the table, almost colliding with NiNi on the way, and slid onto the bench. In record time, he gulped down a chicken leg and reached for another. "You mentioned wolves earlier. Are there really wolves living around here?" asked Deston, using the back of his hand to wipe the juice of the chicken from his chin.

"Oh, oui, wolves, foxes, deer, all kinds of animals live in the forest there," NiNi inclined her head toward the mass of trees a short distance behind the house as she handed him a napkin.

"Really?" Deston turned around and gazed through the screen door. "Have you actually seen any up close? I mean, do they ever come near the house?"

"Oui, occasionally. The animals used to be around a lot more, but not so much lately."

"Wow, that's so cool. I'd love to see a wolf up close. Maybe I could track one and find its den. I'm pretty good at tracking and—"

"Non, Deston! You are not to go into the forest. Not ever," NiNi cried out, cutting him off. "It is very dangerous, and not just because of the animals. You have no idea the kinds of hazards there are in that place. It is, how you say, *imprévisible?* Unprecedented … non, that is not right. It is, um … unpredictable. Oui, it is unpredictable, especially for someone like you. You are unfamiliar with it and could get lost, or worse."

Her voice trembled, but she went on. "You must listen to me and never go into the forest by yourself. I tell you it is not safe inside those trees. Do you understand?"

Deston was taken aback by her outburst. She acted like he was still a little kid, and he was almost fifteen. For a split second his defensive nature flared, but fizzled out just as fast as he realized it was only natural for her to be a little overprotective. After all, she had just met him and didn't know what he was capable of. He could understand that. Joliet was way overprotective at times too. Especially around the autumnal equinox when she would pack them up and take them to an old lighthouse off the coast of Maine. NiNi just needed some time to get to know him and then she would see he could take care of himself. He hoped she would anyway. In the meantime, he figured his life would be a whole lot easier if he just played along with her wishes.

"Yeah, sure" he replied with a shrug of his shoulders, but

before turning back, he stole another glance at the trees beyond the yard. As he did, he remembered something else NiNi had said the day before.

"You mentioned Merlyn yesterday. And something about Mom finding him, or did I dream that?"

NiNi nodded her head eagerly; relieved he had accepted her warning so easily and without a challenge. "Oui, our Jolie was an avid reader of the King Arthur tales."

"That's always been my favorite too. Mom used to tell me stories about him and Merlyn all the time," Deston exclaimed.

"That does not surprise me. But you know, here in these parts it is more than just a story. It is a real part of our lives because of Brocéliande." She tilted her head toward the door. "According to legend, Merlyn's fortress is hidden within the forest. Your maman used to spend hours in there searching for it when she was young."

Deston's brow furrowed. "Wait a minute, I don't understand. Camelot was in England."

"Oui, you are right. Camelot is in the British Isles. But this ..." She swept her arm around to the trees behind the house. "... is the Forest of Brocéliande where Merlyn came to retire. He thought he would find peace and quiet here, but what he actually found was Nimue. You've heard of Nimue, oui?"

Deston nodded and NiNi smiled.

"I bet you do not know that it was here in Brocéliande where Nimue enchanted Merlyn and trapped him in a tower of air bound by nine circles created from his own magic. Some say Merlyn is still trapped there, waiting for someone to release him. Others believe he died and is buried beneath two large slabs of stone in the middle of the forest."

"Really? Wow, I had no idea." Deston's eyes doubled in size.

"Of course, the forest has changed much since Merlyn's time. It is now about half the size it was in those days, maybe even less than that now. Sadly, civilization has taken over what nature spent centuries building," she added.

"Gawd, I can't believe Mom never said anything about growing up next to the forest where Merlyn once lived."

"She didn't?" NiNi's face suddenly fell as she realized in her attempt to distract him, she had inadvertently made the forest even more attractive. "Well, you know, it is just a silly old myth that has been passed down and distorted through time. I doubt there is much truth to the story."

She saw Deston's eyes gloss over with a far-a-way look and wrung her hands, trying to think of how to redirect his attention. "So … how was your bed? Did you sleep well?" she asked.

With his head full of thoughts of Merlyn's fortress, Deston didn't pay attention to what NiNi was asking and she had to repeat the question twice more. Finally, he absentmindedly answered without taking his eyes off the trees, "It was good."

Knowing she needed to draw Deston's attention away from the legend of Brocéliande, NiNi got up from the table and made as much noise as she could as she took a loaf of bread from the cooling oven, sliced it, and placed it and some butter on the table in front of him. As the luscious smell of the fresh bread drifted to his nose, he came back to the present and turned around to grab a slice.

"Was that Mom's room upstairs?" he asked as he chewed.

"Oui. It was. How did you know?"

"I just sorta figured. The ceiling is painted just like mine at home."

"Is that right?" NiNi sat down across the table from him. "So tell me about your home. This Pennsylvania," she prompted, jumping at the opportunity to steer the conversation to safer ground.

Deston wiped his mouth with the napkin. "There's not that much to tell. We lived in a small township in Montgomery County. We moved there from Boston when I was a baby. It's not far from Philadelphia, but Mom doesn't like big cities. She says she needs open spaces. She also likes to have a big garden and lots of flowers around her. She has flowers everywhere, kind of like you do." He took another bite. "Our house was not far from the woods, but they weren't nearly as big as your forest," he gestured to the trees over his shoulder. "We used to take walks in the trees a lot, me and Mom." He stopped to take a drink of milk to wash down the bread.

"What did you do for fun in this Montgomery County?" NiNi asked.

"Hmm, well, I had this friend, Mark, who lived down the road.

We hung out together sometimes." He thought for a moment. "And there was school and my kung fu classes. You know … just normal stuff."

He crammed another piece of bread in his mouth and licked his fingers, thinking about the home he had left behind. After a few minutes, he looked up at NiNi. "Why did Mom leave here?"

The question caught NiNi by surprise and it took her a moment to think of an appropriate answer. "I guess there was nothing to keep her here. Your grands-parents were gone, and she had always wanted to travel." She looked out the window. "I do wish she had not gone. I have missed her so terribly much," she sighed. "And I have often wondered over the years if she was happy in America."

"Yeah, of course she was" Deston snapped. "I mean … I guess she was. Why wouldn't she be?" he added in a softer tone.

NiNi shrugged her shoulders "I do not know. But I think it would be hard to move to a different country where you know no one and where even the language is different. I am not so brave as to do such a thing."

Her words hit home and Deston sobered. "Yeah, it's not a lot of fun." He looked down at the bread in his hand, which no longer looked appetizing.

NiNi noted the sadness in his voice and realized she had once again said the wrong thing. As she silently chastised herself for being an old fool, she remembered the gift she had made him. Turning to a cabinet beside the door, she removed a small object from the drawer.

"I have something for you," she said, holding out her hand. "This was your maman's. She gave it to me, but I know she would want you to have it."

Deston looked up at the beautifully carved wooden cross dangling at the end of a chain.

"Go ahead, put it on," NiNi coaxed. "Wear it beside your heart and your maman will be with you always."

Deston's eyes moved up to her face. "Why do you believe Mom's still alive?"

NiNi's violet eyes turned a darker shade as she struggled with an answer. "Jolie and I have a … how you say, *relation inhabituelle?*" She thought for a moment, but the right English word would not come to her. With a shrug of her shoulders, she added, "I know in here (she touched her heart) and in here (she touched her head) that Jolie is alive. I cannot explain it to you. I just know it is so."

Deston studied her for a moment. "Yeah, me too," he said softly and reached for the cross.

To his surprise, the wooden cross was heavier than it looked. He held it up in front of his face and examined the etched details, which were astoundingly beautiful. "This is really great. Thank you. I didn't get a chance to get anything of Mom's before I left home."

He ran his thumb over the intricate carving and turned the cross over. The back was smooth with only an inscription etched into the wood. He squinted, trying to read the writing, but it was written in a language he'd never seen before.

"What does this say?" he asked without looking up.

"Deliver us from evil," she replied with a small catch in her voice.

"Cool. …So this really was Mom's, huh?"

"Oui. It was her most favorite thing in the whole world. She never took it off until the night before she left for America when she gave it to me."

NiNi picked up the empty plate and took it to the sink. She hated lying to the boy. But what was one small, white lie if it helped keep him safe? She made a mental note to say an extra prayer that night, asking for forgiveness and that the lead-lined cross and small amount of ground St. John's wort and yarrow leaves she had pushed up inside the cavity would protect him.

She glanced over her shoulder as Deston put the chain over his head. A rush of apprehension swept through her. She shuddered and turned back to the window, looking out at the Forest of Brocéliande.

"Oh, Jolie, I will try to take good care of him until you return. But please do not be gone long this time. I am already an old woman and getting older every day. I do not know how much longer I will be around. I am afraid I will not be strong enough to protect him," she silently uttered.

Chapter 5

After Deston finished eating, he helped NiNi clean up the kitchen, and then went to his room to unpack his bags. He was feeling better than he had in months. He had tried so hard to keep from coming to France, but now he was glad he was here.

Walking to the window, he jumped up on the built-in seat and squinted into the sun. He pushed the pane up as far as it would go and leaned on the windowsill, letting the light breeze blow through his hair. The window, which was on the front of the house, looked out onto the gravel drive. Beyond that was a beautiful, lush, green meadow with thousands of lavender and yellow wild flowers scattered amongst the grasses. A short distance down the road, a lone figure worked on a large section of fence that had fallen down.

Deston's gaze moved to the horizon in search of the town and other houses. As far as his eye could see, there was nothing but blue sky, green grass, and trees, and no sign of another house. Leaning farther out the window, he turned his head toward the forest, which looked dark and closed off in comparison.

A shiver of excitement coursed through him as he thought about how close he was to the place where Merlyn had once lived. He fingered the cross around his neck and wondered if Joliet had really found the magician's fortress. He hoped so, because that would mean he might be able to find it too.

As he stared at the trees daydreaming, a soft voice broke through his thoughts.

"The key to finding your mother is in the forest," the voice said inside his head.

Startled by the intrusion, he jerked up and bumped the back of his head on the window. "Oww," he whispered. The phrase repeated and his brow creased as he rubbed the bump on his head. If only it was true. But how could the key to finding Joliet be in France when she vanished in America, thousands of miles away?

He sighed and tried to push the thought away, but it refused to go, and once again whispered the words to him. He put his hands over his ears, trying to get it to stop, but the voice wasn't coming through his ears.

Gawd, all this talk of Merlyn is starting to affect my sanity.

With a puff of air he blew the hair out of his eyes and looked back at the trees. Suddenly, his body tingled all over as if an electrical charge had passed through him. There was definitely something intriguing about the forest, and even if it wasn't the key to finding his mother, he still couldn't wait to explore it—if NiNi ever let him, that is.

A new spark of defiance flared within him as he recalled her outburst. It wasn't fair that he couldn't go into the forest, especially since it looked like there wasn't a whole lot else to do. Other than sit in the house all day with her. And how boring would that be? He would go crazy in a week for sure. Smoldering, he stared out at the trees. How was he going to prove to her he was responsible if she wouldn't give him a chance?

He closed his eyes, mulling over the problem, and just like that the answer popped into his head. It was actually so simple. All he had to do was sneak into the forest for a short time. When he came back safe and sound, NiNi would see he was perfectly capable of taking care of himself. His mind started reeling with the possibilities. The tricky part would be slipping away without her knowing. And that was important, because if she didn't know, she wouldn't worry and be mad. He squirmed on the seat as a plan settled in his head. He didn't like that he had to sneak around, but it really wouldn't hurt anyone and there was no other way to prove himself.

His heart pounded in anticipation as he jumped off the window seat and rushed to his bags. He grabbed out a clean T-shirt and hurriedly pulled it over his head. He stuffed the rest of his neatly folded clothes from the suitcase into several drawers of the chest, and stashed the empty suitcase in a small cupboard under the bed. He then grabbed his favorite baseball cap and casually strolled down the steps.

When he reached the bottom, NiNi, who was kneading bread dough at the counter, looked over her shoulder. "You are done unpacking already?"

"Oh … er … yeah. I don't really have that much stuff."

He fiddled with the napkins on the table for a second and then casually sauntered to the back door. "I was thinking maybe I'd go for a walk. You know, just to get a scope of things," Deston said indifferently, making sure his eye were averted from NiNi. Joliet always said she could see in his eyes when he was up to something, and he already sensed NiNi had that same ability.

"Deston," NiNi called out as his hand reached for the door-knob.

He jumped at the sound of his name and spun around, his guilt shining brightly on his face. NiNi's penetrating gaze swept over him, and Deston knew he was in trouble the second their eyes met and he couldn't look away. Just like the first time they met, he could feel her inside his head, as if she was rifling through his thoughts.

NiNi held his gaze for several seconds before she blinked and cleared her throat. "Actually, I was hoping you would give Peter a hand this afternoon. If you do not mind that is. Some deer broke down the fence last night. He is out there trying to put it back up all by himself."

Deston winced as she continued.

"He is not as young as he once was and I am sure he would appreciate help from a strong lad like you."

Damn! He was caught. "Oh … K," he replied, casting his eyes to the floor. Then, without thinking, he blurted out, "Is Peter your husband or something?"

NiNi let out a hearty laugh, breaking the tension. "Good heavens, non! He is just an old friend who helps me out every now and then with some of the chores."

"Oh, that's good," Deston replied, again without thinking, and immediately wished he could take the words back. His face flamed red and he hurriedly turned to leave, glancing up through his eyelashes at a bemused NiNi as he went through the door.

"Deston," NiNi called softly after him. "I am so very glad you are here. Please remember what I said about the forest. I do not want to lose you now that I have just found you."

Deston's face burned even hotter as he gave a quick nod and raced across the porch and down the steps before she could say anything more. Exiting through the gate, he trudged down the drive toward Peter, kicking the small pebbles along the shoulder and grumbling to himself. As he neared the meadow, he glanced back at the forest and let out a wistful sigh. Then with a great effort, he tore his eyes away and continued, stopping next to Peter. The old man didn't bother to look up, but continued pounding the nail until it was driven home. Peter then reached for another nail as if Deston wasn't standing there.

Deston shifted his weight and cleared his throat. "Umm ... excuse me. NiNi asked me to come help you with the fence."

Peter paused and squinted up at Deston, a blank expression covering his face.

"Oh, this is just great! He doesn't understand English," Deston mumbled under his breath, straining to remember the right words in French. "Er ... *besoin aide?*" he finally stammered out.

Peter turned his head to hide a grin. He had understood what Deston said the first time perfectly well, but he didn't let on. Instead of replying, he pointed to an extra hammer lying on the ground and went back to work.

Deston looked at the hammer and back at Peter, but the old man didn't elaborate further. Finally, Deston shrugged and picked it up; then grabbed a handful of nails and moved to the next section of fence. After checking over his shoulder as to what Peter was doing, he lifted the end of a rail and began hammering it into place just like the old man was doing.

The afternoon dragged on and Deston worked slower and slower as the temperature rose. Two and a half hours later, his back was killing him and several large red blisters had formed on the palm of his right hand. He stood up to stretch and almost cried out loud as his back seized in protest. Wiping the sweat from his forehead on the sleeve of his T-shirt, he looked over at Peter, who was still hammering away and showing no sign of fatigue. Deston rolled his eyes and turned away, leaning against the fence to stare off into the forest. The shade of the trees looked so inviting. He'd give anything to be in there at that moment instead of burning up in the sweltering sun. He absentmindedly massaged his hand to ease the ache as he stared. The day was certainly not turning out as he had planned.

A flock of squawking birds suddenly took flight out of the trees. Deston watched them fly across the meadow until they became small dots on the horizon.

Why can't my life could be like that? Free to soar through the sky with the wind in my face and fly wherever I wanted to go. I'd be able to find Mom then and everything would be back to normal.

He let out a sigh as his thoughts floated to his home in Pennsylvania.

Chapter 6

As Deston watched the birds disappear, a giant pair of yellow eyes watched him. Rellik stayed well inside the forest, silently waiting, drool dripping from his massive jaws. The black of his coat blended perfectly with the shadows of the trees, making him nearly impossible for the naked eye to see. All that moved were his eyes, which followed Deston's every movement.

This was Rellik's first good look at Deston, and what he saw surprised him. He hadn't expected the boy to be so young. The woman had left fifteen years ago, and yet this boy did not look to be that old. Could it be the lad wasn't Oseron's son after all? If that was the case, then he was no threat to Grossard and there was no reason to waste any more time on him.

Rellik stared at Deston and let that thought mull inside his head. He had not been happy when he received the order to come here and get the child. It was risky enough going into the new world to grab the woman. Here on the outskirts of Brocéliande, the people not only knew of his kind, they knew how to fight back. There were rumors about the old woman too, and although the rumors didn't necessarily scare him, she could complicate the situation if they were true.

Taking all that into consideration, he decided it would be safest to wait until the boy ventured into the forest alone before he made a move. That way it look as if the boy just got lost and the old woman wouldn't have to be involved.

The problem with that strategy was waiting was not one of

Rellik's greatest strengths. Neither was relying on someone else.

A low growl rumbled in his throat, sending another flock of birds to flight. He had not bargained on being a child-napper when he joined up with Grossard.

"This is going to cost you extra, Grossard. A lot extra," Rellik grumbled under his breath, watching Deston turn back to the fence and pick up the hammer again.

Chapter 7

By the time the last nail was driven home, it was almost dark. Using what little strength he had left, Deston staggered back to the house. Being from the city and not old enough to have a real job yet, he wasn't used to putting in a full day of manual labor. His acute case of jetlag made it all the worse. Every inch of his body ached, even his pinky finger, which had a long splinter embedded deep under the skin.

As he stumbled through the door, NiNi looked up from her chore of setting the table. "Ahhh, perfect timing, I was just about to call you in for dinner. Go and wash up. I made an extra special treat tonight for my two hardworking men ... coq au vin."

Deston tried to scowl at her cheerfulness, but even his face muscles were too tired to pull it off. If the choice was his, he'd go straight up to bed and forget about dinner altogether. But instead he robotically stumbled to the sink as he was told and winced as the cold water hit his blisters.

He turned back to the room just as Peter came through the back door and went to the old hand pump to wash up. Though Deston was more than a little surprised to see Peter, the old man's appearance didn't annoy him as it had earlier. In fact, he was actually glad Peter was joining them, for he was in no mood to carry on a conversation with NiNi throughout dinner.

NiNi seemed completely unaware of Deston's state and beamed at each of them as she set the food on the table and started chattering non-stop the moment they all sat down. Peter was quite chatty himself, much to Deston's surprise, and the two elders were soon engrossed in a discussion about the fence, the deer that knocked it down, and other matters of the farm that needed attention.

Though Deston listened to it all, the conversation was nothing more than a hum in his head. He sat slouched over and mechanically shoveled bites of food into his mouth, completely unaware of what he was eating. The moment NiNi took their plates away, he mumbled a "good night," and headed up the stairs. He kicked off his shoes and fell into bed fully clothed again and immediately plunged into a deep sleep and dreams of the Forest of Brocéliande.

It was one of those once in a lifetime kind of days and the mile-wide grin on Deston's face conveyed his excitement. And why wouldn't he be excited? One of his long time dreams was about to be fulfilled.

"So how much farther is it?" asked Deston, skipping along a path dotted with small patches of sunlight that lit the way like tiny spotlights.

"Hmm, a little farther," Joliet replied, giving no more away than she had all morning.

Her evasiveness didn't slow Deston down. When he came to a large log that had fallen across the path, he jumped over it as if he had springs on his feet. At the same moment his feet touched the ground on the other side of the log, a chipmunk darted out onto the path in front of him. The startled rodent froze in its tracks and stared up at the two humans with bulging eyes. Deston snickered and slowly knelt down on one knee, cooing softly as he stretched out his hand to coax the small animal over. The chipmunk studied Deston for a moment before taking a timid step forward. Then it stopped and stood up on its hind legs. Its nose twitched side to side, sniffing the air. In the next instant, its eyes grew even larger and it issued a small high-pitched squeak before bolting back under the bush.

Deston chuckled as he stood up, but his laughter died in his throat as he noticed a strange darkness closing in over the path in front of him. He strained to see through the dark, but it was as dense as a black hole, swallowing the light and everything else in its wake. As the darkness inched its way closer to him, a small dot of light appeared in its center and floated up level to his face. It retreated a short distance, came back up to his face, retreated again and waited, as if it wanted him to follow. Spellbound, he watched its antics for several seconds before turning to ask Joliet what she thought it was. To his surprise, the black void had closed in behind him as well. He was completely surrounded and could no longer see his mother.

In a near panic, Deston called out to her, but his voice was devoured by the darkness as soon as it left his mouth. The hairs on the back of his neck stood on end, as the stale air of the black void pressed in around him like an icy, cold fist. Frantically, he reached into the darkness for Joliet, knowing he had to find her and get back to the sunlight.

As he took a step in the direction where she last stood, his toe caught on the log. He crashed to the ground before he could catch himself, tearing his pants and scraping his shin on the rough tree bark. He pushed himself up to his hands and knees and stared at the dirt in a daze.

"Hurry, Deston! Get up and follow the light. You must find your mama and get back, or you will both be lost forever," a beautiful, melodious voice spoke inside his head.

He jerked and scrambled to his feet, looking around in desperation for Joliet like the voice told him to do. But as he started to move, a low growl came from within the blackness. His breath caught in his throat and he froze. He couldn't tell where the growling was coming from, for it seemed to be all around him. He whirled in a circle, searching for the source, but that made him more confused and he wasn't sure anymore which way was forward and which way was back.

And all the while the growl was getting louder and louder.

Chapter 8

Deston awoke with a start and stared wide-eyed at the stars painted on the ceiling. The fear he felt in the dream lingered with him, and the knot in his stomach tightened as a grinding sound from the kitchen reverberated in his head. It wasn't a threatening sound. In fact, it sounded like a coffee grinder, but Deston's heart raced just the same, as the last remnant of the dream floated to the edge of his mind. He sensed there was something important in the dream, something he needed to remember, but as he struggled to hold onto it, the images slipped farther away and then completely vanished.

It's only a dream, he told himself, but the uneasy feeling stayed with him. With a yawn, he lifted his arms above his head to stretch and instantly recoiled as a searing pain exploded through his shoulders and down into his biceps. Every muscle in his body burned and even the smallest movement ignited a new wave of pain. He slowly rolled onto his side, wincing as a muscle spasm seized his back.

"Oh God, make it stop," he muttered, gently massaging his arm and shoulder to relieve the tightness.

Through the open window the faint sound of a hammer pounding somewhere off in the distance floated in. Deston tensed. "Pleassse no more fences," he moaned. He could barely lift his arms now, let alone swing a hammer again all day.

Squeezing his eyes together, he thought of his mother. It was times like this that he missed her more than ever. She had a way of knowing exactly what he needed, even before he did. And no matter what ailed him, she would always come up with a homemade remedy to make him feel better. But she was gone and he had to learn to go on without her.

He groaned again as his mental and physical pain slowly engulfed him. Inhaling a deep breath, he held it in his lungs for as long as he could before blowing it out through his mouth. It was a technique he had learned in kung fu that was supposed to help him focus his mind and take it away from the pain, but it wasn't working so well today. He rolled to his back and immediately regretted his action, as his muscles screamed out again in protest.

Ah man, this sucks!

As he debated whether to stay in bed for the rest of the day or go down and soak away his soreness in a tub of hot water, the heavenly aroma of fresh baked bread drifted up the stairs and filled the room. His eyes flew open as if they had a mind of their own, and his mouth watered. The smell was so tantalizing, he hurriedly pulled the blanket over his nose to block it out. But it was too late. The aroma had already gotten into his head. Within minutes, it penetrated the blanket as well, and hunger pains ricocheted off the insides of his stomach. Knowing the debate was over; he winced and cursed his body for betraying him.

With another moan, he crawled out of bed ever so slowly, grimacing with each movement as the pains traveled from one muscle to the next. He grabbed a clean set of clothes as he passed the dresser and limped down the stairs, leaning heavily on the stair rail as he went. Before his foot hit the bottom step, NiNi turned from the stove with a smile.

"Good morning," she said cheerfully.

"Morning," Deston grumbled.

"I just finished filling the tub with some nice steamy water for you. It will make you feel better to get the stiffness out of your body. And will let you enjoy your breakfast much more."

"Huh? Um ... gee thanks," Deston replied, his brow wrinkling. She was doing it again—knowing exactly when he would come down the stairs.

Throwing a wary look at her out of the corner of his eye, he grabbed a slice of bread from a plate on the stove and made his way into the bathroom. It was getting a little spooky how she seemed to be able to predict what he was going to do before he even knew he was going to do it.

"Breakfast will be waiting for you. After you are finished, we will go into the village," NiNi added as he walked into the bathroom.

Deston automatically nodded, but he wasn't really listening, for the minute he opened the bathroom door, a pleasant, familiar scent greeted him. The smell reminded him of Joliet and with it came a sudden, intense pressure in his chest. Clutching the cross around his neck, he pushed the door shut and crossed to the mirror. As he leaned heavily against the sink and stared at his reflection, it slowly transformed into an image of his mother. At the same time, the soft voice from the day before whispered inside his head, but this time it had a sense of urgency to it.

"The key to finding your mother is in the forest."

"NO, that's ridiculous! You're in America, not here in France," he ground out through clenched teeth.

Pressing his lips together, he closed his eyes and fought back the turmoil building inside him. When he looked into the mirror again, it was his own reflection and his mother's eyes staring back at him.

"Where are you?" he whispered. His mirror image looked as perplexed as he was. He blew out a frustrated breath and bowed his head.

God, I know I don't pray as often as I should, but I hope you're listening anyway. Please watch over Mom, wherever she is. Or actually, what would be even better is if you could just sent her back to me. If that doesn't work for some reason, like she's sick or hurt or something and can't make it back, I could go to her. I just need to know where she is. I've tried to find her, but I can't do it on my own anymore. I ... I need help. I'm sure you know where she is. Mom says you know everything. So I'd appreciate whatever you can do. I guess that's all I wanted to say. I hope you're listening. He started to raise his head then remembered something else. *I really am sorry about not always being as good as I should be. But I promise I will try harder if you help me out. Just think about it ... okay? In Jesus' name, Amen.*

He wiped his hand across his eyes, purposely avoiding the mirror, and pulled his shirt over his head with as little movement as possible. He then stepped out of his dirty jeans and slowly eased into the tub. The herbs floating in the water bobbed as he slid down in the tub until the water lapped at his chin. He laid his head back against the rim and forced himself to relax, allowing the heat to work its way into his muscles.

The water and herbs went to work immediately. As his muscles began to loosen up, his mind wandered back to NiNi. She was definitely an odd one, but it wasn't so bad that she knew some things. It seemed she was trying really hard to make him feel at home.

Suddenly, the words NiNi had said as he entered the bathroom registered in his consciousness. He froze. *We're going into the village?* Water splashed over the side of the tub as he bolted straight up. He was finally going to get to meet some other people and maybe even some kids his own age to hang out with. A shiver of excitement ran through him and he closed his eyes.

Oh God, please let them speak English. And please let them like me.

Deston's plan to take a long soak in the tub was replaced with the anticipation of the upcoming trip into town. With the speed only a teenage boy can achieve, he scrubbed down and completed the rest of his grooming in record time. The only thing he took extra care with was his hair, which, as usual, refused to lay flat. It took lots of water and some kind of salve he found on top of a cabinet before he finally got it slicked down. Once his hair was in place, he took a final look in the mirror and flashed what he considered to be his most charming smile. The deep impression in his cheek irritated him as it always did, but, all in all, he was satisfied with the way he looked.

He walked into the kitchen in a much better mood, expecting to find NiNi waiting for him. For the first time since his arrival, the kitchen was empty. Assuming she was getting ready herself, he grabbed a hunk of bread and some cheese from a plate on the table and sat down to wait.

In no time at all, Deston had finished off the entire plate of food, along with an apple he found on the counter. He drummed his fingers on the tabletop as he sat and waited, checking his watch every few minutes. He didn't know what could be taking her so long.

After another fifteen minutes passed with no NiNi, his patience finally ran out. He walked to the archway that led into the hallway and stuck his head through the opening.

"NiNi?" he called out. There was no answer, so he called

louder, "NINI!" There was still no answer. With a frown, he turned and walked to the back door.

"NiNi?" he called, pushing the screen open and stepping out on the porch.

Deston quickly scanned the yard, then walked to the end of the porch. He shielded his eyes with the edge of his hand and looked out over the meadow. Everything was quiet and he saw no sign of NiNi. He leaned over the railing and gazed down the drive as it rounded the house and sliced through the field. Again there was nothing to see, except for a faint cloud of dust rising up in the distance. As he stared at the dust cloud, his heart lurched with the sudden thought that NiNi had left him behind.

In a panic, he bolted for the steps. At the same time, a red fox with a white-tipped tail came out of the forest and dashed across the drive. Deston caught the red flash out of the corner of his eye and looked over just as the fox came to a stop on the opposite side of the wire fence.

Deston's breath caught in his throat and he slid to a stop. He had read what to do when happening upon a wild animal, but seeing one up close was such a shock, his mind went completely blank. He stared at the fox, and in return, the fox stared back at him just as intently and with no apparent sign of fear. Intrigued by the animal's odd behavior, Deston slowly squatted down, hoping to look smaller so he wouldn't scare it away.

"It's okay. I'm not going to hurt you," he cooed.

The fox tilted its head from side to side, but didn't run away. Instead, it stood on its hind legs, placed its front paws against the fence, and began issuing small yips as if trying to communicate.

Deston put his hand over his mouth to hold back his laughter, but a soft giggle squeaked through.

Hearing the sound, the fox stopped yipping and narrowed its eyes. It glared at Deston, as if it was completely insulted. Then it started up again, yipping more aggressively than before. At that moment, NiNi walked around the side of the house. The second NiNi came into view, the fox's mouth snapped shut and it dropped to the ground. It looked back at Deston, gave one final squeak and a wink, then turned and scampered back into the trees.

"Oh, Deston, there you are. You are ready to go, oui?" NiNi called out.

"Ohmigawd! Did you see that?" Deston exclaimed, running up to the fence where the fox had stood only seconds before.

"See what?" asked NiNi, digging around in her bag for her car keys.

"The fox. There was a red fox standing right here next to the fence. It was making these sounds like it was trying to tell me something, but you scared it away when you came out." His face was alight with wonder as he turned to NiNi.

NiNi looked up. "Non, I did not see it. But there is no need to be scared of foxes. They will not hurt you if you leave them alone," she remarked and headed back the same way she had just come. "Come, we must be going. If we are late, all the best produce in the market will be picked over."

"Wow, that was so cool," Deston said under his breath, looking back to the trees. "I wonder what it wanted. Maybe it was hungry. Do you think?" he asked NiNi, but she had already disappeared around the house. "Poor little thing," he said, throwing another glance at the forest before reluctantly following after NiNi.

He continued talking to no one in particular all the way up to the wooden building at the side of the house. "I can't believe it wasn't scared of me. I bet it would have come up to my hand if NiNi hadn't walked out when she did. I swear it winked at me too." Deston opened the door to the shed and stepped into the enclosed space. "I bet it…" Before he could finish his thought a powerful stench filled his lungs. He gasped out loud and immediately lapsed into a violent coughing fit.

"Just breathe through your mouth until you get used to the odor. It will not be so bad in a few minutes. Keep the door open. That will help," NiNi ordered.

Unfortunately, that piece of advice was a little too late. Deston had already inhaled a large dose of the overpowering stench that hung in the air. Water streamed from his eyes as he coughed non-stop and by the time he ran out of the shed to get some relief, his lips had a blue tint. The fresh air helped, but it still took several more seconds before he could take in a full breath.

"Is everything all right out there? Are you about ready?" NiNi called from within the shed.

Deston swiped his hand under his nose. "Yeah, I'm coming."

Pulling the neck of his T-shirt up over his nose to block the smell, he hesitantly approached the door. As he lifted his foot to step in, he looked up with watery eyes and did a double take. Inside the shed was a grove of trees and in the midst of the trees stood a witch dressed in black and wearing a tall, pointy hat. Her hands were twisting about as if she was performing a spell. The sight of the witch caught Deston off guard and his toe snagged on the threshold. He fell through the door on his hands and knees, but without missing a beat, his head jerked right back up.

It took a few seconds for his eyes to grow accustom to the dim light and to see that it wasn't a witch at all. It was NiNi in a black coat, standing at a table surrounded by dozens of tall potted plants. What he had mistaken for the witch's pointy hat was a black lamp hanging from a long cord over her head. Embarrassed and feeling more than a little ridiculous, he scrambled to his feet, hoping NiNi hadn't noticed his clumsiness.

The room was not much bigger than an oversized walk-in closet and was packed from floor to ceiling with plants of every variety and size, as well as bottles filled with different colored liquids and powders. "What is all this?" Deston asked as he carefully picked his way through the clutter.

"This? This is my ... how you say ... *jardin botanique?*" NiNi replied, tying a ribbon around a small, cloth bag. "I am not sure of the English word for it, but it is what I do in my spare time. I collect and grow plants and herbs from all around the world." She shoved the package into a larger cloth shopping bag as she continued. "I became interested in the healing power of herbs as a young girl while in Tir ... umm ... while away on a trip." She glanced up quickly to see if Deston had caught her slip, but luckily, he was absorbed in the bottles on the table. "Many people think plants are good for nothing more than setting around the house and looking pretty, and herbs should only be used in cooking. But they are so much more than that. I have studied and learned their powers and use them to make special potions and remedies for illnesses and ailments."

"Really? Are you a doctor?"

"Pssssh. First you think I am a gypsy, and now you think I am a doctor?" She winked and gave him a large, toothy grin. "Non, I am not a doctor. My skills come from magical powers that I was given long ago. I use the magic to keep others under my spell," she teased with a twinkle in her eye.

Deston took a step back, silently mouthing the words "magical powers." The rest of NiNi's words were lost to him.

NiNi headed toward a door at the back of the shed, paying no attention to the astonished look on his face. "Well, I think I have everything now. Shall we go?"

Deston stared after her, but didn't move.

"Come now. We have already dallied too long. It is getting late," NiNi motioned for Deston to follow and disappeared through the door.

It took several seconds for Deston to jolt out of his stupor and follow her into a larger room of the shed where an old black Mercedes was parked. NiNi was already seated behind the driver's wheel.

"Will you open the doors, *s'il vous plait?*" she called out.

Stiff as a robot, Deston swung the double doors open and stood off to the side as NiNi backed the car out. Her talk of magical powers and potions had him rethinking his vision of the witch. Along with the psychic abilities he had already witnessed, it seemed too much of a coincidence to ignore.

Once the car cleared the shed, Deston closed the doors and got in the passenger side, keeping his eyes lowered so she wouldn't know what he was thinking. But his flushed complexion and peculiar behavior didn't escape her notice. She shifted the car into park and turned in her seat to face him.

"Is everything all right?" She didn't wait for his reply. "You know I was teasing you back there, oui? I do not put people under spells. I use my magic the same way your maman does," she said tenderly.

Deston jerked around. "My mom is not a witch! She has never made a magic potion, either," he exclaimed.

NiNi was taken aback by his passion. Joliet had hidden more from the boy than she realized. "Magic is not a bad word, nor is it a bad thing," she replied. "You say your maman does not make potions, but let me ask you this...did she ever concoct a special drink for you when you had a cold?"

Deston was reluctant to reply, but after a lengthy pause he mumbled, "Yeah."

"And when you had a headache, did she soak a cloth in an herbal mixture for your forehead?"

He grimaced and repeated "yeah," with the same reluctance.

NiNi smiled. "Well there, you see. That is what I am talking about. It is the same magic I use—the magic of the herbs."

Deston's brow remained furrowed, but his anger slowly began to dissolve. "Mom used to make home remedies whenever I was sick. But I never heard her say she had magical powers."

"Hmm, well maybe I should not use the word "magic." I think it is not right. I sometimes get my translations confused. Whatever the right word is, it is a good thing." NiNi softened her voice. "I did not mean to upset you. I will try to be more careful with my choice of words in the future. Can you forgive me?"

Deston didn't look up. "Yeah ... I'm sorry too. It's just, you know," he stumbled, feeling embarrassed and not knowing what else to say.

"I know," NiNi replied and gave his leg a pat. Then without further discussion, she put the car into reverse and backed out onto the drive.

It was a picture perfect day at the end of May. The sun was shining brightly and white, cotton candy clouds dotted the blue sky. Deston pushed the thought of witches and magic out of his mind and focused his attention on the beauty of the landscape instead.

As NiNi turned onto the highway that led into Lieu de Merveille, a lump formed in Deston's throat and grew larger with each twist and turn of the road. He was both excited and scared at the same time. He had lived in Pennsylvania his whole life, but never fit in with the other kids there. This wasn't Pennsylvania, though, and no one here knew anything about him. It was like getting a fresh start. A second chance. He prayed he wouldn't screw it up this time.

NiNi couldn't help but notice his nervous jitters, and for the first time it dawned on her what a cultural shock Merveille might be to him. "Deston," she ventured, wanting to prepare him for what he was about to see. "I do not think Lieu de Merveille will be much like your big American cities. It is a small farm town, and a very old one at that. Most of the people have lived here their entire life and do things in the old ways ... ways you might consider backward. I hope you will keep an open mind and give it a chance. It is a good place with good people. There are some very pretty girls there too," she added with a wink.

Deston blushed and turned back to the window. "So do a lot of kids live there?" he asked, trying to sound casual.

"A lot? I do not know what you consider a lot, but I am thinking there are enough that you will find some new friends."

They traveled on through several more fields without so much as a sign of a house or the town and Deston became more nervous with each kilometer. "How much farther is it?" he finally asked.

"It is not too far now. All total, it is about thirty kilometers from home. I used to ride my bicycle into the village until two years ago when my arthritis decided it was time for me to quit. So now I drive. The bicycle is still in the shed. You may use it whenever you like."

"Cool," Deston replied automatically as he did a quick calculation in his head. Thirty kilometers was a little over eighteen miles, which wasn't too bad. He could easily handle that. After all, if NiNi could do it ... Deston's train of thought stopped short and he eyed NiNi skeptically.

"You're telling me you rode a bike eighteen miles into town?"

"Oui, I did—every week. It is a pleasant ride. You will see for yourself soon enough."

Deston pursed his lips, finding it hard to believe a woman of NiNi's age would be able to ride a bicycle eighteen miles. However, as they crested the next hill and came upon an entire family pedaling along on bicycles, including an old man who looked to be even older than NiNi, he realized he could be wrong about that.

Each one of the riders turned to him with a wave and a shout of, "Bonjour," as the car drove past them. Their friendliness relieved some of Deston's nervousness. Maybe he wouldn't have trouble finding someone to hang out with after all. Especially if the kids in town were even half as friendly as these folks seemed to be.

Chapter 9

The village of Lieu de Merveille was perched on a hilltop and visible from several kilometers away. As the car rounded a bend and the village came into view, goose bumps pimpled Deston's arms. He scooted forward on the seat as far as the seatbelt would allow, eager to take it all in. However, from a distance all he could make out was a tall stone wall surrounding rows of rooftops that led up to a massive white stone structure at the top of the hill.

When the car reached a point where the highway curved and headed back toward the forest, NiNi turned off onto a side road, which was the only way in or out of Merveille. Deston's pulse hammered harder as they drove the last few kilometers pass an orchard and through an opening in the wall where wide gates once held out the unwanted. Inside the wall, the single road branched out into a maze of streets.

Deston pressed his nose to the window, eyeing the people as they passed. To his disappointment, he saw no one that looked even close to his age until they were more than half way up the hill. Then he spotted three boys standing on a street corner. His stomach jumped to his throat and the three boys seemed to become just as excited as they pointed at the car. He turned in his seat to ask NiNi if she knew them just as one of the boys shouted out an obscenity. Stunned by the boy's outburst and vicious tone, Deston whirled around, twisting his neck so he could look out the back window as the car passed. When the three noticed Deston watching, they shouted out more obscenities and made rude gestures at him until the car turned a corner and Deston could no longer see them.

Deston's face was pale and his eyes no longer held a sparkle as he slowly turned back to the front. He had so hoped it would be different here, but it didn't seem as if it was going to be. His brain knew it didn't matter what the boys thought of him—he didn't know them and they didn't know him—but his heart wasn't buying into that logic.

Hesitantly, he glanced over at NiNi. If she had noticed the boys, she wasn't letting on, and he was glad for her sake. Slumping down in his seat, he stared through the windshield without really seeing anything else, until the car made its way into the village square at the top of the hill.

The square was similar to the rest of the village in that the buildings were all attached, but instead of living quarters, the ground level held small shops with large glass windows displaying a variety of products. In the center of the square, three six-foot tall marble faeries skipped across the water of a large, round fountain. As beautiful as the fountain was, it didn't take away from the focal point of the entire village—the magnificent white stone cathedral, which occupied one whole side of the square.

NiNi drove into the square, skillfully zigzagging through the cars and dodging the people milling about as she searched for a place to park. But every inch of curb was already taken. There were even miniature cars, like what Peter drove, parked on the corners. After circling the square twice and muttering under her breath the whole time, NiNi came to a stop in front of a small shop that had a display of fruits and vegetables spilling out onto the street. She glared and grunted in disgust at the two women with full baskets, who were picking over the crates by the open doorway.

"Ack, look! You see? What did I tell you? There is Josephine and Sophie and I am sure they have already picked out all the good fruit."

NiNi scowled through the windshield at the women who were inspecting each piece of produce as if it was a precious gem. Then with a huff, she threw the car into park, turned off the ignition, and got out. Hurrying up to the produce stand, she yelled and waved at a small, thin man in an apron, who was bustling about between the crates.

Too stunned to move, Deston sat in the car as NiNi push

her way through the women to get into the shop. He couldn't believe she had just left the car parked in the middle of the street. He stared through the windshield, watching NiNi engage in an animated conversation with the man in the apron and seemingly not at all concerned that she had abandoned her car. Sheepishly, Deston eyed the other shoppers, expecting to get plenty of dirty looks, but none of them seemed any more concerned about the car than NiNi was. They all continued about their business without so much as a sideways glance his way.

Deston waited another few minutes, then hesitantly opened the door, got out and stood beside the car. As people walked past him, they smiled and nodded. Some even called out "bonjour", but no one said anything about moving the car. When he finally realized no one cared, he shrugged and trotted over to join NiNi.

As soon as Deston entered the shop, Josephine and Sophie shifted to the table next to him, suddenly very interested in the produce displayed there. NiNi pretended to ignore them, but her voice raised a level to make sure they were able to hear as she introduced Deston to the man in the apron.

"Monsieur LaBelle, this is Joliet's son, Deston. He recently arrived from America," said NiNi, her voice filled with pride.

Deston looked up shyly and nodded to the man.

"It is very nice to meet you, Deston. You are liking France, eh?" Monsieur LaBelle asked in French, keeping his eyes locked on a woman on the other side of the shop.

"I like it fine. Thank you," Deston replied back in French, hoping he had understood Monsieur LaBelle correctly.

As Deston's last word left his mouth, Monsieur LaBelle exploded in a tirade. Deston jumped back in horror, thinking he had said something wrong, but the little man pushed past him and rushed up to the woman he had been watching. Snatching a tomato out of the woman's hand, LaBelle yelled at her in rapid-fire French. The woman looked indignant and held her ground, but within seconds she was yelling right back and a verbal war broke out between the two of them. The screaming went on until LaBelle threw his hands in the air and shooed the woman from the shop.

NiNi turned back to Deston and chuckled at his horrified expression. "Monsieur LaBelle is … how you say *excentrique?*"

"Eccentric? Yeah, no kidding," Deston nodded his head in agreement.

"Oui, Monsieur LaBelle is a little eccentric, but he is also a fair man. His heart is in the right place. And he has the best vegetables in the whole village, so we overlook his occasional fits of temper."

NiNi chuckled again and patted Deston on the arm to reassure him before turning back to the baskets of fruits and vegetables. Deston peered into a basket filled with yellow and green squash, but his interest was not in produce. He was anxious to see the other parts of town and discover where the boys and girls hung out. Shifting his weight from one foot to another, he impatiently fidgeted as NiNi continued to shop.

Several loud sighs and exaggerated glances at his watch later, NiNi finally took notice. With a knowing smile, she reached into her bag for a small velvet purse and took out several coins. She pressed them into the palm of his hand. "Go and have some fun. See if you can find some nice children to play with. On your way back, stop at the *boulangerie* and pick up two croissants for our breakfast tomorrow, s'il vous plaît. It is that shop right down there." She pointed to the bakery.

Realizing NiNi was letting him go off on his own, Deston's face lit up.

"Take as long as you want. When you are finished, come back to the square. I will be waiting for you there in the café," she said, bringing her finger around to a green-striped awning that hung over a group of tables.

Deston looked down at the funny-looking coins NiNi had placed in his hand. He didn't know how much money it was, but when he looked up to ask, she was already engrossed in her shopping and arguing prices with Monsieur LaBelle. Not wanting to waste any more time, Deston shoved the coins into his pocket and headed down the street.

He walked to the end of the square, checking out the shop windows as he passed. Nothing he saw interested him, and to double his disappointment, no one looked to be under the age of thirty in any of the stores. Continuing down the hill, he stopped at the next corner to get his bearings and to decide which direction to go. As he looked up the side street, he noticed a boy and a girl walking his way with the three boys he had seen earlier following closely at their heels. The three boys were taunting the pair in front, yelling vulgar words and calling out rude names in French that even Deston could understand.

The boy, who was walking with the girl, was quite a bit smaller than the others and walked with a slight limp. His hands were stuffed deep into his pockets and his chin was tucked tightly into his chest. Each insult brought his shoulders up closer to his ears as he tried to tuck his head into his shirt like a turtle.

The girl's arm was slung protectively over the boy's shoulder as she pulled him along. Her back was straight and her head was held high, but her face was dark with anger and her lips were pressed into a thin line.

Suddenly, the largest of the three boys reached out, and for no apparent reason, shoved the small boy, who went sprawling to the pavement. The girl instantly spun around, her hands going to her hips as she barreled up to the boy and started yelling in his face. The large boy was unfazed and issued a harsh laugh in response. Then shoved her, sending her to the pavement alongside her small companion.

Without thinking, Deston yelled out, "Hey, leave them alone!"

Five shocked faces turned in Deston's direction as he ran toward them. He slid to a stop in front of the instigator, who was not only the largest of the three, but appeared to be the leader of the group as well. The leader folded his arms over his thick chest and huffed indignantly as he gave Deston a quick once over.

Gawd, this guy not only looks like a gorilla, he smells like one too, Deston thought, as the leader stepped up to close the gap between him and the two on the ground.

The boy was at least a foot taller than Deston and was indeed built like a gorilla. His long arms were covered with black hair, and his fingernails on his thick, stubby hands were ringed with dirt. He had a dark complexion, long greasy hair, and heavy, black eyebrows that met in the middle to make one solid line above his beady black eyes. The other two boys, who also had dark complexions, greasy black hair, and the same offensive odor, stood off to the side with the same arrogant look as their leader.

The leader stared down at Deston and his lip curled up in a sneer. "Well, lookee what we have here. A stinking American who wants to be a hero," he said in heavily-accented English. His two friends guffawed loudly.

Deston clenched his jaw, but didn't reply. His body was tense and his eyes stayed fixed straight ahead as the leader walked around him.

"He doesn't look all that tough to me," the leader said, poking Deston in the shoulder. "In fact, I think he looks like a sissy girl. What do you think, Arnaud?"

The girl, who was helping the small boy up from the sidewalk, spoke up, "Leave him alone, Claude. You can see he is not from here. He has done nothing to you."

"Hey, isn't that the kid we just saw in the car with the crazy old witch?" the second boy commented.

Claude, the leader, stepped back to take a better look at Deston. "Yeah, I think you are right, Vincent. I do believe it is," he sneered.

"I heard Papa talking about him the other night. His mama used to live around here, but she went crazy and moved to America. Now she's run off and left him, so he's living out there with the old witch," Vincent said.

"Hey, you better watch out, Claude. He might have the old witch put a curse on you," jeered Arnaud, the third boy.

Claude pretended to cower in fright. "Ooo ... I'm so scared," he replied in a small, weak voice, and burst out laughing along with his two friends.

"Papa said his mama was a loony witch too," Vincent added.

Claude leaned in close, his nose coming within an inch of touching Deston's. "So I guess that makes you a witch, huh? And here I thought that stench was just because you were one of those filthy Americans."

Deston bristled, but held his tongue. The dimple in his cheek twitched and his eyes stayed glued to Claude's face.

"What's the matter, sissy boy? Are you deaf and dumb?" Claude paused to give Deston a chance to say something, but Deston knew better than to comply. "Oh yeah, that's right. You're American, so that means you're just plain dumb," Claude let out a laugh, then spit in Deston's face. "That's what I think of stinking Americans!"

Deston had no intention of getting into a fight, but his temper had been hovering so close to the surface of late and the spit was just the trigger to set it off. As Claude arrogantly looked over at his cohorts to make sure they had caught his performance, Deston took the advantage. With a loud yell, he jumped sideways and swept his foot around, hitting the back of Claude's knees and knocking Claude's legs out from under him. The large boy crashed to the ground, and before Claude knew what hit him, Deston had him pinned down.

Taken by surprise, Vincent and Arnaud stood and gawked for a split second before jumping in. Each grabbed one of Deston's arms and hauled him to his feet and off their leader. As Deston struggled to get away, his foot accidentally connected with Claude's face as Claude started to rise. The force of the kick snapped Claude's head back and his eyes clouded over as he slumped back to the ground. Claude laid stunned for a moment before he pushed himself up on his elbows. He swiped his hand across his nose and stared in disbelief at the blood smeared on the back of his hand.

"*Salaud!*" Claude hissed through bared teeth. Staggering to his feet, he yelled at his friends, "Hold him down so I can teach this stinking American a lesson."

"No, Claude, don't," the girl cried out, jumping forward to grab Claude's arm.

Claude jerked free and shoved her out of the way. "Shut up, Margaux, and get out of here. This is not about you anymore," he snorted.

With blood streaming from his nose, Claude advanced. Deston tensed, and as Claude raised his fist to take a swing, he used the leverage of Arnaud and Vincent holding his arms to lift his legs and thrust both feet into Claude's stomach. For a second time, Claude went sprawling to the ground and his head smacked hard into the payment as he hit.

Dazed, Claude shook his head and it took him several long

seconds to get back to his feet this time. "Damn it! I said hold him down!" he roared as he advanced once more, although not as steady as before.

Arnaud and Vincent pushed Deston up against the side of the building and anchored their legs over his, rendering him virtually immobile. Claude pulled his arm back and swung. Deston jerked his head to the side, timing it as Claude's fist came around. Still, the fist clipped the side of his face and sent a jolt of pain through his jaw. Claude immediately reared back and threw a second punch into Deston's stomach. Deston crumpled over, coughing and gasping for air.

"So it looks like this stinking American is not so tough after all," Claude spat, raising his fist for a third punch.

As his fist started forward, a gnarled, leathery hand reached out from behind and closed over it to hold it back.

"Hey now, what's this? I hardly think three against one is a fair fight. Break it up right now," the owner of the hand said sternly.

Claude looked over his shoulder at the old man standing behind him. The old man had straggly gray hair and a scruffy strip of beard with one long, pure white strand that hung down from his lower lip to several inches below his chin.

A fiendish grin spread over Claude's face as he jerked away from the hold, not at all intimidated by the look of the frail old man.

"Go on now and get yourself out of here. I have already called the *gendarme*," the old man continued before Claude could make another move.

Hearing the word "gendarme," Arnaud and Vincent let Deston go.

"Let's get out of here," Arnaud said, taking off with Vincent up the street. He grabbed Claude's arm as he went by to drag his leader along with them. Claude staggered a few steps; then dug in his heels in a show of defiance.

"You better watch yourself, you stinking American witch, because you can bet your life I'll be coming for you." Claude gave out a wicked laugh as he made an obscene gesture at the old man and ran off to catch up with his friends.

"Tsk, tsk ... it is truly sad how the young of today's society have no respect for their elders," stated the old man with a shake of his head as he watched the three boys round the corner and disappear from sight. He then looked back at Deston, who was bent over and clutching his stomach. "Are you all right, young man?"

Deston, still struggling to take a breath, couldn't answer. He held his stomach and coughed as the girl stepped up next to him.

"That was very brave of you. But also very stupid," she said in perfect English, with only the slightest accent.

Deston tilted his head and looked up through his hair that had fallen over his eyes. The girl wasn't very tall, maybe an inch or two taller than he, and was quite thin. Her hair, which was a brilliant copper-color, was pulled into two long braids that hung down over each shoulder. Her pale skin was covered with freckles, and her exotic almond-shaped eyes, the color of honey, showed her concern, even though she had a slight smirk on her lips.

"Claude will never let this rest. So you will need to be careful and watch out the next time you come to Merveille," she stated matter-of-factly. "But it was very nice of you to come to our defense like you did and I would like to thank you. My name is Margaux Labonté, by the way. This is my brother, Philippe," she added, offering her hand.

Deston stared at her hand for a minute before taking it. "Deston Lespérance," he croaked in reply.

"So you really are American, yes?"

"Yeah, how'd ya guess," Deston replied dryly, struggling to stand a little straighter.

Margaux wasn't fazed by his sarcasm. "Are you living at Madame Jolicoeur's as Vincent said? Is she really your aunt?"

Deston tried to take a full breath and coughed again. "Yeah, I'm staying there, but she's not my aunt. She's my mom's cousin," he finally answered.

"Groovy! Will you be staying there long?"

"I don't know ... hopefully not."

Philippe tugged on Margaux's shirt. "Come on, Margaux. We need to get home," he said in French.

Margaux flashed him a "just a minute" look and turned back to Deston. "I guess I have to go. I do hope to see you again soon."

There was an awkward pause as she waited for Deston to reply, but he was in no mood to be cordial to her or anyone else at the moment.

With a quick, embarrassed smile, Margaux turned to the old man. "Thank you for your help, Monsieur," she said, dipping into a small curtsy. Looking back at Deston, she added, "It was nice to meet you, Deston. Please give my regards to Madame Jolicoeur." With that said, she took Philippe's hand and the two of them hurried down the street in the opposite direction of the other three.

Deston leaned back against the wall and let his head drop as a wave of nausea passed. He lightly touched his jaw where Claude's fist had connected and winced. What was NiNi going to think? How could he explain how he had gotten into a fight with the very first person he met? It seemed his bad luck had followed him to France after all. And his dream of making new friends was completely shattered.

Forgetting about the old man standing off to the side, Deston pushed himself away from the wall and began to retrace his steps to the square.

I'm such a dope. Why couldn't I just stay out of it?

"My boy, you could never turn your back on an injustice. It is not in your heart to do so," commented the old man as he fell in step beside Deston.

Startled to a stop, Deston looked up at the old man. "Huh?"

"Do not waste your time on those three. They are not worthy of your concern or worry. There are many others—nice children, that is—here in Merveille. Like the girl for one."

"Oh, yeah, sure. Thanks a lot. I'll try to remember that," replied Deston. With a nod of his head, he started walking again, only a little faster this time.

Without missing a beat, the old man fell in stride with Deston. "Lieu de Merveille might seem quite different from your Pennsylvania on the surface, but it is not really. The nature of people is the same in every country, and you will find good as well as evil no matter where you venture. The thing to keep in mind is that each encounter, no matter how distressing at the time, will make you a little stronger and more prepared for the next."

Deston stopped walking again and narrowed his eyes suspiciously at the old man. "How did ya know I was from Pennsylvania?"

"Well, you *are* an American, and you are wearing a Philadelphia Phillies T-shirt. I just added two and two together."

Deston looked down at the front of his shirt and back at the old man. "Yeah, well ... thanks Mr. ..."

"Monsieur Zumwald," the man offered with a slight bow.

"Okay, Monsieur Zumwald, I appreciate you helping me out back there. But I'm supposed to meet someone now, you see, so I've got to go. Thanks again," Deston said and continued up the street. To his annoyance, the old man fell in step beside him once more. Gritting his teeth, Deston looked over at Zumwald, and with a sterner tone, said, "Look, really, I—"

"Have you experienced any of the mysteries of the forest yet?" Zumwald interrupted.

"What?" Deston stopped short for a third time and stared guardedly at the old man.

"The Forest of Brocéliande—have you had the chance to discover the wonderful mysteries it holds?"

"What mysteries?" asked Deston, suddenly very interested in what the old man had to say.

"You don't know?" The old man looked astonished. "Surely you can feel it. The forest is ... well, let's just say there's a lot more to it than trees. It is a wondrous place, but holds different treasures for each person who ventures into its borders." He bent his finger, motioning for Deston to move in a little closer. "It's enchanted, you know," he whispered as Deston leaned in. He paused a moment to let his words sink in. "If you look hard enough, I mean really look, I'm certain you will be able to discover the magic that lives there."

Deston's eyes widened and he stared transfixed, unsure what to think of this strange old man.

"I personally know of some who have been fortunate enough to find the stone fortress where Merlyn once lived. Did you know it exists there inside the forest?" He didn't wait for Deston's reply, but hurried on. "It's true. Though in order to find it, one has to be very special, as well as dedicated in the search for the clues," Zumwald added to lock up Deston's interest.

"Merlyn's fortress? So it really does exist?" Deston asked, taking the bait.

"Yes, it does. But as I said, it takes someone special to locate it—someone with a clear mind. To find your true reward, you must first let go of the pain, anger, and doubt that you carry with you."

Monsieur Zumwald reached into his pocket and with a grand gesture pulled his hand out and turned it over palm side up. He slowly opened his fingers to reveal a small, dark object wrapped in cellophane. "This good luck charm has helped me through many times of trouble. It is very special and holds great power. But I am an old man now and do not have the need for such luck. You, on the other hand, are in need of some from what I've witnessed. So I want you to have it, along with my blessing. I pray it guides you to good fortune, as it has me all these many, many decades."

Deston hesitated, uncertain whether or not to accept a gift from a stranger. Although technically, Zumwald wasn't really a stranger since he had helped him out of what could have turned into a very nasty predicament. And it wasn't as if Zumwald was asking him to get into a car with him or anything. It was just a small good luck charm. Heaven knows he could use some good luck for a change.

At Deston's hesitation, Zumwald lifted his hand and pushed it forward, gesturing with a nod for Deston to take the offering. After another short pause, Deston shrugged his shoulders and stretched out his hand. Zumwald hid his smile as he unwrapped the object and reverently laid a blackened leaf, about the size of a silver dollar, in Deston's palm.

As Deston eyed the object, his nose wrinkled in distaste. *It's a rotten, old leaf?* The old man was indeed as crazy as Deston first thought. But as his thumb brushed over the surface, he realized it wasn't a decayed leaf at all. It was thin and an exact replica of an oak leaf, but it was also hard like metal. He lightly scratched the surface with his thumbnail. Some of the black grime came off, displaying a shiny, gold underneath. He scratched at the black again and more of the gold showed through, along with part of an inscription. Curious, he rubbed until the writing was fully uncovered, but the engraving was not written in English and there was too much black grime in the grooves to make it out clearly.

Deston looked up to ask Monsieur Zumwald what it said. To his surprise, he was alone. He spun all the way around, looking up and down the street, but Zumwald had completely vanished.

Wow, if he can move that fast, he isn't as old as I thought. Deston rubbed his thumb over the engraving once again. *Humph, it probably just says, "Made in China" or something.*

With one more look around, Deston shoved the leaf in his pocket and hurried off to buy the croissants and meet up with NiNi.

Perched on the rooftop of a nearby building, a large black crow with a white tuft under its beak watched Deston make his way up the street. The crow waited until Deston entered the bakery and then circled once over the square and flew off toward the forest.

Chapter 10

NiNi was sitting at a table in the café, enjoying tea and fruit crêpes with two other women when Deston walked into the square. He was hoping to get to the car and assess the damage to his face, but, as luck would have it, NiNi saw him crossing the street and yelled out before he made it to the safe harbor.

"Deston, over here. Come join us. We are having tea."

Deston grimaced and walked awkwardly to the table as asked, taking the chair NiNi pushed out for him. He could feel the heat rising to his face, but there was nothing he could do. He sat uncomfortably in the chair with his elbow on the table and his chin propped in his hand, hoping to cover any tell-tale mark Claude's fist might have left on his jaw.

"Deston, I would like to introduce you to Marie and Cosette," NiNi said, pointing out the two women sitting across the table from him.

She pushed a plate of crêpes at Deston as he gave a slight nod to each woman.

"Er ... no, thanks. I'm not hungry," he said, keeping his face turned away from the table.

At Deston's response, NiNi's hand stilled and her sharp eyes narrowed. She had never known a teenage boy to refuse the offer of food, especially when it involved sweets. The two other women took no notice and resumed their gossip. NiNi nodded and pretended to listen as she studied Deston out of the corner of her eye.

Deston had been so excited about meeting new friends before

he went off on his own. She couldn't imagine what had changed in such a short time. But the way he held his head and diverted his eyes, even when answering a question, convinced her something was wrong.

"Well," NiNi suddenly exclaimed, cutting Marie off mid-sentence. "We have a lot of work to do before the day is done. I am afraid we must go. Deston, will you please take my bags to the car for me. I will be right there."

Deston jumped up and grabbed the bags, glad to get away from the scrutiny of the women. As he headed to the car, NiNi apologized to her friends and assured Marie she would send a poultice for the swelling in her knee by the end of the week. With one last goodbye, NiNi hurried to the car and got behind the wheel as Deston settled into the passenger seat after having put the bags in the back. He kept his back turned toward her and pretended to be intrigued with the activities going on outside the window. She wasn't at all fooled by his charade, but she said nothing. She started the car, put it in gear, and headed down the hill.

Deston's face remained plastered to the window as he stared solemnly at the passing houses, wondering how he was going to explain the incident. He didn't want to tell NiNi he had gotten into a fight. She was the only person who believed in him, and he didn't want to disappoint her or jeopardize their relationship. But no matter how hard he tried to come up with a plausible explanation to have at the ready in case Claude had left a bruise on his jaw, nothing came to him.

"So tell me, what did you think of my little village of Merveille?" NiNi asked, interrupting his thoughts.

"Huh? Oh ... um ... it was okay, I guess," Deston replied without turning away from the window.

"Did you meet any of the children?"

"Yeah ... a couple."

"Wonderful! Maybe you will be able to see them again when you go back to deliver a package for me."

"What?" Deston flipped around, forgetting all about his jaw for a moment.

In the brief instant Deston faced her way, NiNi got a glimpse of a purple welt rising along his jaw line. Her heart skipped a beat, although she managed to mask her shock.

When Deston saw his face reflected in the pupils of NiNi's eyes, he quickly turned back to resume his position at the window. He didn't think it was possible, but he was more miserable than before. For now not only did his jaw ache, but he had to worry about returning to Merveille too.

As the car drove through the intersection where Deston first saw Claude and his friends, he mumbled, "They called you a witch."

NiNi grasp on the wheel tightened as she stole a glance at Deston. The reflection of his forlorn expression in the glass of the window broke her heart. "Ignorant people say ignorant things. And you must know, people like that feel the need to put labels on whatever they do not understand. But you cannot let ugly words upset you. Words hold no power unless you allow them to."

She would have said more, but at that moment a girl stepped out of a house a short distance ahead and waved wildly at the car. "Oh look, it is Margaux Labonté," NiNi said waving back. "Such a sweet child. Now she is someone you should meet. I believe she is about your age and she speaks very good English. I am sure you two would get along splendidly. I shall invite her over and introduce you."

"No!" Deston exploded. "I mean you don't have to. I've already met her and her brother," he explained, frowning at Margaux through the window as they passed.

"Oh?" NiNi was truly puzzled. She knew Margaux and her brother well, and also knew neither were capable of doing such a thing to Deston's face. She was also certain they would never have called her a witch. There had to be something more he wasn't telling her. When Deston didn't offer up any further explanation, NiNi prodded on, "Did you meet anyone else?"

"Oh ... um ... there were a couple of other kids around, but I didn't really meet them."

"Non? That is too bad. Maybe next time," NiNi said, with a quick sidelong glance at the back of Deston's head.

"Yeah, maybe."

The rest of the trip home was filled with silence, as both Deston and NiNi were lost in their own thoughts. Deston endeavored to find a suitable explanation that didn't make him look like a trouble-maker; but everything he thought of sounded lame, even to him. As the time rapidly sped by, his anxiety level escalated and his stomach twisted into a tighter knot.

He still hadn't come up with a solution when NiNi turned off the highway onto the gravel drive of the cottage. The only hope he had left was that there was no mark on his chin to give him away. He prayed for that to be true so he wouldn't have to tell NiNi anything about what happened—at least not right away.

He touched his jaw again and felt the tenderness, but he didn't give up hope. Soreness didn't necessarily mean a mark. He could be worrying about nothing, although his gut told him he was going to be in big trouble.

NiNi stopped in front of the shed and let Deston out to open the doors. She then sped in, turned off the ignition, and jumped out of the car before it had even stopped rocking. She was almost sprinting as she rounded the corner of the shed and headed toward the house, yelling out for Deston to get the bags from the backseat as she went.

Deston waited for her to disappear, and the second she was out of sight, he rushed to the front seat and turned the rearview mirror around to look at the damage to his face. But there was no light in the shed and the inside car lights weren't working either, so the mirror did little good. He scooted in closer and turned his head back and forth, comparing one side to the other. Strangely, no matter which way he turned, the shadow hit his chin just right, darkening both sides of his jaw equally so it was impossible to tell for certain if there was any noticeable damage.

He slammed his fist down on the dashboard. *Damn it! Why can't anything ever go my way?*

His jaw was throbbing as he tried to think of what to do next, but the mental clock in his head was ticking loudly and he knew if he stayed in the shed much longer, NiNi was bound to get suspicious. He closed his eyes and ran his hand along his jaw line. There was only one option left—head straight into the bathroom and check it out before NiNi saw him. If there was a mark, he could try to cover it up with the face powder he saw on the cabinet next to the salve he had used on his hair.

With his heart thumping wildly against his ribs, he stepped out of the car and grabbed the bags from the backseat. Then, tugging the neck of his T-shirt up higher around his chin, he reluctantly started for the house.

Ah shit, I'm doomed, he thought as he approached the porch and saw NiNi standing in the doorway holding the wooden screen open for him.

He hastily shifted his gaze to the ground and gulped hard. A multitude of thoughts and excuses flooded his brain as he lifted his foot to the porch stairs and to his horror, his toe caught on the edge of the step. He stumbled forward, but caught himself and didn't fall. Heat rushed up his neck as he awkwardly shuffled the bags around in hopes of disguising his misstep.

Cursing under his breath, he tucked his chin and trudged up the last few steps. At the door, he darted a quick glance up at NiNi before starting through. At that very moment, the screen slammed shut with such force it shook the porch. He jumped back with a yelp and a look of surprise as the door whacked him hard in the side of his arm.

"Oh my goodness," NiNi cried out in alarm, pushing the screen open. "You poor bébé. I am so sorry. I do not know what happened. The door slipped right out of my hand. Are you all right?" she asked, pulling him into her arms before he could respond.

"I'm fine," Deston tried to reply, but his words were muffled as she held his head against her coat.

NiNi pushed Deston back an arm's length and looked him over. Putting her hand under his chin, she tilted his face to the light. "Mon dieu, look what I have done. Your face ... your sweet face," she cried, pulling his head into her coat once more.

She rocked back and forth as he awkwardly tried to pull away. When she finally released him, it was only enough to guide him to the table. "Sit here while I go to the shed and make you something for that bruise. I know just the thing. It will take away the sting and keep it from coloring any worse," she said with tears in her voice as she pushed him down on the bench. She patted his other cheek and gave him a pitiful look. "You must forgive this clumsy old woman."

Deston was speechless as he watched NiNi hustle out the back door, muttering to herself in French. He couldn't believe she actually thought she had done this to him. Lightly fingering his jaw, he winced at the soreness and rushed to the bathroom to assess the damage. As he stood in front of the mirror and turned his face to the light, he staggered a bit and grabbed hold of the sink for support. A deep purple color covered the full length of his lower jaw-line. However, instead of feeling relief that he'd gotten away with it, he remembered the grief-stricken look on NiNi's face. Closing his eyes, he sagged against the sink. If he told her the truth now, he'd look like a complete jerk and he wouldn't blame her for getting really angry. Yet, he knew it wasn't fair to let her think she had done this to him.

"Ah, damn it," Deston muttered, hearing the back door open and slam shut.

Steeling himself for the scene that was about to take place, he turned and slowly walked back to the kitchen. His head was hung low and his eyes were focused on the floor as he stopped beside the stove.

"I need to—"

"Non, Deston, there is nothing you need to say. Come and sit," NiNi instructed, taking his hand and pulling him to the bench. She pushed him down on the seat and handed him a small, warm bundle of leaves tied around some herbs. "Hold this against your face. It will help."

NiNi walked around the table and sat on the bench across from him. "I do not know how the door slipped out of my hand. I think the spring must be too tight. I will have Peter check it tomorrow." She shook her head sadly, but there was a glint in her eyes. "I am not used to having someone else around, is what it is. But I will be more careful in the future. It was one of those unfortunate accidents that sometimes happen. Your grand-mère used to have a saying for just this sort of thing. She would say, "the milk has already spilt so do not cry."" Her brow wrinkled. "Non that is not right." She thought for a second and then dismissed it with a wave of her hand. "Oh, I do not remember how it goes, but her point was, we must forget about the obstacles life throws at us and move on without wasting precious time worrying about them. ... Agreed?"

With that said, she patted his hand and stood to retrieve the bags that were still sitting on the floor by the door.

"Yeah, but—"

"Non, Deston. Please. Nothing more needs be said. It was an accident. We both know that. Now we will put it behind us and go on to more pleasant things." She gave a nod of her head to emphasize her words.

"But—"

NiNi's look turned obstinate as she held her hand up, cutting him off a third time. In the next instant, her face brightened. "Look, I got you a surprise … American wieners. I am told boys from Pennsylvania love them, oui?" she exclaimed, holding up the white package she had retrieved from one of the bags.

Deston pressed his lips together as he stared at her. If she wouldn't listen to the truth, what was he supposed to do? He let out a sigh and replied, "Yeah, I like them. We call them hotdogs."

"*Hotdogs?* That is a strange name. They do not look much like a dog to me," she stated, looking down at the long sausages. "But no matter, we shall have hotdogs, as you say, for lunch. How does that sound?"

Deston nodded and NiNi started huming and bustling around the kitchen, putting the groceries away and preparing lunch. Somehow, without doing a thing, he had accomplished exactly what he wanted, but it didn't make him feel any better. Not telling NiNi what really took place felt like lying. He studied the herb pack in his hand. The truth would eventually come out one way or another. He knew that, and he'd rather it come from him. But it wouldn't hurt to wait until they knew each other better before he brought it up. Then she might have an easier time believing it wasn't his fault.

With another sigh, he set the herb pack on the table and got up to help NiNi unload the grocery sacks. She gave him a mischievous smile and a knowing wink before turning back to the stove to tend to the fire.

Ohmigod, she already knows the truth. He stared at her back more perplexed than ever. It didn't seem possible, but he was pretty sure she somehow knew. He shook his head and silently vowed to be more careful around her in the future.

Chapter 11

After lunch NiNi went out to the shed to work with her plants while Deston sat at the table reading. Though it was a book by one of his favorite authors, and one he had been looking forward to reading for some time, he couldn't keep his mind on the story. After re-reading the same paragraph three times and having no idea what it said, he gave up and wandered outside. He sprawled across the seat of the porch swing and absentmindedly pushed it back and forth with his foot as he stared at the trees beyond the fence.

As his gaze moved from one tree to the next, his foot suddenly stilled and he bolted upright. He'd been waiting for an opportunity just like this to go and explore the forest and here he was wasting it. He jumped up, rushed to the end of the porch, and peeked around the corner. As he hoped, the door to the shed was closed and NiNi was nowhere in sight.

"Yes," he muttered under his breath and hurried down the steps, resisting the urge to run. At the gate, he stooped and pretended to admire the flowers while sneaking another look behind him. Then, without so much as a thought of NiNi's earlier warning, he pushed the gate open and ran across the drive.

His heart was pounding in his ears as he stepped into a world as different from the outside as day is to night. He stood for a moment spellbound, breathing in the cool damp air as his eyes adjusted to the dim light. Though his excitement was on the verge of overflowing, he had the mind to check his watch and make a note of the time. He didn't want to be gone for too long and have NiNi discover he was missing and start to worry. That would definitely not be good.

And would also probably be the end of any future explorations for him. He figured an hour would be just about right. That would allow him do a little exploring and make it back before NiNi knew what was going on, thus, proving he knew what he was doing and would not get lost.

He pulled Mark's pocketknife out of his pocket and gazed down at the compass to mark his location. Instead of pointing out the direction as it should, the needle spun haphazardly without stopping. He tapped the instrument against the palm of his hand a few times, but the needle continued to spin, first one way and then the other. With a frown, he lifted his eyes and scanned the area. He knew the compass had worked just fine the last time he looked at it, so there was no reason for it to act the way it was. Unless there was something magnetic in the area. He slowly turned in a circle, but from what he could see, there was nothing out of the ordinary that would make the needle spin in such a fashion.

He looked back the way he had come and shuddered at the thought of going back. But no matter how badly he wanted to explore, he knew enough to not head into an unknown forest without a compass or path to follow; and he had neither.

With a long drawn out sigh, he put the knife into his pocket and turned back to the cottage. He was just about to step out of the trees when he noticed a carving on one of the trunks. He stopped and stared at the initials "OL" for a long moment, wondering who had put it there. All of a sudden, he let out a gasp.

"Oh my gawd, I'm so stupid. I don't need a compass. I can mark the trees and leave a trail to follow back," he stated out loud, reaching into his pocket again. He pulled out the knife, etched a shallow X on a tree trunk, and stood back to inspect his work. It was perfect. With his spirits soaring high once again and a grin on his face, he confidently walked into the trees, humming softly to himself.

The forest floor was soft and spongy with a thick layer of leaves and pine needles, and the air was heavy with a strong odor of earth and mold mixed in with a light scent of pine. An occasional shaft of sunlight was all that could make it through the dense canopy of foliage, and it cast an ethereal, greenish glow over everything.

Deston could feel the magic hovering around the trees, just as the old man from town said. It was like a living, pulsing energy and it made him shiver as goose bumps ran up his arms. Absentmindedly, his hand went to the cross hanging around his neck and he thought of how Joliet used to spend her days here. He could almost feel her presence and that gave him a sense of peace that he had been missing for a long time.

With no particular direction in mind, Deston ventured deeper into the forest, walking in a half daze and paying no attention to how the forest was changing around him.

The giant oak trees gradually disappeared. In their place grew spindly beech trees between broad conifers. The conifer limbs were long and thick with needles, and the trees were so close together, one intertwined with the next, forming a natural barrier.

When the tangled confusion of trunks and branches finally snapped Deston back to the present, he looked around in surprise, unaware he had stumbled into the midst of a thicket. As he squinted into the mass of green and black in front of him, he thought about turning back, but a small voice in the back of his mind urged him on. And he really did want to see what was on the other side of the trees. With a jerk of his head, he flipped the hair out of his eyes and plowed ahead without a thought about the time.

Slowly and painstakingly, he picked his way through the dense foliage, wincing each time a rigid pine needle scraped an angry welt up his arms. The farther into the thicket he went, the harder the limbs were to pull apart, and once again he began to entertain the idea of turning back. But within the next few feet, the thick vegetation miraculously ended and opened into a small clearing.

Deston lifted the hem of his T-shirt and wiped the sweat off his face as he looked back at the thicket. His path had already been swallowed up by the wild plant life and showed no sign of his passage. With a heavy sigh, he sat down on a fallen tree trunk and stretched out his legs, letting his eyes wander the area for an alternate way back.

On the ground, not far from where he sat, fresh tracks of what looked like a deer or elk were stenciled into the soft dirt. The tracks brought to mind NiNi's comment about the animals that lived in the forest. For a split second his eyes lit up at the thought of finding a wolf or a bear track. Then, just as quickly, his delight faded and he looked back at the thicket. An animal could easily hide within the dense brush and he'd have no idea it was there. There could even be one in there right now watching for its chance to attack.

He sat up straighter and looked around nervously. He'd been in such a hurry to sneak out before NiNi saw him, he didn't stop to think about what he was doing or how foolish it was to go into the wild completely alone and unarmed. He hadn't even brought along water, and he knew better than that.

Deston looked down at his watch. Seventy-five minutes had already gone by since he started on his trek, and he still had to make the return trip.

"Ah man, I'm going to be so grounded for this," he moaned, swatting at a large flying insect buzzing around his ear. The insect flew out of range of his hand and circled his head to buzz loudly in his other ear.

He stood and as he swatted at it again as it passed in front of his face, he caught a flash of light out of the corner of his eye. He looked over and did a double take at the sight of a beautiful, pure white deer standing between two trees a few feet away. He shook his head and rubbed his fists into his eyes, sure that he was seeing things. But when he removed his fists and opened one eye a crack, he saw the deer in the same spot, just staring back at him. And there was no doubt about it—it was white. So white, in fact, it sort of glowed against the backdrop of the dark forest.

This can't be real. I gotta be dreaming, he thought and pinched his arm to wake up. Not only did the deer not disappear, it took a step closer. Then it took a couple more steps toward him, stopping within an arm's reach. Deston sucked in his breath as he looked into the emerald green eyes of the deer.

"Ah man, this is the coolest dream I've ever had. And since it's just a dream, I can walk up and touch you and you won't run away. Right, big guy?" he said softly, hoping what he said was true.

The deer lowered its head and snorted, but stayed where it was. It didn't even flinch when Deston moved closer and reached out to touch the side of its nose.

"Hello, beauty. Where did you come from?" Deston cooed, stroking the deer's velvety muzzle. He gently ran his hand up the silky fur to the bridge of the deer's nose. Just above its eyes there was a noticeable change in the fur. "What's this?" he asked, looking closer at the spot. "How did you get this, boy? Is that a tattoo?" he added, noticing a blue tinge on a small crescent moon shape. As soon as he said the words, he snorted incredulously. "Humph, yeah right. That's pretty ridiculous, huh? How would you get a tattoo? It's probably a scar from a fight. I bet you won that fight too, didn't you, boy?"

Reaching up to the large rack of antlers, sitting like a crown on the deer's head, Deston added, "You probably win all the fights with beauties like these."

He touched the deer's antlers and a sharp spur pierced his finger. "Owww," Deston whispered under his breath, yanking his hand back and shoving his finger into his mouth.

The deer suddenly lifted its head high and its ears stood alert. It stared into the forest directly behind Deston, pawing the ground with its hoof and shaking its antlers fiercely. Then with a flick of its tail, it leapt past him and into the trees. In the time it took Deston to spin around, the deer had disappeared into the darkness.

"Hey, wait," Deston yelled, but it was too late. The deer was gone.

He shook his head and pulled his finger out of his mouth. The small cut on the tip was evidence he hadn't been dreaming.

"Oh man, wait until I tell NiNi about this. She's is not going to believe it." The minute he said those words, he knew them to be true. He had seen the deer with his own two eyes and still found it hard to believe. So there was no way NiNi would believe him. He looked back at the trees where the deer had disappeared, wishing he had brought his camera. Unfortunately, it was one more thing he'd left back at the cottage.

Deston stalled for as long as he possibly could in hopes the deer would return, but he was already pushing it for time. If he stayed any longer, NiNi would undoubtedly discover he was gone. With a sigh of resignation, he turned toward the thicket. The tangled barrier looked as uninviting as he knew it was, and he was no longer in the mood for new adventures.

He glanced over his shoulder every few seconds to see if the deer had returned as he walked along the edge of the clearing to find an easier route back. But once he came upon an area that didn't look as wild as the other, his hopes of seeing the deer again evaporated. With mixed feelings he gave one last longing look at the clearing before he stepped into the trees to head back to NiNi's.

His mind was half on the deer and half on where he was going as he made his trek back through the brush. When he came upon a large fallen tree blocking the way, he mechanically lifted his leg to step over it. But just as he did he caught a glimpse of a pile of fur lying on the ground on the other side of the log. His foot stalled in midair and he looked down his nose. The trunk hid all but a portion of the animal, but from what he could see, it looked like a small wolf or coyote.

Cold sweat broke out on Deston's forehead and his heart began beating so loudly he was sure the beast would hear it. However, it didn't move a muscle. Holding his breath, he lowered his foot and carefully leaned over the log to get a better look. It was definitely a wolf, but its eyes were closed as if it was sleeping. Then he saw the blood on its fur and the metal claw trap clamped around its neck.

With a gasp, Deston jerked back. NiNi hadn't said anything about there being traps in the forest. A shiver of disgust ran through him, and a bitter taste crept up his throat. With trembling legs, he carefully stepped over the fallen log and squatted next to the wolf to get a better look. He sat back on his haunches and stared at the limp body.

The wolf was just a pup with a solid black face and a beautiful silver coat with black tips. He reached out and touched the sleek fur. Its soft silkiness reminded him of his mother's hair and an incredible sense of loss suddenly paralyzed him.

Deston wiped his hand over his face. The pup never had a chance. He balled his hands into fists and scrambled to his feet as his anger flared. He wanted so badly to punch the brute that had set the trap, or punch anything for that matter. He quickly scanned the trees, but the forest was dark and silent. He was all alone and there was no one else to witness the hideous crime—or so he thought.

He clenched his jaw and looked down at the wolf. There was nothing he could do to save it, but he could take it back to NiNi's and bury it so no one would profit from its death.

"You aren't going to get this one, you sick son of a bitch," he shouted, even though he knew there was no one around.

He glared at the chain attached to the trap and saw it was wound around and padlocked to the tree trunk. It wasn't going anywhere, which meant the only way he could take the pup back to NiNi's was to free it from the trap.

Okay, I can do this, he thought, positioning himself with one foot on either side of the wolf's head. Gritting his teeth, he grabbed hold of each side of the trap and pushed down with all his might. The trap gave a small creak, but the teeth barely moved apart. He wiped his hands on his jeans, took a deep breath, and tried again, struggling and pushing until his muscles ached. When that didn't work, he sat on the ground and pushed with his feet as he pulled back. The trap's claws remained tightly clamped together.

Deston tried every way he could think to get the trap open, but nothing worked. He just wasn't strong enough to get it open by himself. Letting out a frustrated yell, he buried his hands in his hair. Several ideas flew in and out of his head, but the only one that was remotely feasible was to find something to use as a lever and try to pry the trap open.

It didn't take him long to find a sturdy limb. He carefully wedged it into the small gap between the trap's teeth, then placed one foot on the base to hold the trap in place and pushed down with all his strength. The teeth opened a little wider than before, but still not enough to pull the wolf out. And the instant Deston released the pressure, the jaws snapped back together. Shifting his position to use the whole weight of his body, he once again leaned onto the limb. The trap slowly opened more and more. He grimaced with the strain, but didn't let up.

All of a sudden, a loud crack shot through the quiet as the branch snapped in two. Deston fell to his hands and knees in the dirt beside the wolf. The ground was cold and damp, and the metallic smell of blood was strong, but he hardly noticed. He sank back on his heels and placed his forehead on the ground as a wave of grief passed through him. He had failed and he didn't know what else to do.

((●))

Caught up in the dilemma of the pup, Deston didn't notice the giant pair of yellow eyes watching him from behind a tree less than fifteen feet away.

Rellik had arrived shortly after Deston, but stayed hidden in the background. He watched Deston try to free the pup, his brow wrinkling in confusion. His kind had always been feared and hated by humans, yet, there was an unmistakable look of grief on the boy's face. That didn't sense. And having never felt compassion himself, the emotion puzzled Rellik. He became all the more intrigued. Running his long tongue around his lips, he decided to wait and see what Deston would do next.

((●))

Deston opened his eyes and turned his head toward the dead wolf. From his new vantage point, he noticed a small lever on the side of the trap that hadn't been visible from above. He narrowed his eyes, got to his knees, and slowly reached out a finger. The second he pressed down on the lever the trap sprang open with a loud snap and such force it made Deston jump. He fell backward and sat on the ground for a moment, staring wide eyed at the open trap. He then let out a hearty laugh. It never occurred to him to look for a release latch.

He shook his head at his own stupidity as he got to his feet and began dusting the dirt off the butt of his jeans. As he leaned down to swipe his legs, a cool puff of air blew by his ear, sending a chill down his spine. His hand stalled midair and the hairs on the back of his neck stood on end. He whipped around as an intense feeling that he was being watched came over him. His gaze darted from tree to tree, but the shadows were too deep to make out anything past a few feet. He did notice the birds had stopped chirping, and in fact, there was no sound in the forest whatsoever as if he had suddenly been placed inside a vacuum. Another chill ran down his spine and his whole body gave a shudder.

Wiping his sweaty palms on his pants, he looked down at the wolf he had freed from the trap. "I hope some animal isn't expecting to have you for dinner," he said, bending down and pushing his arms under the pup. "If there is, it'll have to go through me first before it gets to you."

Deston let out a groan as he straightened his knees and lifted the wolf in his arms. It was a lot heavier than it looked. Adjusting his hold, he took a deep breath and started back to NiNi's, with the limp body dangling from his arms.

((●))

As soon as Deston disappeared into the trees, Rellik lumbered out into the open. His long, sleek body was three times the size of a normal wolf, and his powerful physique gave him the ability to jump higher and run faster than most other creatures of the forest. His massive jaws could chomp a small tree in half with one snap, and his upper lip was curled in a permanent snarl from the four-inch-long canine teeth, jutting up from his lower jaw. He was known and feared by all creatures throughout the forest, not only because of his size, but because he was Grossard's henchman. And Grossard was, without contest, the most feared and hated of them all.

Rellik walked to the spot where Deston sat a moment earlier and sniffed the ground. He then sniffed the trap, more bewildered than before. It did seem as if Deston was genuinely distressed by the pup's death. Or was it just a trick? Rellik's eyes narrowed. It had to be a trick. What other reason would the boy go to so much trouble. And why would he take the pup with him?

A low, sinister growl rumbled in Rellik's throat, but a seed of doubt stuck in his mind. He lifted his nose in the air and immediately picked up the scent. He wasn't worried about Deston getting away— he knew he could overtake him any time he wanted. But there was something unusual about the boy, and Rellik's curiosity had risen to a level that he knew he wouldn't be able to rest until he found out what. Plus, this might be his only opportunity to see how cunning the boy really was.

With one last look around, he dispassionately loped off in the same direction, following at a safe distance to keep out of sight.

(((●)))

Deston trudged through the forest with his heavy load, following the Xs he had etched on the trees. The wolf pup was getting heavier with each step, but he was determined to keep going.

One foot in front of the other, he chanted over and over to himself, trying to keep his mind occupied. The minutes, however, seemed to drag by, and it wasn't long before his arms began to quiver from the strain. Just when he thought he wouldn't be able to carry the weight another foot, a ray of sunlight and a flash of color shown through the trees ahead.

"NiNi," Deston called out, as soon as he broke free of the trees. He stumbled across the drive with the wolf pup and yelled again, "NiNi!"

"Oui?" NiNi yelled back, wiping her hands on her apron as she came out of the shed. Seeing Deston with a pile of fur in his arms, she hurried forward. "Mon dieu, Deston, what have you got there?"

"It's a baby wolf," he huffed, kneeling down and carefully depositing the wolf on the ground by the gate. "It was caught in a trap in the forest."

NiNi came to a dead stop and her hand went to her chest as her heart flipped over. Deston had gone into the forest alone. She swallowed back her panic and rushed to him, throwing a quick glance at the trees before bending over the wolf. The minute she saw the angle of its head and the blood around its neck, she knew it had been a cruel, but swift death. She also saw the pain etched on Deston's face and realized it wasn't the right time to reprimand him for going against her wishes.

Reaching up, she brushed the wet hair off his forehead. "Ah, mon garcon, do not be upset. The world is full of cruelty, and it pains me to say there are many people who do not appreciate nature.

They only care about what they can gain from it. They use what the earth gives and then discards it as if it is their right. I know it is hard for you to understand. I do not always understand it myself and I have lived much longer than you.

"You took a big risk bringing the wolf back here, but I am glad you did. It was the right thing to do. Your maman would be proud of you, as I am." NiNi gave Deston's shoulder a squeeze and stood. "There is nothing more we can do for this creature. He is in a better place and no one can hurt him now. Get the shovel from the shed, s'il vous plaît. We will bury him in the meadow where the ground is soft. He will be happy there."

Deston sniffed and wiped his nose on the sleeve of his T-shirt. He knew NiNi was right, but her words didn't ease the pain in his heart. He rose slowly and shuffled off to retrieve the shovel, as NiNi went to get the wheelbarrow from the side of the porch. When he returned, they lifted the wolf into the barrow and NiNi walked beside him with her arm over his shoulders as he pushed the load to the meadow.

Chapter 12

Rellik stood as still as a statue at the edge of the forest, his black coat melting perfectly into the background and his giant yellow eyes fixed on Deston. He watched as the boy and old woman buried the wolf pup in the ground. It wasn't until the pair disappeared inside the cottage that he realized the consequences of his lack of action. He had been given the perfect opportunity to take Deston undetected and he let it slip away. What had he been thinking? He allowed his curiosity to get the better of him and now, without a doubt, he was going to pay for that error.

A tremor traveled down Rellik's legs at the thought of what Grossard would do upon learning of today's incident. A wave of paranoia engulfed him. He jerked around and quickly scanned the trees to make sure he was alone. The forest appeared empty, but he knew that didn't necessarily mean he was safe. Grossard always seemed to have ways of finding things out.

A sneer lifted the corner of his mouth as he turned back to the cottage. The night wasn't over yet. There might be another chance for him to snatch the boy.

He waited in the shadows. Even after the sun set and the sky turned dark, he stayed on. Although by that time, it was more out of the need to concoct a good story to tell Grossard then because he expected Deston to reappear. However, he found it hard to focus on an excuse to give his master as his thoughts kept turning to the one question that bothered him most. Why didn't he grab the boy in the forest when he had the chance? That puzzled him more than anything else did. It was so unlike him.

Chapter 13

That night at dinner, Deston's thoughts were on the forest, and instead of eating, he pushed the food around on his plate. Noticing his lack of appetite, NiNi did her best to engage him in conversation, but she could only get him to occasionally respond, and even then it was half-hearted. It broke her heart to see him so upset and as the evening wore on, she grew more desperate to find a way to distract him.

Finally, in a last ditch effort to avert his attention from the events of the day, she cleared her throat and began to recount outlandish stories of her younger years. It took a while for Deston to start listening, but the minute NiNi noted his interest, she exaggerated her narratives to capture him completely. By the end of dinner, the tales had become so outrageous they were both doubled over with laughter.

NiNi continued the stories through the clearing of the table and washing of the dishes, but after the kitchen was cleaned and everything put away, an uncomfortable silence grew between them. NiNi folded and refolded the dish towel, knowing she could no longer put off talking to Deston about going into the forest. He had no idea the danger that awaited him in the forest, and it was up to her to impress upon him the importance of not venturing into it again. And she had to do so without revealing the true reason for her concern.

Pulling two cups from the cupboard, she set them on a tray along with a pot from the stove. "It is such a beautiful night. Let's go out and sit on the porch. I've made some of my special recipe hot chocolate. Some say it is the best hot chocolate in all of France, but you can be the judge of that yourself."

NiNi led the way to the porch swing and poured the rich, dark liquid into the cups. As they silently sipped their drinks, she pushed the swing back and forth with her foot. Her heart was heavy, but she steeled herself, took a deep breath, and turned to him. The moon was little more than a sliver in the sky and provided very little light, but there was enough coming from the kitchen to give her a silhouette of his face.

"Deston, do you remember the first day you were here and I told you about the dangers of the forest?" NiNi asked.

Deston's cheeks turned a deep shade of pink and he turned his face away from her before answering, "Yeah."

"So do you now understand what I am talking about?"

"Yeah," he repeated after a short pause, although it was barely audible.

"Deston, look at me please," NiNi said taking his hand. "I need you to listen to me and believe me when I tell you I am doing this for your own good. The forest is an extremely dangerous place. You must not step foot inside it again."

"But nothing happened ... to me, anyway. I left markers on the trees so there was no chance of me getting lost. And I saw a really cool white deer," he replied in defense.

NiNi's foot stilled the swing and the blood drained from her face. "A *white* deer?" She looked toward the forest, as the memory of another time and place flashed through her mind. After a moment, she closed her eyes and forced herself back. "Non, Deston, you are mistaken. There are no white deer in Brocéliande."

"Ah, seeee. I knew it. I knew you wouldn't believe me. But I did see one," Deston argued. "And if I hadn't gone into the forest today, I wouldn't have found that wolf pup. Think of what would have happened to it then. It would have been ..." His throat closed up and his words trailed off.

NiNi squeezed his hand. "You are a smart boy and you know animals die in the wild all the time. It is how Mother Nature is able to keep the balance of things."

"I know that, but Mother Nature didn't kill it."

NiNi sighed. "Oui, you are right. It was not Mother Nature.

Unfortunately, there are people who set traps in the forest as a business. There are even some who set traps for the fun of it. Right or wrong, that is the way it is, and the way it has been for hundreds of years."

Deston sat up straighter. "You mean there are more traps out there?"

"I am sure there are many more. They are one of the dangers I was referring to. What do you think would have happened if you had been the one to step on that trap instead of the wolf? I do not know if I would have been able to find you before the … er … I may not have found you in time. I would never forgive myself if anything happened to you. You have no idea how fortunate you are to have made it back here safely."

Deston's chin dropped to his chest.

"Please, promise me you will not go into the forest again," NiNi pleaded.

Deston remained silent as he looked across the yard at the forest. In the dark of the night it looked like a gigantic, black curtain had been draped across the land to shut out the rest of the world. A lengthy pause went by, and NiNi was about to ask him again when he finally spoke in a voice so soft it was almost a sigh.

"They say wolves have families just like we do. So somewhere out there is a family looking for its lost baby. They don't know where she's gone and they're probably searching all over for her and worried out of their minds. I know how horrible it is to lose someone you love and have no idea where she's gone."

"Oh, mon garcon." NiNi reached out and brushed the hair off his forehead, realizing there was more to his sadness than the death of the wolf. "I am sure the wolf's family is sad that one of their own is missing. But you must remember wolves live by the laws of nature every day. They understand the price of freedom comes with the bad as well as the good. I am sure they endure it and accept it as part of their fate, just as we have to endure the bad things that happens to us. They will mourn their loss, but they will also go forth with their lives, as we must."

NiNi put her arm around Deston's shoulder, pulling him into her side as she gave the swing another push with her foot. "I have just found you, mon garcon. I do not want to lose you again so soon," she whispered into his hair.

She could feel Deston's resistance and her chest tightened with fear. There had to be a way to get across to him and make him understand how important it was to heed her words. She stared off into the darkness as the swing rocked up and back, and gradually a thought formed in her mind.

"You know when Jolie was very young ... well, maybe she was not all that young, but her age is not important. One day she went into the forest, as she had so many times before. Your grands-parents let her come and go as she pleased and thought nothing of it since she had grown up here and knew the forest better than they did. But on this one day, dinnertime came and went and Jolie did not return. The sun set and the sky darkened, and still no Jolie. Your grand-mère became very worried. Jolie had never stayed out so late before, and it is well known in these parts that you do not go into the forest after dark. There are twice the dangers at night."

She gave Deston's arm a squeeze. "Your grand-mère, God rest her soul, sat right here in this very swing the entire night waiting for Jolie to find her way home. Then at the first hint of dawn, she collected everyone who would come, including me, and sent all of us out searching."

NiNi stopped her story and stared into the forest. Deston pushed away from her shoulder and looked up. "So what happened?" he prodded.

"Hmm?" NiNi started, coming back from an ancient memory. "Oui, well, we searched many, many hours and found no sign of Jolie. Most of the others assumed either an animal had gotten her and she was hurt, or she had fallen into the lake." She let out a hearty chuckle. "You should have heard your grand-mère then. She gave them a piece of her mind, I tell you. "Your negative thoughts are only blocking the Universe from showing us the way. You cannot expect to find my bébé if you have already given up."" NiNi did her best imitation of Deston's grandmother and then paused and shook her head. "Your grand-mère was a remarkable woman—very strong, but also very stubborn. Jolie is a lot like her in many ways. And I think you may have inherited some of those same traits too."

Chuckling softly, NiNi stood and took their cups to the small table on the other side of the door to buy some time to think of how to continue the story without revealing too much. After stacking the dishes, she came back, cleared her throat, and continued. "We searched and searched, but many things are never found when they are lost in the forest. This is why I tell you it is not safe for you to go into the forest alone. You see, Jolie was a girl who knew the forest better than anyone else in the land, and yet she was lost. The forest is like that. It is, how you say, *imprévisible?*"

Satisfied she had made her point, NiNi stopped and a far-a-way look settled over her face.

Deston looked up, waiting to hear the end of the story, but it quickly became obvious NiNi wasn't going to continue. He gave her a nudge. "So how did you find her?"

"Hmm?"

"Mom ... you had to have eventually found her, because she went to America and had me."

"Ack ... well," NiNi fumbled with her words, realizing she had unintentionally backed herself into another corner. "Let me see. My memory is not so good as it once was. As I recall, sometime later, Jolie found her way out of the forest. It was a miracle, I tell you, and if she were here this minute, she would agree with me and tell you herself that she was very fortunate to make it back unharmed."

Deston waited for NiNi to elaborate further, but again she grew silent. "What did Mom say when she came back? Did she tell you where she was?" he pressed.

"Mon dieu, that was such a long time ago. I ... er ... I do not remember what she had to say. She left for America shortly after she reappeared, so I never had the chance to talk to her about it. But I do not want you to miss the important message of the story. That is, even with Jolie's vast knowledge and many previous trips into the forest, she got lost. It truly was a blessed miracle she came back. And miracles do not happen every day."

Deston leaned back against the swing and quietly digested the story. "Do you think she found Merlyn's fortress that day and that's where she was?" he asked after a short while.

"Non, non—that is just an old myth."

"But this man I met in town told me it's really there. He says he knows people who have discovered it."

"What man is this?" NiNi questioned, tensing and stopping the swing once more. "You did not mention meeting a man."

"I didn't think it was important. He was just an old man I met walking up the street. He said his name was Monsieur Zumwald."

"Zumwald?" NiNi repeated, trying hard to keep the alarm out of her voice. "That name has not been around Merveille in a long time. You must be mistaken."

Deston shrugged his shoulders and started the swing up himself this time. As he stared at the forest, a faint pinpoint of light materialized in the middle of the darkness. Slowly, it expanded and became brighter as it moved forward. Once it broke free of the trees, it separated into hundreds of tiny flying lights that blinked off and on. The tiny lights crossed the drive, skirted the outer edge of the fence and headed straight to the meadow. There they hovered and danced in a circle over the very spot where the wolf had been buried.

"Oh look," Deston exclaimed. "Fireflies!"

NiNi, lost in her own thoughts, didn't notice the flying lights until Deston pointed them out. As she turned her head and saw them bouncing across the dirt, her breath caught in her throat. She had not seen Them come out of the forest in a long time. In fact, They had not appeared since Jolie left for America. A feeling of helplessness overcame her and she closed her eyes. She thought she was prepared to protect Deston, but with the appearance of the white deer, Zumwald, and now this, she realized she was wrong.

"I didn't know you had fireflies in France. I'm going to go catch some," Deston remarked, remembering how much fun he had doing that as a kid.

"Non!" NiNi yelled, and then cleared her throat to cover her distress. "I mean, it is better if you watch them from here. You could step in a gopher hole in the meadow and break your leg, or worse. I am sure They will not stay long. They never do."

NiNi pulled Deston in closer to her side and held him tightly, as if she was afraid he would fly away if she let go. And just as she said, less than five minutes later the lights gathered into a tight little ball and headed back toward the trees, skirting the outer edge of the fence as before. As the swarm crossed the drive, Deston ran to the steps of the porch and watched one of the tiny bugs break away from the group and dance back and forth in front of the gate, blinking its light on and off, but never crossing over the barrier of the fence.

"Look, it's checking me out," Deston laughed and made a face at the bug.

As he started down the steps, the tiny light flew high into the sky and made a dash for its fellow compatriots, who had already begun to fade into the darkness of the forest.

NiNi shivered, even though the night air was still warm. "We should go in before we catch cold," she said, moving to the door and holding it open for him.

Deston turned without an argument. As he was just about to step inside, a sorrowful howl echoed through the night air. The sound tore through his heart like an arrow and a lump lodged in his throat. He paused and looked over his shoulder. "I know how you feel," he said under his breath, then hurried through the door and up the stairs before NiNi could see the tears that were floating in his eyes.

Chapter 14

Rellik gave up his post at the cottage shortly after the lights went out. Still, he took his time getting to Grossard's cave. He stopped just inside the entrance and waited patiently to be acknowledged by Grossard, who was lounging next to the fire, gnawing on the leg of a deer. Saliva dripped from Rellik's jaw at the sight of the blood dribbling down Grossard's chin onto his shaggy chest.

"Since you aren't watching the old woman as I instructed you to, am I to assume you have information for me?" Grossard inquired through a mouth full of raw meat.

"Yes, Master. The boy has arrived at the cottage."

Grossard's muscles tightened and his arm froze in midair, "Humph. Is that right? I thought you said he knew nothing of our world."

"That is what I was told. I still believe it to be true since he went to the old woman and not to Them."

Grossard turned his head and his steely eyes drilled into Rellik. "I see. So you are here to tell me you have taken care of him, then?"

"No, not exactly, Master. I—"

With an earsplitting howl, Grossard threw the deer leg aside and jumped to his feet. "No? If you don't have the boy, why are you standing here?"

Rellik flinched at the outburst and hastily retreated a few steps. "I ... um ... I thought you would want to know of his arrival. I haven't taken him yet, because I haven't been able to get near him. The old woman is guarding him well. She hasn't let him out of her sight," he lied.

Grossard's brow furrowed as he studied Rellik. "The old woman is guarding him and that's why you can't get near him?" He snorted in disgust and turned his back. "Do They know he's arrived?"

Rellik's gaze nervously flicked around the room. "Y-yes. They came to the cottage this evening. But as I said, the old woman has taken precautions and They didn't … They couldn't get near him."

"Could not get near him." Grossard pursed his lips as his head slowly bobbed up and down. *"Could not get near him,"* he repeated louder. "COULD NOT GET NEAR HIM?" he roared, throwing his hands in the air and whirling around to face Rellik. "Have you any idea what will happen if They do get near him? My plan and everything I've worked for these last years will be ruined!"

Rellik held his tongue and lowered his gaze. In the next instant Grossard was standing right in front of him and Rellik jumped back in surprise.

"I gave you one simple task and you have bungled it from the very beginning. If I didn't know better, I'd say you are purposely trying to sabotage me. Or is it that you don't wish to be my second in command anymore?"

Rellik remained silent.

"Maybe you're in need of another reminder of what will happen if you fail me?"

"No, Master," Rellik swiftly replied, keeping his eyes down.

Grossard opened and closed his fists as he stared at Rellik. "Go back and take care of the boy—the old woman, too, if she gets in the way." He started to turn away, then hesitated and turned back. "Just so it's perfectly clear," Grossard growled, enunciating each word. "You and you alone will be held responsible if that boy interferes with my takeover in any way. Need I tell you what that means?"

Rellik shook his head, but Grossard continued anyway. "You will watch your entire bloodline be obliterated from this earth, and not in a pleasant way, I might add. Then you will follow."

Grossard walked back to the fire and retrieved the deer leg from the ground. Without brushing the dirt off, he took a bite, but his appetite had vanished. With a sneer, he turned to throw the leg out the door and saw Rellik still standing quietly by the entrance.

"What are you still doing here? Didn't I just tell you to go and take care of the boy before They get to him?"

"But, Master—" Rellik abruptly stopped as Grossard bared his teeth and took a step forward.

"Was there something else you wanted to say to me?" Grossard said, blood oozing from the corners of his mouth.

Rellik shook his head and stepped backward. He knew when to keep his mouth shut.

"I'm warning you again … do not fail me. And do not come back until the boy is dead," Grossard hissed.

Rellik bowed and ran from the cave, disappearing into the fog.

Chapter 15

Deston tossed and turned all night, unable to get the image of the wolf caught in the trap out of his mind. The thought of the white deer or some other innocent creature falling victim to one of the remaining traps made him sick to his stomach. As the purple hues of dawn chased the black of the night across the sky, he finally came to the conclusion that he had to do something to stop the cruelty. He would search the entire forest all on his own if need be to find and destroy every remaining trap there was.

Having made a decision on a course of action, his mind eased somewhat, though only until he realized there was one major hurtle he would have to get over before executing his plan—NiNi. She had made it obvious after her talk the previous night that she wasn't as sympathetic to the animals' plight as he was, and her unyielding resolve to keep him out of the forest had turned into an obsession, which he still didn't understand. Though he was pretty sure there was more to the story than she was telling him. He had thought once he proved he could go into the forest and return safely as he had done that would remove her objection. But she seemed to be incredibly stubborn about the subject. His mother was stubborn like that too, but over the years, he had learned how to get around her. He was fairly confident he'd be able to find a way around NiNi as well. It just might take him a while to do so. In the meantime, more animals would die.

Massaging his temples, he tried to think it through, but his mind refused to cooperate, and his stomach grumbled so loudly it broke his concentration. He hadn't eaten much dinner the night before and he had never been good at thinking on an empty stomach. But he knew it was too early for NiNi to be up, so he rolled to his side, pulled the pillow over his head, and tried to ignore the hunger pains. He had never been good at that either, though, and finally gave up trying.

With the thought of NiNi's delicious cooking taking over his mind, Deston hurriedly threw on some clothes, hoping he might be able to scrounge up some leftovers from last night's dinner. He bounded down the steps two at a time. Much to his surprise, NiNi was already and sitting at the table with a pencil and notepad in front of her.

The events of the day had weighed heavy on NiNi's mind all night long as well, and she hadn't slept a wink. All through the dark hours she agonized over what to do. In the end, the only scenario that made sense was to take Deston far away, just as Joliet had done. It broke her heart to think of leaving her home. The best years of her life had been spent on the farm and she loved it. But when it came down to it, she loved Deston and Joliet much more.

For the past few hours, NiNi had sat at the table making a list of arrangements she would need to attend to before leaving. The hardest part, and what took up most of her time, was deciding how to break the news to Deston. She pondered that problem until the dawn light was breaking the horizon, and by then her head was aching so badly she gave up. She still had several days to decide whether to tell him the truth or not. Until then, she would tell him nothing. And to keep him from discovering what she was up to, she decided to send him into the village for the day while she packed and made the preparations. It was the only place she felt comfortable about leaving him, as They stayed clear of Merveille.

NiNi looked up as Deston jumped off the last three steps and rushed to the table to sit down in front of a big plate of croissants and fresh fruit. "Did you sleep well last night?" she asked.

"Yeah," he replied, stuffing his mouth full of the buttery roll.

"That is good to hear. I was hoping you would be well rested. I need you to do an errand for me. If you do not mind, that is."

"Yeah, sure," replied Deston, licking his fingers before taking another bite.

"I have a package that needs to be delivered to a friend of mine. I would do it myself, but something has come up that needs my immediate attention. And I thought you would enjoy taking the bicycle into Merveille and deliver it in my place."

Seeing the stricken look cross Deston's face, she hurried on, "As I said, I would do it myself, but this is a very pressing matter that has come up and I cannot manage both. If you would do me this favor, it would help me out *immensément*."

Deston opened his mouth to speak, but NiNi held up her hand. "I know what you are going to say … you do not know your way around Merveille. I have already thought of that and made arrangements for Margaux—you know that nice girl you met yesterday—to show you where Marie lives. Afterwards, you can spend the whole day with Margaux and she can introduce you to some of the other nice children she knows. That will be fun, oui?"

At the mention of Margaux, Deston choked on a piece of fruit he had just put in his mouth.

"Are you alright?" NiNi asked with a feigned look of concern.

"Yeah," he coughed, "it just went down the wrong pipe."

"Good. Then it is all settled. You will stay in the village and have some fun today with people your own age."

Deston's mind was racing. Getting out of NiNi's sight was exactly what he wanted to do; however, going into Merveille was not how he wanted to do it. The odds of running into Claude and his friends in such a small village had to be incredibly high. If he came home with another bruise, or worse, he'd have a lot of explaining to do. Plus, the thought of spending the day with Margaux after she witnessed him being pummeled was not what he would call fun.

"Deston?" NiNi prompted when he didn't reply.

"Huh?" Deston looked up.

"I cannot force you to do this for me if you do not want to. I suppose I can put everything else I have to do aside."

Deston inwardly cringed, "Nooo, I will do it. But I was just thinking there's no reason to bother Margaux. I'm sure I can find your friend's house on my own. Just tell me how to get there. I'm really good with directions. And I have a compass," he added as an afterthought.

"Non, that is ridiculous. It is no bother. Margaux is happy to take you to Marie's and I will feel better if I know she is with you. The streets of Merveille can be tricky."

"I don't want to see Margaux again," Deston inadvertently blurted out. As soon as the words left his lips, his face turned scarlet.

NiNi's eyebrows went up in mock surprise. Margaux's mother had mentioned Deston might not be too enthused to see Margaux again, but she had not said why. "Mon dieu, I am sorry. I did not think you would mind. I have already called and made the arrangements with Madame Labonté. Margaux is expecting you and is very excited to spend the day with you."

Deston put his head in his hands and inwardly groaned.

"I told Madame Labonté you would be there within two hours, so you do not have to rush. You have plenty of time to get ready," NiNi added with an innocent smile.

Chapter 16

Since NiNi had to go that way, she drove Deston and the bicycle to the turnoff into Merveille. He scowled at the car as she drove off down the road, then jammed his arms through the straps of his backpack, got on the bike, and started pedaling toward the village. It was bad enough he had to go into Merveille again, but doing it on a girl's bike that was at least thirty years old made it all the worse. That, however, wasn't the only reason he was in such a sour mood. He was dreading the thought of seeing Margaux again. Before getting out of the car, he had tried once more to persuade NiNi to give him the directions to her friend's house, but she was adamant Margaux needed to show him the way. And since he couldn't explain why he didn't want to see Margaux, there wasn't any way he could get out of it.

His legs felt like lead as he pumped the pedals, and his agitation grew with each downward stroke. Though he was stuck having to let Margaux show him the way, he was determined he would not spend the entire day with her as NiNi expected. He would ditch Margaux as soon as he dropped off the package and then head straight to the forest.

As he thought about different excuses to give Margaux, he suddenly remembered she had a brother. *That's it! Maybe I can get Philippe to show me the way and I won't have to deal with Margaux at all.* He couldn't believe he hadn't thought of that earlier. *This might just turn out to be a great day after all.*

As his mood picked up, so did his speed, but only until he

reached the orchard and saw Margaux sitting on a large rock waiting for him.

"Oh crap," he muttered, as she jumped up with a big grin and a wave.

"Hi, Deston! Mama told me you were coming into Merveille today, so I thought I would come out to meet you. I didn't know if you'd be able to find your way," she said in a rush.

"I could've found the way. I'm not stupid," Deston replied and pedaled right past her.

Undeterred, Margaux got on her bike and hurried to catch up. "Wait up. I didn't say you were stupid," she yelled after him. "Wait! You don't know where you're going."

Realizing she was right, Deston slowed.

Margaux pulled up beside him and gave him a toothy grin. "It's so groovy you could come into town today. I was hoping to talk with you again. Few Americans ever come to Merveille, so I seldom get to practice my English. And people here in town don't particularly like speaking English. I've tried practicing on my own, but it's not the same as talking to someone." She rushed on without giving him the chance to respond. "I used to watch the Brady Bunch on television all the time. It was the only American show we got and it stopped broadcasting a few years ago. But now that you are here, *you* can teach me all the American slang words. I will need them when I go to America to study."

Deston kept his lips clamped together, his eyes on the road, and pedaled as fast as the old bike would go, singing silently to himself to block out her babbling. He could still hear her, though, and when she abruptly stopped talking, he mistakenly looked over to see why.

"Oh, my stars, that's a real shiner," she blurted out. "Did Claude do that to you?"

"It's not a shiner. A shiner is only if it's on your eye," Deston grumbled.

"Oh? So what do you call it then?"

"A bruise. It's just called a bruise and that's all."

"Does it hurt?"

Deston brought his bike to a stop and straddled it as he scowled at Margaux. "Look, if you don't mind, I would rather not talk about what happened yesterday. Please just show me the way to Marie's place so I can get on with my life, okay?"

"Oh sure, sorry. I didn't mean to bring up a sore subject," Margaux replied, and snickered as Deston blushed at her intended pun. "Marie lives on the east side of town. Follow me."

Margaux started up the road with Deston right beside her. They pedaled along for a few minutes before she shyly looked over at him. "I wanted to tell you how sorry I am about your mama's passing. It must be really hard—"

"She didn't pass. She's not dead," he snapped, cutting her off. "She's just missing. But I know she's out there somewhere."

"Oh ... I thought—"

"Yeah, well you thought wrong, just like the police and everyone else back home. Just because they couldn't find any trace of her in the woods, they assumed she had gotten swept away in the creek when her car went off the bridge. But they're wrong. There's no way she could have gotten out of the car once it was in the water. There was no water inside the car and all the windows were rolled up. The doors were all closed tight too. So she obviously wasn't in the car when it went over."

"Oh," Margaux said again. "What do you think happened?"

"I don't know. I was trying to figure that out before they sent me here. The car had these three long scratches that looked like claw marks down each side of the hood. There was also a big dent in the passenger side door like something had rammed into it. I haven't figured out how those things play into her disappearance yet, but I don't think her car slid off the bridge like they said. I think someone kidnapped her, then pushed the car off the road to make it look like an accident."

Deston's words shocked Margaux into silence and she spent the rest of the ride through the orchard processing the information.

After they passed through the gate into Merveille, Margaux led Deston down every street in the village, or so it seemed to him. By the fifth turn, she had him so disoriented he began to wonder if she was purposely trying to get him lost. On top of wasting time, he feared if they continued to travel down every single street in town, they would eventually run into Claude and his friends. And he wasn't relishing the thought of going home with a real shiner this time. But since he was at her mercy, all he could do was grip the handlebars tighter and try to remain calm.

By the time Margaux finally stopped in front of Marie's house it felt like they had been riding for hours. Deston hastily delivered the package and politely declined Marie's invitation to come in for tea and croissants. As he hurried back to the bike, he couldn't help but smile. He was almost free. All he had to do was get rid of Margaux and find his way back to the main road, which he hoped would be a cinch.

He was giddy with anticipation as he straddled the bike and turned to Margaux. "Thanks for showing me how to get here. So, um … I guess that's everything. I'll see ya round."

"No, wait," Margaux called out, catching hold of the bike's handlebars before he could take off. "Madame Jolicoeur said you were to stay in town today. She asked me to show you around and introduce you to some of the other boys and girls."

Deston hid his groan with a fake cough and turned on his most charming smile. "Yeah, well, things have changed. It was great of you to show me the way here, but I don't need you anymore. Sooo, I'm going to take off. It was nice seeing you again, and, um … maybe we can get together some other time," he said without sincerity, and pushed down on the pedals. As he rode off, he waved and called out, "Later."

"*That* was rude," Margaux said, letting out a huff as she glared at Deston's back. But when she saw him take a wrong turn at the next corner, she smiled, got on her bike, and took off after him. She followed him all through the village and giggled loudly each time he went the wrong way.

Deston had been fairly confident he would be able to find his way back to the main road by himself; however, it didn't take long for him to realize he was wrong about that. All the streets and houses looked the same, and he quickly became so turned around he didn't know if he was coming or going. With a frown, he looked down at his watch. Being stubborn was costing him valuable time that he

could use to find traps. He knew Margaux was following him—
he heard her laughing several times—and though he wasn't overly
thrilled about having to ask her for help, he swallowed his pride and
pulled over so she could catch up.

"You know, it would have been nice if you had said something
when I took a wrong turn," Deston snapped at Margaux as she
pulled up beside him.

Margaux cocked her head to the side and raised her eyebrows.
"I don't speak to rude people. Especially those who don't *need* me
anymore," she stated. Sticking her nose in the air, she pedaled on
down the street.

"Crap," Deston said under his breath, and shook his head as he
let out a heavy sigh. "Wait … I'm sorry. I didn't mean it that way.
Hey, wait up," he yelled out.

Margaux stopped her bike and turned, giving him a satisfied
smile. "Is that all you have to say to me?"

"What? I said I was sorry."

"Men," Margaux replied, rolling her eyes as she pressed her lips
into a firm line and folded her arms over her chest.

Completely baffled, Deston looked around for help, but he was
on his own. "Oh, for crying out loud, what more do you want? I'm
sorry, okay? I shouldn't have just left you back there. Will you please
help and show me how to get back to the highway?"

"Oh, I thought you didn't need my help?"

It was Deston's turn to roll his eyes. He then counted to ten
before replying through clenched teeth. "I do need help and I'd
appreciate it if you would show me the way out of here."

Margaux beamed. "Why, I would be happy to assist you,
Deston," she replied sweetly.

Deston bit down on his tongue to keep from countering, but as
soon as Margaux started down the street, he mimicked her behind
her back.

He followed her down the hill and with each new turn, he felt
like a bigger jerk. He would never have found his way out of this
maze without her.

Maybe I shouldn't have been so hard on her. It's really not her fault that

NiNi asked her to show me around. And she's kinda cute, he thought.

At that moment Margaux stopped and got off her bike in front of one of the houses.

"What are you doing? This isn't the highway," Deston stated the obvious.

"No, silly, this is my house."

"What? Look, can you please just show me to the highway? I told you I need to get home," Deston protested.

"No you don't. Madame Jolicoeur told Mama you didn't have to go right back. She's expecting you to spend the day here with me."

Deston felt the heat creep up his neck, and it took a great deal of effort to remain calm as he lied. "Yeah, well that might have been true earlier, but something came up after NiNi talked with your mom. I have something I need to take care of."

"What do you have to take care of?" Margaux asked.

"It's none of your business."

"Well, I could just go with you on this business."

"No, you can't. It's too dangerous," Deston blurted, and immediately regretted his response when he saw Margaux's back stiffen and her eyes grow wide.

"Dangerous?" she repeated.

"Well actually, what I meant to say is, it's just something I'd rather do by myself. You know, it's not something a girl can do."

"Oh *really*?" Margaux replied, planting her hands on her hips.

Deston grimaced. *Oops, wrong again.* "You know what? I think I can find my way from here, after all. Thanks for the help. Maybe I'll see you around," he said in a rush, knowing if he stayed any longer, he would get himself in deeper trouble.

Margaux's eyes narrowed and her lips pressed into a thin line as she watched Deston speed down the street. "We'll see about that," she huffed, getting on her bike. This time she kept a good distance behind him so he wouldn't know she was following.

Through sheer luck and directions from a friendly woman, Deston made only one wrong turn before reaching the gate that led out of town. As he pedaled through the orchard, he breathed a sigh of relief. He was free of the town, free of Margaux, and the only thing he had to worry about was getting back to NiNi's in record time. The sun was already high in the sky and every second he wasted put an animal in jeopardy.

Thankfully, the road into Merveille was an easy ride, just as NiNi had said. If Deston had his own bike, it would have taken him no time at all, but NiNi's old piece of junk was a disaster. It not only wobbled uncontrollably, but the chain also slipped constantly, costing him precious time. He pushed the bike to its sorry limit and prayed it wouldn't fall apart before he made it back to the farm.

His original plan had been to stop at the end of the driveway and circle around the back of the meadow to the forest behind the house. But as the bicycle limped along the highway that paralleled the forest, he realized there was no need to go all the way back to NiNi's. Seeing as how it was all part of the same forest, it was just as likely the trappers would have traps set in this section as in the section by the farm.

His stomach tightened with excitement as he slowed the bike to a crawl and looked for a good place to stop. A high wire fence separated the highway from the forest, but a few kilometers down the road, the fence came to an abrupt end.

Deston coasted to a stop and walked the bike to the edge of the trees. There he let it drop in the bushes and used the sleeve of his t-shirt to wipe the sweat from his nose and forehead. As he opened the backpack to retrieve his water bottle, he spied the neatly wrapped sandwich NiNi had made him. He winced at the thought of how furious she was going to be when she found out he went into the forest again. She would ground him for sure this time, and this could very well be his one and only chance to trigger the traps. So he needed to hustle and make the best of it.

Letting his pack drop to the ground, he took a big swig of water and thought about a strategy.

"What are you doing?" said a voice behind him.

Deston jumped and twirled around to face the intruder. As he did, he stepped on his pack, twisted his ankle, and fell to the ground. He hurriedly sat up and pushed his hat back off his eyes. Then seeing it was Margaux, he gave a disgusted snort. "What are you doing here?"

"I asked you first," Margaux replied with a satisfied smirk as she crossed her arms over her chest.

Deston scrambled to his feet, embarrassed she was able to sneak up on him. "I told you already. I have stuff to do this afternoon," he snapped.

"I know. I remember. And I've decided to come along."

"No! I mean, I already told you, you can't come."

"Yes, I remember. It's dan—ger—ous," she mocked.

With an exasperated sigh, Deston picked up his backpack. "It's not that it's dangerous, it's just not something a girl can do. So go home. I don't want you here," he retorted.

Without another word, he pulled his pocketknife out of the pack, heaved the strap over his shoulder and walked into the trees.

Margaux's eyes shot daggers at Deston's back. "Not something a girl can do," she mimicked under her breath. "I'll have you know girls can do anything boys can. And I'll prove it to you."

Gently, she laid her bike next to Deston's, and without reservations, followed him into the forest.

Chapter 17

Deston wasn't sure which way to go, or exactly where to look, for the traps could be anywhere. But he hoped as long as he kept his eyes on the ground in front of him, he would be able to spot them. He had managed to get out of town pretty quickly, so he had plenty of time to search. And this time he had come well prepared, with water, food, and his camera, in case he ran into the white deer again.

He walked into the trees until he was sure Margaux couldn't see him before picking out a sturdy stick to use as a trigger. As he clicked on the pocketknife's penlight, a rush of adrenaline sent a shiver up his back. He might get into a bunch of trouble for doing this, but if he could save the animals, it was well worth it.

His muscles were tense and his senses were all heightened as he slowly moved forward, sliding his feet through the underbrush to avoid accidentally stepping on a trap. Suddenly, a loud crack interrupted the silence and he nearly jumped out of his skin. He froze in his tracks and listened. A few seconds later, there was another snap—this one louder and directly behind him.

Very slowly he turned and squinted through the trees. The forest appeared to be empty and peaceful, but he sensed something was out there. And whatever it was, it was coming his way. His heart thumped in his ears, and in that instant, he realized he wasn't as prepared as he thought. He had brought along all the basic essentials, but forgot the most important item—something to use to defend himself with.

He looked down at the thin branch in his hand and gulped as he took a step backward. Before he could take another, the large bush in front of him rustled and he realized it was too late to turn and run. He grabbed up a larger, sturdier stick from the ground and crouched for an attack. Slowly, he raised the stick and swung just as Margaux stepped out from behind the greenery.

Deston stopped the stick an inch from her head and croaked, "Geez, Margaux!" Heat rushed to his cheeks and his heart raced as he looked at the stick that could have crushed her skull. With a growl, he threw it to the ground and turned his back. He walked a few paces away, put his hands on his knees, and dropped his head as he inhaled and exhaled to calm his nerves.

After a few minutes, he straightened and turned back, his eyes hard. "Don't you know better than to sneak up on someone like that? I could have really hurt you."

"I didn't sneak up on you," Margaux replied, flashing him a false smile. "I was just walking through the forest, enjoying nature. Is it my fault you just happened to be here in the same vicinity?"

Deston let out an exasperated sigh. "I told you to go home. What do I have to do to get rid of you?" he asked in a sterner tone than he intended.

Two large splotches of pink colored Margaux's cheeks. "You don't have to get *rid* of me," she said, scorn dripping off each word. "And just so you know, I can go wherever I want. Maybe it's not so in America, but here in France we are free to come and go as we please. If that bothers you, I suggest you go somewhere else."

Deston inwardly groaned. He had very little experience dealing with girls, and this was one of the reasons why. "Look, I'm sorry. I didn't mean it that way. But you're a girl." As Margaux arched her right eyebrow, Deston rushed on, "I mean, I don't want you to get hurt or anything."

"Why would I get hurt? I have been in this forest a hundred times. In fact, I know it a lot better than you do."

"Look, I'm not here on some nature walk. I'm searching for traps. But don't tell anyone, okay?" he added hastily, realizing he probably shouldn't have mentioned that.

"Traps? What makes you think there are traps around here?" asked Margaux.

"I *know* there are traps. I found one yesterday. A baby wolf had been caught in it. It was horrible and I don't want any other animal to have to suffer like that. So I'm going to search for the traps and trigger as many as I can find."

Margaux's eyes widened and her expression softened. "Ahh, a baby wolf, really? Was it dead?"

"Yeah, it had gotten caught around the neck. There was blood everywhere. It was really gross," Deston added as a second thought, hoping the mention of blood would turn her away.

"Ohhh," Margaux breathed softly, then immediately brightened. "But I can help ... really, I can. Just think how many more traps two people could find."

"No, I—" Deston started to protest.

"Besides, it would be a lot safer," Margaux interrupted. "Didn't Madame Jolicoeur warn you about going into the forest alone? Everyone around here knows that. But if we do it together, it'll be better, because there will be someone to go for help if we run into trouble," she finished quickly.

Deston was shocked. The girls he knew back home would never go traipsing through the forest looking for traps. The mention of blood alone would have sent them away screaming in hysterics. "I don't know," he said, still uncertain. Although the more the idea bounced around inside his head, the more sense it made. Having Margaux along would take away NiNi's main objection of him going into the forest alone. Plus, if NiNi does find out and gets mad, he could say it was Margaux's idea, which technically wasn't a lie.

"Come on. I won't get in the way. I promise," Margaux coaxed. "I'll be a big help. Really, I swear I will."

Deston let out an exaggerated sigh, although he had already decided it was the perfect solution to his problem. And even if he told her no, she would probably just follow anyway.

"Fine. But don't get in my way. And if you see a trap, don't touch it. Let me trigger it." He started to turn, then looked back with an afterthought. "And just so you know... I'm not going to babysit you. If you can't keep up, you'll get left behind. Got that?" He turned and started on his way without waiting for Margaux to agree.

"Groovy," Margaux beamed and skipped after him with a triumphant grin plastered on her face.

Chapter 18

Deston's nerves were stretched to the limit and his patience was wearing thin with Margaux's endless babbling. On top of that, she would continuously stop to check out some fuzzy caterpillar or a strange looking mushroom and wasn't keeping up. Each time she stopped, he would snort in disgust. Finally, he couldn't take it any-more and trudged on ahead without her like he told her he would do, hoping that she would take the hint and go home.

However, it wasn't just Margaux's delays that had deflated his mood. They had been at it for over two hours and so far had only found one trap. That was far less than what he had thought and hoped he would find. And the shadows were lengthening fast, which meant he would soon have to turn around and start back. But before he did, he really wanted to find just one more trap. Especially since he didn't know when, or even if, he would have another chance to come back.

As he trekked deeper into the forest, it began to change, just as it had the day before. The trunks of the trees gradually become broader and were spaced so closely together their branches and leaves became one as they reached for the sky, which effectively sealed out even the smallest ray of sunlight. A strange wild vine had also appeared, growing up between the trees and weaving back and forth to link one tree to the next.

After fighting through an exceptionally thick net of vines, Deston leaned his shoulder against a tree trunk to catch his breath. He looked down at his watch and winced. If he turned around at this very minute, it would still be almost dark by the time he made it back to NiNi's. He looked up wistfully at the jungle ahead of him and shook his head. There was really no point in going on if the probability of finding a trap within the thick underbrush was nil.

As he looked around, debating whether to go back the way he'd just come or try a different route, a movement in the trees caught his attention. He squinted into the darkness, trying to make out what it was, and suddenly, the white deer stepped out from behind a tree. Its emerald eyes stared at him as calmly as before and he was once again awestruck by its beauty.

The odds of coming across the same white deer twice in a row in a forest the size of Brocéliande was astronomical. But the odds were the last thing on Deston's mind, as he was thanking God he had remembered his camera so he could get proof for NiNi this time. But as he lifted his arm to get the camera out of the pocket of his backpack, the deer shied away and took several steps back into the trees. Deston immediately froze and locked eyes with the deer. If it got away before he was able to get a photo, he would be in the same boat as yesterday. He had to get the picture.

Making soft mewing sounds, he slowly rotated his body to keep the deer from seeing the movement of his arm. The deer stayed in place, but its ears stood up straight and a quiver rippled up its neck as Deston pulled the zipper open. For a split second he thought the deer was going to bolt again, but miraculously it stayed where it was.

"Hey, boy, it's alright. It's just me," he said soothingly.

The deer cocked its head, snorted, and took a step forward. It studied Deston for a brief moment, then turned and sauntered off into the trees.

"Hey, wait a minute!" Deston cried, still fumbling to get the camera out of the pocket.

At Deston's cry, the deer took off in a run.

"No, wait! Come back!"

Deston streaked after the deer, vaulting over bushes and darting around trees to catch up. He did his best to keep the white glow in his sights, but the thick foliage slowed him down and he was losing ground fast. The white blur continued to grow fainter and fainter, and then all at once, it completely vanished. But Deston didn't slow down. He noted the direction the deer had been heading and barreled forward, ignoring the vines and branches slapping at him and snagging his skin and clothes.

Seeing a speck of white light sparkle through the heavy mesh of vines ahead, Deston surged in that direction, using the stick to slap the vines out of his way. His breath was coming in short bursts from the adrenaline pumping through his veins, but he finally broke through the vines and stumbled into a small, sunlit clearing. The brightness took him by surprise. He shielded his eyes from the glare and slid to a stop.

The small patch of sky was the first he'd seen in over an hour, but he cared little about the beauty the light displayed. All he could think about was that he had stupidly put the camera in the pack and out of reach, which had allowed the deer to get away a second time without him snapping a photo. He silently berated himself as he clipped the strap of the camera to his belt loop in case the deer returned. Then he tilted his head back and exposed his face to the sun's rays.

Slowly, the warmth of the afternoon began to penetrate his tension, but his mind remained on the deer and he took no notice of how extraordinary the clearing was. The perfect round circle didn't have a single tree or bush of any kind within its boundaries. A lush carpet of grass, more suited to a golf green than to the wilderness, covered the ground, and a wide border of tiny purple violets and white lily of the valleys encircled the perimeter, acting as sentries to keep the wild foliage at bay. It was a beautiful oasis in the middle of the dark forest, but the circle's perfection was lost on Deston.

Dropping his backpack to the ground, he sat down on the velvet blanket of grass and took out the lunch NiNi had prepared for him. He looked back through the trees every few seconds, hoping to catch sight of the deer, even though he knew the possibility of it returning was slim.

As he chewed a bite of sandwich, he looked to where he had broken through the vines and thought of Margaux. When they first started out he had tried to ignore her, but her tedious ramblings were impossible to block out. He kept thinking she would give up and go home, but she never did. That surprised him the most. No girl he knew from the states would have lasted more than a half hour.

He took another bite of sandwich. As he chewed, a muffled "ouch" came from within the bushes. In the next moment, a disheveled Margaux came crashing into the clearing. She had dirt stains on the knees of her khaki slacks and a small twig standing straight up out of her hair on the top of her head. She paused for only a second; then angrily swiped at a piece of hair hanging over her eyes and stomped across the grass, mumbling to herself.

Deston tried to hold back his laughter, but the sight of her was too much and a small snicker leaked out.

Margaux's eyes filled her pale face and her hand flew to her chest as she jumped back in alarm and screeched, "*Merde!*"

Deston let out a loud guffaw at her shocked expression, spewing the bite he was chewing across the lawn.

It took Margaux a moment to realize it was just Deston. As soon as she got her breath back, she gave him her best glare. "What are you doing?" she demanded.

"Nothing," Deston replied. "I'm just sitting here enjoying a snack."

"Well, you nearly scared me to death," Margaux panted, still a little breathless from the scare and the effort of breaking through the vines. "Why did you leave me back there? I thought we were going to do this together."

"Hey, I told you I wasn't going to wait around for you. It was your choice to come not mine, so don't start ragging on me now," Deston fired back as he got to his feet.

"Oh, you are such a … such a nerd," Margaux spit out, her face darkening with anger. "And what does that mean, this "ragging on me?""

Deston's temper flared to match hers. "Look, first of all, no one uses words like *nerd* and *groovy* anymore. They haven't for like decades. Second, I told you upfront this wasn't a place for girls," he shouted, glaring back at her.

Margaux stomped her foot on the ground, "Deston Lespérance. You … you make me so mad," she said through clenched teeth.

"Oh, yeah? Well, good. You're no fun fest, either, so why don't you just go home," he yelled back.

"Humph, maybe I should. Then where will you be? I doubt you'd find any more traps, because need I remind you, it was *me* who found the first and only one. *You* walked right by it."

"Yeah, well if you hadn't distracted me with your constant jabbering, maybe I wouldn't have been in such a hurry to get away from you, and maybe I'd have seen it for myself," he shot back.

Margaux opened her mouth to respond, but a sudden flash of light behind Deston averted her attention and she forgot what she was about to say. "What is that?" she exclaimed, stepping around him to get a better look.

With a sigh, Deston stuffed the sandwich back into his pack and turned as Margaux knelt in front of the heavy curtain of vines at the edge of the clearing.

"There is something in here," she said, trying to push the vines aside.

"Come on. There's nothing ..." Deston's words trailed off as a spectrum of color suddenly splashed across the leaves.

"What is that? Is it a trap?" he asked, hurrying over to where she was kneeling.

"I don't know what it is, but I don't think it's a trap," she said, struggling to pull down a mass of the twisted vines.

"Here, move over. Let me do it," Deston said in a macho tone, nudging Margaux out of the way.

He grabbed hold of the vine with both hands and immediately cried out. Jerking his hand back, he sucked on his palm where a thorn had pierced deep into his skin.

Margaux giggled into her hand and Deston shot her a murderous glance.

"Very funny, ha, ha," he scoffed. He could feel the tips of his ears heating up and hurriedly turned his attention back to the vines to hide the red he knew would follow.

The vines were not the same as the ones they had navigated through to get to the clearing. These had hundreds of needle-like thorns covering the stalks, leaving very little space to grab hold without getting pricked. Deston sat back and studied the situation. Unless he wanted to turn his hands into a pin cushion he would need a pair of gloves or some kind of padding. For a brief second, he thought about taking off his shirt and using it, but the thought of Margaux seeing him shirtless sent another round of heat to his cheeks.

As Margaux leaned in to get a closer look, one of her braids draped across Deston's shoulder. The scent of cherry blossoms instantly infused his mind and sent him into a tailspin as a warm sensation flared to life in the pit of his stomach. His palms began to sweat and he was suddenly very conscious of her nearness.

"What about the knife on your flashlight? Do you think it would cut through this?" Margaux asked as she put her hand on his shoulder and moved in even closer.

Margaux's touch sent a shockwave coursing through his body and he jerked involuntarily. He stared blankly at the penknife in his hand. He knew he was supposed to be doing something, but for the life of him he couldn't remember what it was.

"Deston, will your knife cut through those vines?" Margaux repeated.

He looked up and saw his blank expression reflected in her eyes. "Huh?"

She cocked her head and frowned. "What's the matter with you?"

Suddenly feeling foolish, he blinked and quickly looked down. "Nothing," he mumbled hastily and scooted a couple of inches away from her.

His cheeks burned as he turned to the vines and started hacking away. The thick stalks were incredibly tough and after a few minutes of sawing at them, Margaux was pushed to the back of his mind. The saw blade of the knife was barely able to cut through, and in the end, he still had to use his hands to pull the vines apart. By the time he had created a big enough hole for them to look through, his hands were red, sore, and bleeding.

Man, this better be worth it, he thought as both he and Margaux stuck their heads through the opening at the same time.

It was pitch black beyond the curtain of vines, and even after Deston's eyes adjusted, he still wasn't sure what he was looking at.

"What is it?" Margaux whispered.

"I don't know," Deston replied, also in a whisper, even though they were the only two around. "It looks like a dried-up riverbed.

But a riverbed wouldn't have such high walls or be as symmetrical as this is."

"There aren't any rocks, either. A riverbed usually has rocks," Margaux added.

Deston flicked on the penlight and shined it through the hole. The ravine was enormous, approximately twenty five feet across and at least that deep. He slowly moved the light about and found it was the same as far as the beam hit, which confirmed his assessment that it was too perfect to be a natural formation.

Oh my God, it's a moat! he suddenly realized.

Margaux nudged him in the ribs. "Will you please shine the light across to the other side so we can see what's over there?"

Without saying a word, Deston obeyed and pointed the light at the opposite bank. However, the light wasn't strong enough to penetrate the dense, swirling mist rising out of the ravine and all they could make out were a few dark shadows.

"Hmm," Margaux sighed. "That's strange. I don't see anything that would have created that flash of light we saw. What do you think that could have been?"

"I don't know. Maybe it was just a rock or something caught in the vines."

Scooting back, Deston moved the flashlight over the vines.

"There, that's it," Margaux called out as the beam flashed on something to the left of them.

She crawled to mark the spot. Deston joined her and quickly discovered that whatever was there was buried deep inside the vines. With an inward moan, he began cutting through the next section of vines, which were twice as thick as the others and so tightly wound around each other, it was like sawing through a log. Sweat broke out on Deston's forehead, but he kept attacking the stalks. Then, all at once, they fell away in a clump and exposed the source of the sparkle.

"Whoa!" Deston said, expelling a whoosh of air at the sight of a large crystal pyramid sitting on a stone plinth.

"It's beautiful," Margaux whispered, leaning in closer. "What is it?"

"I have no idea," Deston replied.

He got to his knees and reached out. The crystal was ice cold to the touch. As his fingers came in contact with the surface, the core of the pyramid lit up with a soft, orange glow. Startled by the light, he jumped and fell back onto his butt. The second his fingers lost contact with the pyramid the glow went out.

"That was groovy," Margaux exclaimed. "Do it again."

Deston got back to his knees and slowly reached out, placing his hand on the pyramid. As before, the core of the crystal lit up as soon as his skin made contact, and this time he didn't take his hand away. The glow grew brighter and brighter, filling the inside of the pyramid. It then shot out of the pointed top, illuminating the opposite bank of the ravine.

"Oh, *mon étoiles*," Margaux breathed, looking across at the large, stone archway standing magnificently in front of a mammoth, wooden door.

Deston's mouth dropped open and he stared in disbelief. He had found Merlyn's fortress, just as the old man said he would. And thankfully he had his camera with him so he could prove to NiNi it really did exist. He reached for the camera at his belt without taking his eyes off the giant door. As before, as soon as he let go of the pyramid, the light went out.

Margaux punched his arm in dismay. "What did you do?"

"Nothing ... I just took my hand off the crystal so I could take a picture," replied Deston, more harshly than he intended. "You hold it so I can get a picture. Otherwise, no one will believe what we've found."

Margaux knew he was right, but for some reason she was nervous about touching the crystal. Holding her breath, she reached out and grasped the base of the pyramid. Nothing happened. Frowning, she switched to her other hand and tried again.

"Come on, what are you doing? Light it up so I can get the picture," Deston said, moving the lens back and forth to get it focused.

"I'm trying, but it's not working," Margaux replied.

Deston lowered the camera. "Oh no. What if it's one of those things that only lights up once every hundred years or so, and that was it a minute ago?" he said, watching Margaux try one hand and then the other with no success.

"Maybe ... why don't you try it again," she suggested.

"Okay, here, hold this." He handed her the camera and they changed positions.

He reached out, but his hand stopped inches from the base of the pyramid. What if he was right and it didn't light up again? He threw a nervous glance up at Margaux, then bit down on his lip and took hold of the base. The crystal lit up the second his fingers made contact. He sagged in relief.

"I guess it doesn't like you," he teased.

"I'm sure. How would a crystal know one person from the next?" Margaux replied, trying to hide her disappointment, but failing miserably.

"Well, obviously this one does, because it didn't light up for you, did it? I guess it's smarter than you give it credit for," he said with a big grin.

"Fine ... you sit there and hold onto the stupid thing. I'm going to find a way to get to the other side and see what that is over there." She gave him a tweak of a smile and dropped the camera on the ground as she rose.

"Wait. How are you going to see where you're going?" Deston retorted, letting go of the crystal and turning the area into darkness once more.

Margaux turned and held out her hand, "Give me your pocket-knife."

"No way! Absolutely not," Deston squeaked as his voice cracked. Embarrassed, he turned away and retrieved his backpack and camera before facing Margaux again.

"Look, let's just think about this for a second," he suggested. "How are we going to get across the moat? It's too deep and the sides are too smooth to climb up."

"Moat? Who said it was a moat?"

"No one ... I mean that's just a guess. But it could be a moat, don't you think? In the olden days, they built moats like that to protect the entrance to a fortress. And that is a door on the other side. So if it is a moat, there is also a bridge or some way to cross, and it should be close by."

Margaux's brow furrowed, mulling over his theory.

"The bridge typically led straight to the front entrance," Deston continued, thinking out loud as he knelt beside the plinth, trying to rationalize it all in his mind. "That door looks like the entrance, so then the bridge should connect somewhere right around here."

Margaux sank down beside Deston, picking up his train of thought. "Yes, and the pyramid could be a key or a switch or something that lowers the bridge. Or maybe the key is inside it." She leaned over to examine the pyramid closer.

With her nose nearly touching the crystal, Margaux looked up and down all three sides, but there was no switch or lever of any kind on the surface. Thinking it might be on the bottom, she tried to pick it up. It was stuck tight to the stone. Undeterred, she simply shifted her weight and used both hands to try again. She pulled with all her strength, but the pyramid didn't budge. However, as her fingers pressed hard against the base, she felt an indentation on the side.

"I think I've found something," she said. Her voice was muffled as her mouth was right next to the pyramid. "It feels like a … like the shape of a leaf," she added as her fingers traced along the edge of the shape.

"A leaf?" Deston said confused, and then brightened. "A LEAF?"

"Yes, I am pretty sure it's a leaf. An oak leaf, I think," Margaux confirmed, fingering the shape once again before looking over her shoulder to find Deston furiously digging through his pockets.

With a smug look on his face, he pulled his hand out of his pocket and dropped down beside her. "Like this?" he asked, holding out the good luck charm Monsieur Zumwald had given him.

"What is that?" Margaux questioned, wrinkling her nose as she looked down at the small black object.

"It's a good luck charm. I got it from that old man in town the other day."

Margaux took the trinket and held it next to the shape in the pyramid. "I've never seen a good luck charm that looks like this, but it does—" She stopped mid-sentence as the leaf slipped into the indentation on the pyramid.

Immediately, the crystal began to vibrate with a low hum.

Margaux jumped back and fell into Deston. They both landed on the ground. Seconds later, the hum escalated to a loud whirring sound, and the pyramid started spinning on the plinth. Without taking her eyes off the spectacle, Margaux groped for Deston. Arm in arm, they sat on the ground and watched the pyramid spin faster and faster and then levitate off the stone.

Margaux gasped out loud and cowered into Deston's shoulder, as an intense blue beam of light exploded from all sides of the pyramid.

Blinded by the intensity of the light, Deston threw his arm up to shield his eyes and Margaux buried her face in his chest. After several minutes, the whirring sound changed to a rumble and the ground beneath them began to vibrate. Deston opened one eye a crack to get a glimpse of what was happening, but the light was still too intense for him to see anything. The noise continued and a few minutes later, a soft popping sound joined in amidst the rumbling.

"What's happening?" Margaux shouted above the noise, her eyes still tightly closed.

"I don't know. I can't see," Deston shouted back.

"What should we do?"

"I don't know," he replied again. "But I think we—"

Before Deston finished his thought the noise abruptly stopped; leaving behind an eerie silence. Lowering his arm, he opened his eyes and gasped out loud as his heart leapt into his throat, and for a moment he forgot to breathe.

Margaux heard his gasp and peeked through her fingers. "Oh, mon étoiles!" she said under her breath, making the sign of the cross over her chest as she had seen her mother and her mother's friends do many times.

The thick vines had completely vanished and in their place, directly in front of Deston and Margaux, stood a glistening golden bridge, arching across the ravine to the colossal door on the other side. Although there were no visible supports of any kind holding the bridge up, other than where it was attached to each side of the bank, it didn't sag in the middle, and it glowed with a light of its own making.

Deston stared in wonder. Then, without saying a word, he

peeled Margaux off of him and picked up the knife, his camera and backpack from the ground. He calmly closed the knife blade and put it into the pocket of the pack. He stuck the camera in another pocket and got to his feet. Slinging one strap of the pack over his shoulder, he headed toward the bridge, as if in a trance. He reached the entrance before Margaux came out of her stupor and realized what he was doing.

"Hey, wait. You're not going to leave me behind this time," she cried, scrambling to her feet.

She ran to catch up, but when she reached the bridge, an invisible force threw her backward. She pushed herself up onto her elbows and stared at the bridge, stunned and unsure what had happened.

Warily, she got to her feet and walked on wobbly legs to the entrance. She waved her arms up and down in the air over the golden planks, feeling for a barrier or force field. There didn't seem to be anything there, yet something had stopped her. She gritted her teeth and pressed her lips together as she lifted her foot to step out onto the bridge, but she couldn't place it down. She tried again and again to place her foot on the planks, but no matter how hard she tried, the bridge would not let her step onto it. Or someone or something else was keeping her from crossing.

Chapter 19

Deston was almost to the halfway point of the bridge and completely unaware Margaux was still on the bank.

"Deston, wait. There's something here. It won't let me on the bridge," Margaux cried out, but her plea didn't penetrate his thoughts, as he was tuned out to everything, except for the door on other side of the ravine.

"Deston, please, wait for me," Margaux called, trying again to step onto the bridge.

When Deston walked on, her heart sank. He was going on without her and she was going to be left alone in the middle of the dark forest. She stared at his back and crumbled to the ground. Her shoulders shook as small sobs racked her body and tears coursed down her cheeks.

Though the sound of Margaux's sobs were no louder than a whisper, they blasted through Deston's head like an amplifier turned up to full power. He came to an abrupt halt and looked over his shoulder, shocked to see Margaux sitting on the ground with her face buried in her hands.

"Margaux, what's the matter? Come on," he yelled back.

At the sound of Deston's voice, Margaux's head whipped up. She scrambled to her feet and wiped away the tears with the back of her hand.

"Deston," she cried out. "I can't. There's something here. It won't let me on the bridge." To prove her point she lifted her foot and tried to place it down on the boards.

"Oh, for crying out loud," Deston grumbled to himself. Then

to Margaux he yelled, "I didn't have any trouble walking out on it. Nothing stopped me. Just walk forward."

"I've tried. I'm telling you, something is here. It won't let me through."

Heaving a frustrated sigh, Deston retraced his steps and stepped off the bridge beside Margaux. "Look, see ... nothing." He stepped back on the bridge to prove his point. "If there was something here, it'd stop me too, wouldn't it? So come on. It's getting late. I want to see what's behind that door before we have to go home." He walked a couple paces out onto the bridge and waited for Margaux to do the same.

Holding her breath, Margaux crossed her fingers and tried again. As before something prevented her from stepping out. Her foot wavered in the air and her face turned red with the effort of trying to place it down. But no matter how hard she tried, she couldn't make contact with the surface.

"See!"

Deston frowned and walked back to where Margaux was standing. If he hadn't seen it for himself, he wouldn't have believed it. Squatting down beside her, he waved his arm in the air in front of and beneath her foot. There was nothing, but even when he pushed on her knee, he couldn't get her foot to touch the planks.

"I don't get it," he said with a shrug, stepping off the bridge. "Maybe only certain people are allowed to cross. I guess you aren't one of them. Sorry, but it looks like I'm going to have to go over there and check it out by myself."

"No, you can't leave me here alone," Margaux cried out.

"Well, what am I supposed to do? You said yourself you can't go on the bridge and there's no other way to cross the ravine."

Margaux looked at the wooden door and sniffed. "You could carry me across," she suggested softly, sneaking a peek at Deston through her eyelashes.

"What?" Deston took a step back. "You've got to be kidding?"

"No wait, listen. I think it will work," Margaux continued in a rush. "Take off your backpack."

"What? No way. I'm not leaving my backpack here. There's stuff in there I might need," Deston protested.

"I'm not asking you to leave it behind. I just want to prove something." She held out her hand for the backpack.

Reluctantly, Deston slipped it off his shoulder and handed it over. Margaux took hold of it, reared back, and slung it as hard as she could toward the bridge.

"Hey!" Deston watched his backpack fly up into the air and then drop like a rock in front of the entrance.

"See, I told you. There is something there." Margaux flashed him a triumphant smile.

Deston cautiously walked out on the bridge and turned around. "I don't get it. I can walk out here just fine. Nothing is stopping me."

"Yes, but remember you were the only one who could make the pyramid light up. So maybe there is something special about you."

Deston shrugged. It made no sense at all, but things had stopped making sense the moment they found the pyramid.

"Think about it. When you had the backpack on your back, it could go onto the bridge. The minute you took it off, it couldn't. So the only way we can both cross is if you carry me."

Deston looked at the hope shining on her face and turned back to the bridge. He knew he was setting himself up to look like a fool, but there seemed to be no other way for Margaux to get across. He took in a long, slow breath and blew it out through his mouth.

"I guess it's worth a try. Hold my backpack and hop on up," he said, bending over and putting his hands on his knees to brace himself for her weight.

Deston tensed as Margaux jumped onto his back and a small "oomph" escaped through his clenched teeth. She was a lot heavier than she looked. After adjusting her weight, he wrapped his arms over her legs and took a shaky step toward the bridge. "Ha—" his voice cracked. He cleared his throat and tried again. "Hang on. Here goes nothing."

He picked up one foot and tentatively placed it on the bridge, then did the same with the other. "Yes," he said under his breath as Margaux let out a whoop.

He adjusted her weight and started across the bridge once

again, praying he would be able to carry her the whole way without embarrassing himself. His legs started shaking from the effort a short distance in, but he gritted his teeth and walked on.

The forest was strangely quiet, except for the sound of Deston's heavy breathing. It was creepy, and the thick gray mist rising up from the depths of the ravine made it even more so. The mist swirled over the planks of the bridge and around Deston's legs, making it looked as if they were floating in midair. Margaux shivered as she looked down at the illusion and pressed in closer to Deston's back, suddenly not so sure it was a good idea to cross over.

Deston's gaze was fixed on the massive door at the other end of the bridge and he was completely oblivious to the mist swirling around them. As they drew nearer to the bank, he didn't notice Margaux's weight any longer either. All he could think about was the scene in horror movies where the star would inevitably open the spooky door, even though it was obvious there was something bad on the other side. He used to laugh at the absurdity of it. Who in their right mind would do that? Yet here he was in a somewhat similar situation, in front of a strange door in the middle of a dark forest, and the irony of it didn't escape him.

This, however, wasn't a movie lot with a fake monster waiting on the other side. This was the real thing and he had no idea what he would find behind that door. But no matter how ridiculous it was, his curiosity far outweighed his fear. He also had a nagging feeling that he had been guided to this spot and was supposed to find this place.

As soon as Deston stepped onto solid ground on the other end of the bridge, Margaux hopped down. He stood up straight and stared in awe at the archway in front of them, forgetting all about the ache in his back. The arch was made up of two gigantic black stone slabs, leaning together and supporting each other to form an inverted V. There was a faint trace of an engraving on each slab, but it was too high up and too worn to be able to read what it might have once said. About twenty meters beyond the archway, a wall of stone blocks rose into the sky and disappeared into the darkness. Each stone in the wall was green and pitted with age and was as tall, if not taller, than Deston, and twice as wide as it was tall. A mammoth wooden door, at least twenty feet wide and a full two stories tall, stood in the middle of the wall. Unlike the wall, the door looked new or recently made and was hewn out of a single piece of wood, anded smooth as glass with no visible hinges or door handles. Anchored high on the stones next to the door was a tarnished metal, claw-shaped torch holder with a sturdy, unlit torch sitting in the basket.

"What do you think it is?" Margaux whispered, unable to hide the quiver in her voice.

"I don't know," Deston replied, although several different thoughts were running through his head. He flipped around, his face a glow with excitement. "Do you want to find out?"

Margaux stared at him dumbfounded and then looked back at the door. She thought he was crazy, but she didn't want to voice that thought out loud and sound like a sissy. "I don't know. It's getting kind of late. Maybe we should do this another time."

Suddenly, a low rumble erupted behind them. Margaux let out a scream and whirled around at the same time Deston twisted with a jerk to see the bridge pull away from the bank. One plank at a time, it folded in upon itself with soft pops, all the way across until it disappeared into the opposite side of the ravine. When the last plank vanished, the rumbling stopped and the unnatural silence returned.

Deston and Margaux stared at the place where the bridge had stood a moment before, then turned to each other with the same astonished expression on their faces. As Margaux began to tremble, Deston quietly took her hand. He was a little shaken himself, but he didn't want her to know that. Giving her a weak grin, he lightly squeezed her hand in reassurance and let it drop.

"Looks like we're going to have to find a pyramid on this side too, huh?" he said, trying to make light of the situation even though he wasn't feeling all that lighthearted.

He slowly scanned the clearing for a stone plinth like the one on the other side. The ground had a cover of gravel over hard-packed dirt from the archway up to the door, but there was nothing else in the clearing except for a few random boulders and bushes. About thirty feet on either side of the door the forest closed in, looking dark and uninviting.

Deston frowned. It seemed odd there wouldn't be a mechanism

to call the bridge forth on this side as on the other. "Check that way and see if you can find anything. I'll look over here," he told Margaux, pointing to the left side of the door.

For the next fifteen minutes they searched every inch of the area around the clearing and door. To their disappointment, they found nothing. And to make matters worse, the mist from the ravine was moving onto land and it was becoming harder to see.

Deston blew out a breath. "I don't get it. There's got to be a way to bring the bridge back from this side." He turned in a complete circle and sat down on a rock. "There should be another pyramid right here by the door," he continued, thinking out loud. "I mean, wouldn't you think it would be easier for a person to summon the bridge from here? So where the heck is the pyramid?" he hollered.

Margaux looked up from the bush she was inspecting. A lock of hair that had been snagged by a branch hung over her right eye. "Well, I suppose the pyramid could be inside the door?" she said as more of a question than a statement.

Deston jumped up and turned to the door. "You're right. Why didn't I think of that?"

His gaze traveled up the height of the door. Once again he noticed there were no hinges or handle, and as it was set inside the stone walls, it could not slide sideways. That left only one way it could open. He walked to the door and lifted his arms to give it a push. But right as he was about to place his hands against the wood, a silly notion popped into his head. He stopped and looked over his shoulder at Margaux.

"Do you think we should knock first or something?"

Margaux walked up beside him. "I don't know. I guess if some-one lives here, it would be rather rude to just walk in." She shrugged. "But I don't think anyone lives here. I don't see any recent footprints in the gravel. So I'd say it's been quite a while since anyone has been to this place. I think it's okay. Go ahead." She took a step back to give him room.

Deston's heart pounded in his ears as he stared at the door. He then blew out a big breath and wiped his sweaty palms on his T-shirt. He wiggled his fingers before he reached out and tentatively placed both hands on the door. The second his flesh came in contact with the wood, a sensation shot through his fingertips and quickly exploded throughout his entire body. He jerked his arms back in alarm and hugged them to his chest.

"What's the matter?" Margaux whispered from behind.

Deston stood in silence for a moment trying to collect his thoughts. The sensation was the most exciting, yet scariest thing he had ever experienced. Every cell in his body tingled as if an electric charge had passed through him—except it was a pleasant feeling instead of being painful. He had also seen and felt vibrant colors and sounds that weren't there. His brow wrinkled as he looked down at his hands. Colors weren't something you should be able to feel, and sounds weren't something you should be able to see. Yet, he could describe the feel and look of both. There was something else—he had felt a draw from the other side, as if something or someone was trying to pull him right through the door.

Margaux softly placed her hand on Deston's shoulder, breaking his concentration. "Are you all right?"

He jumped at her touch and looked up with dazed eyes. It took him another moment before he shook his head and rubbed his palms together. "Yeah, I'm fine," he said weakly.

He turned back to the door, closed his eyes and took another deep breath. *This is just my imagination going wild again. It's a regular door and nothing more. Just push it open.*

He opened his eyes and blew on his hands for luck. "Okay … here goes." He put both hands on the door and pushed.

Chapter 20

Deston pushed with all his might, but the door didn't budge. Taking a step back, he wiped his hands on his pants and threw a quick embarrassed glance over his shoulder. Though it was a giant door, he didn't think it should be that hard to open. Digging his feet into the dirt, he pushed until he was red in the face and out of breath. Margaux joined him then and together they pushed, but the door didn't give an inch.

"Is it stuck?" asked Margaux.

"I don't know," Deston panted, resting his forehead against the wood.

"Maybe it's locked."

"Maybe. If it is, it has to be locked from the other side, because there's no keyhole or locks out here." Deston stepped away and looked up at the door. "And if it is locked, we're screwed."

Margaux's brow puckered. "What does that mean, "we're screwed?""

"It means we aren't going to get the door open," he snapped, taking his frustration out on her.

"Oh," she said flatly. "So what do we do now?"

Deston had no answer. He looked back at the ravine, which was now completely hidden by the mist. *Aghh, there has to be a way to get inside. What am I missing?* He walked away deep in thought and sat down on a large boulder.

Margaux craned her head back and looked up. Her mind was also wrapped up in the problem, and several things in particular nagged at her. For one, she didn't understand why someone would need so much protection in a place that was already so secluded. She also thought it strange that the key was fairly easy to find on the other side, but was well hidden on this side. It almost seemed as if someone had set them up and was trying to keep them here.

As she pondered those mysteries, another thought came to her. They'd almost missed the key indentation on the pyramid. In fact, if she hadn't re-examined it very closely, she wouldn't have found it at all. Maybe the key to this door was just as inconspicuous.

Margaux leaned in close, her nose almost touching, and lightly placed a hand on the icy cold wood. Slowly, she moved her fingers up its silky surface feeling for an indentation. There was nothing. She moved to the wall and did the same, inching her fingers up and over the stones that framed the doorway as far as she could reach. The stones were surprisingly smooth along the edge of the frame, but again she felt no place for a key. She wasn't tall enough to reach a good portion of it, though, and as the mist had moved into the clearing, the light was becoming more limited.

She stood back and chewed on the side of her cheek, her eyes going to the torch on the wall. If she could get it down and get it lit, it would at least solve the problem of the fading light.

"Deston, do you by chance have any matches with you?" she asked.

Wrapped up in his own thoughts, Deston didn't look up. "What?"

"Do you have any matches?"

"Yeah ... there're some in the backpack," he replied.

Margaux flipped her hair over her shoulder and scurried onto the rock that was set directly under the torch. Standing on her tip-toes, she stretched up, but her fingertips didn't even come close to brushing the bottom tip. Not to be discouraged, she pressed her lips together and looked around for something else to stand on.

"Can you please come over here for a second?"

Deston looked up at the second interruption, but didn't move.

"Come on, hurry. I need you," she persisted.

Deston rolled his eyes, but got up and walked over just the same.

As soon as he got close, Margaux grabbed his arm and pulled him up on the rock beside her.

"Stand right here while I get on your shoulders," she stated bluntly, positioning him right below the torch.

"What?" Deston cried out. "Are you kidding? Why?"

"Because we need light if we're going to find the way to get this door open. And that torch up there can provide a lot more than your small penlight can."

Deston didn't have time to argue for Margaux had already placed her foot on his leg to climb onto his back. He wobbled a little and his knees buckled as she hoisted herself up onto his shoulders. He automatically locked his knees in place and grabbed her ankles to steady her and keep them both from falling.

Margaux slowly straightened her legs as she walked her hands up the wall. Once she was standing erect, she reached up and pushed on the tip of the torch. It didn't even budge. "Merde," she uttered under her breath and tried pounding on the handle to get it loose.

"What are you doing?" Deston demanded breathlessly, as Margaux's foot rocked back and forth on his collarbone.

"It's stuck. I'm trying to … Oh!" Margaux shrieked, as her foot slipped off his shoulder. She grabbed for the torch to regain her balance, but the handle was slick with oil and her hand slid right off. She grabbed for it again and the torch and basket both twisted to the side. The unexpected movement sent her tumbling down onto Deston and they both crashed to the ground.

Margaux's scream drowned out the soft click of the door unlocking, but they both felt the whoosh of cold, stale air blow over them as they hit the ground. In an instant, they untangled themselves and sat up as the giant door swung outward to reveal a stairway leading down into darkness.

Deston and Margaux turned to each other at the same moment, their eyes bulging wide. Slowly, a grin lifted the corners of Deston's mouth.

"That was so awesome. Way to go!" He raised his hand for the ceremonial high-five, but Margaux, not understanding the meaning of the gesture, didn't reciprocate. Unfazed, he dropped his hand, jumped up and ran to the doorway to peer down the dark staircase.

Margaux sat where she had fallen, too shocked to move.

"This is so incredible," he said under his breath. "It's got to be Merlyn's fortress. The old man said it was here, but I thought he was crazy."

Margaux's courage had fled the moment the door opened. She stared up at Deston as if he was insane. "You cannot seriously be thinking of going in there." When he didn't reply, she sprang to her feet and ran to him. "Listen, Deston, this is not a good idea. I think we should go home and tell my papa. He'll know what to do. We can bring him back to go in there with us. It'll be a lot safer," she tried to reason with him as she pulled on his arm to get him away from the stairs, but Deston shook her off.

"No, are you kidding? I'm not leaving now!"

"Really .... I think we should—"

"No!" Deston roared. "*I – am – not – leaving.* We may never find this place again," he stammered, glaring at her. "Don't you see? This may be our one and only chance of finding out if this really is Merlyn's fortress."

Margaux's eyes turned glassy and her hand fell to her side.

"Ah, man," Deston sighed, turning away. He knew this would happen. She just didn't get that this might be the greatest discovery of recent times. He ran his hand through his hair and tried to think. She wanted to go home and that was fine, but he was staying. Taking a deep breath, he turned back with what he hoped was a resigned look on his face.

"You know what? You're right. Maybe we shouldn't go in there alone. So how about this ... you run home and get your dad, and I'll stay here. You know, to make sure the door stays open."

Margaux sniffed and wiped her nose on her sleeve. "You won't go in there without us, will you?"

"Nooo, of course not." Deston crossed his fingers behind his back to cancel out the lie.

"But how am I going to get across the ravine?"

Deston looked over his shoulder. "Oh, yeah ..." He had forgotten all about that little problem. He looked off through the trees. "I'm sure there's a way around it. Why don't you walk down there a bit and see if the ravine gets narrower. Or maybe there'll be a shallow spot you could get across. I'm sure there's another way," he added with a nod of his head.

Margaux looked over her shoulder in the direction he was pointing. "Do you really think so?"

Deston nodded more earnestly. "Yeah, I do. There *has* to be way."

"I guess it's worth a try." She narrowed her eyes at him. "But you'll stay right here and wait for me to come back, right?"

"Sure. Just hurry, though, okay?"

Feeling more than a little apprehensive, Margaux gave Deston a wary smile. She walked the few feet to the edge of the tree line, hesitated, and looked back.

Deston gave her a thumbs-up in encouragement and sat down on the rock. "I'll be waiting. Just hurry."

She swallowed hard and nodded, then stepped into the trees.

(((●)))

Margaux pushed a branch out of her way as she fought through the thick underbrush. The mist was closing in fast and visibility was getting poorer by the minute. With each new step, she became less certain this was the right thing to do. And the more she thought about it, the less sense it made. If there was some other way to cross the ravine, there would be no need for a bridge. As that logic lodged in her brain, something else occurred to her. They hadn't looked for the pyramid or key on the inside of the door. The solution she was looking for could very well be back where she had started. In a huff, she turned and headed back, glad she hadn't gone far.

She broke through the trees into the clearing and came to an abrupt halt. Deston wasn't on the rock where she left him, nor was he anywhere in the clearing. She hurried to the open door and looked down without getting too close. In the dust on the second step was a perfect imprint of a tennis shoe. There was also a faint glow flickering on the wall below. Margaux's mouth dropped.

He went without me!

"Deston!" she cried out. Without a second thought, she bolted down the steps in pursuit of the fading light. "Deston Lespérance, you were supposed to wait," she yelled, flying down the stairs so fast her feet scarcely touched the steps.

As Margaux rounded the second curve of the spiral stairway, a shadowy figure holding a light came into view. "Deston? Is that you?" Margaux called.

Her voice echoed off the walls and the figure stopped and turned in her direction.

"Margaux?" Deston answered, surprised to see the dark shape racing down the steps toward him.

She was out of breath and her eyes were blazing when she came to a stop beside him. "How—dare—you," she gasped between breaths. "You said … you would wait."

Deston bristled. "Yeah, well, I decided I didn't want to wait."

Margaux pressed her lips into a thin line and stared at him in disbelief and anger.

"Don't look at me like that. You didn't want to come. You were too scared. So why are you here anyway?"

Margaux's nostrils flared. "I was not scared. I was only being reasonable. You know as well as I do it would be smarter to have an adult with us. You're just so pigheaded you won't listen to reason."

"Yeah, whatever," Deston said coldly. "Go on back and wait for your adult. I'm going to see where these stairs lead." He turned and started down the steps, adding over his shoulder, "By the way, there's a lever on the inside of the door jamb to bring the bridge back, so you can go home. I'll tell you all about it the next time I'm in town."

He started down the stairs again without waiting for her reply, leaving her on the step with her hands still on her hips.

"You are not leaving me behind again, Deston Lespérance," Margaux called after him, hurrying to catch up.

Deston shrugged, but didn't turn around. "Do whatever you want. But I'm warning you, you'd better keep up this time."

Chapter 21

The stairs wound around and around, becoming steeper and narrower the farther down they went. The stale air within the confined space had a strong, wet, earthy smell, and the only sound was their breathing and footfalls. Goosebumps lined Margaux's arms and she unconsciously squeezed closer to Deston as second thoughts ran through her head. She was just about to voice her trepidation out loud when the stairs came to an abrupt end. At the bottom was a small landing and a glistening black wall that blocked any further advancement.

Deston stopped on the last step and stared in disbelief at what appeared to be a dead end. He stepped down and lightly touched the wall in front of him. It was freezing.

"This is solid ice," he exclaimed, running his hand across the surface, feeling the cold, wet texture of the ice. "How in the world did this get here? ... And how does it stay frozen? It's not cold enough in here," he wondered out loud.

Margaux didn't comment. She just stood on the last step staring at the wall, her uncertainty displayed prominently on her face.

"I don't get it. Why have a stairway that leads to nowhere?" he pondered as he pointed the light at each corner of the wall of ice.

"I think we should go back. I don't think whoever built this place wanted to have visitors," Margaux said softly.

Deston looked around at her and let out an exaggerated sigh. "Listen, for the last time, I am *not* going back," he stated with passion shining in his eyes. "Don't you see? This is the chance of a lifetime. Who knows what we'll find on the other side of this wall. I mean you've heard of Merlyn the Magician, haven't you?" Assuming she had, he went on. "This could be his place and we're the first to discover it. We'll be famous.

"Come on, Margaux, you can't want to turn back now—not when we've come this far and are so close."

Margaux didn't reply. She stared at the wall and chewed on the inside of her lip.

"Can we just try to find a way through this? If we can't, we'll have no choice but to go back. ... But I have to try. Please, do this for me?" Deston coaxed, thinking he might need her help to get through the wall.

Margaux's eyes shifted from the wall to Deston. The grin on his face accentuated his dimple and his eyes shone with a mixture of hope and excitement. Her heart gave a little twinge. "I'm probably going to regret this," she mumbled under her breath as she stepped down on the last step.

"You have to promise me that if we find any more barriers, we'll go home and get Papa, okay?"

Deston let out a hoot and jumped into the air with joy. As his feet reconnected with the wet, slippery floor, they shot out from under him and he fell backward. His arms flailed in the air as he tried to regain his balance.

Margaux couldn't help but giggle at his exaggerated antics, and it helped relieve some of her tension. But her humor was cut short as Deston landed on the ground.

"Very funny," Deston growled, lifting his head and rubbing the spot that had hit the floor.

"Deston," Margaux whispered.

Hearing the apprehension in her voice, Deston froze. Moving only his eyes, he looked up and saw Margaux's face had drained of all color and she was focused on something behind him. He gulped and his heart started thumping wildly against his ribs as he very slowly turned his head, expecting the worst. To his surprise, and annoyance, there was nothing behind him but darkness.

Deston let out a disgusted snort. "Are you trying to mess with me or something? There's nothing there," he barked as he scrambled to his feet.

Margaux didn't appreciate the tone of his voice. Squaring her shoulders, she matched her tone to his. "Exactly! There is *nothing* there. No wall ... nothing."

Deston jerked around and saw that he was standing in a narrow passageway to the side of the wall of ice. Keeping his eyes locked on the passageway, he took a step backward, and then another and another until the passageway disappeared, or so it seemed. As soon as stepped forward, the passageway reappeared. He repeated the movement twice more and then turned back to Margaux, his face aglow.

"It's just a light trick," he exclaimed. "See, the way the light hits the ice makes it look like there's a wall here, but there isn't. Check that side and see if it's a passageway too."

Margaux reached out and touched the wall on the other side of the stairs. "It's solid."

"Great, so we don't have to make a decision on which way to go," Deston said, beaming.

Retrieving his backpack and penlight from the floor, he gave Margaux a wink, and with a spring in his step, he started into the passageway. "Come on, let's see where this leads."

Margaux's excitement didn't match Deston's, and she became even less enthused once inside the passageway. The air was heavy with moisture and the path was so narrow they were forced to walk single file. She squeezed in as close to Deston as she could get without walking on his heels and held tightly to the strap of his backpack so he wouldn't get away from her.

Deston held his small penlight out at arm's length and slowly moved forward, but the darkness was so dense the light only penetrated a couple of inches. It was unnerving not being able to see where he was going, and each time he bumped into the wall or kicked something with his foot, his heart skipped a beat.

A short distance in, the tunnel took a turn and started on a downward slope. As Deston followed the descent, an uneasy feeling of déjà vu swept over him. And even though it was cool in the tunnel, he began to sweat as a memory floated to the edge of his consciousness. It all seemed so familiar, yet, he couldn't put a finger on why that was.

Suddenly out of nowhere, an intense pinpoint of light appeared in the darkness several feet in front of him. Deston stopped short and Margaux bumped into him.

"What ..." she started to ask, but her words trailed off as she looked around him and saw the light too.

The light was incredibly bright and hard to look at, especially as their eyes had become accustomed to the dark. However, as intense as the beam was, it didn't light up the passageway. Deston held his breath and his heartbeat boomed in his ears as the light came closer.

"What is it?" Margaux whispered in his ear.

"Ssshhh," he replied.

The light stopped about a foot in front of him, but due to its brightness, he couldn't tell if there was someone behind holding it up or not. The light hovered in midair for several minutes; then slowly retreated the way it had come.

"Hey," Deston shouted, his voice echoing off the walls.

At Deston's call, the light paused and returned to the same spot in front of him. It hung there briefly, then retreated several feet and stopped. Deston didn't move, but waited to see what it would do next. After a few seconds, the light retreated another foot and stopped again. Deston took a hesitant step forward and then another. With his second step, the light started moving slowly down the passageway, as if leading the way.

"It wants us to follow it," Deston said, pulling Margaux along with him, since she was still holding onto the strap of his backpack.

"Do you really think we should?" Margaux asked in a trembling voice.

"Yes, I do," Deston stated emphatically.

"But we don't know what it is or where it's going."

"Ssshhh," Deston said in reply and picked up the pace to keep from losing sight of the light.

They followed in silence a good distance into the tunnel before the light came to a stop. As Deston closed the gap, the light suddenly veered to the right and went out, leaving no trace.

"No, wait!" Deston cried out.

He swung his penlight around to where the light disappeared and gasped out loud. Cut into the side of the earthen wall was a wooden door with a round, brass door handle. Hesitating for only a fraction of a second, he held his breath, reached out with a trembling hand, and pulled on the metal ring.

Chapter 22

What the heck? Deston thought.

The door had swung wide to reveal a small room. Across from the door an old man sat hunched over a small desk. The man's back was to them and he was so immersed in his book he didn't look up or even acknowledge the sound of the door opening. After the initial shock of finding someone else in the tunnel passed, Deston turned to Margaux with a silent question in his eyes. She shook her head and shrugged her shoulders in reply. She was as baffled as he was.

Deston looked around the room, uncertain what to do. He'd been taught it was bad manners to enter someone's home without first being asked, and though this hardly seemed the time for protocol, he didn't feel comfortable walking in uninvited. He cleared his throat loudly to get the man's attention and waited.

At the sound, the old man stiffened and slowly closed the book. Pushing his chair back, he got to his feet and turned with a look of pure pleasure on his face.

"Ah, Deston, how nice to see you again, and so soon," said Monsieur Zumwald. "And I see you have brought your friend with you. What a pleasant surprise."

Deston's mouth dropped open. He never expected to see the old man again, let alone find him in the tunnel. It took a jab to his ribs from Margaux's elbow to jolt him out of his stupor. "You … what are you doing here?" he finally blurted out.

Zumwald's right eyebrow lifted and his smile vanished.

"I mean … er … how did you get here? Do you live here or

something?" Deston asked, noting a small cot in the corner and shelves piled high with books on the far wall.

"Why yes, I do. At the moment anyway," Zumwald said, his smile returning. Sweeping his hand in front of him, he bowed stiffly at the waist. "Please forgive my rudeness … come inside. I've been waiting for you."

Margaux slipped her hand under Deston's arm and stepped in closer, but he was too shocked by Zumwald's words to notice.

"You were expecting me? How could you be expecting me? I didn't even know I was coming," Deston replied.

"Ah, you will soon learn there is much you do not know," Zumwald said, putting a hand on Deston's back and ushering him and Margaux into the room so he could close the door.

"What is this place?" Deston asked, turning in a circle to take in the whole room.

"It is … let me see, what would you call it? Hmmm … well, I guess you could say it's a lobby of sorts." Zumwald chuckled softly to himself.

Deston, however, didn't find anything amusing about it. "A lobby to what? What do you do here?"

"I am the gatekeeper. But Deston, you're forgetting your manners. I've never been properly introduced to your friend here," Zumwald rebuffed.

Deston threw a quick glance at Margaux, "Oh, sorry, this is Margaux," he replied automatically and quickly added, "Gatekeeper to what?"

Zumwald gave Deston a reproachful look before bowing again at the waist. "Mademoiselle Margaux, it is very nice to see you again. Welcome to my humble abode."

Margaux dipped in a small curtsy in response, but didn't utter a word.

Straightening, Zumwald turned his back to the pair and walked to the desk, ignoring Deston's question. "Deston, I believe you've been looking for your mother, have you not?" he asked, turning slightly to look over his shoulder.

Deston bristled. "What does this have to do with my mom?"

"If I'm not mistaken, your mother is the reason you came to France. When she disappeared you had no other place to go and were sent here to her family. Correct?" he looked at Deston for acknowledgement.

Deston held Zumwald's stare. He didn't know what was going on and he wasn't about to give out any more information until he got some answers of his own.

A knowing smile lifted the corners of Zumwald's mouth. "Well, I have some good news for you. If you still wish to find her, I believe I can be of service."

Deston's heart did a flip and he rushed to Zumwald's side, forgetting all about his previous reservations. "You know where she is? Have you seen her? Is she okay?"

Zumwald held up his hand. "I didn't say I knew where she was. But I do know someone who can help you find her."

"Who? Where is he? Can I talk to him now?" Deston cried out, ready to burst with excitement.

Putting his hand on Deston's shoulder, Zumwald looked solemnly into his eyes. "Retrieving your mother will not be easy. I venture to say it will in fact be very dangerous and will require a long journey and a commitment that should not be entered into lightly. You'll be asked to make sacrifices and you'll face challenges unlike anything you have ever faced before. So before you agree, I want you to think it over. Much will be asked of you. I'll need your assurance you are ready and willing to give all."

"What do you mean? Where do I have to go? Are you sending me back to America?"

"Like I said, I have no knowledge of where your journey will lead you. I'm only the messenger." Zumwald turned back to the desk and opened a large, leather-bound book. "But I do know that if you decide to take on this quest, your life will change forever. There is also a possibility you will not return from it."

Facing Deston again, Zumwald looked him in the eye. "Think about what I just said carefully before you answer. It is a matter of life or death that I'm speaking of." He gave Deston a moment to absorb what he was saying. "Are you willing to accept the risks and do *whatever* it takes to save your family?"

"Are you kidding? Of course, I'll do anything. I'd go to hell and fight the devil if that's what it took to get Mom back. Just tell me what I have to do," Deston rushed out without giving it one second of thought.

As Zumwald studied Deston, a strange lightning shaped glint passed through his right eye. "Yes ... I believe you are ready."

Picking up a feather quill from the desk, Zumwald offered it to Deston, "All I need is for you to sign right here on this line and I will send you on your way."

Deston stepped up to the desk and took the quill from Zumwald's hand. The pages of the book were made of very thin parchment paper, yellowed with age. Each page was divided into two columns. Signatures filled the first column three quarters of the way down the page. In the second column were dates lined up directly across from each name. Deston scanned the page, paying more attention to the dates in the right-hand column than to the names. The first date at the top of the page was October 1523. The last date on the line above where he was to sign was April 1930. His gaze traveled across the line, and upon seeing the name, his breath caught in his throat. The name was written in a girlish scribble, but there was no mistaking it was Joliet Lespérance.

Deston stared in bewilderment. "That's impossible," he said under his breath. "It ... it can't be right. Mom wasn't even born in 1930." He looked up at Monsieur Zumwald. "Who is this?" he asked, pointing to the name. "Is this a relative of mine?"

Zumwald lowered his gaze. "I cannot answer your questions. You'll have to discover the answers on your own, but in order to do so, you must first sign," he said, pointing to the blank line in the book.

Deston looked back at the name on the page. It had to be a relative. There was no other explanation. Joliet Lespérance wasn't that common of a name. Maybe this Joliet was the one Zumwald spoke of—the one who would help him find his mother. Pressing his lips together, he bent over the book to sign.

Margaux, who had been standing back watching and listening, rushed up and grabbed Deston's arm. "What are you doing?" she whispered.

In the excitement of finally getting some information about his mother, Deston had forgotten Margaux was with him. He looked around at her with a strange spark in his eyes. "I'm going to get Mom back," he stated calmly.

"But you don't know this man. He could be lying. How would he know where your mama is?" she whispered.

"I don't know how he knows. I don't even know if he knows, but I have to find out. This is the first lead I've had in eight months. And look at this," he said, pointing to the page in the book. "That's my mom's name. It can't be her, of course. She hadn't been born yet in 1930. But it might be a relative, and maybe finding this Joliet will help me to find Mom."

He bowed his head to hide the tears gathering behind his eyes. "Don't you see? I have to do this," he said softly. He took a deep breath and looked up, his eyes shining with the pain he held inside. "You don't know what it's like. If there's any chance at all of finding her, I gotta take it."

He gently lifted Margaux's hand off his arm and bent down, scribbling his name in the book without further hesitation.

"Very good," Zumwald said as he took the quill from Deston and filled in the date in the right-hand column, next to Deston's name. The handwriting was identical to all the other dates in the column.

"Well, then … everything is set," Zumwald said, closing the book and putting the quill back in its holder. "Are you ready?"

Deston looked at Margaux once more and licked his lips nervously. "Yup, I guess so," he said, turning back to the old man.

Zumwald put his hand on Deston's shoulder and squeezed as he guided him toward a door on the side of the room—a door Deston was pretty sure wasn't there when he entered the room.

"Someone will be on the other side to greet you once you step through this door," Zumwald said.

"What? Wait a minute … you aren't going with me?" Deston asked in alarm, wrenching his eyes away from the door and looking up at Zumwald.

"No, my boy, I cannot go with you. It is not my journey."

Deston gulped. He hadn't expected to be going alone.

"Deston, wait," Margaux ran to his side. "I'll go with you." She turned to the old man and tugged on his hand as she pleaded. "Please, let me go with him, Monsieur."

Zumwald's brow furrowed, as two pairs of hopeful eyes stared up at him. "This is not your journey, either, Mademoiselle," he said. "And as I told Deston, there are no guarantees of its outcome."

Margaux fidgeted for a moment, rubbing her hands together as she gathered her courage. "I understand, but I want to go anyway. I can help. Deston and I make a good team. We can accomplish anything as long as we do it together."

With one eyebrow raised, Zumwald looked questioningly at Deston. Deston looked at Margaux.

"You don't have to do this," Deston said, but the look on his face stated the opposite.

Margaux pressed her lips together and a fire sparked in her eyes. "Yes, I do. Like I said, we're a team. You helped my brother and me yesterday and you didn't even know us. I told you before we came into the forest that two people are better than one and that's still true." She looked back at the old man and pleaded again, "Please Monsieur, please let me go with Deston."

"I'm afraid it's not my decision." Zumwald looked over at Deston. "Deston?"

An unexpected sense of relief coursed through Deston, but he tried not to let it show. Margaux could be annoying at times, but she was also smart and had proven to be helpful. And he was beginning to like having her with him, though he would never admit that out loud. With a shrug and a nod of his head, he answered. "Sure, why not."

"Very well," said Zumwald, hustling back to the table and enthusiastically opening the book. "Margaux, if you please. You can sign right here below Deston's name."

Margaux took the quill and signed her name. As she set the quill back in its holder, Zumwald clapped his hands together.

"Wonderful! I believe this calls for a celebration, and I have just the thing. I made some berry scones this very morning. I use a secret ingredient, which I believe you'll find really sets them apart from any others you've ever tasted before." He guided Deston and Margaux toward the table. "Please sit and I'll get us some tea to go with them."

As Zumwald hustled off, Deston leaned close to Margaux. "You really don't have to do this, you know," he whispered.

"I know I don't."

"So why are you? You heard Zumwald say it might be dangerous."

Margaux's eyes flashed. "Everything is dangerous to you, Deston. But I'll have you know I'm just as strong as you are. I can do anything you can."

"Okay, okay, take it easy. I didn't mean it that way. I just don't want you to think you owe me anything, because you don't."

Before Margaux could reply, Zumwald returned to the table with a plate of scones, three cups, and a teapot. He ceremoniously poured the tea and held his cup up for a toast.

"Here's to good friends, good journeys, and happily-ever-after endings," he said. With a wink he clicked his cup to the other two. As Deston and Margaux each took a sip of the tea, he smiled and set his cup on the saucer.

"Please, help yourself," Zumwald urged, picking up the plate of scones and offering it to each of them. The funny-shaped, blue triangles did not look at all appetizing, but to be polite, Deston took one and set it on his napkin.

"Go ahead, try it. I'm telling you my secret recipe is the best," Zumwald urged, smiling proudly.

Deston looked at Zumwald's beaming face and picked up the scone, nibbling off the corner. To his amazement, the scone was as good as Zumwald said, and without further hesitation he consumed the entire biscuit.

"What did I tell you? I wasn't lying, was I?" Zumwald chortled.

"No, you weren't," Deston replied.

Margaux nodded her head in agreement as she licked the last crumb off her finger.

Deston picked up his cup and took another sip of tea. As he looked over the rim, Zumwald, who was sitting across the table from him, suddenly became blurry. He moved the cup away from his mouth. Before he could set it down, it dropped from his grip, spilling tea all over the table. He blinked a couple of times, trying to focus his eyes, but the room was spinning.

"Wass … gooing … onn?" Deston's tongue was thick and his words wouldn't come out right. He looked over at Margaux. She was slumped over with her head resting on the table. He reached his hand out to her, then everything went black.

Chapter 23

Deston's laughter trailed across the field as he raced toward his mother. The sweet smell of heather filled his head, and butterflies flitted from one flower to the next to get out of his path. Joliet smiled back and held her arms open to him. He ran until he was panting and his lungs felt as if they would burst, but each time he looked up she was no closer than she was before.

Something cold and wet suddenly touched his cheek and then his nose. Deston's eyes flew open. Two large, soft brown eyes stared down at him, inches in front of his face. He let out a yelp and scooted backward until he was butted up against a wall and could go no farther.

"Firefly, get away from there," a musical voice called out from somewhere close by.

The miniature horse turned its head in the direction of the voice and flared its nostrils. It swished its tail once in defiance and leisurely moved away, exiting through an open door. Deston's bewildered gaze followed the small horse. A strong scent of heather lingered in his nose and his mind was cloudy, but the horrible pain pounding inside his head told him he wasn't dreaming. He closed his eyes and strained to remember where he was and how he had gotten there. Slowly, his memory returned.

Margaux! Deston reared up and immediately regretted his action as a hot, searing pain shot through his head. He pressed his fingers to his temples and eased back down, trying to move his head as little as possible. However, in that brief look around he'd seen enough to know Margaux wasn't in the room with him. He squeezed his eyes shut and tried to piece together what had happened. He remembered walking down a long, dark passageway and finding Monsieur Zumwald sitting in a room. There was also something about going on a journey to find his mother. Margaux was going to go with him and Zumwald had given them tea and scones to celebrate. That's as far as his memory went.

Deston sucked in his breath. *Ohmigawd, I've been kidnapped!*

He held his body stiff and stared up at the ceiling as that thought took root in his brain. But what would someone gain by kidnapping him? He had no money or anything of value that anyone would want. And what about Margaux? What did she have to do with this? A twinge of guilt gripped him. If he hadn't agreed to let her come along, she wouldn't have gotten in this mess. He was responsible for her and he had to find her and get them both out of wherever they were.

Ignoring the pain in his head, he pushed the blanket back and swung his legs over the edge of the cot. He stood and received another unpleasant surprise. His clothes were gone and all he had on was a short, flimsy, almost see through linen shirt, which barely covered his butt. He hurriedly slipped back under the blanket and pulled it up to his chin, hoping no one saw him. As he did, his hand brushed across his neck—his mother's cross was gone too.

His heart raced and dozens of questions bombarded his mind, such as, how did Zumwald know he would be in the tunnel? No one told him to go there. He'd gone of his own free will, so he had to be missing something, but the pain beating against the sides of his skull made it impossible to think clearly.

Deston gently rubbed his temple to ease the throbbing, and moved his head around very slowly to scan the room. In direct contrast to Zumwald's dull, drab room, this one was alive with colors, sounds, and smells, and the intensity of it all pushed his senses to the verge of overload. What was even stranger, he could not only see, hear and smell everything, he could feel them as well. The reds were hot and loud, the blues cool and distant, and the yellows soft and mellow, just like what he experienced when he first touched the door to the tunnel. It was an amazing sensation, but at the same time, it was too much to take in all at once. As the throbbing in his head intensified, he closed his eyes and pulled the blanket over his nose to shut it out. If the pain didn't stop soon, he was going to be sick to his stomach for sure.

"Deston?" an unfamiliar voice said close to his ear.

At the sound of his name, he squeezed his eyes together even tighter and shrank into the covers, trying to become invisible.

"Deston, you must get up. We don't have time to waste," the voice said a little louder, as a small hand shook his arm.

Deston noted the urgency in the voice and hesitantly cracked an eye to peek out from under the blanket. The minute he saw the young woman standing beside the cot, the blanket dropped from his hand and all other thoughts fled from his mind. She was undeniably the most beautiful woman he'd ever seen in his life. Her hair was like a sunset, the perfect blend of gold and copper, and hung long and straight down past her waist. Encircling her head was a thin delicate band of gold that held a teardrop-shaped amber crystal, dangling directly above a blue crescent moon tattoo on the bridge of her nose. Her almond-shaped eyes had a slight upward tilt at the outer corner and were a deep emerald green color. Minuscule flecks of amber dotted the outer rim of the iris and sparkled when she smiled.

Deston didn't move a muscle. He didn't even blink. She looked like a model, only much, much prettier. As that thought passed through his mind, the young woman's eyes twinkled and the corners of her mouth turned up, as if she had heard his thought.

"Welcome to Tir na-nÓg, Deston. My name is Lilika. I'm so happy you've come to us at last," she said in a musical voice that matched her beauty.

Deston was completely mesmerized and unable to take his eyes off Lilika, and not just because of her beauty. Something very odd was going on. She was speaking in a strange dialect, one he'd never heard before, but he could understand every word.

Deston's brow furrowed. *This has GOT to be a dream. Or am I dead and she's the angel who's come to take me to heaven?* His eyes swept over Lilika again. *If this is heaven, why do I still have this awful pain in my head? You aren't supposed to feel pain in heaven, are you?*

"You don't feel pain in what you refer to as heaven. But you aren't in heaven," a woman's voice answered inside his head—a voice that sounded remarkably like Lilika's.

Deston's eyes opened wider.

At that moment, a very small child carrying a wooden cup on a leaf-shaped tray stepped out from behind Lilika. Lilika picked up the cup and offered it to Deston. "Drink this. It will help you to feel better," she urged.

Deston's eyes moved to the cup, but he made no attempt to take it.

Lilika knelt down beside him and gave him an understanding look. "Don't worry. It's only tea with willow oil and nothing more. It will take away the pain in your head, which is there because you aren't accustom to this realm as yet. Your brain is more or less overextended and trying to comprehend too much at once. This will help," she said, her eyes beseeching him to take the cup as she pushed it toward him.

Deston was still skeptical, but the throbbing in his head was more than he could bear. Reluctantly, he took the cup, eyed the brown liquid and looked back at Lilika. She smiled reassuringly and gave him a nod to indicate it was all right. He looked at the liquid again and took a small sip. Within seconds, the pounding in his head eased. He took another sip and the pain became even less. By the third drink, it was completely gone. He slumped against the wall, letting the tension drain from his body. It was such a relief to be rid of the pain that for a moment he forgot about everything else. However, as his mind cleared, the questions flooded back in.

He sheepishly looked up. "Did you take my mom's cross?"

Lilika gave him a sympathetic look and shook her head. "Don't fret about that bauble. You have no need for it here. It wasn't your mother's anyway. Nicolette made it herself and told you what you wanted to hear so you would wear it. Her heart was in the right place, but sometimes she doesn't understand. She believed the lead lining in the cross and the St. John's wort she filled it with would be enough to—"

Her words were interrupted by a loud commotion outside the

room, drawing her and Deston's attention to the doorway. Deston leaned forward on the bed and looked through the opening to see what was going on.

A group of people had gathered just outside the door. The mob seemed agitated and was pushing to get past the two men who were standing guard. Deston didn't know what was going on, but from where he sat, it didn't look good. He nervously surveyed the room for another way out. His gaze had only traveled halfway around when the commotion outside abruptly ended. He turned back to the door and watched as the crowd split apart to make an open aisle across the grass. Seconds later, a sweet trumpet sounded and a man appeared at the far end of the opening. He marched down the aisle, carrying an emerald green flag with a golden tree embroidered in the center attached to a tall pole.

Deston leaned forward until he was teetering on the edge of the bed to get a better view of the man, who looked as if he had just stepped out of King Arthur's court. The man was decked out in a purple surcoat with long panels trailing down from each sleeve. Gold shin guards were strapped over his brown leather boots and he wore a gold helmet adorned with three peacock feather tips that danced and shimmered softly in the breeze as he marched to a silent beat. Everything about the man was magnificent. However, once Deston's eyes fell on the long, jeweled sword hanging off the man's wide belt, everything else became a blur, including the transport bearing an old woman on a throne carried by four men dressed exactly as the first. It wasn't until the transport was placed on the ground outside the door and the trumpet had quieted that Deston finally took notice.

The two men who had been guarding the door gently lifted the old woman off the carrier and set her on the ground. They then bowed and backed away as the woman strode purposely through the door and straight up to the bed.

Up close the woman appeared much older than Deston first thought, but her eyes were bright and intense. Her features softened, though, as she scrutinized his face, showing a hint of her former youth. She reached out and gently pushed the hair off Deston's forehead the same way his mother used to do.

"My boy, I never thought I would live to see this day. You look just like your father when he was a child," she said in a voice a lot more youthful than her looks.

Deston watched a wave of grief cross the old woman's face and for a moment, he thought she might collapse. But just as quickly, she straightened her back and regained her composure.

"Leave us," the woman commanded in a tone accustomed to being obeyed.

Lilika and the child immediately bowed their heads and exited the room, closing the door behind them. When all was quiet, the old woman took Deston's hand and looked into his eyes. "This must seem very strange to you. I am sure you have lots of questions."

Not sure what to make of her, Deston just nodded in response.

"You have entered the high realm of Tir na-nÓg, the land of your ancestors," she replied, the softness returning to her voice.

"Who are you?" Deston asked.

She smiled. "I am Titania, your grandmother."

"My..." Deston fell back onto the bed in shock.

"Yes, dear, I'm your father's mother," she nodded her head in affirmation.

Deston looked into her eyes, as a seed of doubt and hope both sprouted within him.

Titania cocked her head and her eyebrows arched. "You seem surprised. Have you not heard of me before?"

"I ... I don't know my father. I've never met him."

"I'm fully aware of that. But surely your mother has told you about us—about your family?"

Deston halfheartedly shook his head no.

"Oh dear, it's true," Titania swayed a little. "I had so hoped those rumors were false." She looked down at her hands to collect her thoughts. "This makes things so much more complicated. I don't understand why Joliet wouldn't have told you *something* of your heritage—something about us."

She turned away for a moment. When she turned back, there was sadness in her eyes. "There is so much you need to know and so little time. I cannot begin to tell you everything, but I'll do the best I can." The old woman patted his leg, signaling him to move over so she could sit beside him. "Your father's name is Oseron."

Deston nodded his head. "Yes, I know."

"You know?" Titania's brow creased.

"His name is on my birth certificate, but that's all I know. Mom never told me anything else about him, or about you."

"I see," Titania said and continued. "Your father is my only son. My husband, Oberon, was killed in battle when Oseron was about your age. After his father's death, I'm afraid I doted on Oseron more than I should have, but even in spite of my many mistakes, he grew to be an incredible, selfless man. I'm extremely proud of him." She hesitated and looked away. "It has recently come to my mind if only I had done things differently, maybe we could have avoided this mess we are in now." With a wave of her hand she dismissed the thought and focused back on Deston. "I'm sorry. That's neither here nor there. I shouldn't be wasting time or energy on things that cannot be changed. Anyway, let me see ... where was I?"

"You were telling me about my father," Deston replied, eager to hear more of the man he had wanted to meet for so long.

"Oh yes ... as I was saying, in spite of everything, Oseron grew to be a strong and wise leader. Yet, he was always restless and kept searching for that one thing he insisted was still missing in his life. Then when he met your mother in the Forest of Brocéliande everything changed." Titania's eyes stared off at a spot over Deston's head. "I fully believe their union was ordained by the gods, for no one could fall in love so deeply and as quickly as those two without some help from above. From the first moment he laid eyes on Joliet, he was completely obsessed with her." She looked down at Deston. "Of course, I and everyone else in the village did our best to dissuade him, but he is stubborn that one—just like his father."

Deston's back stiffened. "What's wrong with my mom? Why didn't you want him to be with her?" he interjected.

Titania held her hand up. "You misunderstand. There's nothing wrong with your mother. She is a lovely woman—intuitive, gracious, and the kindest human I've ever known. But she is not from our world. Our people have worked hard over the centuries to distance ourselves from the human race. It is extremely rare for one of our kind to marry a human, for we feared bringing one of them into our midst would undo everything we've achieved. And I must say, after what has recently transpired, that fear was justified and is now a very real possibility."

Deston's brow drew together as he listened. Little of what she was saying made sense. And the way she kept referring to humans as if they were something alien was unsettling. His eyes narrowed and he looked at her more closely.

Except for her face, Titania was covered from head to toe. Fine age lines were etched around her eyes and mouth, but her intense blue eyes were as clear and bright as a child's. She had a perfectly sculptured nose that turned up slightly at the tip and a blue crescent moon, like Lilika's, just above the bridge of her nose, although hers was faded and barely noticeable. Her white hair sparkled as if coated with a fine layer of glitter and the golden diadem she wore was adorned with jewels that were arranged in a way to look like peacock feathers. A shimmering veil so fine it looked as if it would disintegrate with a touch was attached on each side of the diadem and draped under her chin to frame her face.

Titania watched Deston studying her and knew it was time he learned the rest of the story. She pulled the veil loose from one side of the gold band and turned her head toward the window to give him a clear view of her profile.

Deston's eyes were immediately drawn to her ear and his hand automatically reached up to touch his own. Her ears had the same odd petal shape as his; only hers were much more exaggerated and longer, coming to a very pronounced point at the tip. He'd never seen an ear such as hers on a real person before.

His gaze traveled back to her face, and for the second time, he asked, "Who are you?"

Titania reached for his hand and held it between hers. "We are the fae, although you may have heard us referred to by other names, such as the Fair Folk, or as the lower realm prefers to call us, faeries."

Deston gasped out loud and his face took on a look of pure horror. Wrenching his hand back, he held it tightly to his chest. "But you ... er, how can you be a faerie? You don't have wings."

A point of light sparked in Titania's eyes, but her face remained neutral. "Not all faeries have wings. I know humans think we do, but they're wrong. Our bodies vibrate at a faster rate than a human body, and because of this, we can move very quickly, so they assume we must all have wings."

"No." He shook his head side to side and shrank back. "I don't believe it. You can't be a faerie."

Titania lowered her eyes. She feared it might be hard for him to learn who he was and she had tried to prepare herself for his reaction before she came in, but his pulling away hurt more than she imagined it would. And knowing he was also in pain made it all the worse. If only there was enough time to let him get to know the fae first. Unfortunately, time was not a luxury they had. She steeled herself and went on.

"It's not what you think. I know the way the lower realm depicts our people. They lump us together into a single category, portraying us as either evil mythical creatures, or tiny comical beings, flying around and sitting on flower petals. But the fae are neither. Believe me when I tell you we are more like humans than you think. We have families, we work and play, we laugh, we cry, just as humans do.

"Of course, there are differences," she added. "Those differences are the reason our two realms were separated. The light energy of the Universe is purer and stronger within us, because we never passed through the veil and our connection to the gods and the spiritual plane was not severed. We also live much longer, are stronger of mind, spirit, and body, and have powers humans don't have. None of that makes us evil. Actually, we are quite the opposite. The purpose of our life on this earth has never been a question for us, which makes it easier to live true to the laws of the Universe. We consider life to be sacred and precious, no matter what form it takes—animal, plant, human or faerie. But we differ most from the human race in that we denounced the darkness long ago and have little experience with greed, prejudice, and hatred. Those traits are simply not taught nor accepted here amongst the fae."

Her brow rose and her eyes pleaded. "Being a fae is not a bad thing. Once you're around us a while you will see for yourself that we lead very normal, boring lives—very much like what you've lived in the lower realm these past years."

She saw the uncertainty in his face and could feel the turmoil raging within him. She reached out and took his hand again. He let her take it, but his eyes remained wary and unblinking. She took a deep breath and braced herself for his response to what she was about to tell him next.

"Many thousands of years ago, almost back to the beginning of time, the ancient gods constructed a barrier between the two realms. The dark energy had found its way into the humans by that time and they were distancing themselves from the truths. They had already become arrogant and started believing they were superior to all other living beings. They took over the land as if it were theirs and theirs alone to do with as they pleased. And they were easily swayed by words, glory, power, and the false promises the darkness had to offer. The Wise Ones saw this and knew if our two realms remained as one, a war would be inevitable, as humans had become unable to live peacefully with their own species, let alone coexist with other kinds.

"When the realms split, the fae were granted the higher realm and we became known as the Children of Light. It was a tremendous honor, but with it came a great responsibility. For one, the balance and protection of the earth was placed in our hands. We right the wrongs of the other earthly inhabitants and diminish the darkness the best we can. That in itself is an arduous task and has cost our people dearly, as the darkness gains strength every year. I doubt we would have been able to succeed if the gods hadn't given us the Light Crystal to keep our powers strong."

Deston's blank look told her he had no clue as to what she was talking about.

"The Crystal is the seed of the Universe—a direct link to the source energy and to the gods. Its clear, pure energy is what gives us our powers and provides the earth substance to thrive. Through this energy we are sustained and renewed season after season, together with all life on this planet. Without it, the earth, as we know it, would cease to exist."

Titania paused for a moment, her eyes darkening with renewed vigor. "Our king is the Keeper of the Crystal and governs this realm, making sure the balance remains in check. He keeps the Light Crystal in a medallion around his neck and close to his heart, so its strength and wisdom is always available to him to shield the earth from the destructive forces that are constantly at work.

She squeezed his hand. "As I said before, it's been this way for a very long time. But now our realm is in grave danger. One of our enemies has plotted to take the Crystal from us. He plans to use it to bring in the dark energy from the farthest corners of the Universe and destroy our realm. That would ultimately lead to the destruction of the earth. He has already captured our king, Oseron, and his queen."

Titania waited for her words to sink in. After several seconds passed with no response, she realized Deston hadn't grasped what she was telling him. "My son, Oseron—your father—is king of the fae. He's in danger and we need your help to save him."

Chapter 24

Deston's eyes grew even rounder than they already were and he stared unblinking at the old woman sitting beside him. He heard her words but they took a moment for his brain to process. A look of sheer horror came over his face and he shook his head side to side in denial as his heart pounded furiously in his chest and his stomach roiled, threatening to bring up the scones he'd eaten earlier.

Titania reached out to him, but he withdrew and rolled to his side, facing the wall. He pulled the blanket over his head wanting to disappear. Or just go home so everything would go back to the way it was before. But how could it ever be the same after learning the terrible secret his mother had kept from him his entire life? *My father is a faerie. How can that be?*

He wondered if it was a joke. But then another unimaginable bombshell hit him. If his father was a faerie, then he was a faerie too. He flinched as if he'd been punched in the stomach. *Oh my God, I'm a faerie? Noooo, I can't be. They've got it wrong. I'm not a faerie. Please, please don't let it be true.*

Deston curled into a ball and squeezed his eyes together. A vision materialized behind his eyelids of the tiny, fluttering form of Disney's Tinker Bell, except it had his face and head. He hid his face in his hands to block the image. It didn't help.

For his entire life he felt there was something wrong with him. He had always been different from everyone else, and Joliet had dismissed his concerns, even though she knew the truth. Now he knew the truth as well, and there was no more denying it.

The words *"I'm a faerie"* rolled over and over in his head until he wanted to scream. What would everyone back home think when they found out? And Margaux—what was he going to tell Margaux? He had endured being called a freak for years, but this was so much worse—he was more than a freak. He wasn't even human. How could he not have known that?

I'm not even a good faerie. I can't do magic, or fly, or anything, he thought as his disbelief simmered into anguish.

Burying his face in the pillow, Deston tried to push the thoughts away, but an image of his mother floated into his mind and he lost his concentration again. "How could you marry a faerie?" He whispered to the image.

She had always been one of the smartest people he knew, which made it doubly hard to believe she would do that. Deston went rigid and his heart flipped over. Maybe Oseron enchanted her and made her marry him? Maybe he was the one who kidnapped her too? He pondered that possibility for a moment until he recalled the day Joliet talked about his father. She hadn't been faking it when she said how much she loved Oseron.

You married a faerie by choice, didn't you? Why? Why would you do that to me?

He pressed his fingertips hard into his temples to stop his mind from racing wild, but fresh questions popped in so fast he couldn't keep up with all of them. In amongst those thoughts a small voice whispered to his subconscious, *"The fae are the god's chosen ones, and the purest and most beloved of all living beings on this planet. Why would you think it bad to be a custodian of the Light of the Universe?"*

That question gradually worked its way into the forefront of his conscious. Deston's mind went still as it slowly took over all other thoughts. *Is it a bad thing to be a fae?*

He pictured all the different races living around the world and the many kids at school from other nationalities. They all mingled together with everyone else and no one cared where they came from or that they looked and talked differently.

Another thought suddenly came into his mind. He flinched. *I've been part fae my whole life and never knew it … never even suspected it. No one else did either. So I can't be that different after all.*

That startling admission stopped him cold and the harassing

thoughts faded to the back. His own mother had married a fae. She wouldn't have done that if the fae were bad. And Titania said the fae were just like regular people, except with powers. A trickle of excitement ran through him and his mind did an abrupt change of course. *Do I have special powers too?*

Titania, sitting on the edge of the cot, stared at the lump under the blanket. Her heart ached for Deston and she wanted so badly to comfort him, but she knew better than to interfere. His battle was one he had to resolve on his own. She had no doubt he would eventually accept who he was and realize being a fae was a blessing, but there was so little time remaining and that was the problem.

She lifted her hand to reach out, then pulled it back. He didn't want or need her support at the moment. He needed time alone. She took a deep breath and felt a tightness grip her heart. The least she could do was give him a few minutes before adding to his burden. The others may not like it, but she was his grandmother. That gave her the right to do what was best for him.

Deston felt the bed rise as Titania stood and heard the sound of her soft footfalls walking away. From out of nowhere, a pang of longing seized his heart. He gasped out loud and his breath caught in his throat. He barely knew her, but she was a part of him and he had already lost so much. All of a sudden, it didn't matter who he was, or that she was anything other than the family he had wanted to meet for so long. He threw back the blanket and sat up just as Titania reached the door.

"Grandmother," he cried out.

Titania stopped and turned, giving him a quizzical look, which flustered Deston even more. There were so many raw emotions rolling around inside of him he suddenly couldn't remember what he had wanted to say.

"Do I ... will I have magical powers too?" he blurted out.

His question amused her, but she held back the urge to smile. "The fae can do some magic, yes. But you're half human and still young. There is no way to know to what extent your powers will manifest," she replied.

"Oh … I was just wondering, 'cause … well, I was thinking it might be kind of cool if I did have some powers, you know," he stammered, embarrassed that of all the things he had wanted to say, he had asked a stupid question like that.

Titania breathed a sigh of relief as Deston's words filled her heart with joy. He was more like his father than she realized. "You may not be aware of this yet, but the fae are the most revered of all the species on this planet. Seeing so many of our virtues in you brings me great pleasure," she cried, opening her arms in welcome.

Deston jumped out of bed and raced to her, wrapping his arms around her waist. She rested her cheek on the top of his head and silently thanked the gods for sending her this small miracle.

It felt good to be in the warmth of his grandmother's arms. He didn't know she existed until a few minutes ago, but still something deep inside him had always missed her. For as long as he could remember, he had felt alone and out of place and never understood why. Now he truly belonged somewhere. In just one amazing day he went from having no one to gaining a whole new family—a grand-mother *and* a father.

However, as quickly as his joy came, it faded as Titania's earlier words came back to him. He pulled away and wiped his sleeve across his eyes. "Did you say someone took Oseron … er, my dad?" he asked with a sniff.

Titania's face fell. "Yes, I'm afraid so. Grossard, the enemy I mentioned earlier, used your mother—"

"Mom? My mom is here?" Deston shouted.

"Well, yes and no. As I was saying, Grossard took Joliet and used her to lure Oseron into the open alone, so his henchmen could strike. There were too many of them and Oseron didn't have a chance. They overpowered him and locked him inside the monastery where Joliet was being held. Now—" Titania's explanation was again interrupted by someone clearing their throat.

Deston turned at the sound and was surprised to find a group of people standing directly behind him. His brow drew together as he wondered how long they had been standing there.

A flash of annoyance crossed Titania's face as she looked up at the group, but she quickly hid it and regained her regal stature.

She pulled Deston around to stand beside her and face the group. "Deston, I'd like to introduce you to the Council of Elders. This is Lan, Pora, Aren, Frayne, Sadria and Rehan."

As Titania called out their names, they stepped forward one by one and bowed at the waist in acknowledgement. Deston nodded back to the group, which appeared to be comprised of three men and three women—although their looks were so similar it was hard to tell male from female.

All six were strikingly good looking and had long, pale golden hair, fair complexions, pointed ears, and almond-shaped eyes with the same upward slant at the outer corner as Lilika's and Titania's. Each was dressed in the same long, iridescent-colored robe; the only difference being the runes embroidered around the neck, the hem, and the cuff of the sleeves. Encircling their heads was an inch wide gold band that dipped to a small V shape at the center of their forehead. The three Deston assumed were women had a teardrop-shaped crystal similar to Lilika's dangling from the V of their bands.

As Deston eyed the new arrivals with skepticism, Titania turned to him and looked sadly into his eyes. "I wish we had more time to spend together, just the two of us, but there is something more pressing at the moment." She smiled encouragingly, but the smile didn't reach her eyes. She took a big breath and sighed. "Do you recall me telling you that our realm is in danger?"

"Yes," Deston replied hesitantly.

"The Elders are here to ask for your help."

Deston tense beneath her hands. "There's nothing to worry about. No one is going to force you to do anything against your will. It's not our way. The choice is completely yours. All I ask is that you hear them out," she said, lightly squeezing his shoulders to show her support.

She pulled him into another hug and gave a slight nod to the group over the top of his head.

Chapter 25

On Titania's signal, the one named Lan lifted his hand and waved it through the air. As he did, the colorful, brightly lit room transformed into a large dark chamber with bare walls and a high arched ceiling. The chamber was sparsely furnished with eight high-backed chairs, seven of which were arranged in a semicircle in the middle of the room. A shaft of sunlight, shining down through a circular skylight in the ceiling, showcased the eighth chair, sitting in front of the others. The Elders and Titania moved to the chairs in the semicircle and motioned for Deston to take the lone chair facing them.

As Deston walked to the chair and sat down, he was shocked and relieved to discover the room was not the only thing that had been transformed. His clothes had been too, and he now had on a long, brown suede, sleeveless jerkin over top of the flimsy linen shirt he had woken up in, a pair of tight-fitting moss green pants, and soft leather boots that were laced up to his knees. He looked down at the garb in bewilderment, but as the one introduced as Aren stood and addressed him brusquely, he lifted his head.

"It is said you had no knowledge of our realm until you arrived here."

Deston tensed at Aren's tone, which was more suited to an interrogation than to a request for help. He looked questioningly at Titania, who smiled and nodded. His eyes went back to Aren, but he paused before replying. "That's right, sir. I didn't."

"You mean you were never told of your birthright?" the one called Sadria exclaimed.

"No," Deston repeated, switching his attention to the woman. "What birthright?"

A soft murmur filled the room, as the Elders turned to one another, whispering soft exclamations. After several seconds, Lan held up his hand and the room went silent.

"My lord, permit me to explain. As the king's only son, you are heir to the throne of Tir na-nÓg. If anything were to happen to King Oseron, you would become our new king," Lan stated.

Deston drew back as if he'd been slapped. He stared at the group with bulging eyes, his mouth suddenly so dry he couldn't have commented even if he had known what to say.

Aren cleared his throat. "As your grandmother aptly mentioned, a vile creature by the name of Grossard is currently holding the king prisoner in a monastery in the lower realm. Grossard's plan was to kill the king, secure the Light Crystal, and marry the queen to gain the throne of Tir na-nÓg." Aren paused and lifted his chin a little higher. "Should I assume you know nothing of the Crystal, as well?" He raised one eyebrow accusingly.

Deston stared back, too flabbergasted to follow what Aren was saying.

Aren rolled his eyes and shook his head. "The Crystal is what separates our realm from you ..." His eyes darted a quick look at Lan. "...from the lower realm. It holds the source energy of the Universe, which in turn empowers us, and thus, the earth. It can never fully lose its light, but the demand the earth takes from it, which is mostly due to the human realm, does drain its energy.

"Recharging it—I use that term loosely and only so you'll be able to understand—will take place as the full moon rises on the autumnal equinox. However, to ensure the Crystal is renewed with positive light energy, it must be here in the high realm at moonrise. It must also be in the possession of the rightful king to ensure the fae's powers and reign continues. If it remains in the lower realm where it currently is, it will be susceptible to the dark energy, and whoever is in possession of it at the time will gain the power to reign over the earth.

"So I'm sure even you can see how imperative it is to bring the Crystal back to Tir na-nÓg. If Grossard were to gain both the throne and the Crystal, the essence of light will be extinguished and the world as we know it will end." Aren paused for a dramatic effect before resuming. "But your birth has changed all that. As you are Oseron's legitimate heir and have so conveniently arrived in our realm at the appropriate time, you have eliminated Grossard's advantage." Aren's voice turned hard as he went on. "According to the law, the throne will automatically go to the king's heir at his death, whether the queen remarries or not. So as long as you're here, you are the only one who can legally hold the throne and take possession of the Crystal ... if you outlive Oseron that is," Aren added, lifting both corners of his mouth in a sadistic smile.

"Oh, really, Aren, stop being so melodramatic," Titania scoffed. "What he's trying to say, Deston, is—Grossard's plan cannot work now that we've found you. You've stopped him. You've saved us."

"Your Highness, if you please," Pora said, stopping Titania from saying more.

"The boy's arrival may have delayed Grossard from gaining the throne, but it will *not* stop him. I know better than any the lengths Grossard will go to get what he wants. He's blinded by the darkness and is intent on revenge against all the Fair Folk, not just Oseron. Deston's arrival hasn't changed that. He is young and knows nothing of our ways. Without Oseron at the helm, our realm will remain in grave danger. It will take his strength and experience to obtain our freedom from Grossard's tyranny."

A small murmur of accord circulated through the room, as the others in the group nodded their heads in agreement. When the room quieted, Lan stood and addressed Deston.

"My lord, as you are new to this realm, I'm sure you find this all very confusing and may think we're asking a lot of you. In that I agree, we are. But I assure you, if there was any other way, we would most certainly take it. Unfortunately, we're limited to the resources we have available, and time is as much our enemy as Grossard is.

"From what we hear, he hasn't learned of your arrival as yet, but it's inevitable he will before long. That's why we must act swiftly or run a greater risk of losing the battle." Lan paused, searching for the right words. "I think you should know it was not an easy decision to bring you here. If Grossard had chosen any other prison, it wouldn't have been necessary to do so. But you see, our kind cannot enter a holy place in the lower realm. To pass through the doors of such a venue would immediately strip us of our powers, as well as our strength. We would be dead within minutes."

Lan saw Deston's stricken look and hurriedly added, "Do not fret—that does not pertain to the king. The monastery will most certainly take away Oseron's strength and powers, but as long as the Crystal remains in his possession, he'll live. That's a blessing to us all, but it creates another problem. With the Crystal inside the monastery, its life force energies have been cut off to us. Each minute that passes, our realm grows weaker and our people lose more of their powers. Already we're seeing difficulty in crossing between the two realms. If any of us were to make it into the lower realm, what little power we still hold would completely vanish. Because of this, we were forced to bring you here. If you decline to help us, or fail to bring Oseron and the Light Crystal back to our realm, we may not be able to stop Grossard."

The Elders sat rigid in their chairs, all eyes trained on Deston.

"You may not have previous knowledge of your father or know anything of our world, but we are beseeching you to help us defeat Grossard and return the Crystal. I must forewarn you, however, it will be a dangerous endeavor, and once you cross through the gateway into the lower realm you'll be on your own, for none of us can follow. It's important you understand that and also accept the possibility of failure," Lan added.

The room went deathly quiet, as everyone waited for Deston's response. Bewildered and more than a little scared, Deston stared at the group. He was only fourteen years old and here they were asking him to fight a person who had already captured his mother and father. He looked down the line of solemn faces and felt incredibly small. He had some fighting experience from different kung fu tournaments he'd attended. He'd even faced adults in some of his matches, but what the Elders were asking of him was hardly the same thing. In the tournaments, no one intentionally tried to hurt the other and opponents were matched by skill level. He knew nothing about this Grossard or what Grossard was capable of.

His eyes stopped on Titania. "Who is this Grossard? Why does he want revenge on you guys?"

No one said a word, but all heads turned to Pora. Pora's back was rigid as she stared blankly at the wall behind Deston's head. When she finally spoke, her voice was a raspy whisper.

"Grossard is from a different sect of our people. I know Titania explained to you how the fae are inherently good. You'll witness that for yourself once you're able to spend more time with us. As Children of the Light, we consider it an abhorrence to hurt or destroy another living thing. Even in times of war and in matters of self-preservation, we try to incapacitate unless there is no other alternative. But sad to say, it's not so with all species of faeries. Long ago the darkness infected some of our ancestors, and just as dark is the opposite of light, they became the opposite of us. Their numbers are not large, but they have caused much turmoil by spreading their hate and darkness throughout both realms. These few are called solitaries faeries, the children of Erebus. From the time of the Crystal's first renewal, we fae have shouldered the burden of undoing the harm the solitaries cause. Up to this point they have been fairly easy to manage, and that is mainly because they are lazy creatures and care only about themselves and instant gratification. They are also ignorant being for the most part. That is where Grossard differs."

Pora's voice broke and she looked down at her trembling hands unable to continue. Lan placed a hand on her shoulder for support. After a few minutes of silence, he resumed the story himself.

"As Pora was saying, Grossard isn't like the others. He is a child of Erebus and just as lazy and self-centered as the rest, but he has two major differences. The darkness seems to be stronger in him, and he was raised and educated here in Tir na-nÓg so he is not ignorant."

Seeing Deston's puzzled looked, Lan added. "As an infant, he was abandoned and left to die. A fae woman, who longed to have a child of her own, happened upon him. That woman convinced herself that with the love and influence of the Good Folk he would take on the fae attributes and not those of the darkness and his own kind. Because she was a woman of influence, she convinced the Elders of this as well. It had never been tried before, but after much pleading the Elders relented and allowed him to stay and be raised amongst us.

"So Grossard grew up and was educated alongside our own children. For a while he did very well and it seemed as if the woman would be right. We've learned since, however, that was only an act. He showed us what we wanted to see. As he got older, it became harder for him to hold back the ugliness of his true nature. It seems those born of the darkness will always have darkness inside them and nothing can take that away. And as is the nature of darkness, once he opened his heart to it, it consumed him."

Lan paused and looked at Pora. Her head was still lowered, but after a few seconds she looked up. Her eyes were dull with sadness, but she nodded her head for him to continue.

"Grossard's thirst for attention and power grew as he did. In the best interest of the village we decided he must be returned to his own kind. When he heard of this, he went on a rampage ..." Lan's voice cracked and he stopped to collect his emotions before going on. "... Grossard killed one of our men and abducted the man's wife. A short time later, we found the woman, but he had already fled into the lower realm. There he kidnapped a human child, thinking the child would be a good bargaining tool, as she was a relative of the queen's."

Deston tensed. *NiNi?*

"Oseron discovered Grossard's plan and when Grossard came back through the gateway with the girl, he was captured. Punishment was delivered quickly and was harsh—banishment from the high realm for all eternity. In addition, due to the nature of Grossard's unforgivable crimes, Oseron put a curse on him, which changed his outer appearance to match the ugliness of his soul. The transformation was instantaneous and staggering. Grossard had disguised his true self for so long, we had no idea how black his soul was until it was out in the open. Anyone who looks upon him now will see him for whom he is—a repugnant, monstrous creature."

Lan looked down at his folded hands and said no more. Deston blinked and tried to ignore the tightness that was growing in his chest and inhibiting his breathing. He stared at Lan, waiting for him to continue, but the Elder remained silent along with the others.

"So where is he now?" Deston asked tentatively.

"We're told he occupies a cave in the lower realm that once belonged to Morgane le Fae."

The crease in Deston's brow deepened. "So if this guy is really as bad as you say, why just let him go? Why not throw him in a dungeon, or a prison or something?"

"Ahhh, that is the kind of question I would expect from someone outside our realm," Lan stated. "The lower realm has always been unable to comprehend our ways. But you will soon come to realize the high realm is so much more than a place for our kind to live. It's part of our essence and is as important to us as water and air. Being removed from all of this is indeed a more horrendous punishment than being caged. In hindsight, I guess you could say it was a mistake for us to let him wander unsupervised, but in our defense, it has been a very long time since we've faced true evil. We wanted to believe, as Pora did, that if she loved Grossard enough, gave him good examples, and taught him right from wrong, he would grow to be a different person."

Deston's eyes darted to Pora. *She's the one who found Grossard as a baby?*

"Unfortunately, that didn't happen. And our history has shown us what will occur if Grossard succeeds and acquires the power of the Crystal. Our realm will undoubtedly be destroyed and the lower realm will quickly follow as the darkness grows. That is why it is crucial we do everything we can to stop him."

Deston felt numb. He didn't know what true evil was, much less how to fight it. He looked at Titania and then at each of the Elders questioningly, but there were no answers on any of their faces.

"So ... does this guy have magic powers too?" he inquired, hoping with all his might the answer would be no.

"Yes, he does. Probably more than we are aware of. Our spies informed us some time ago that Morgane was teaching him the dark arts and that he was becoming adept at controlling the elements. How much he has actually mastered, though, we don't know."

Deston shook his head in disbelief. "How am I supposed to defeat him then? I don't have any magic powers. ...I'm just a kid!"

Lan opened his mouth to answer, but Titania held up her hand

and cut him off. "Magic is only a tool and extremely overrated, Deston. The intelligence and integrity you were born with, as well as the love in your heart, are all the powers you need. Those are much more potent than magic and you have all that inside you. Believe me, I can see your strength. You're so much stronger than I expected you to be, and you're more intelligent and more courageous than Grossard will ever hope to be. You don't need magic."

Deston bit his lip. They all seemed to think he could do it, but he wasn't so sure. Closing his eyes, he tried to picture himself in a real fight—a fight for his life.

The Elders shifted uncomfortably in their seats. Their whole existence rested on Deston's shoulders. If he declined, there was no one else to call upon.

Titania knew what they were thinking, but she also knew more about Deston than they did. She walked to his chair and knelt before him. "Are you aware of the meaning of your name?" she asked softly.

He opened his eyes and gave her a curious look.

"It means destiny', she continued before he could respond. "And it's no coincidence you were named this. Your destiny was decided when you were conceived and your mother was fully aware of how it would rule your life. I know Joliet didn't want to leave Tir na-nÓg. She fought with Oseron to stay at first. Then out of the blue, she relented and left with no explanation. I didn't understand why until recently, when I learned of her secret. She left to protect you." She took Deston's hand and gave it a squeeze. "You have to know your mother is more intuitive than most humans, so it shouldn't surprise you she was the one person who saw through Grossard's façade. I now believe she also knew what was coming. That's why she took you to the lower realm. You see, we age very slowly here in Tir na-nÓg. If she had stayed, you would still be an infant and wouldn't be able to take on this challenge. She gave you the greatest gift she could to ensure your success—the gift of time. I'm sure she would change your destiny if she could, but no one has control over that. Not even us with the powers of the Crystal." Titania squeezed his hand again. "Look into your heart." She placed her hand over his chest to emphasize her words. "You have all the knowledge and answers you need right in here."

Deston gawked at her, not following or understanding what his name, or time, or looking into his heart had to do with any of it. He looked to the Elders for clarification, but all he saw was their worried expressions. Suddenly, he realized they all thought he was going to decline. That amazed and appalled him at the same time. Did he really look like the kind of person who would turn his back on his family and his own mother and father? He had told Monsieur Zumwald back in the tunnel he'd do whatever it takes to find his mother, and he meant every word of it. He'd do *anything* to get her back.

Feeling strangely calm, he scooted the chair back, stood, and faced the Elders. "Where do I have to go and when do I start?" he asked.

A couple of the Elders looked surprised, but they all rose, clapping their hands in delight.

"You will leave immediately," Lan replied. "As I mentioned earlier, time is the most important element right now. The Crystal must be back in the high realm by the rise of the full moon on the autumnal equinox to keep the light from being extinguished and to keep the barriers from coming down," Lan said, stepping forward to shake Deston's hand.

The others swarmed Deston, buzzing congratulations as they patted him on the back until Lan raised his voice and yelled over them. "Everyone ... please. Step back. Let the boy breathe."

The room quieted and Lan turned to Deston. "We have everything prepared for your journey. Two of our best warriors will be traveling with you. They'll show you to the gateway and be your protection along the way. They're waiting for us now, so if you will please follow me." He turned and walked toward the exit.

One by one the Elders filed out of the chamber after Lan. Titania brushed Deston's hair out of his eyes and kissed his forehead. A combination of pride and sorrow reflected in her eyes as she opened her mouth to tell him how proud she was, but her words stalled in her throat. She took his hand in hers, squeezed it, and led him to the door after the Elders in silence.

Chapter 26

Deston's mind was far away as he stepped through the doorway of the great hall and into the sunlight, but the loud cheer from the crowd gathered outside instantly brought him back. His eyes bulged and he pulled back as he gazed in wonder upon the throng of people who were waving and clapping. He could feel the tips of his ears burning and he tried to retreat into the doorway, but Titania's strong hold on his hand prevented him from running back inside as he wanted.

Titania, paying no attention to his discomfort, moved on and practically dragged him down the steps. As they made their way through the spectators, the crowd bowed their heads and dropped to one knee. Deston tried not to gawk, but he found the reaction extremely puzzling.

"What are they doing?" he asked under his breath, his face becoming hotter with the added attention.

"They are showing their respect, as is customary. You are their prince after all," Titania replied.

Prince? The word sent a jolt through him. He hadn't thought of himself as a prince. But of course, if his father was the king, that would make him a prince. *Prince Deston*, he repeated silently in his head as a small smile tugged at the corners of his mouth. He liked the sound of it. Straightening his back, he lifted his chin the way he imagined a prince would.

What I wouldn't give to see the look on Larry's face when he hears this! The thought of Larry's reaction brought an even bigger smile to Deston's face.

Titania escorted Deston through the crowd and proceeded along a path that separated a field of tall straight stalks from a field of vibrant-colored wildflowers. Just as when he first woke up in Tír na-nÓg, all the colors, smells, and sounds were so intense it was surreal, like walking into a canvas of one of the great master painters where everything was perfectly drawn and placed in the right spot to please the eye. But thankfully this time it didn't give him a headache.

They made their way up the side of a rocky hill and stopped at the crest. There Titania lovingly looked out upon the valley below as she spread her arms wide in front of her. "Welcome home," she said, pride filling her voice.

Deston stared down upon a scene that was not only breathtakingly beautiful, but also familiar. He labored to recall why, and all at once it occurred to him—this was the picture hanging above his bed back home. The picture his mom had painted when she first came to America. He hadn't paid much attention to it for years, but there was no mistaking it was a picture of this very place.

The valley was horseshoe shaped with sloping hills on both sides, a sheer rock-faced mountain along the curved end, and a forest of trees on the open end. Twin waterfalls cascaded down the mountain's rock face, churning the water of the turquoise lake below into a cloud of haze. Two identical rivers flowed from each side of the lake and circled around a portion of land, one to the right, the other to the left, making a large island between them before they joined together and became one. Several arched bridges crossed the two rivers, giving access to the lush hillsides where fields of grains, orchards, and vegetables were planted in neat, precise rows.

His mother had done an amazing job of capturing the beauty of the valley, especially the enormous oak tree standing in the middle of the island between the two rivers. It was the part of the painting that had always intrigued him the most. But never in his wildest dreams did he imagine it was a real place.

The trunk of the tree was at least a block wide, with limbs rising into the sky higher than the clouds and leaves the size of a car. Clustered around the base of the oak were small, brightly colored shops bustling with activity. A road was notched into the thick bark and circled the trunk from the base up until it was lost within the branches. Scattered amongst the leaves, small islands of twinkling lights and faint shapes of peaked rooflines, doors, and windows of houses were visible.

Deston's face lit with wonder as his gaze traveled up the tree to above the clouds where a crystal shrine in the shape of a pyramid sparkled like a beacon at the very top and created a vivid rainbow that arched across the sky and hung like a banner over a magnificent golden palace sitting directly below the shrine. A lump rose in Deston's throat and any lingering doubt of whether or not his mother had actually been here vanished. The painting was too accurate to be a coincidence. Remembering how she used to stare lovingly at the picture, he realized how much she must have missed this place and how much she had sacrificed for him.

Titania waited silently, letting Deston soak in the splendor before urging him down the hill. She loved Tir na-nÓg almost as much as she loved Oseron, and the chance to show it off to someone new seldom came along. But the Elders were waiting and time was of the utmost importance.

As they started down the hill on a well-worn path, a small group of children ran through the field below, chasing one of the miniature ponies. Deston's gaze followed them, but stopped short as he spied a girl picking flowers. The girl's bright red hair triggered a spark of recognition. At that same moment, Margaux looked up and let out a squeal. The flowers were tossed aside and quickly forgotten as she raced up the hill waving and shouting ecstatically.

"Deston! ... Deston! Can you believe it? We're actually in Tir na-nÓg, and it's just like I always dreamed it would be," Margaux shouted, hurrying toward him.

With all that he'd recently learned about his mother, father, and Grossard, Deston had completely put Margaux out of his mind. But the second his eyes landed on her, his spirits soared and he took off down the hill to meet her. As they came together, Margaux threw her arms around him, knocking them both to the ground. They rolled down the grassy slope, laughing and squealing like two little kids until they came to a stop. Out of breath, but still laughing, they sat up and hugged each other. For just a moment, Deston was caught up in the delight of seeing Margaux again, and he forgot about everything else as he watched the sunlight turn her hair to fire.

"Where have you been? When I woke up in that room all alone, I didn't know where you'd gone. But this really nice fae woman told me I would see you again. I've been looking and looking for you and no one would say where you were," Margaux rushed on without taking a breath.

Her question instantly brought back the task at hand and Deston's moment of joy evaporated. "I ... er, I've just been talking to some people." He stammered, unsure how much he could divulge.

"Oh, are they the ones who know where your mama is?" Margaux asked, just as Titania caught up to them.

"Yeah, I'm actually on my way right now to meet the guys who are going to take me to her," he said, keeping his head diverted as he got to his feet so Margaux couldn't read his face.

Margaux scrambled to her feet along with him. "Really? That is so groovy. Is she here in Tir na-nÓg? When will I get to meet her?"

"No, she's not here," Deston replied and turned away.

Margaux stared at Deston's back and frowned. "Is something wrong? Where is your mama?" she yelled at his back.

Deston kept walking, pretending not to hear as he desperately tried to think of what to say to pacify her. However, before he could think of a plausible answer, Margaux ran up behind him, grabbed him by the arm, and pulled him to a stop.

"What's going on? Why don't you want to talk about your mama?" she asked, her eyes showed her concern along with a hint of annoyance.

"Because I don't know where she is. I ... I have to go find her. She's not in this realm," he replied, looking everywhere but at Margaux, which made her suspicions grow stronger.

"Oh ... I see. I'll go with you to find her."

"No!" Deston snapped. "It's better if I go by myself. It's going to be danger ..." He stopped himself from finishing the word and darted a quick glance up at Margaux. Her lips were pressed into a thin line and she had that look on her face that was becoming quite familiar. Crap, he thought, realizing she wasn't going to let him off that easy. He ran his hands through his hair and shifted his weight awkwardly from one foot to the other. "Look, there's this guy who's holding Mom hostage. I have to go rescue her, because I'm the only one who can enter a monastery. That's all I know, okay? So that's why you can't go with me."

Stunned into silence, Margaux stared at him with wide eyes. But after a minute, her eyes narrowed and her expression made it clear she wasn't buying his story. "Humph. Yes, I see," she said coolly. "And what I see is that I can go into a monastery the same as you, so there's no reason why I can't go along."

"No, Margaux, don't you get it? This really will be dangerous." He took a big breath, blew it out through his mouth, and counted to ten. "Look, this guy is a really bad dude and he isn't going to just turn Mom over to me. I don't know what's going to happen and I have more than enough to worry about without having to worry about you too."

Margaux's eyes darkened and her nostrils flared. "You do *not* have to worry about me, Deston Lespérance. I can take care of myself. But go ahead and go. I'll just follow behind," she shouted back, planting her hands on her hips.

Deston shook his head in disbelief and looked over at Titania, pleading with his eyes for help. "Will you please tell her she can't go?"

Titania had recognized Margaux the minute she laid eyes on her. But the shock of seeing the girl in Tir na-nÓg was quickly replaced with delight at how much Margaux was like her mother. After giving Margaux a wink, Titania smiled sadly at Deston. "I'm sorry, Deston, but here in Tir na-nÓg it is everyone's prerogative to choose his or her own actions. Margaux's destiny led her here the same as yours did. Who am I to stand in the way of destiny? And I must say, she does seem quite determined to go. If I were you, I would save my strength for the more important battles ahead."

Deston's mouth flopped open and the look on his face was one of total astonishment.

Titania brought her hand up to her mouth to hide her smile and started down the hill to keep from laughing.

Margaux gave Deston a satisfied smirk and happily skipped off after Titania.

"This is just great," Deston mumbled under his breath, as he watched the two walk off together. "How come I never get to win any of the arguments?"

Grumbling about his bad luck, he grudgingly headed down the hill after them.

At the bottom of the hill, they crossed a bridge to a small house set on the bank of the island. The Elders were waiting for them inside and turned as a group as the three entered the house, Margaux being the last to walk in. As Margaux stepped through the door, Lan rushed forward, putting a hand out to stop her. Before he could say a word, Titania spoke up.

"This is Margaux. She is Deston's friend and will be going with him," she announced matter-of-factly, leaving no room for debate.

All eyes turned to Margaux and she took a step back, but Titania quickly moved beside her and put an arm over her shoulder to guide her and Deston into the middle of the room.

Pora was the first to break the silence that followed. "Deston ... Margaux," she added with a nod of her head. "We have gathered together some items you'll need for your journey." She held out her hand, indicating three small children. Two were holding identical stacks of clothing. The third was holding Deston's backpack. "We hope to keep word of your arrival from Grossard for as long as possible. The clothes you see here will help mask your true identities by giving you the appearance of being one of our soldiers."

Deston and Margaux took the clothes the children offered them as the third child set the backpack at Deston's feet. Deston looked down at the garments and the polished silver breastplate and helmet sitting on the top of the pile. The look of wonder on his face reflected back to him in the shiny metal. His eyes glazed over and the rest of Pora's words were lost as he pictured himself on the back of a black stallion racing toward a castle, his sword flashing in the sun. But as Grossard's name pierced his daydream, his attention was drawn back to Pora.

"Grossard thinks you're still with Nicolette," Pora was saying. "As long as he thinks that, you'll be able to travel along the main road, which will save time. However, we know Grossard has spies everywhere and once he gets word you're here, he'll send his minions out to find you. It's vital to your success that you travel fast and stay alert." She swept her arm around to two men standing at the back of the room. "This is Torren and Keir, two of our very best warriors. They'll accompany you as far as the gateway. Listen to them, follow their lead, and learn as much as you can from them in the time they are with you."

Deston looked at the men standing at attention, their unblinking eyes staring straight ahead. They were quite tall and very impressive with broad shoulders and bulging biceps. They each had on a long hauberk of finely woven chainmail over green tunics and brown trousers, similar to what was in his stack of clothes. Their helmets had a long metal piece that covered their nose and another long piece following their jaw line down and around, almost coming together in front of their chin, leaving only their steely eyes visible. Each also had a bow and a quiver of arrows slung over their left shoulders and a long sword attached to the broad belt at their waist. Deston eyed the swords, then looked back at the pile of clothes in his arms. There was no weapon in his stack.

Pora stepped back into the line of Elders and nodded to Rehan who hesitantly walked up to Deston. She kept her eyes lowered as she held out a dark green box.

"This special gift is a great treasure and will be extremely valuable to you on your journey," she said in a timid voice not much louder than a whisper. "If you get into a situation you don't know how to get out of, open the lid and you'll find whatever you need inside."

As Deston took the box, Rehan's eyes lifted to his. The glance lasted no more than a nanosecond, but it was long enough for him to notice the fear reflected in them. Taken aback, he mumbled an uncertain, "Thank you," as she bowed and backed her way out the door, keeping her head down the entire way.

Margaux leaned over and pushed down on Deston's arm to get a better look at the mysterious box. To her surprise, it was just a plain, trunk-shaped box with a tree carved into the top. It didn't look very wondrous at all, nor did it look like it could produce much that would help, as it was no bigger than a shoebox. She exchanged a questioning look with Deston, but he was as puzzled as she was and shrugged his shoulders in reply.

"Keep this box safe and use it wisely when you arrive at the monastery, for what Rehan said is true. It will be invaluable to you. But only use it as your last recourse and after you've exhausted all other options, for it can only be opened three times," Pora added.

Deston and Margaux both looked down at the box again as Frayne stepped forward carrying a small, leather bundle.

"This is an eternal flame," Frayne announced, holding the bundle up for Deston and Margaux's inspection. "Whenever you're in need of light or warmth, place this on the ground and untie the lace. A flame will immediately appear. When you no longer have need of it, tie it securely and store it away for another time. It will never burn you or burn out and will provide protection from the darkness."

He handed the bundle to Margaux and placed a hand over each of their heads. He closed his eyes as his lips moved silently; then he bowed to each of them and backed out of the room as Rehan had.

As soon as Frayne left, Aren approached the two. He laid a thin coil of rope on top of the green box in Deston's arms. "This rope is woven with faerie hair. It cannot be broken," he stated bluntly and turned, showing Deston his back as he walked swiftly to the door without bowing.

Deston looked down at the rope, unaware that Aren had been disrespectful.

Lan didn't miss the slight, however. He held his tongue, but his steely glare followed Aren out of the room. Lan knew Aren had been unhappy when Deston's arrival was announced, as Aren had anticipated being named the next in line for the throne. But Aren had assured everyone he harbored no ill will. But his attitude of late and now this deliberate snub, said otherwise.

Sadria was the last to approach, carrying a wooden bowl in her hands. She smiled sweetly as she held it up in front of Deston and Margaux. "This faerie oil will allow you to hear and understand nature and the animals. Listen to them, for they are wise and can teach you much," she said.

She dipped her fingers into the bowl and rubbed the oil on the inside of their ears and looked solemnly into each of their eyes. "May the gods grant you the eyes of the hawk, the ears of the bat, and the speed of the cheetah. Rely on the animal spirits and they'll guide and protect you." She smiled encouragingly, bowed, and left as the first two had.

As soon as Sadria was gone, Lan gestured for Torren and Keir to leave as well. The soldiers quietly exited as Pora turned to Deston.

"These gifts may look insignificant, but they'll help you a great deal on your journey, I assure you. Although, as your grandmother has already told you, your intelligence and fortitude will be your best weapons against Grossard." Pora reached out to caress Deston's cheek, but her arm stalled, then dropped back to her side. "I'm truly sorry you have to endure this burden and undo my mistake. I wish there was another way. More than that, I wish I could be of more help. But I will make you this promise that regardless of the out-come, I will see that the world sings the praises of your bravery for all the generations to come."

She hesitated and looked at Titania and Lan before continuing. "I'm afraid it's time for you to get ready. Margaux, you can change in the other room through that door," she pointed across to the far wall. "Deston, you'll change here. When you are ready, come outside. We'll be waiting there for you.

Chapter 27

Pora's words echoed in Deston's head as he stood beside Margaux in the middle of the room and watched Titania and the two Elders walk out the door. When the room had emptied, Margaux looked down at the pile of clothes in her arms and back up at Deston.

"I guess we had better change," she said, although she didn't make an attempt to move.

"Yeah," Deston replied, lost in his own thoughts. The magnitude of what he was about to do weighed heavy on him. On top of that, second thoughts about letting Margaux come along were starting to fester in his mind. This wasn't her battle. It said a lot about her character that she was willing to go with him and help out, but if anything happened to her, he'd never be able to live with himself. The thought of going alone was a little scary, but this time it really was for the best.

Hesitantly, he turned to her. "I—" His voice cracked. He blushed as he cleared his throat and started again. "I've been thinking ... maybe I should just do this by myself."

Margaux pressed her lips together and looked at the floor.

"Those two soldiers will be with me until I get to the gateway, and I just think it'll be a lot easier for one person to sneak into the monastery than two. And ... well, this is my battle and there's no reason you should risk getting hurt. So you should just stay here and I'll see you when I get back."

Margaux didn't respond right away, but when she looked up, her eyes were glassy. "No, I have to go with you," her voice quivered.

"For as long as I can remember I've dreamt about what it would be like to come here and be with the fae. Now here I am, and it's all because of you." She stopped and blinked several times to hold back the tears. "This may sound crazy, but for the first time in my life, I feel like I'm where I'm supposed to be. Don't you see? This isn't just about you. Titania said it herself ... my destiny brought me here for a reason. I think at least part of that reason is to help you do this."

Without giving him a chance to counter, she set the eternal flame on the ground next to his backpack and hurried across the room, closing the door with a bang behind her.

Deston stared after her, completely flabbergasted. *I will never understand girls. Especially* that *one!* He looked down at the armor in his arms and his concerns for Margaux were instantly pushed to the back of his mind as his excitement flared back to life.

He dropped everything on the floor and quickly changed into the fae uniform. The tunic was exceedingly long and had to be cinched up with the belt, which was also too big. He wrapped it around his waist twice to make it work. He was anxious to try on the armor, but knowing it would be difficult to pack the backpack with it on, he flopped down on the floor and emptied the contents of the pack beside the stack of fae gifts he had been given.

As he watched the items tumble out, he frowned. There was way too much stuff for him to take all of what he had, plus, the gifts from the Elders. Clenching his jaw, he sighed and began rummaging through the items, sorting them into two piles—a "must have" pile and a "don't need" pile. In the "must have" pile he added all the Elders' gifts, plus his pocketknife, a whistle, waterproof matches, two water bottles, his jacket, a framed picture of his mom, and the half-eaten sandwich and cookies NiNi had sent. In the "don't need" pile went his camera, his cell phone, earbuds, and the clothes and shoes he had just taken off.

Deston chewed his lip as he studied the first pile, mentally prioritizing each item. He reached for the green box since it was the largest item, and according to the Elders, the most essential to take along.

"Damn," he muttered under his breath as he slid the box in and saw that it took up a good portion of the available space. Realizing he was going to have to leave more behind than he had planned, he hovered his hand over several other objects, trying to decide what else was absolutely essential to take along. Finally, deciding on the eternal flame, he turned back and let out a loud gasp as he looked upon the pack lying flat on the floor as if it was completely empty. He dropped the eternal flame and frantically grabbed up the pack.

"No, it can't be," he muttered, thrusting his arm into the empty hole and patting the fabric on the inside, praying his eyes were deceiving him. But they weren't. The box was gone.

"Oh gawd, how did I lose it already?" he asked the empty room, looking around helplessly. He'd only turned his back for a moment. How could it have just disappeared? Out of desperation, he reached his hand all the way to the bottom and inched his fingers along the seam. His stomach twisted in panic as lint and a tiny block lodged in the folds of the fabric was all he could feel. Though the block was too small to be the box, he pulled it out just the same and gaped in disbelief at a minuscule replica of the green box.

He cocked his head from one side to the other, and then brought the small block up closer to his face. At that moment, the box unexpectedly snapped back to its original size and thumped him in the nose. He jumped and let out a yelp at the suddenness of the transformation and nearly dropped the box on the floor. With trembling hands, he hurriedly set it down and scooted back several inches.

His gaze remained glued to the box and slowly his face lit up. *It's a magical box!* Laughing out loud, he picked it up, slid it back into the pack and held his breath. In just a few seconds, the bulging shape sank flat again. Even though he watched it shrink with his own eyes, he still couldn't believe it.

Excitedly, he reached for the eternal flame and the coil of rope and pushed them into the pack as well. He didn't know if all the fae gifts were magical or if the box was special, but he didn't have to wait long for an answer. As with the box, the pack collapsed flat in no time after the two items had been placed inside.

"YES," he hooted and gleefully stuffed everything from the "must have" pile into the pack, stashing his camera in the front pocket as well since there was enough room.

Satisfied he had everything he needed, he zipped the pack closed and turned to the armor lying beside him. A shiver ran up his back as he lifted the breastplate, which consisted of two metal pieces secured together with leather straps at the shoulder and silver chains at the waist.

Just as he started to lift the armor over his head, Margaux came out of the other room. He glanced over at the sound of the door opening and did a double take as she walked toward him, her helmet bouncing around on her head and her hands in a constant state of motion, either pulling up her breastplate as it slid off one shoulder and then the other; pushing up the sleeves of her tunic, which hung down almost to the floor; or moving the helmet back on her head so she could see where she was going. She looked like a small child dressed up in her daddy's clothes and he couldn't hold back his laughter. He laughed so hard he could hardly breathe and each movement she made triggered another fit. Even after she stopped in front of him, it took him several minutes to regain his composure.

At last, he bent and retrieved his T-shirt from the floor to wipe his runny nose on and dab the water from his eyes. "I'm sorry," he said, struggling to suppress another chuckle. "I didn't mean to laugh, but if you could see how ridiculous you look in that outfit."

"I know. I'm not sure who they think I'm going to fool. I certainly don't look like either of those other two soldiers, that's for sure," she replied with a grin.

Deston lapsed into another fit of laughter and had to turn his back to stop. As he lifted his own breastplate over his head, he snickered again, but when the armor slid right past his shoulders and the neck hole came to stop mid-chest, he instantly sobered. Margaux burst out laughing at the sight, but this time Deston didn't think it so funny.

With a red face, he struggled to get out of the armor, but his arms were pinned to his sides and were completely useless. He was too embarrassed to ask Margaux for help, so the only way left was to bend over and wiggle until the breastplate slid down and over his head. After several minutes, it landed on the floor with a loud clang.

"I guess they aren't equipped for extra small soldiers in their army," Margaux said teasingly between giggles.

Deston mistook her remark as a slam about his height and fired right back, "Yeah, well yours doesn't fit you any better."

"Yes, I know. Like I said, they must not be accustom to outfitting teenagers," she giggled, ignoring his tone.

Deston felt more embarrassed and more foolish than he did before. He'd been trying so hard to impress Margaux, but it seemed like all he did was screw things up whenever she was around.

Man, I'm such a jerk, he thought, stooping to pick up his backpack and armor to hide his humiliation. He counted to ten and took a deep breath before straightening. Then, as casually as he could, he turned to face her, pretending he hadn't just snapped at her. "Okay, I guess this is it. Are you ready?"

Margaux smiled and walked up beside him, threading her arm through his. "Yes, let's go," she said with a wink.

Together they walked outside, Margaux holding up her armor as she walked and Deston carrying his in his arms.

Chapter 28

Deston and Margaux stepped through the door to find the Elders huddled in a group, except for Lan and Aren, who were standing off to the side deep in conversation. Lan turned his head and glanced over his shoulder at the sound of the door opening, his face still dark with anger. Aren, who was standing with his arms crossed over his chest and an obstinate look on his face, switched his steely glare from Lan to Deston. As Titania rushed to Deston and Margaux, Aren's chin lifted a little higher in the air and his jaw hardened.

"No, no, no! This will not do," Titania stated.

Taking hold of Margaux's arm, the older woman led her into the sunlight and walked around her, looking her up and down. "Tsk, tsk," she declared and held her hand out over Margaux's head.

Slowly, Titania lowered her hand down in front of Margaux all the way to the ground. As it went, the uniform and armor instantly adjusted. When Titania finished it looked as if the uniform had been custom made for Margaux.

Titania next turned to Deston. "Yours doesn't look too bad, but I need to see all of it together. Please put on the armor," she instructed.

Deston darted a quick sidelong glance at Margaux as he stuck his head through the neck hole, keeping a tight grip on the breastplate so it wouldn't slip down like before. Still, his cheeks turned a bright pink as Titania walked around him. She repeated the movements she had done to Margaux and within seconds Deston's uniform was a perfect fit as well.

Stepping back, Titania cocked her head and examined each of them once more. She made a few more adjustments, then turned to the Elders for their nod of approval.

"You two look very impressive," Pora exclaimed. "I think you will pass nicely as one of our own. What do you think, Lan?"

Lan inspected the pair, his sharp eyes taking in every detail. "Yes, I think they'll do very nicely," he agreed.

"Sir, what about a sword? Those soldiers have one, so I thought..." Deston began, but his words trailed off as Lan's right eyebrow shot up and an amused look crossed the Elder's face.

"Of course, you're right. Every good soldier carries a sword. That was an oversight on my part, but one that is easily rectified," Lan exclaimed. The words had no sooner left his mouth than a small boy came through the doorway holding two swords in his outstretched arms. Lan picked up the first, bowed to Deston and handed the weapon to him. He offered the second to Margaux.

At the sight of the sword, Margaux let out a small squeak and her bottom lip quivered as her eyes locked on the sharp edge of the blade. "Do I have to take that?"

Lan briskly pulled the sword back. "Certainly not ... not every soldier needs to carry a sword. Perhaps you would feel more comfortable with a bow?"

Margaux looked relieved at the suggestion and before she could open her mouth to respond, another child appeared at the door with a bow and quiver. As Margaux donned the bow, Deston proudly slid the sword into its scabbard and tucked it into his belt while Lan gave last minute instructions to Torren and Keir. The two soldiers stood at attention, their expressions blank as they listened. When Lan turned back to the group, the two did an about-face and began walking down the road, loaded down with weapons and knapsacks.

From deep within the city came the blare of a loud trumpet. The Elders, with the exception of Aren, immediately fell into single-file and followed the soldiers. Titania put her arms around Margaux and Deston and escorted them along after the others.

The procession progressed along the road and into an orchard where neat, even rows of sculptured trees were weighed down with pink and white blossoms, filling the air with a heady scent. Lost in his thoughts, Deston took no notice of his surroundings until the sound of cheering roused him out of his daze. He looked up and was startled to find they had not only reached the base of the giant tree, but a crowd had gathered and were lining both sides of the road. Having been through this once before, he quickly looked down, but the cheers became increasingly louder. As they did, doubts formed in his mind. It was one thing to imagine himself a hero rescuing his mother and saving the fae, but actually doing it was an entirely different matter. These people were counting on him and he didn't know what would happen to them if he failed. The thought made him feel sick, and it got worse when he realized that giving his all may not be enough.

The crowd of people continued to cheer as they followed the group over a bridge at the junction of the two rivers. A short distance before the road was swallowed up by the forest, the procession came to a stop and the crowd quieted in anticipation.

Lan turned to Deston and Margaux. "This is as far as we go. The four of you will continue along this road to Mirror Lake. The gateway to the lower realm is on the far side of the lake. Torren and Keir will remain with you as far as the gateway, but once you cross through, you will be on your own.

"Your parents are being held in the Monastery of Leinad. Think that name as you step into the gateway. On the other side, take the road along the sea cliff and follow it to the monastery. It's a large structure situated on the edge of the cliff a few kilometers from where you arrive. You should have no trouble locating it. There's nothing else around. Stay on the cliff road and it will lead you straight there. Grossard will undoubtedly have some kind of defense set up in the lower realm, so please stay alert at all times and be cautious. Your return is as important to us as the return of Oseron and the Crystal."

Lan hesitated and his eyes turned sad. "I realize I have not given you much to go on, but I simply don't know any more. No news has been able to get through to us for over a day and our information is limited." He paused and added, "Do you have any questions?"

Deston looked up incredulously. Of course he had questions— hundreds of them, but at that moment he couldn't bring a single one to mind. Stalling for time, he sputtered, "What about food? I ... er ... I only have part of my lunch, which won't be enough for all of us."

"Torren and Keir have all the food and supplies you'll need. Don't worry about incidentals. Anything else?"

Deston strained to recall some of his earlier questions, but no matter how hard he tried nothing came to mind. At last he gave up and shook his head no.

Lan nodded grimly, took a step back and closed his eyes. As he turned his face to the sky and lifted his arms in the air, the Elders and the crowd dropped to their knees. Out of nowhere, a gust of wind whirled up around Lan, and only Lan, lifting a circular column of leaves straight up into the heavens. The funnel lasted only a few minutes and gave way to a soft glow, which bathed Lan in an ethereal light. His eyes sprung wide open and he called out in a booming voice that shook the trees.

"We thank you Gaia for sending us this deliverer in our time of need. We now look to you for guidance and ask you to watch over both of these young people as they set out to fulfill their destinies. Fill them with your light and let your wisdom and strength be theirs. Send the spirit of the earth, wind, water, and fire to guide them and lead them along the right path. And protect them from evil so they may triumph and return back to us safely."

As Lan's words faded, a soft hum filled the air. It came from beneath Deston's feet and escalated in volume until the ground was trembling. A warm energy seeped in through the soles of Deston's boots, spreading throughout his body all the way to the top of his head. He closed his eyes, letting the energy consume him and replace his apprehension with a calm, peaceful feeling. But as soon as Lan lowered his arms, the hum left and so did the feeling.

Lan looked down on Deston and Margaux, his face still aglow. "Remember, time is limited. Go with speed and trust no one," he warned. With that said, the glow around him vanished.

Titania stepped up to Margaux and pulled her into a tight hug. She kissed her on the forehead, then turned to Deston with tears in her eyes.

"I wish I could go with you, but it's not meant to be," Titania said, cupping his face in her hands as she looked deep into his eyes, trying her best to impart to him some of her knowledge. "You are your father's son, never forget that. Though you have never met him, you can still gain from his strength. It is in your blood. Be strong ... be true ... be careful, and come back to me soon," Titania said, as she wrapped her arms around him. She hugged him tightly and kissed him on each cheek twice before stepping back.

Deston and Margaux looked at each other, and then at Torren and Keir who were waiting for them just inside the trees. Margaux sucked in a breath, took Deston's hand and gave him a weak smile. He squeezed her hand and smiled back as a warm tingle, which had nothing to do with the journey they were about to embark on, filled the pit of his stomach. A loud cheer went up from the crowd as the two stepped forward. It continued until they were well inside the forest.

Chapter 29

Rellik was in a dark mood as he raced through the trees. He'd taken a detour to visit his pack on the way to the cottage and the hours had flown by much faster than he realized. Now he had to race like the wind or he wouldn't make it back to the cottage before dark. Still, he wasn't sorry he had made the stop. It had given him the chance to sit down and analyze Grossard's plan. In doing so, he realized it wasn't so grand after all. There were too many variables involved and that didn't even take into consideration the glitches that had already surfaced. He also came to realize he had been duped from the beginning and the abundant rewards Grossard had promised were nothing more than empty words.

Rellik's pace slowed as his mind returned to the situation at hand. He should have left the minute Grossard involved the humans. It wasn't that he had any particular love for humans, but he knew how relentless humans could be in their pursuit when one of their own kind was killed. Especially if that one was a child. He also knew he and his family would be the ones to suffer and pay the price, not Grossard.

"We'll see about that," Rellik sneered under his breath. "I'll bring you the boy, but if you want him killed, you'll have to do it yourself."

Picking up speed, Rellik's enormous feet pounded the ground and echoed like a bass drum through the quiet of the forest. His long tongue lolled out of his mouth and his permanent snarl was in place. However, for the first time in months, he felt strangely calm.

He didn't slow again until he had reached the edge of the forest across from the cottage, arriving just as NiNi's car drove up the driveway. His body tensed with anticipation as he waited for Deston to appear. To his disappointment, the only person to emerge from the building at the side of the house was the old woman. Shifting his position, he kept his eyes locked on the door, impatient to be finished with the task. Minutes turned into hours, and as the sun sank low in the sky, Rellik swallowed back the uncomfortable tightness growing in his chest.

Suddenly, the back door of the cottage swung open. Rellik's muscles twitched with expectation, but once again he was disappointed as it was just the old woman.

NiNi walked to the end of the porch, looked down the road and checked her watch. With a frown and a shake of her head, she turned back to the house. Rellik watched her, but made no move. His only interest was Deston.

A short time later, the door opened again and NiNi walked to the porch stairs, wringing her hands as she stared down the road. The light continued to fade, but she stayed on the porch until a small dot appeared on the horizon. Letting out a loud sigh of relief, she hustled down the steps and hurried through the gate, waiting anxiously by the end of the fence. Her hand went to her forehead as she squinted into the fading light.

Drool dripped from Rellik's muzzle as he too watched the dot grow.

When it became clear the dot was a bicycle and rider, NiNi rose up on her tiptoes and gave a joyous wave, but as the rider straightened up on the seat, her body went stiff and her brow puckered in confusion. The rider rode straight to her and stopped. She stared at the apparition with a look of horror and then her legs began to tremble and she grabbed hold of the fence to steady herself.

"Zumwald, what have you done?" she cried out.

Zumwald swung his leg over the seat and let it drop in the dirt as he rushed to NiNi's side before she crumpled to the ground. At that same moment, a strange wind picked up, blowing in the opposite direction and Rellik could not hear the words being said. He knew who Zumwald was, however, and his heart skipped a beat. He told himself Zumwald's arrival was nothing more than a coincidence and didn't necessarily mean They were involved. Still, nervous perspiration ran into his eyes as he watched Zumwald walk NiNi to the porch.

Rellik stayed at the forest's edge, watching the two on the swing, deep in conversation. Not being able to hear what they were saying was maddening, but at the same time, it allowed him to hold onto the desperate hope that Zumwald's visit was inconsequential.

The couple seemed to talk for hours, although in reality it was only a few minutes. Finally, just as the sun was slipping below the horizon, NiNi got up and walked to the edge of the porch. She was trembling as she stared off into the forest and silent tears rolled down her cheeks. For several minutes, she stood there stoically; then her face crumpled.

"Titania, please … he is just a boy. Send him back to me before he gets hurt," she yelled to the trees, and then buried her face in her hands and sobbed.

With NiNi's words, Rellik's earlier bravado disintegrated and his legs went weak. There was no more speculating. They had the boy. He had failed Grossard. He closed his eyes as the panic he'd been holding back took over.

What was he going to tell Grossard? Or did Grossard already know? He spun around, half expecting to find the monster standing behind him, but the forest was dark and empty. His eyes darted frantically from side to side as his mind raced. He needed to find the boy before Grossard heard the news—it was his only chance for a reprieve. Turning into the trees, he ran faster than he ever had in his life. He had to find the boy. He had to.

Chapter 30

As army officers, Torren and Keir were as accustomed to taking orders as giving them and their current orders were to get Deston to the gateway as quickly as possible. That was their mission and they were concerned with nothing else. The second Deston and Margaux walked into the forest, the warriors started off at a brisk pace without looking back, expecting the other two to fall in line, as any good soldier would.

At first, Deston and Margaux tried to keep up, but their legs were not as long as the adults and they had to run full out just to keep the warriors in sight. Margaux did her best to maintain the speed, but after a short distance her lungs felt as if they would burst. When she could no longer catch a breath, she came to a halt.

"I don't know—how far this gateway is—but I don't think— I can run like this—the entire way," she panted.

Deston nodded his head in agreement and walked circles around her, struggling to catch his own breath. The Elders had warned him that time was of the essence, but like Margaux, he knew he couldn't keep up that kind of pace the whole distance.

By the time he and Margaux started on their way again, Torren and Keir were so far ahead Deston couldn't see them at all. But he hoped as long as they stayed on the road and kept up a steady jog, they would eventually catch sight of the warriors again.

The dirt road was hard packed from years of use, which made it easy to jog on. Tall, lush trees lined each side, acting as silent sentries, but they also provided plenty of cover for anyone who didn't want to be seen. With the loud beating of his heart no longer pounding in his head, the sounds of the forest were finally able to penetrate Deston's thoughts. However, it wasn't the sounds of birds chirping and animal calls he expected to hear. It was the sound of voices talking—lots of voices. At first he thought he was being paranoid, but as the voices persisted, he began to suspect it was more than just his imagination. Clearly, there were people within the trees, and the fact they were hiding didn't bode well with him.

His gaze darted from left to right at every little sound in hopes of catching sight of someone, but the only thing he saw were two brown squirrels chasing each other up a tree trunk and out onto a limb. The squirrels jumped from one tree to the next and as they disappeared amongst the leaves, someone shouted out, "Hey, come back!"

Deston and Margaux both jumped at the shout and whirled around at the same time. Without thinking about it, Deston pushed Margaux behind him and did a quick scan of the area.

"Did you hear that?" he whispered out of the corner of his mouth.

"Yes, I did," Margaux whispered back.

Knowing Margaux had heard it too did nothing to alleviate Deston's anxiety. He swallowed hard and hesitantly walked to the side of the road. As he peered into the shadows, another shout came from behind him. He went rigid. Then very slowly, he walked backward to where Margaux was standing, keeping his gaze locked on the trees.

"I heard something over there," Margaux whispered as he got near, tilting her head in the direction of the sound.

"I know. I did too. It sounds like we're surrounded," he whispered back. "Pretend like nothing is wrong. Just turn around and start jogging. Jog fast, but don't full out run. I don't want them to know we suspect anything."

Together they turned and started jogging like before, making an effort to act casual. Deston kept his head facing forward, but his eyes flitted wildly from side to side, looking for any sign of movement. *Where the heck are Torren and Keir?* he thought, moving his hand to the hilt of his sword, even though he didn't know what he'd do with it if someone attacked as he had never used a weapon before in his life.

Beads of sweat broke out on Deston's forehead and his nerves were stretched as taut as a guitar string. Even the slightest movement of a leaf caused his heart to skip a beat and when a squirrel darted out from under a bush a few feet in front of him, he jumped back with a yelp and pushed Margaux behind him again.

The squirrel froze in its tracks at Deston's cry and let out its own screech. Visibly shaking, the rodent stared up at the two humans, its nose twitching in the air. Then with an audible sigh it relaxed and stood up on hind legs to address the two.

"Forgive me, but you startled me," the squirrel squeaked. "I wasn't expecting the fae to be outside of the city today with all that is going on. You must be on an important mission. I pray I have not delayed you. Please excuse me." With a little wave of its paw, it scampered to the other side of the road. When it reached the bramble, it looked back. "You two watch yourselves. Word has it the forest is filled with darkness today," the squirrel warned before vanishing under the branches.

Deston's heart was racing from the start and his mouth hung open as he stared after the rodent.

Margaux was startled too, but she recovered first and started laughing. "It's only the animals. Remember? They put that oil on our ears and we can hear them now," she said through her laughter.

Deston went limp and it took him another minute to remember to breathe. "I really thought we were under attack," he said with a nervous laugh.

High over their heads, Keir's panicked voice suddenly yelled down. "Deston! Margaux!"

In the next second two enormous hawks dropped from the sky and landed on the road. Before the hawks' feet had even touched the ground, they transformed into Torren and Keir. The warriors sprinted directly to Deston, drawing their swords as they ran.

Seeing the warriors wielding swords, Margaux let out a shriek and jumped behind Deston. The top of her head was all that could be seen as she peered out over his shoulder.

"Are you alright, Your Highness?" Keir questioned.

Deston, still not one hundred percent recovered from the

talking squirrel incident, stood transfixed and stared at Keir with bulging eyes.

"Is something wrong? Have you been hurt?" questioned Keir again, examining Deston for any sign of injury.

"No, we just heard voices—" Margaux replied when Deston didn't answer.

The soldiers didn't wait to hear the rest of Margaux's sentence, but immediately turned back-to-back and faced opposite sides of the road in preparation for an attack. Their steely eyes searched the trees as they gripped their swords with both hands.

"—but it was only the animals," Margaux finished timidly, shrinking further down behind Deston.

Keir and Torren paid little attention to Margaux's last words and plowed into the trees, each taking a different side, while Deston stood in a trance in the middle of the road.

As soon as the two disappeared, Margaux straightened. "Oh, I wish they wouldn't swing those nasty swords around like that. Someone is going to get hurt!"

Deston turned to her, his eyes still wide with wonder. "Did you see that?" he asked in a voice that was more of a squeak. "They can turn into hawks. I mean, one minute they were hawks and the next they were men. You saw it too, right?" His words tumbled over each other in his excitement.

"Yes, I saw them. The fae are masters at that—shapeshifting, that is," she replied in a slightly surprised tone, implying it was common knowledge.

Deston gawked at her. "Have you seen them do that before?" he marveled.

"Well, no … not Torren and Keir anyway. But I did see one of the boys back in the city turn into a cat. Everyone knows the fae have the ability to do that. Didn't you recognize Keir's voice when he called out our names?" She wrapped her arms around her chest and shivered as she looked into the trees. "I just wish they wouldn't swing those swords around like that," she repeated.

Margaux never ceased to amaze Deston. A man changing into a hawk didn't seem to bother her in the least, but the sight of a sword had her trembling.

"Oh, and why did Keir call you, Your Highness?" Margaux added in an afterthought as she looked back at Deston.

Deston shook his head in disbelief and walked away.

Margaux watched him go and repeated. "Deston, you didn't answer me. Why did he address you as, Your Highness?"

Deston let out a sigh. "Because my father is the king of Tir na-nÓg," he replied without turning around.

Margaux's right eyebrow shot up as she shifted her weight to one leg and planted her hands on her hips. "Your father ... the king? Is that so? I thought your name was Lespérance?"

"That's Mom's maiden name. She had to use it so no one would find us," he responded in the same sarcastic tone.

Margaux pressed her lips into a thin line and glared at him. "You *really* expect me to believe King Oseron is your father and yet you don't even know the fae can shapeshift?" she demanded.

Deston bristled at her tone and glared back. "Look, I could care less what you believe or don't believe," he said and walked to the other side of the road to avoid any further discussion. There were too many other issues, important issues, on his mind at the moment and he wasn't in the mood for long explanations.

Margaux clenched her teeth and folded her arms over her chest, as her eyes shot darts at his back. With a harrumph, she turned her back on him and fumed as she stared into the trees.

A few minutes later, Keir and Torren returned to find Deston and Margaux standing on opposite sides of the road. Margaux still looked angry, and Deston was still marveling over the fact the two fae could transform into hawks.

Keir went straight to Deston, dropped down on one knee and bowed his head. "Your Highness, I beg your forgiveness for leaving you behind. We didn't realize you had stopped. We assumed you were right behind us."

Margaux looked over her shoulder just as Keir bowed his head. Her eyes widened in surprise. Then her brow drew together in confusion as she heard Keir address Deston as "Your Highness" once again. Hesitantly, she crossed the road as Deston explained why they had fallen behind.

"It was actually my fault," Margaux interjected. "You were

going so fast I couldn't keep up." Her words trailed off as Keir shot her a piercing look.

Ignoring her, Keir addressed Deston, "For your own safety, Your Highness, I must ask that you stay close to us. I apologize that we were going too fast for your comfort. In the future, if you feel the need to stop, I must ask that you inform us. We'll be happy to accommodate you in any way we can."

Deston nodded. "I'm sorry. I didn't mean to be any trouble."

"You are no trouble, but we do need to continue … if you are ready that is."

"I'm ready," Deston replied, anxious to get out from under Keir's scrutiny.

Keir nodded to Torren and they started off at a brisk pace, with Keir in front and Torren bringing up the rear to make sure Deston and Margaux did not fall behind again.

Margaux, deep in thought, jogged in silence a few paces behind Deston. She thought back to the procession through Tir na-nÓg and how the crowd had bowed as Deston walked by. It hadn't registered with her at the time, but now it did seem rather strange. Her nose crinkled as she also recalled Titania's words to Deston, *"Don't forget you're your father's son."* All of a sudden everything fell into place. She gasped out loud.

"King Oseron really is your father, isn't he?" she called out.

"Yup, he is," Deston replied without looking back.

Margaux stopped short and stared at Deston's back. "Oh … mon … étoiles," she said under her breath. "It really is true." She jolted back into action and ran to catch up, her face split into a wide grin. "Far out—that is so groovy. Why didn't you say anything before?"

Deston rolled his eyes and squeezed his lips together to keep from smiling.

"Can I meet him? Where is he? Why wasn't he in Tir na-nÓg?" Margaux fired off questions without allowing him time to respond. Then she gasped out loud, "Oh, no … does that bad man you told me about, the one who took your mama, have the king too?"

"Yeah, I guess Grossard used Mom as bait and Oser … er, Dad

was totally outnumbered. He didn't have a chance."

Margaux stopped firing off questions for a moment to absorb the new piece of information.

"You know one thing I don't understand, though, is why Grossard waited so long to capture Oser—Dad? He took Mom back in September," Deston said, speaking his thoughts out loud.

"Well, that actually makes perfect sense when you figure in the time difference between the realms. It's only been a couple of days here since your mama was taken, not eight months," Margaux answered matter-of-factly. Seeing the bewildered look on Deston's face, she added incredulously, "You don't know about the time difference, either?"

"Time difference?"

Margaux was dumbfounded. "How can Oseron be your father and yet you know nothing at all about this realm?"

Deston shrugged. "Simple. I grew up in America and wasn't told anything about my father or this place. The only faeries I knew about were the ones in Disney movies. I've never even heard of a fae until just a little while ago."

Margaux straightened her back. There was nothing she loved more than talking about faeries, but usually no one wanted to listen. "Well, you see, time runs slower in this realm," she explained. "Each day here is equivalent to approximately four months in our realm, give or take a few weeks. So it is completely possible for Grossard to take your mama eight months ago in America, but here in Tir na-nÓg it would only be two days. Do you see? September makes perfect sense too, since the gateways from the lower realm are only open at certain times of the year. The fall equinox is one of those times."

Confused by her last statement, Deston looked over to insert a question, but Margaux held her hand up in anticipation, "That only applies to the gateways *into* the high realm. Although, there are a few places in the world, Forest of Brocéliande being one, where the gateways are permanently open. But those gateways are well hidden, so very few people have ever actually been to Tir na-nÓg."

Deston considered Margaux's explanation as he walked. It

explained so much, but it also made him realize how much he had to learn about this new world. "So what else do you know about the fae?" he asked.

Margaux smiled with enthusiasm. "Plenty. I've read every book that's ever been written on the high realm and on faeries. And there's this old gypsy woman who comes into Merveille every once in a while. She has visited Tír na-nÓg and has told me all about it. What do you want to know?"

Deston didn't know where to start. "So I guess there are different kinds of faeries?"

"Yes, quite a few different ones actually. The fae are the most human-like and lead the rest, but some of the others are very similar to us too. The pixies and sprites, for example, look just like us humans, except in miniature size, and they have—"

"Pora said Grossard was a solitary faerie. What about them?" Deston interrupted.

"Oh, of course, he would be a solitary." Her eyes squinted and her nose wrinkled as she tried to recall what she knew. "The term solitary faerie is more of a classification than a species. It'd be like calling a person a *félon*, or ... um, a *criminelle* in our realm. All the dark faerie groups have been lumped under that one classification." She paused to collect her thoughts. "I guess you could say the solitaries are the terrorists of the high realm. They are mean, nasty creatures, and scary too. They've hurt a lot of people throughout the centuries and have caused a lot of destruction—especially in our world. It's them that have given faeries a bad name. When you hear someone talk about monsters, it's probably a solitary they're ta—"

Margaux abruptly stopped speaking as Keir raised his hand and motioned for her silence. At that same instant, Torren materialized next to Keir. The warriors' expressions were somber and their eyes were riveted on the dense forest as they stood side by side.

Deston had been so engrossed in what Margaux was saying he hadn't been paying attention to anything else; but as Torren silently slid his sword from its scabbard, Deston instantly became alert. He followed their stares, but saw nothing out of ordinary.

Margaux stepped up closer to Deston and took hold of his arm, as Keir silently gestured for them to stay put. The two soldiers took a step forward. Before they could take another, small monkey-like creatures fell from the trees and jumped out of the bushes.

"Spriggans!" Torren yelled, instantly dropping his knapsacks to the ground and drawing a short sword from his waistband to have a weapon in each hand. At the same time Keir threw his own knapsack down and knelt on one knee as he shrugged the bow from his back.

Margaux covered her mouth with her hand to stifle a scream as the small creatures with large heads, hairy pointed ears, and stout stubby bodies slowly advanced on the soldiers, waving their own short-bladed swords in the air.

Though Torren and Keir were vastly outnumbered, they calmly held their stance and waited for the spriggans to come closer.

A group of the little creatures moved in and formed a wide circle around the soldiers. Another group split off and created a line separating the two pairs. They had no particular interest in Deston and Margaux, since those two weren't carrying supplies, but they wanted to make sure the two didn't interfere.

The spriggans circling the soldiers darted in and out, jabbing their short swords chaotically in an attempt to intimidate the fae and draw them away from the knapsacks. Torren and Keir didn't fall for their antics and held their ground. After playing that game for several minutes, one of the spriggans lost patience and charged. Torren waited until the last possible instance before he jumped sideways and swung his sword so fast, it was nothing but a blur. A high-pitched scream filled the air and the creature fell to the ground. The remaining spriggans stilled momentarily, their ears twitching. Then in a rush, the entire group stormed the soldiers.

Keir let an arrow fly and followed with more in rapid succession, as Torren's swords sliced through the air. Within seconds, none of the small creatures were left standing. As the last spriggan fell, Keir slowly stood, an arrow still nocked at the ready and aimed at the trees.

Margaux was paralyzed with fear and was clutching Deston's arm so tightly his circulation was nearly cut off, but he barely noticed. He'd never seen anything like what Torren and Keir had just done. Even the most spectacular combat scene in the movies couldn't compare. And it had happened so quickly and the soldiers had remained so calm, it was almost as if they had choreographed the battle.

Deston opened his mouth to yell out to them, but a shrill whistle from deep within the forest came first. The piercing sound bounced off the trees and before it ended, dozens of spriggans bounded from the forest on both sides. They hurled themselves onto the road in two units, one running toward Torren and Keir, the other toward Deston and Margaux.

Seeing the sunlight reflect off of the blades of their short swords, Margaux let out a scream. In response, Deston quickly pushed her behind him and reached for his own sword. As he pulled up on the hilt, the cross guard caught on his belt and stuck.

The lead spriggan saw Deston look down to free the sword and took the advantage of the distraction. It threw its sword down, leapt onto Deston's back and started clawing at the backpack. Within seconds, the creature had the zipper torn open and grabbed out what was on top. Hoisting the package high in the air for its colleagues to see, the spriggan let out a victory shriek. The others raised their swords in a responding cheer.

Deston felt the weight of the creature land on his back and spun around, jerking side to side to dislodge it. The spriggan's strong back legs held tight. Not knowing what else to do, Deston flung his arm behind his head and tried to knock it off. The creature reared back and easily dodged Deston's arm, then seized it and sank its jagged teeth into Deston's flesh.

With a cry of shock and pain, Deston wrenched his arm to get free, but the creature was amazingly strong for its size. No matter how Deston twisted or pulled, he couldn't get his arm loose from the spriggan's grip.

Deston could feel warm blood dripping down his forearm as he groped for his sword with his free hand. But as he fumbled to get the cross guard untangled from his belt, he heard a loud "thwack," and his arm was suddenly released. He whirled around and found the spriggan lying on the ground with Margaux standing over it, holding her bow like a bat. She looked over at him with her green eyes blazing and her lips pressed into a thin line.

At that moment another creature leapt into the air straight for them. Deston opened his mouth to yell out a warning, but Margaux saw it at the same time and swung her bow. There was another loud "thwack" as the bow met the spriggan in midair. The creature sailed across the road and into the trees.

Deston gave Margaux a bemused smile as he pulled at his sword again. It came free just as another spriggan flew at him. Deston saw the creature coming out of the corner of his eye and stooped low just in time so that it sailed over the top of him. In the next instant, he rose up, spun around and planted his foot in the middle of the creature's back in one fluid motion. There was a loud crack as the spriggan's bones snapped in two and it collapsed to the ground in agony.

Deston didn't have time to think about what he had done as more spriggans came rushing at him and Margaux. He had never handled a sword before, but he had seen sword fights in movies. He mimicked the moves he remembered and slashed the blade through the air to keep them at bay. Two of the spriggans continued to advance cautiously. Deston took a step back and bumped into Margaux, who was wildly swinging her bow in a wide sweep instead of using it to shoot arrows.

Though spriggans are extremely dim-witted creatures, it didn't take them long to figure out the two small soldiers were not the typical fae warrior. Banding together, they began to circle Deston and Margaux just as they had Torren and Keir. Each time Deston and Margaux took a step back it boosted their confidence and they were soon advancing two and three at a time to close in on the pair.

A few feet away, Torren's sword flashed like a laser light show and Keir fired arrows with rapid intensity. However, more spriggans were appearing from every side.

"Deston, you must escape. Get into the trees and find a place to hide. We'll take care of the spriggans and catch up with you. You must go now!*"* Keir spoke inside Deston's head.

Deston didn't question Keir's order, or how he had received it. He saw the number of creatures increasing and knew he didn't have the skill to hold them off much longer. With a bravado he wasn't fully feeling, he lunged forward and slashed the sword in a wide arc.

The spriggans scurried out of the way of the blade and a small break opened in the circle. Deston took hold of Margaux's arm and pulled her through the gap before the spriggans could regroup.

The spriggans stopped and looked from one to another in confusion as the two sprinted off. They had never witnessed a fae running away from a fight before. A second later, one of them let out a shriek and started after the pair. As soon as the first took off, several more followed his lead.

Deston heard the shriek and glanced over his shoulder. "This way," he yelled to Margaux, veering to the left and into the trees for cover.

Torren was battling his own onslaught of spriggans, but at the same time, he was keeping an eye on Deston's flight. As the creatures set off in chase, Torren leapt high into the air, performed a perfect double flip and landed on the road between the teens and the spriggans. He raised his sword to fend the creatures off, but at the same moment another whistle sounded from within the forest.

The spriggans slid to an immediate halt and turned in unison to look back at Torren's knapsacks lying unattended in the middle of the road. With a scream of delight, they scrambled over each other to get back to the sacks. As the first reached them, he snatched the bags from the ground. The others were right behind and dove on top of him to claim the treasure for themselves and a scuffle instantly ensued.

In the midst of the mayhem, a third whistle blared. At once the creatures quieted, their ears twitching. To Torren and Keir, the third whistle was no different from the first two; but the minute it ceased the creatures jumped up and fled into the trees, dragging the knapsacks behind them.

Torren flew across the road and into the forest after the spriggans. Keir took off in the opposite direction, chasing the second group. Neither of them cared about losing the knapsacks, but they knew if the spriggans made it back to Grossard, the mission would be in greater jeopardy.

Chapter 31

Deston ran hard, pulling Margaux along with him. His lungs burned and tree branches tore at his arms as he barreled his way through, but he didn't stop. When the second whistle blasted, he assumed it was sending more spriggans after them and real panic set in. Instead of watching where he was going, he glanced over his shoulder to see how far behind the creatures were and promptly tripped over a fallen log. He went down hard and landed on his stomach, taking Margaux down with him.

He jerked up out of the dirt, spit dried leaves from his mouth and frantically looked around for a place to hide. There were numerous bushes and trees in the area, but nothing substantial enough to conceal both of them. Then he noticed a bush sitting directly in front of a giant tree. The bush was taller and thicker than any of the others. If there was enough room for both of them to squeeze in between it and the tree, it should work.

"Stay here," Deston whispered to Margaux and crawled to the bush, silently praying the spriggans had lost their trail.

His stomach plummeted when he got to the bush and realized there was no way both of them would be able to fit behind it. Afraid he had wasted too much time to start running again, Deston looked around for another hiding place. As he tried to think over his panic, the memory of a soft voice entered his head. *"When you're in need of help, open this box and you'll find whatever you need inside."*

Deston's heart was in his throat as he hurriedly shrugged off his backpack and dug inside all the way to the bottom. When his fingers touched the tiny block in the corner, he pulled it out and held it in both hands ready for it to spring back to full size. Even though he knew what it would do, he still jumped as it popped back.

With trembling hands, he held his breath and lifted the lid, expecting to find something inside to make them invisible. Something along the line of a camouflage net, but instead, there was only a small piece of gum wrapped in silver foil, sitting grandly on a purple velvet lining.

Oh crap, I did it wrong! Deston thought back to what the Elders had said, but he couldn't recall them giving any instructions. Picking up the silver foil, he held it to his nose. It smelled like bubblegum. He turned it over in his hand, hoping to find a hidden message, but it was only gum.

What the heck am I supposed to do with this? Chew it? It suddenly occurred to him that maybe that was exactly what he was supposed to do. Chew it to become invisible.

Nervously, he took off the wrapper and broke the piece in half, saving some for Margaux. He popped it into his mouth and chewed, and then cringed. The gum tasted like rotten eggs. He continued to chew and gagged as the taste intensified. His eyes began to water and he retched again. He tried not to think about the taste, but it so horrid he could think of nothing else. After a couple of seconds, he looked down at his hands through watery eyes to see if they were fading. To his dismay, he could still see them clearly. It wasn't working. He wasn't becoming invisible, and the taste was getting worse by the second.

When he couldn't take it anymore, he spit the gum out and picked up the hem of his tunic to wipe the taste off his tongue and dab the water leaking from his eyes. When he looked up again, he gasped. In the trunk of the giant tree, exactly where he had spit the gum, there was a large hole. He rubbed his fists in his eyes, thinking the horrible gum was giving him hallucinations. The hole was still there when he looked again.

He scrambled to his knees and reached into the void. To his utter amazement it was not only a hole, it was an ideal hiding place. The box had worked after all, just as the Elders said it would. Behind him a flock of birds squawked loudly as they rose out of the trees. *Spriggans!* Deston thought and anxiously looked back at Margaux, who was lying on the ground with her arm over her eyes.

"Margaux, come here, quick," he beckoned in a loud whisper.

Margaux turned her head and looked at him wearily. She had taken her helmet off. Her hair was matted to her forehead, and a dried leaf was stuck to her cheek. She blankly stared at Deston and he once again gestured with his hand in an urgent appeal for her to come. She let out a tired sigh, sat up and started to get to her feet, but he whispered an explosive, "No!" and motioned for her to stay low. Too emotionally exhausted to argue, she crawled over to him on her hands and knees.

"I've found us a hiding place. Quick, get in. They'll never find us in here," he ordered.

Margaux peered into the dark hole and wrinkled her nose. "Are there bugs in there?"

"What?" Deston exclaimed. "Are you kidding? There are little monkey creatures with swords chasing us and you're worried about a few bugs?"

Margaux still looked uncertain. "Where will you be?"

"I'll be right in there next to you. Now come on, get in. I think they're coming."

"Let me have your flashlight," Margaux asked, still hesitant to crawl into the hole.

"Oh, for crying out loud!" Deston exploded. "We don't have time for this. Will you please just get in?"

Margaux shuddered, but she knew Deston was right. A bug or two was not going to kill her, but the spriggans might. Reluctantly, she crawled into the tree, praying there were no spiders inside. As soon as she was in, Deston threw his backpack in next to her.

"I'm going to get a few more branches to make sure they can't see the hole. I'll be right back," he whispered and hurried off on his hands and knees.

While Deston was gone, Margaux inspected her surroundings. It was amazingly roomy and incredibly clean, given it was a hole in a tree in the middle of a forest. Even more remarkable was the fact there were no cobwebs, no bugs, and no dried leaves on the floor. She ran her hand over the wall and felt grooves, as if a giant drill had bored through the trunk. It seemed odd, but even stranger was the fact that this perfect hole was in the exact place where they had tripped. Her intuition screamed that something wasn't right, but she was too drained from the spriggan attack to follow it through. And there was a much more important issue troubling her at the moment.

Scooting in as far as she could, she leaned her back against the wall and stretched out her legs as doubts about her decision to come along bombarded her. What had she been thinking? She didn't know how to use a weapon, and it was obvious she was slowing them down. As she toyed with the idea of telling Deston she was going to return to Tír na-nÓg, a dark shadow appeared in the opening. Her stomach lurched and she opened her mouth to scream just as Deston's head poked through and he crawled in.

"Deston, will you quit sneaking up on me? You nearly scared me to death," she barked when she could speak again.

"Oh, sorry," he responded without feeling as his concentration was on the branches he was arranging in front of the opening. Once he was satisfied they couldn't be seen from the outside, he settled back, and for the first time since leaving the village, he felt safe. Letting out a long sigh, he took off his helmet. It felt so good to be able to relax, he didn't notice how unusually quiet Margaux was.

Leaning back, Deston rested his head against the wall and let his gaze roam the space, stopping when it came to Margaux. The light coming in through the branches was just enough for him to see that her eyes were closed and her face was pale. The dried leaf was still stuck to her cheek and a small twig was caught in her hair. His stomach tightened as the memory of how her hair smelled like cherry blossoms floated through his head. He reached up to brush the leaf off her cheek and she jumped at his touch.

"Are you okay?" he asked.

Margaux laid her head back and closed her eyes again. "Yes. I'm just tired and thirsty—and hungry."

Deston reached for the backpack and pulled out a water bottle. He handed it to Margaux and rifled through the bag, looking for the sandwich and cookies he had packed.

"I know there was some food in here …" his words trailed off. "Oh damn, I think that spriggan that jumped on my back got it." He looked over at her. "Sorry. Guess you're going to have to wait until we hook up with Keir and Torren to get some food."

The silence grew between them as they were both lost in their own thoughts. After a short time Margaux raised her head and asked the question Deston was thinking himself.

"Do you think they'll be able to find us … Torren and Keir?"

Deston turned his face away before he replied, so Margaux wouldn't see that he was lying. "Yes, of course, they will." He tried to sound confident, even though he wasn't so sure. Torren and Keir had no idea which way they had gone once they entered the trees. And if the spriggans couldn't find them, how likely was it that Torren and Keir would be able to?

Deston peered through the opening at the large bush in front of the hole. He hadn't paid much attention to it before, but now that he was looking closer, he noticed small, blue clusters of berries attached to many of the branches.

"Hey, I think this is a blueberry bush," he said, reaching through the opening to snap off a small clump of the berries. "Look, blue-berries." He beamed, holding his hand out to show Margaux. "Just what the doctor ordered to hold us over until we can get some real food."

Margaux's eyes shot open and she sat up. "Are you sure those are blueberries?"

Deston picked one off and popped it into his mouth. "Of course they are. Do you know any other berry that is blue?"

Margaux watched him chew and swallow the berry. When he didn't retch or fall over dead, she warily tried one herself. The berry had a similar taste to a blueberry, but was much sweeter. Within a matter of minutes the two had cleaned the branch of all its berries, as well as several other branches Deston broke off. With a little food in their stomachs, their moods lightened.

"Did you see how fast Keir could shoot those arrows?" Deston marveled. "You couldn't even see him reach back for another one. And Torren was incredible with the swords."

"They were pretty amazing. Although, I don't think those

spriggans have had much fighting experience. Actually, I'm not sure they even know how to use a sword. They didn't really fight with theirs. They just sort of jabbed them around. That one that jumped on your back dropped its sword on the ground instead of stabbing you with it," Margaux replied.

"You may be right," Deston agreed, and yawned. "But I don't think it would have made a difference. I bet Keir and Torren still would have won."

He yawned again, suddenly feeling so exhausted he couldn't keep his eyes open. The excitement of the fight and the chase had drained him of his energy. He laid his head back and closed his eyes. It wouldn't hurt to rest for a few minutes before going out to find Keir and Torren— as long as it was just for a few minutes.

Chapter 32

The sun's glare had turned the water to a white sheet of glass, as the small sailboat bobbed gently on the waves. Deston had nothing to do, no homework, no chores, nothing. It was just one of those rare, treasured days that were few and far between. A whole day all to himself, and he couldn't have been blessed with a more perfect one. A light breeze teased and pulled at the rainbow-colored sail and Deston closed his eyes, inhaling the clean salty air as the mild rocking lulled him to the edge of sleep.

As he let the boat drift where it may, it slowly inched its way to the mouth of the cove and out into open water. The minute it freed the confines of the cove, a brisk wind caught the sail and the boat plowed into the waves. Deston dived for the rudder as the boat dipped precariously on its side. He turned it into the wind and it glided across the water, catching the attention of a pair of dolphins that decided to swim alongside.

Even though Deston had never been in a sailboat before in his life, he skillfully steered the boat around and into the sun, which to his amazement was sitting low in the western sky. It had been such a wonderful day he hadn't noticed the hours slipping by. He was tempted to forget about the time and keep sailing, but then thought better of it. If he were late for dinner, he'd be in big trouble with his mom.

Halfheartedly, he steered the boat in a wide, sweeping circle and headed back for the cove. He hadn't realized he'd gone out so far, but the wind was with him and he approached the entrance to the cove faster than he would have liked. As the boat rounded the rock outcrop that protected the cove from the open sea, he saw his mom standing on the shore, frantically waving her arms at him.

"What's she doing? I'm not that late," he grumbled to himself. However, as he got closer to the shore, he realized she wasn't waving at him, she was signaling *him. He sat up straighter in alarm and his heart started racing. He reached for the rudder to guide the sailboat to the shore, but something was wrong—he couldn't reach the rudder. He looked down at the empty sleeves of his T-shirt flapping in the breeze. His arms were gone. He stared at his torso in utter amazement and then looked up helplessly. The boat was moving away from the shore and heading back out to open sea with the current, and without arms he had no way to turn it around.*

A knot of panic lodged in his stomach as the boat neared the mouth of the cove. In a matter of seconds, it would be in open water again, unless he got it turned around. He stood and pushed his shoulder into the boom, trying to use his body to steer the boat. At that moment the boat hit a wave and the sudden pitch knocked him off balance. With no arms to catch himself, he fell over the side of the boat.

Deston's whole body jerked awake and his eyes flew open. He blinked rapidly and stared up at the dark sky above him until a few sparkling stars came into focus.

Gawd, another weird dream, he thought, closing his eyes and breathing a heavy sigh. Taking in a slow, deep breath, he tried to rid his mind of the anxiety the dream had left behind. The gentle rolling up and down helped to ease his tension and he relaxed into the movement. Gradually, the dream drifted away with the soothing ripples, but a strange sense that something was wrong continued to nag at him.

All of a sudden, his eyes sprang open. *If that was just a dream, why am I still rocking?*

He looked up through the tree limbs that formed a black net above him, allowing only small patches of the night sky to show through the holes. From what he could see, it was a clear night and the stars were shining bright. Rolling his head to the right, he focused on the trees that looked like grotesque statues, barely distinguishable through the shadows. The forest was dark and extremely quiet, except for the sound of his beating heart, but he didn't see anything out of place.

I'm becoming a paranoid freak. Before he could push his apprehension aside, something else caught his attention. He narrowed his eyes and stared at the trees, which seemed to be moving away from him. He blinked to clear his vision and squinted harder into the gloom. They *were* moving—but he knew that wasn't possible.

Is this still a dream? He tried to lift his arm and wipe the sleep from his eyes, but to his surprise, his arms wouldn't budge.

"What the hell?" Deston exclaimed, raising his head and looking down. It took him a moment to comprehend what he was seeing. Even after it registered, he still couldn't believe what was in front of his eyes. He tried lifting his hands to confirm the vision, but as before, he could only raise them a fraction of an inch for a vine rope had been wrapped around his wrists and secured to another vine that circled his body several times, pinning his arms to his chest. He looked down at his feet and tried lifting them, but his ankles were also bound to something.

He laid his head back and tried to make sense of it. Who would tie him up? Grossard's name immediately came to mind and he felt like a hundred pound weight had just been dropped on his chest. He fought back the nausea that moved into his throat. Was he really that incompetent that he could lose the battle before it even began? He was his mother's only chance of rescue. He couldn't just give up. He closed his eyes to think and as if on cue, the recurring dream that had haunted him over the past months began to play in his mind clearer than it ever had before.

Joliet was in the small, stone room, sitting beside the bed as always. She looked tired and drawn. However, the person on the bed was more than just a shape this time. It was a man—a man with finely chiseled features and long sandy-blonde hair. Deston's heart flipped as he looked into the face of his father for the first time.

Joliet leaned close and kissed Oseron softly on the lips. A look of love softened the worry lines on her face, leaving no doubt as to her feelings about him. As she straightened to dip the cloth into the bowl, an enormous shadow filled the doorway. The creature making the shadow was still not visible, but Deston could feel the evil sucking the air out of the room and an all-consuming heaviness enveloped him.

As the shadow advanced farther into the room, Joliet turned toward Deston. But this time her face was filled with pride—the same look she had when he won the science fair and received his three black belts in kung fu.

Deston gazed into her violet eyes. When she smiled back, tears gathered in the back of his throat.

"Deston, you are smart and strong. Just use your head and think it through. You can do this. I know you can. I have faith in you," she said. She held his gaze until the shadow moved over her and then she was gone.

Deston squeezed his eyes tightly together, trying to hold onto the image of his mother's face as it faded to black. He couldn't imagine how she knew he was coming to save her, but it seemed she did. And she believed in him.

I can do this. No, damn it, I'm GOING to do this. Nobody is going to stop me. Not Grossard ... not anybody. Mom and Dad are counting on me. I can't let them down.

Cautiously, Deston tilted his head back and opened his eyes a crack to sneak a peek at his adversary. Seeing there was nothing behind him but trees, he turned his head to the left and peeked out again. Margaux was there beside him, tied to the top of a giant centipede. A shadow was splayed across her face so he couldn't tell if she was awake or not, but since she was lying perfectly still, he assumed she was still asleep. He opened his mouth to wake her; then decided against it. He wasn't sure how she would react when she discovered she was tied up and he didn't want to risk her calling attention to them until he figured out what was going on.

He closed his eyes and reviewed the facts in his head. There was no sign of guards, although that didn't mean there weren't some hidden within the shadows. He also reasoned that if Grossard was behind this as he thought, they could very well be on their way to the monastery. And if he was still tied to the centipede when they arrived, his chances of rescuing his parents would be zilch, so the first thing he needed to do was break free of the ropes.

Deston tugged on his hands, testing the strength of the vine. It gave a little, but not enough to make a difference. He pulled harder and gritted his teeth as the vine cut into his skin. Painful as it was, he didn't ease up until he felt the vine stretch a little, giving him enough room to twist his right hand around so his fingers could reach the knots.

Silently, he went to work on getting the knot loose, keeping his eyes shut so it would appear he was still asleep. He felt certain if they discovered he was awake, they would keep a closer eye on him, and that would make it harder to escape. But he didn't realize how difficult it would be to untie a knot with his eyes closed. After picking at the vine for several minutes and getting nowhere, he began to fret they would arrive at the monastery before he was able to get loose.

Deston opened his eyes ever-so-slightly, but his head was too low for him to see much of anything. He groaned to himself and racked his brain for a solution, but it seemed clear that if he wanted to get free, he needed to see what he was doing. Finally, he decided to try raising his head for a few seconds at a time. He hoped that would be enough and wouldn't catch anyone's attention.

Gritting his teeth, he lifted his head and looked down at the knot. At that very moment a large, dark object flew directly over his head. Deston slammed his head back and went stiff; hoping whatever it was didn't see him and alert the guards. Minutes ticked by and he stayed tense, waiting for something to happen, but everything remained quiet. Slowly, he let his muscles relax. Whatever it was must not have noticed he was awake.

Deston went back to work on the knots, keeping his eyes shut and trying hard to limit his movements as the centipedes progressed through the forest. The forest was eerily quiet. No cricket sounds, no birds chirping, no rustle of leaves, no sound at all until he heard a faint whisper call his name.

Turning his head, he looked into Margaux's bulging eyes. She opened her mouth to say something, but he shook his head slightly and rolled his eyes upward. His lips pursed in a silent "ssshhh" as he closed his eyes again, hoping she would understand. To his relief, she remained silent.

Knowing that Margaux was awake sent a new sense of urgency surging through him and his fingers plucked harder at the knots. When it finally came loose, he almost shouted out loud with joy. Adrenalin surged through him and he went to work on the next one with renewed hope. The second knot wasn't as tight as the first and he was able to get it loose fairly easy. Again his hopes soared and he could feel success looming nearer. There were only a few more knots to go. He pulled at the rope and felt the knot give, but then without warning he was pitched violently backward.

Deston yelled out in alarm, all pretense of being asleep forgotten as he slid down the back of the centipede. His fingers grabbed onto the rope around his chest and held on tightly. The rope vines tightened and strained against his body weight, but they held as the front end of the centipede raised in the air and he was turned upside-down. Blood rushed to his head and the ropes cut painfully into his wrists and stomach. He didn't know what was going on, but it was obvious they'd left the forest. A full moon, shining like a beacon high in the sky, exposed the landscape around him. However, being upside-down severely limited his range of sight to what was directly behind him—the forest and a few scattered boulders.

Deston's toes were tingling and his head was pounding by the time the centipede reached the top of the mound and began its climb down the other side. Slowly, Deston started to slide the other way. Within a few minutes, he was in an upright position with an open view of his surroundings, including the gigantic mountain sprawled in front of him like a sleeping giant. There was no vegetation of any kind on the surface of the mountain, just a stark, foreboding rock face with jagged, protruding boulders and crevices that cast unearthly shadows across its surface to add to its sinister appearance.

Deston's eyes traveled up the face of the mountain and stopped about one hundred meters above the ground, where a significant black mark marred the surface and swallowed the light. He knew it had to be a cave, but in the dim light it looked like a giant, gaping mouth screaming in terror.

With a great effort, he tore his eyes away from the black hole and looked to his left where two other centipedes were trudging over the rough terrain a short distance away. One centipede was carrying Margaux; the other carried his backpack. There was nothing to his right other than more boulders of varying shapes and sizes, and there was nothing overhead in the clear night sky. More importantly, he saw no guards anywhere.

The centipede came to a stop near the base of the mountain and Deston lifted his head for a better view. However, there was still nothing new to see. A light breeze blew off the mountain, spreading a strange odor and a faint, unrecognizable sound along with it. Deston turned his ear toward the mountain and listened. The sound was barely audible, but it made the hairs on the back of his neck stand on-end. As he strained to make it out, the sound escalated and became more of a high-pitched squeal. Immediately, other squeals from different points on the mountain joined in to make a deafening noise. Deston flinched and instinctively tried to raise his shoulders to shelter his ears as the sound slammed painfully into his eardrums. But the vines binding his wrists to his waist limited his movements.

The noise increased in volume until it was more than he could bear. Just when he thought his eardrums would burst, the screech abruptly ended, leaving a low, ominous rumble coming from deep within the mountain. The rumble grew louder as it traveled up through the mound, and the ground trembled, which in turn shook the centipede. Then all of a sudden, hundreds of dark, flying shapes exploded out of the mouth of the cave.

Deston ducked his head and closed his eyes and Margaux screamed, as the dark objects dove straight for them. He could feel the breeze of their wings as they skimmed back and forth mere inches above him and their horrible stench made him gag.

The onslaught continued for several minutes before it began to dwindle and Deston felt it safe to open his eyes. All but a few of the dark shapes were gone and those that remained circled overhead like a large black cloud. He squinted up at them but couldn't tell for certain what they were. They didn't look like birds, but it was hard to them see against the night sky.

Without warning, the ropes binding him to the centipede gave way. Deston sharply sucked in his breath and groped for something to hold onto, but there was nothing. Helpless to stop himself, he slid off and his shoulder slammed hard into the ground. Pain shot down his arm like a burning arrow, taking his breath away. He rolled to his stomach, gritting his teeth against the ache and rested his forehead on the cold, hard ground. His hands were still attached to a vine wrapped around his waist, and his ankles were also still tied together, but his arms were no longer strapped down to his chest.

A short scream broke the quiet and was followed by an "oomph."

He turned his head in the direction of the sound and saw Margaux lying on the ground a few feet above his head. There was another thud, and his backpack was deposited on the ground right above her head. As soon as he saw the backpack, he remembered his knife was in one of the pockets and his aching shoulder was forgotten. If he could get to the knife, he could cut them free and they might have a chance of getting away before the guards, or whoever, decided to show up. He didn't give much thought to the creatures flying above, for they were too high up to see what he was doing on the ground. However, he moved cautiously, inching his way over to Margaux just in case they or someone else was watching.

"Are you okay?" Deston asked breathlessly, as he worm crawled up beside her.

"Yes, I think so."

"Are you still tied up?" he whispered.

"Yes. My ankles are tied together and so are my wrists," she raised her hands to show him.

His eyes widened. "Your hands aren't tied to your waist?"

"Yes, they are," She raised them higher and he could see the rope running from her wrist to her waist, but it was a long piece, which allowed her a lot more movement than what he had.

"Yes," he whispered under his breath, and quickly looked over his shoulder to make sure they were still alone. "Look, my backpack is right above your head. Do you think you can reach it and get my knife out?"

Margaux tilted her head back at the pack. "Maybe. What about those things up there?" she replied, gesturing to the dark shadows flying over them.

"Don't worry about them. I think they're just birds, or maybe bats."

"They don't look like birds, and they're kind of big for bats, don't you think?"

"It's hard to tell. They probably just look bigger because it's dark. I'm sure they won't be able to see what we're doing. We've got to get that knife. It's the only way we're going to get out of here. My hands are tied to my waist and I don't have as much give as you do, so it's up to you."

Margaux shot Deston an uncertain look, but didn't argue. She craned her neck around and dug her heels into the ground to propel backward. At the same time, Deston wormed his way alongside of her.

When the backpack was between them, Deston whispered, "The zipper pocket—there on the front. See it?"

"Uh-huh," Margaux replied as she started to rise up.

"No!" Deston hissed. "Don't get up. I don't want them to know what you're doing. Try to be inconspicuous."

"But I can't reach the pocket if I'm on my back like this."

Deston was silent for a moment. "Okay, get on your side and I'll tilt the pack up a little so you can reach it. Just don't let it be obvious what you're doing. I haven't seen any guards, but that doesn't mean they aren't around."

"I'll try," Margaux replied.

Deston squirmed into position, wedged his elbow underneath the pack, and lifted up. With the pack between them, he couldn't see what she was doing, but he could feel the tug. The sound of the zipper sliding open one tooth at a time was like music to his ears. He held his breath as Margaux rummaged through the pocket. After what seemed like an eternity, she finally whispered, "I can't find it. The only thing in the pocket is your camera."

Deston let his breath out in a whoosh, realizing their captors might have taken the knife when they tied them up. As likely as that was, he refused to give up so easily.

"Check the side pocket," he whispered, letting the pack fall flat so Margaux could get to it.

He felt Margaux fumbling with the pocket. After a few seconds she whispered back, "It's not there. Are there other pockets?"

Deston swore softly under his breath. "Yeah, there's one on the back. We'll have to tip the pack all the way over to get to it." He knew that wouldn't be easy to hide from anyone who might be watching, but they had no other option.

"I'll push the pack up and you pull. Take it slow and try to cover what you're doing," he whispered.

He wiggled in closer, wedging the pack between him and Margaux, and pushed up with his elbow as Margaux pulled. The rope tugged mercilessly at his wrists, cutting a red welt into his skin, but they finally got it up on its side. With one last nudge, it rolled over. A few seconds later, Margaux whispered, "I got it!"

Deston sagged with relief and hastily shifted so his hands were just below the backpack. "You should be able to get to my ropes if you move in a little closer," Deston whispered as Margaux fumbled to get the blade out.

"I will in a minute. After I cut mine."

"What? No ... cut mine first. Then I'll cut yours," Deston whispered, forcibly wiggling his hands for emphasis.

Margaux tucked her body into a ball, ignoring him and started sawing awkwardly at the ropes on her own wrists. Deston couldn't see what she was doing with the backpack in the way, but when he didn't feel the pressure of the knife against his ropes, he lifted up and looked over the pack.

"What are you doing? I said to cut my ropes first," he said through clenched teeth to keep from screaming.

"I heard what you said," Margaux replied just as haughtily. "But you're going to have to wait, because I'm cutting mine."

Deston gritted his teeth and fought back the urge to yell. Margaux was without a doubt the most pig-headed person he'd ever met. She was also completely lacking in listening skills. But what irritated him the most was that there wasn't a thing he could do about it at the present time. He was at her mercy and she seemed to be moving at a glacial pace.

Every few seconds, he lifted up, looked over the pack and sighed loudly. With each new sigh, Margaux shot daggers at him from the corner of her eye. At the sixth interruption, she stopped sawing on the vine and looked up with a scowl. "Oh, for—" she began, but the rest of her words were drowned out by a forlorn trill coming from the mouth of the cave.

At the sound, the dark shapes circling above responded with their own high-pitched screech and dove toward the ground, landing in an open circle around Deston and Margaux. Now that they were closer, Deston saw they weren't birds at all. They were bats—six foot tall bats, covered with a sleek black fur so dark he wasn't able to make out a single detail other than the shape of their small, pointy heads, unusually large ears, and two long, wicked-looking incisors that shone brightly in the moonlight.

When the last bat touched down, the wail abruptly ended, leaving an unnatural silence in its wake. Deston craned his neck back so he could see around the entire circle. Each bat stood stiff and straight as an eerie silhouette, its wings folded at its side and its face turned toward the mountain.

Deston's heart pounded in his ears as he followed their stares up to the black hole of the cave. A cold sweat ran down his back and he held his breath, waiting for something to happen.

Within seconds, two black figures emerged from the cave and floated to the ground, filling in the empty spot left by the others to complete the circle.

Deston raised his head to peer over the tips of his boots at the new arrivals. They were identical to the others, and even with the moonlight shining directly on them, he couldn't make out any details other than their teeth and their ghostly, glowing eyes.

Margaux made a small sound in her throat and wiggled closer to Deston, pressing the backpack into his side.

On some silent cue, the last two arrivals took a step forward and turned to face each other, forming an entrance into the circle. Deston raised his head higher and strained to see into the darkness as a scuffing sound came from somewhere beyond. Seconds later, a tall, menacing form stepped out of the shadows. The new arrival walked with a limp, dragging one leg behind, as it purposefully moved into the circle. At once, the other bats bowed low and raised their right wing in the air in a salute, as the tall, thin bat limped its way to the center, stopping at the captives' feet.

Deston spotted the reddish stain on the bat's two long, needle sharp incisors and swallowed hard. Unlike the other bats in the circle, the newcomer's features were clear. Its sleek black fur had streaks of gray, and where the others had small pointed heads, its head was large and out of proportion to the rest of its shriveled body. Its beady eyes were close set, it had no nose to speak of other than two long slits for nostrils, and a chunk of one ear was missing. Perched on the top of its head was a crown of sorts, made from a variety of small white bones, twined together into a ring. A long, scarlet cape was draped over its narrow shoulders and held together in front by a wide ribbon supporting a large jeweled medallion. Its skeletal hand held a white staff made from two leg bones and a human-like skull mounted on the top.

Deston felt the backpack press into his side again, as the bat stared down at them.

"Who are you?" the bat demanded in a high, grating voice that made Deston shudder. "Who sent you, and why are you here?"

Deston's eyes grew to the size of golf balls as he looked up at the bat. The bat's size was intimidating enough, but to hear it speak as well, stunned Deston into silence.

The bat's penetrating glare didn't waiver as he waited for a reply. When none came, the slits of his nostrils flared and his thin lips pulled back into a sneer. "So you do not wish to answer?" he said, walking up beside Margaux. Leaning forward to give her a better view of his teeth, he hissed, "You think I, Vérosse, King of the Sangcou, am a fool? You think I would not recognize the scent of Tir na-nÓg? Or maybe that was your plan, hmm? A ruse to get me to think Oseron has broken our treaty and sent his soldiers here to spy on me?"

The king straightened and walked a few paces away, then made a swift twirl and retraced his steps. "Who sent you?" he bellowed, raising his staff in the air over Margaux in a threatening manner.

Margaux screamed and tucked her head between her shoulders, anticipating the blow, as Deston cried out, "No! Noo—one sent us."

The king's glare immediately shot to Deston.

Deston faltered a second before rushing on. "We were ... umm ... we got lost hunting and ... and ... stopped to rest, and fell asleep. When we woke up, we were tied to the back of a centipede and brought here."

"Ha!" Vérosse spat. "I told you, I am no fool. Do not insult me further with your lies."

He slammed his staff into the ground next to Margaux's head. She jumped and screamed again. Vérosse smirked arrogantly and walked back to stand at their feet. He looked down his nose at them as his long bony fingers drummed the skull on the top of the staff.

"You come into our land uninvited and deface our sacred

Temple—a Temple that has stood since the beginning of time. Then you insult us further by eating the forbidden fruit of the gods. Yet, you do not run or hide. My men find you asleep within the Temple itself, as if you were waiting to be discovered. I find that peculiar, and it makes me wonder—are you that brave? Or are you that stupid?"

He paced slowly alongside Deston, his one leg scraping a trench in the dirt behind him. "If you think that was a show of bravery, let me assure you, you are misguided. Knowing Oseron as I do, he would never have such foolish soldiers in his army." His gaze narrowed. "Your ploy has failed, my friends. I know you're not part of Oseron's army. You may have the smell of the fae, but you're not one of them—although, you do not have the smell of the solitaries, either, which I find peculiar."

Vérosse continued to stroke the skull as he walked back to stand at their feet. "So I ask you one more time, and this will be the last. Who sent you and why did you accept this fool's assignment?"

Deston and Margaux both stared up at the king in silence.

Focusing on Deston, Vérosse cocked his head and hissed, "Tell me what I want to know and perhaps I'll be lenient with your companion."

Deston didn't know what to say. If he told Vérosse where they were going, it might jeopardize everything. And he still wasn't one hundred percent sure Grossard wasn't behind this.

The deafening silence grew as Vérosse waited for a response. Finally, he straightened his back. "Very well. Since you refuse to cooperate, you leave me no choice."

Turning his back on them, he walked a few steps away and lifted his staff in the air. Immediately, several bats stepped out of line and gathered around him in a small huddle.

Deston looked nervously at Margaux. Her terrified expression made him more anxious than he already was. She was his responsibility and he couldn't let anything happen to her. "Wait," he yelled out in desperation.

Vérosse slowly turned back to Deston, a knowing leer on his face.

"I ... umm ... we ... umm," Deston cleared his throat, stalling for time to come up with a convincing story." Grossard sent us," he finally said.

As soon as the words left his mouth, he wished he could take them back, as Vérosse's expression instantly changed to one of immense rage and angry murmurs rumbled around the circle.

"No, I mean—" Deston tried to recant, but Vérosse cut him off.

"Grossard thinks he can manipulate me by penetrating our boundaries and defiling our land?" Vérosse's tone was ripe with malice. "That may have worked with the others, but it will not work with me. The Sangcou will not cower. Nor will we be intimidated. That fiend has underestimated us and our strength for the last time."

Vérosse turned back to the huddle and voices rose into squeals as the bats expressed their fury.

Deston was horrified. What had he done? He should have known if Grossard was as evil as the Elders said, he'd have more enemies than just the fae.

A new sense of urgency coursed through Deston and he feverishly pulled at the knots to get free. He had made very little progress when Vérosse lifted his staff to hush the voices in the huddle and turned back. Vérosse moved to stand at their feet and glared down at them.

"You're as arrogant and devious as your master," he said, contempt dripping off each word. "I have no doubt this is Grossard's doing, as you stated. But because you came willingly and defiled our Temple with your own hands, you will pay with your life. You'll be an example to show Grossard and all others how we deal with those who try to cross us."

Vérosse looked purposely around the circle. "Grossard, the Vile, believes the Sangcou are mindless and weak," he shouted and was immediately rewarded with a roar of anger. Holding up his staff to silence the others, he continued. "I say we send him a message written on the skin of his own men. We will show him how we crush our enemies, and how we deal with those who wish to do us harm."

Again, the bats erupted in cheers, and Margaux shrieked. Rolling to her side in a fetal position, she buried her face in the back-pack and sobbed loudly.

Vérosse stepped back and raised his arms in victory. The circle broke as the bats rushed their king to bestow on him the praises he deserved.

Deston stared at the spot the king had stood a moment before. *This can't be real. They're going to kill us for eating some stupid fruit?*

His mind went numb and several seconds passed before he realized something was tapping his arm. Looking down, his mood went from despondency to joy in a nanosecond at the sight of Margaux's hand holding his pocketknife in the crack between him and the backpack. His eyes shot up to her face, and though it was mostly buried in the pack as she pretended to sob, one eye peeked out. She winked at him.

Deston wanted to kiss her. He turned his gaze to the king, who was basking in the admiration of the bats surrounding him. It was the perfect diversion. Rolling to his side and making a big act of comforting Margaux, just in case someone was paying attention, he wiggled in and positioned his hands at the same level as the knife. He held his wrists against the blade and cautiously moved them up and down until he felt the vine give away. A rush of adrenalin coursed through him. He darted a look at the bats, who were still gathered around the king, rejoicing in their supremacy, as he pulled his hands out of the vines. He then took the knife from Margaux and cut the vine that was wrapped around his waist.

"Can you bring your legs up more? Just enough so I can cut the rope around your ankles," he whispered.

Without replying, she let out another loud sob and drew herself into a tighter ball. In no time, Margaux felt the release of her bindings.

"Okay. On the count of three, crawl down behind that mound and run for the trees," Deston whispered.

Margaux lifted her head and looked down at Deston's tied feet. "What are you going to do?"

"As soon as you get to the trees, I'll cut my ropes and will be right behind you."

"But what if they notice me running away before you get free?"

"Don't worry about me. I'll be alright. Just get to the trees as fast as you can and keep going. Don't look back."

"No. We go together or I'm not going anywhere," Margaux stated with a look on her face that said her mind was set.

Deston was aghast. "Look, Margaux, don't be ridiculous. We'll be easier to spot if we go together. Just listen to me for once and do what I say. This is the best way."

Margaux's eyes narrowed as she stared at him, but he ignored her inflexible look and began counting, "One ... two ..."

"No, wait. I have an idea," she whispered.

Deston gave a frustrated sigh, as he felt the backpack move.

"Look, we don't have time." He stopped as she pulled out the camera and gave him a silly grin.

"You have got to be kidding," he hissed.

"No, wait—think about it. Bats are nocturnal. They live in the dark."

Deston didn't grasp her line of thinking for a second. Then it clicked. "You—" Deston didn't have a chance to finish what he was going to say, as the bats suddenly went silent and turned to face them.

Margaux hurriedly shoved the camera down between them and out of sight, as Vérosse squared his shoulders and walked back to stand over them. The army of bats followed, forming two lines on either side of their king.

After a dramatic pause, Vérosse spoke. "As king of the Sangcou, I find you guilty of high crimes against our state. Restitution for these crimes will be death. Your hearts are to be sacrificed to the gods and your blood will be served at the feast of our victory. The skin of your bodies will become the parchment we'll use to deliver our message to Grossard. Your bones will be scattered at the entrance of our land to deter any who think they can overthrow us."

The army squealed with delight. Vérosse paused to let the commotion die down.

Margaux used the noise to whisper to Deston. "On the count of three I'm going to press the flash. Close your eyes and get ready."

Deston nodded his understanding and tightened his grip on the knife.

Margaux started counting quietly, "One ... two ... three!" she yelled, bolting upright and pressing the button on the camera.

A look of surprise flickered across Vérosse's face in the instant between Margaux's yell and the flash. But as soon as the flash went off, he and the other bats shrieked in pain and draped their wings over their eyes.

Deston reared up and sliced through the ropes at his ankles, as Margaux clicked the flash a second time to make sure all the bats were sufficiently blinded.

As soon as Deston was free, he grabbed his backpack and Margaux's hand and together they sprinted over the mound toward the trees. The piercing screams of the bats echoed off the mountain and followed them into the darkness.

Chapter 33

A thunderous wail reverberated off the walls, sending the nesting birds on the rocks outside the cave into flight. Grossard's look was murderous as he searched for something to destroy.

"Incompetence!" he snarled. "I am surrounded by nothing but incompetence."

Finding nothing in the cave to satisfy his wrath, he turned to the small gremlin who had brought him the news, and who was still standing in the middle of the cave, shaking uncontrollably. As Grossard advanced toward it, the gremlin's eyes widened in horror and it bolted for the exit. But Grossard was too quick. Vanishing from his spot, he reappeared in the doorway before it could get away. He grabbed the gremlin by the neck and hoisted the small creature in the air.

"Where is he now?" demanded Grossard, squeezing the tiny creature to make it speak.

The gremlin's eyes bulged, as Grossard's hand tightened around its midsection. It wrestled to get free, but its strength was nothing compared to Grossard's and the lack of air was weakening it even faster. Grossard didn't really need an answer, though. He already knew where Deston was going and his rage sparked anew at the thought of the boy making it to the monastery before moonrise.

"Rellik, you had better be dead, or you're going to wish you were," Grossard roared.

Grossard unconsciously twisted the gremlin in his hands, snapping the tiny creature's bones in two and splitting its body apart. Blood sprayed into Grossard's face and the warm liquid ran down his nose, jolting him back to his senses. He looked down at the two limp pieces of the gremlin's body dripping blood onto the floor of the cave.

"Weak creatures," he grunted in disgust as he walked to the entrance. He threw the remains of the body at the two ogres lying outside the cave and yelled, "Leahcim! Iccasor!"

The two ogres raised their heads and looked up through blood-shot eyes.

"Get in here. There's work to be done," Grossard added.

Grossard was accustom to his minions jumping to attention the second he issued an order. However, the two ogres remained where they were and stared hungrily at the body parts as the smell of fresh blood drifted their way on the breeze and saliva leaked from the corners of their mouth. Leisurely, they pushed themselves to their feet and coolly gathered the remains together, stashing them away for later. When the last of the gremlin was safely stored, they ambled into the cave unaware Grossard was waiting just inside the entrance with a giant log at the ready. They were only a few steps in when Grossard swung the log at the side of Leahcim's head and knocked the ogre off his feet.

"When I say get in here, I mean now," Grossard hissed, holding the log over his shoulder like a baseball bat, ready to swing again.

Iccasor shuffled backward, putting a safe distance between him and the log. He locked eyes with Grossard as Leahcim staggered to his feet, blood oozing from a large gash in his temple.

Leahcim stood upright and swayed slightly, trying to focus on the two images of Grossard swimming before him.

After a moment, Grossard snorted in disgust and threw the log on the fire, turning his back on the pair without fear of retaliation.

"Oseron's son has joined up with Them and is on his way to the monastery as we speak. I want you and the rest of your clan at the gateway outside of Leinad keeping watch for him. When he comes through, secure him and alert me with this." Grossard flicked a black crystal orb at Iccasor without turning around.

Iccasor caught the stone out of the air and grunted his under-standing, as he stuffed it into a small pouch at his waist.

"Rellik has already failed me on this task, so I suggest you get to the gateway before They do, or you'll end up in pieces like that gremlin," Grossard added, looking over his shoulder with a sneer.

"Do we kill them all?" Iccasor grunted.

"I don't care what you do with the rest. Just bring the boy to me. I want to meet this son of Oseron's who was able to elude Rellik."

Iccasor nodded and left without another word, pulling Leahcim along with him.

Grossard walked to the doorway and stared vacantly at the waves pounding the shore outside the cave long after the two ogres disappeared. He had been told Deston didn't have knowledge of Tir na-nÓg, but with the recent turn of events, he was beginning to suspect otherwise. He absentmindedly rubbed his chin and wondered what had happened to Rellik. If Deston had indeed killed the wolf, that would be proof his powers were already strong. However, with the Crystal locked in the monastery, those powers would be growing weaker by the minute.

Grossard shook his head to clear his thoughts. "What am I worrying about? He's just a child. He can't hope to stand up next to me." He spoke the words out loud to make it so. "I can't wait to see Oseron's face when he sees I have his son. I'll let them have a little father-son reunion and then he can watch his boy be torn apart. Better yet, maybe I'll challenge the child to a duel and take down both father and son at the same time."

He smiled at the thought and walked to the broad sword that was leaning against the wall. He pulled it out of its scabbard and examined the blade. He didn't particularly like fighting with swords; they were so messy and laborious. Using dark magic was so much more to his liking, but if he used dark powers to kill Oseron or Deston, he'd forfeit the right to possess the Crystal. That was the law of the Universe and there was no way around it. Only through a fair fight to the death could the throne and the Crystal be transferred to someone other than the direct descendants of the present king.

Grossard ran his hand down the blade and forced himself to look at his horrific reflection in the shiny metal—something he rarely did. "You did this to me, Oseron, and I swear to Erebus I'll make you pay for," he spat.

As he stared at his image, a tic appeared in his right cheek and quickly traveled to his right eye. His arm also began to twitch violently and shrivel in size. The potion was wearing off. He hurriedly scanned the cave to make sure he was alone and moved to a niche in the wall. He glanced over his shoulder again as he reached for a vial hidden behind a box on a high shelf. Pulling out the stopper, he took a swig of the crimson liquid and shuddered involuntarily as he swallowed. As the liquid ran down his throat, the twitching stopped at once. With a satisfied sigh, he corked the bottle, taking note there was very little of the liquid left.

Humph, maybe I should have secured the formula before killing Morgane, he thought, then quickly brushed the thought aside. He wouldn't need the potion much longer. The Crystal would soon supply him with all the power he wanted or needed to create a whole new image for himself—one no one would suspect or could resist. A vicious smile lifted the corners of his mouth in anticipation of his revenge.

He slid the sword back into its scabbard and stuffed it into his belt as he headed for the back of the cave, stopping on the way to light a torch from the fire. Facing the back wall, he ran his hand along the ceiling joint until he felt the indentation in the rock. He pushed on the spot and felt the whoosh of cold, damp air on his face as a large section of the wall rotated outward and revealed a long dark tunnel. The tunnel, an old passageway from the monastery, ran for kilometers through the rock and was used by the monks in ancient times to smuggle dissidents out of France. As he held the torch out in front of him, he snickered at the thought of how the fae would react when he arrived in Tir na-nÓg with the Crystal. The thought brightened his mood immensely and he chuckled softly to himself as he stepped into the dark, dank passageway.

Chapter 34

Once Rellik reached the meadow at the edge of the orchard, he skidded to a stop. His sides were heaving from exertion and foam coated the sides of his muzzle as he struggled to catch his breath. His eyes were locked on the empty path as he paced back and forth impatiently and tried not to think of the consequences that came with Grossard finding out he had let Deston get away.

A short time later, a lone figure of a man appeared in the distance. The man leisurely strolled up the path as if he had all the time in the world. A low growl rumbled in Rellik's throat and it took all of his willpower to keep from rushing out and attacking the man as he came closer. The only thing that stopped him was he needed the information the man was bringing.

When the man finally reached the trees, Rellik snarled, "I thought my message was clear about the urgency of this meeting."

Aren raised an eyebrow and arrogantly looked Rellik in the eye. "Panicking are we, now that you failed in your mission?" he remarked, not realizing Rellik's patience had already been stretched to the edge of its breaking point.

In the next instant, Aren was on the ground and a monstrous paw was forcefully pressing on the center of his chest. Fear suddenly replaced Aren's smugness, as sharp claws pierced his skin and small, dark splotches appeared on his robe.

"Don't you think you're in enough trouble?" Aren stuttered, trying to push the crushing weight off.

Rellik ignored the comment and leaned in close, his nose almost touching Aren's. "Tell me what you know," he demanded, adding pressure to push his claws deeper into Aren's chest.

Aren started to protest, but thought better of it as the pressure was already more than he could bear. "The—boy was— brought in—this morning," he sputtered between gasps for air.

Rellik showed a little more of his teeth, but that was the only sign of his distress.

"He met with the Elders—and agreed to help—" Aren couldn't continue as the weight on his chest was making it impossible to fill his lungs. He struggled once again to push the paw off.

Rellik stared off into the distance, digesting the news and forgetting for a moment about his paw on Aren's chest. On the way to Tir na-nÓg, he had held onto the hope that there was still time to get to Deston before They did. That hope was now gone. Countless images of what Grossard would do to him and his family pummeled his mind. But then it dawned on him—if Grossard was already aware of what had happened, his goons would be all over the place, and Rellik hadn't seen a single one. His hope sparked back to life and he looked down at Aren.

"Is the boy on his way to the gateway or still in the village?" Rellik growled.

Aren offered no more words. His face was a peculiar shade of blue and the whites of his unseeing eyes had turned red.

Rellik yanked his paw back and put the side of his muzzle against Aren's nose. There was no hint of breath. Panic seized him once again. He needed more information if he was to find Deston before Grossard did. He picked up Aren's lifeless arm and let it go. It dropped to the ground with a soft thud.

Rellik's anger boiled inside him. He let out a loud, gruesome howl that shook the trees as he kicked out at Aren's body and sent it rolling into the tall grass.

Stupid! Stupid! Stupid! He silently berated himself.

He dropped his head and took in several deep breaths to sift through his thoughts. Time was growing short, so it was logical to think Deston was already on his way to the monastery. But he couldn't be that far ahead. Rellik lifted his head and sniffed the air. There was no scent of the boy, but that didn't mean anything, for the safest and quickest route to the gateway was through the forest on the other side of the village.

"He will be mine," Rellik growled to the wind, turning into the trees to skirt the village.

As he approached the forest, he picked up Deston's scent and knew he was on the right track. Without hesitating, he raced into the trees. It wasn't over yet and when he caught up to the boy this time, he would not hesitate to do what must be done.

Chapter 35

Deston and Margaux reached the cover of the forest and ran headlong into the darkness, dodging trees and jumping blindly over fallen logs. Deston didn't know where they were or which direction to run, but he figured as long as it was away from the bats, it was the right way. He looked for something familiar to give him a reference, but since his eyes had been closed the whole while he was on the centipede, everything was foreign to him. The only thing he was certain of was they were no longer in the forest of Tir na-nÓg. He knew that because the trees here were stumpy and twisted, as if something had stunted their growth. There was also a strong smell of decay in the air, and the ground was littered with broken, dried branches and twigs. More than once Deston stubbed his toe and almost tripped. But falling wasn't his only worry. The loud crack the twigs made when stepped on gave away their exact location to anyone in pursuit. Unfortunately, there was nothing he could do about it.

Deston threw a quick glance over his shoulder to see if anyone was coming. There was no one behind him. But when he checked a moment later, a faint, white glowed through the trees. Without waiting to see what it was, he changed direction, pulling Margaux along with him. He ignored the stitch shooting daggers into his side and ran as hard as he could, but the change in direction made no difference. In the blink of an eye, the white glow was beside him and called him by name.

Hearing the sound of his name caught Deston off guard and his head jerked around. At the same moment, his toe caught on a tree root. It was by sheer strength of will that he managed to stay upright, but his floundering caused Margaux to crash into him and they both ended up on the ground.

Deston wasted no time scooting out from under Margaux. He jumped up, spread his feet wide and yelled out, "Eeee yaahhh," as he cut through the air with the side of his hands. In the next second, his hands dropped and his mouth fell open as he looked into the green eyes of the white deer.

"Hurry and get on my back. I must get you off this land before the Sangcou recover," the white deer cried out.

Deston didn't have to be told twice. He grabbed Margaux by the hand, pulled her up from the ground and hoisted her onto the back of the deer. He then jumped up behind her. He barely had his seat before the deer leapt into the trees. The jolt nearly threw Margaux off and she hastily grabbed for the deer's neck to keep her balance. As she did, the camera hit the deer's antlers and was knocked out of her hand.

"Oh no," Margaux cried out, but it was too late. The deer was already speeding away.

Deston saw the camera drop, but there was little he could do. It took all his strength just to stay on the back of the deer. Locking his arms around Margaux's waist, he prayed she had a good hold of the deer's neck.

"Keep your heads down," the white deer shouted back.

Deston leaned into Margaux's back and could feel the wild thumping of her heart, as well as the sides of the deer heaving in and out. If the bats caught them, they would be hard pressed to escape again, but even with that knowledge, he felt strangely calm. He didn't know how the white deer had found them, but its familiar presence was enough to comfort him and give him hope.

The deer raced through the trees at such an amazing speed it felt as if they were flying. But the smell of rotting vegetation permeating the air as the deer's hooves struck the piles of moldy leaves gave witness to the fact they were still earthbound. However, as they went deeper into the trees, the rancid odor intensified and began to smell more like bats than moldy leaves.

Suddenly out of nowhere, a black shape dropped from

a tree in front of the deer. The deer dodged to the right, nearly throwing Deston and Margaux off again. Immediately, several more black shapes landed in front of them, blocking their new path. The deer swerved once more, only to find more black shapes in the way. In no time, the area was full of bats, dropping to the ground and swooping overhead. Margaux screamed and clutched the deer tighter.

"Stay on my back," the deer yelled as it skidded to a stop in front of a tree and swung around, lowering its head so it could use its antlers to keep the attackers at bay.

Deston craned his neck from side to side, searching for a get-away, but bats were converging on them from every direction. They would soon be completely penned in if he didn't do something. Spying a long stick on the ground gave him an idea. He thrust the backpack at Margaux and slid off the back of the deer. He had trained with a staff at one time in kung fu, and though that was long ago, he still felt confident of his ability.

"No, Deston, stay on my back. There're too many of them," cried the deer as Deston's feet hit the ground. He ignored the warning, for unless the deer had wings, it wasn't possible for them to get away, and he had no intention of going back to face King Vérosse.

Grabbing up the stick, he skillfully balanced it in his hands to get the feel and twirled it a couple of times for practice. *I can do this*, he reassured himself and lunged forward, thrusting out with the end of the stick. The bats closest to him jumped out of the way and Deston quickly sliced the stick through the air, scattering more of them.

Though the bats were as black and nasty looking as the ones from the mountain, they weren't as large—only about three feet tall at best. Deston sized them up, picked his target, and executed a couple of moves he remembered from his training. To his delight, several of the bats went down and the remaining bats hissed loudly as they backed away outside of the stick's range. The bat's eyes remained glued on Deston as more dropped from the sky. As their numbers grew, so did their confidence and they slowly closed in once again.

Deston planted his feet and gripped the stick tightly, ready to take out as many as he could.

All at once, from high overhead, a piercing squawk shot through air. The bats looked up and squealed in terror, and more than half of them took to flight.

Deston didn't dare look up, even though he desperately wanted to. He kept his eyes locked on the bats in front of him, knowing if he looked away, he would lose the advantage. He assumed the commotion was the king's guards arriving to take them back and he wasn't going to go without a fight.

Another shriek sounded, this time only a few feet away, and out of the darkness, two immense hawks dove at the group, scattering bats in all directions. The hawks pulled up effortlessly, snatched the bats out of midair, and crushed them in their powerful claws before discarding them to pick off another. Pandemonium quickly took over as the bats scattered to evade the hawks.

The hawks chased one group across the sky, but another group circled back. When Deston saw them advancing toward Margaux and the deer, he shoved the stick down the back of his tunic to free his hands and leapt onto an old stump. From there, he jumped up and caught hold of a limb overhead. His momentum launched him forward and he landed between the bats and Margaux. In one swift move, he pulled the stick out, gave it a twirl, and struck out with a one-two jab, catching a bat on the side of the head with each end. The first fell to the ground and Deston swiftly brought the stick down to make sure it was knocked out. He then flipped around and jabbed the staff into the side of the other.

The last few bats on the ground assembled into a tight group and rushed him before he could turn back. At that same moment, a brown blur whizzed by his head and landed behind him. The bright yellow light of the eternal flame instantly erupted from the leather pouch and roared to life, lighting up the darkness. The bats shrieked and covered their eyes with their wings, but it was too late, they were already blinded by the light. The hawks had circled back and were waiting for them as they awkwardly tried to take flight, and the bats barely made it off the ground before they were snatched up.

Deston looked back at Margaux. Her eyes were huge and her face was pale in the firelight. He mouthed a "thank you." She blushed as she ducked her head and looked away. A smile tugged at the corners of his mouth and he looked up to watch Torren and Keir finish off the last of the bats.

"Deston!" Margaux screamed out.

He spun around, his stick ready for another attack. His eyes darted from left to right, but the only bats he saw were already crumpled on the ground. Then he saw it. It looked like a large, black blanket draped over the white deer, who was pitching violently side to side in an effort to shake the bat off. The bat hung on, though, its fangs sunk deep into the deer's neck and the deer was weakening fast.

Deston yelled and sprinted toward the deer, ducking out of the way of its antlers, which came dangerously close to spearing him in the stomach. He slammed the stick down on the bat's head as hard as he could again and again, but it held fast to the deer.

Margaux ran to a tree and broke off a stick of her own, but before she could get to the deer, a loud, ear-piercing squawk came from behind her. Startled by the closeness of the sound, she ducked as one of the hawks zoomed over her head, its sights set on the bat. It swooped down and seized the bat with its razor sharp talons, ripping it off the deer. The hawk then soared into the sky and dropped the bat to the second hawk as it flew under. The second hawk caught it in its beak and snapped it in two, letting the pieces fall into the trees as it nose-dived for the ground.

Immediately upon landing, Torren transformed and ran to Deston. "Your Highness, are you alright?" he cried, kneeling down on one knee and bowing his head.

"We need to get you two out of here," Keir stated without ceremony before Deston could reply. He rushed to the deer and looked at the blood oozing from the two holes on its neck. "Are you able to take them?"

The deer took a wobbly step, but held its head high. "Yes," was all it said.

Keir didn't question it further. He just lifted Margaux and Deston onto the deer's back.

Deston felt the deer tremble, but as soon as he was seated, it took off at the same breakneck speed as before. Margaux leaned over nearly flat and locked her arms around its neck. Deston hugged her tightly and stayed as low as he possibly could as well.

As they raced through the knotted, misshapen trees, Deston tried to keep watch for more bats, but there were too many dark shapes and shadows and at the speed they were traveling, everything merged into one big blur. When the motion started to make him dizzy, he gave up and closed his eyes, feeling safe enough with Torren and Keir flying guard.

The deer sprinted on and Deston tried not to think about his aching buttocks or thighs, which were shaking from squeezing them to stay on the deer's back. Even his jaw hurt from grinding his teeth, and every time the deer jumped over something, his head banged painfully into Margaux's spine.

After what seemed like hours, the deer finally slowed its pace and came to a stop. Deston groaned as he sat up and rubbed the grit from his eyes. With the feel of the sun on his face, he looked up and breathed deeply of the fresh, sweet-smelling air. As the deer sank to its knees, he looked around in relief at the sight of the tall, straight trees and their rich, green foliage.

All Deston had to do to stand was bring his leg over the deer's back, but even that small task was a challenge as he was stiff all over. His knees wobbled when he put weight on them and a tingling sensation of a thousand pin pricks ran up and down his legs. He walked back and forth along the road to work out the kinks and get his blood circulating again.

Margaux was just as stiff as Deston and bent at the waist, letting her fingertips brush the dirt to stretch her quivering muscles. Neither her nor Deston noticed Torren and Keir kneeling on the ground next to the body of a woman.

As feeling slowly came back to Deston's legs, he tilted his face to the sun, letting the rays melt away the chill of the Sangcou. His anxiety drained away bit by bit, but in its place came a small nagging in the back of his mind. Something was amiss, but he couldn't put a finger on it. He looked up at the beautiful azure sky and the sun shining brightly. Suddenly, he went pale as it hit him that it was daylight again.

A feeling of doom washed over him and a hollow emptiness filled his insides. When they were with the Sangcou, it had been night and now it was light. One whole day was gone, and the Elders said he had to reach the monastery before the full moon rose on the equinox. Deston looked around frantically.

"What day is it?" he asked no one in particular as he turned in a complete circle. Before anyone could speak up, he added, "I've got to go." He took off down the road in full panic mode, but he didn't get far before Torren appeared in front of him and stopped him.

"It's alright. It's not that late. The land of the Sangcou is enchanted. It stays in a state of perpetual night. You have lost but a few hours. There is still time," Torren said, taking hold of Deston's arms.

Deston squirmed to get free of Torren's hold, the panic in him overriding reason. "What? Are you sure? How do you know?" he stammered.

"Yes, I am sure. Your grandfather is the one who put the enchantment on the land to fortify the treaty with the Sangcou."

Deston struggled against Torren's grip, but Torren wasn't about to release his hold. They had almost lost the prince twice already and he was determined not to let it happen again.

"Your Highness, please forgive my insubordination, but I beg your indulgence and ask you to hear me out. What I told you is true, but we still have far to go to reach the gateway and there is still much danger. Keir and I have been assigned to protect you, but we can only do so if you stay by our side. We were fortunate the Universe stepped in this last time. If Lilika hadn't followed you and alerted us to your location, all could have been lost." He gave Deston's arm a slight shake. "Please, I beg of you. I must have your word that you will not take off again or I cannot let you go," Torren stated firmly, but with a tone of respect.

Deston stopped struggling at the mention of Lilika's name. "Lilika? She followed us? When?" Deston looked around and for the first time noticed Lilika lying on the ground at the side of the road. Keir was kneeling next to her with his head bowed.

Margaux also looked up when she heard Lilika's name and rushed to Lilika's side. With her hand over her mouth and her eyes wide, Margaux knelt down beside the body.

More confused than ever, Deston pulled free of Torren's hold and ran to Lilika too. Her eyes were closed and on her neck were two perfect, round holes, along with a trickle of blood where the bat's teeth had sunk in. As soon as Deston saw the marks, he realized Lilika was the white deer. That startling revelation hit him like a punch to the stomach and he dropped to his knees beside Margaux. He gently placed his finger against Lilika's carotid artery. He could feel her heart beating faintly, but it was irregular and her breathing was shallow and labored.

Deston looked up at Keir. "What's wrong with her?"

Keir's jaw clenched and his eyes did not leave Lilika's face as he replied. "She was injected with the bat's poison. We have no antidote with us and there's no time to take her back to Tir na-nÓg."

"So what are you going to do?" Deston asked.

"There is nothing we can do for her now."

Margaux lifted her head and exchanged a look of horror with Deston.

Deston turned to Torren for help. Torren's expression was as sullen, and with a somber shake of his head he confirmed Keir's words.

"I don't understand. What do you mean? You can't possibly think of just leaving her here to die," Deston cried out.

"I'm sorry, Your Highness. There is nothing—"

"No, don't say that," Deston bellowed, jumping to his feet with his hands clenched at his side. He looked down at Lilika's still body, and then back at Keir. "I'm not leaving here without her."

"Your Highness."

"No! And don't call me that again. My name is Deston, just plain Deston." He was nearly screaming as he glared at Keir and then at Torren. "If I'm your prince, like you say, you have to do whatever I command. Isn't that right?"

Both Torren and Keir tensed, but Deston went on belligerently before they could say anything. "As your prince, I order you to do something to help her."

Keir's eyes hardened and a slight tic twitched in his jaw, but his tone was neutral. "Your Hi—Deston," he said in a deadly quiet tone. "You have no idea how much I want to help Lilika, but there's nothing Torren or I can do for her. I—we, have been assigned to take you to the gateway and to protect you along the way. That, along with the task of retrieving the king and the Crystal, is the highest priority for the sake of all of Tir na-nÓg. Lilika was ordered not to follow us. She disobeyed and knew the risk she was taking in doing so. She made her own choice." Keir looked down at Lilika and lowered his voice. "Believe me, I would save her if there was any possible way. But the future of our world is at stake and too much time has already passed."

Deston couldn't believe what he was hearing. Lilika had saved his life, and here they were expecting him to turn his back and leave her to die. He looked at Margaux for support, but her head was down and tears were dripping into her lap. She was as helpless as he was. He looked back at Lilika, his own eyes burning. She was so beautiful lying there, just like a faerie princess. If only this was a faerie tale, then all he'd have to do is lean down, give her a kiss, and she'd wake up. But this wasn't a make-believe tale. This was the real thing and unless some kind of miracle happened, there would be no happily-ever-after ending.

Torren and Keir waited silently for a moment more before Torren picked up the backpack and held it out to Deston. "I'm sorry, but we must be going," he said.

Deston stared at the pack, feeling numb all over. He just couldn't come to terms with the idea of leaving Lilika behind, but he didn't know what else he could do. With a sniff, he wiped the back of his hand across his nose and took the pack from Torren. The second his hand touched the fabric, he remembered the green box.

Without saying a word, he hurriedly pulled the pack open and turned it upside down, spilling everything out on the ground. Dropping to his knees, he dug through the contents until he found the small green cube. He snatched it up and didn't even flinch as it returned to its normal size. His eyes were shining with renewed hope as he looked up at Margaux. At the same moment, Keir and Torren yelled "No!" in unison, and Keir lunged forward, seizing Deston's wrist to stop him from opening the box.

"Your High—Deston. Need I remind you the box can only be opened three times? Its purpose is to help you defeat Grossard, not this. You'll need it when you arrive at the monastery. You must not use it now," Torren cried.

Deston's eyes locked on the box as Torren's words planted seeds of doubt in his mind. No one knew he'd already opened it once. If he used it again to help Lilika, that would leave only one more time he could do so. Would it be enough? He closed his eyes and bit his lip as a battle raged within him. He didn't want Lilika to die, but he didn't want to jeopardize his mother's rescue either.

Margaux moved closer to Deston and gently laid a hand on his shoulder. He looked up, hoping she would have the answer and would tell him what to do. Her lips were pressed together and she said nothing, but she didn't need to. He could see her thoughts written plainly on her face.

Deston looked down at the box, feeling nauseous. How could he possibly make a decision, knowing that either way someone may lose their life? His brain was telling him one thing and his heart another, but when it came down to it, there was really only one decision he could live with. With a weary sigh he set the box on the ground and bowed his head.

Keir hesitated a moment before relaxing his grip on Deston's wrist, and an uncomfortable silence enveloped the small group.

Deston stole a quick sidelong glance at the two fae, then without warning, he flipped the lid of the box open.

Torren started and gasped out loud. Keir closed his eyes and bowed his head to hide his face. At the same time Margaux exhaled the breath she'd been holding and sagged with relief.

As Deston peered into the box, Margaux rose up on her knees and looked over his shoulder. It surprised her to see the interior of the box was nothing more than plain, rough wood with no lining. Even more surprising was that the only thing it held was a handful of rocks and a few colored gems.

"Is that it?" Margaux whispered. "Are those going to help Lilika?"

"I don't know," Deston replied, his chest tightening with dread.

For the second time, the box had produced something that made no sense. First it was the gum, and now it was rocks. Baffled and more than a little put out, he dumped the stones into his hand, hoping for some kind of clue. However, they looked just the same in his hand as they did in the box. Consumed with disappointment, he didn't notice the slight surge of energy running up his arm from the stones.

"They're just rocks," he stated flatly.

Torren knelt on one knee in front of Deston and held out his hand. "Your Highness, may I, please?"

Deston handed him the stones. "It was supposed to give me an antidote, not rocks. What did I do wrong?"

"You did nothing wrong. This is exactly what is needed," Torren replied, picking out a clear quartz with what looked like gold toothpicks embedded in it and a brown stone speckled with red and yellow flecks. He handed both to Keir.

Keir took the two stones, walked a few feet away, and knelt on the ground. "Margaux, will please see if you can find a large round rock. Deston, I need you to locate a flat rock," Keir instructed as he took out a short bladed dagger and began chipping away at the two stones.

Deston hurried off and immediately brought back a long, black rock that was flat on one side. Keir positioned the rock on the ground and placed the stone fragments he had broken off on the flat surface. When Margaux returned with the round rock, he took it and slammed it on top of the other so forcefully both Margaux and Deston jumped. Keir lifted the rock and examined the small chunks, which had broken into several smaller pieces. Again and again he slammed the rock down until the chips were reduced to small grains. He then grated the round rock back and forth until the grains were ground down to fine granules. Once it had reached the consistency of a coarse powder, he scooped it up on the tip of the dagger and carried it to Lilika. Carefully, he poured the powder over the two holes in her neck and gently patted it into the wounds.

While Keir was making the powder, Torren had been kneeling at Lilika's feet in silent prayer. Once the powder was in place, he helped carry Lilika to the center of the road and gently aligned her body to face the sun, straight from head to toe with her arms at her side.

"I need everyone's concentration now," Torren said as he knelt once again at her side. "Send your energy and strength to Lilika to cleanse her body of the poison."

Torren closed his eyes and started chanting a mesmerizing melody in a tone as sweet and pure as an angel's harp. At the end of the song, he placed a ruby on Lilika's lower stomach in the approximate position of the base of her spine. He then placed an orange colored crystal in the center of her stomach. Next, he placed the quartz with the gold toothpicks in the center of her rib cage, a green stone in the center of her chest over her heart, a pale blue crystal at her throat, a dark blue stone with white veins on her forehead, and lastly, a purplish stone at the top of her head. As each stone was placed, Torren chanted a short verse. When the last stone was laid, he looked to the sky and lifted both arms up. Keir mimicked his pose and the air suddenly became electrified. The forest went deathly quiet.

Deston wasn't sure what exactly to do, so he raised his arms as the others and closed his eyes, concentrating hard on seeing Lilika awaken and sit up. As each second ticked by, his anguish doubled. When he couldn't stand it any longer, he peeked through slits in his eyes to see what was happening. He had hoped to find a miracle, but it didn't look as if anything had changed at all.

After a short time, Torren and Keir dropped their arms. Keir sat back on his heels and placed his forehead on the ground with his arms stretched out straight to the side in the shape of a cross.

Torren moved to Lilika's head and held his hands, palms down, an inch above the purple stone. His breathing was loud and his lips moved silently, as he systematically traced small figures in the air above the stone before moving on to the next. He spent more time at some stones than at others. When he reached the ruby at her lower stomach, his breathing changed to short, powerful bursts that sounded as if he was trying to force something through her body. After a half dozen bursts, Lilika's body jerked and Torren's breathing returned to normal, but he didn't move away from the ruby for several more minutes.

Finally, Torren opened his eyes and slid his hands down her legs as he moved around to her feet. He pulled firmly on each toe individually and threw his hands behind him as if discarding something. When he finished with the last toe, he let out a long, weary breath and placed the palms of his hands together. He bowed at the waist and then sat back on his heels in the same position as Keir.

Deston's eyes remained fixed on Lilika, but nothing seemed to be happening. *Wake up. Come on, please. Just wake up,* he repeated over and over, but her eyes remained closed. He stared unblinking, trying to convince himself she didn't look as pale as she had before, but in reality, there was no difference. His chest was so tight he could hardly breathe and his guilt sat like a lead balloon in his stomach. *Oh God, this is all my fault. That freakin' bat wouldn't have bitten her if it weren't for me. The poison wouldn't have spread through her so fast either if she hadn't had to carry me back.*

Margaux put her arm over Deston's shoulder and leaned close to his ear. "It's not your fault," she whispered, as if knowing what he was thinking.

"Yes, it is," he spit back and dropped his head into his hands. *Please don't let her die, please. She's got to wake up. She's got to.*

Suddenly, he felt Margaux's grip tightened on his shoulder. He spread his fingers and peeked through, but it took him a second to comprehend that Lilika's eyes were open. His nose burned with unshed tears as he slumped back and dropped his chin to his chest. He didn't even acknowledge when Margaux grabbed his hand and gave it a squeeze.

Lilika blinked and turned her head to the side where Keir was still kneeling in a prone position on the ground next to her. Slowly, she lifted her hand and touched the back of his head. As her fingers brushed his hair, he reared up and their eyes met. He took her hand and brought it up to his lips and smiled.

"Welcome back, my love," Keir whispered and took her in his arms.

Margaux tried to hold in her sobs, but failed. Lilika heard her and turned her head. Seeing the two teens sitting there safe and sound, she started to rise, but Torren stopped her.

"You must rest a moment longer and drink this," he ordered, handing her a flask.

After Lilika drank, Torren collected the stones from her body and helped her to her feet. She stepped forward, gave Margaux a hug, and then turned to Deston. Keir took Margaux by the arm and guided her to the side of the road to let Lilika and Deston have a few minutes alone to talk.

"I'm so glad to see you weren't harmed. Joliet would never have forgiven me if anything happened to you," Lilika said, wrapping her arms tightly around him.

Deston pulled back. "You know my mom?"

Lilika laughed. "Of course I do. I have known her since she was a toddler. I used to play with her in the forest. It was I who introduced her to Oseron. I also knew about you, but I gave an oath not to tell."

"You were the deer I saw that day I found the baby wolf, weren't you?"

"Yes. I also led you to the pyramid." She smiled and reached out to brush the hair off his forehead. "I've been keeping an eye on you ever since you arrived in France. But when my powers began to weaken, I knew I had to bring you into our realm so others could help watch over you. I didn't know then the Elders were planning to send you on this journey. I learned of it the same time you did. I can't say I agree with it, but I want you to know you'll not be alone. I'll be at your side until the end of the journey to see no harm comes to you. That was my oath to your mama long before you were born, and it remains so. In this realm we are bound by our oaths and nothing comes above them."

Before Deston could say anything, Keir rushed forward. "Excuse me, Deston, but we must leave. We just received word that Grossard has learned you are headed to the monastery. He has sent men out to find you, so it's imperative we get you through the gateway before they catch up."

Torren was already stuffing the items back into the backpack. After zipping it closed he handed it to Deston and held out his other hand to display two stones which weren't used for Lilika's cure.

"The gods sent these stones to you." He pointed to the deep green stone. "This is malachite, a very powerful stone that will absorb pain when placed on an injury. But its greatest value is in its protection. It breaks into pieces when danger is nearby and will thus warn you." He pointed to the other stone in his hand. "This one is called tiger's eye. It too is very powerful and has great protective abilities. It will help you focus and clarify your mind. Keep both of these stones close to you at all times. They'll protect you and give you strength." Torren placed the stones in a small leather pouch similar to what he and Keir wore around their necks and handed it to Deston.

"Lilika return to the city and check in with the healer," Keir ordered before turning back to Deston. "We'll continue on this road for as long as we can. It's even more important you stay close to us now. If you can't keep up the pace, let us know," he looked pointedly at Margaux, then back at Deston.

Deston nodded and Margaux blushed.

On Keir's signal, the group started off and Lilika rushed up, falling in line beside Deston. Keir's arm immediately shot out and stopped her short. The whole group came to an abrupt halt. Keir's face was red and the veins on his temples were pulsing as he squared his shoulders and swung around. He looked as if he was about to explode.

"I ordered you to go back to the city," Keir stated with a tone of authority. "You need to regain your strength. You won't be needed here. Deston is in our charge and you have nothing to worry about. We will not let him out of our sight again."

Deston and Margaux shrank back at his tone, but Lilika stood tall, matching Keir's stance. "Do not use that tone with me, Keir. You can take that look off your face, as well, because I am not leaving. Wherever Deston goes, I go."

"Lilika—"

"Nothing you say will make a difference. I should think you would know that by now. But if you wish, we can stand here and discuss it all day, wasting more valuable time. Just be aware that regardless of what you say, I will follow one way or another."

Keir's eyes narrowed and his jaw clenched. After two years of marriage he did know her and also knew how obstinate she could be. "So help me, if the king's life wasn't at stake, I *would* stand here and argue this out and *make* you obey me, not only as your husband, but as the captain of the guard." He wiped his hand over his face. "I swear your stubbornness will be the death of us both one of these days."

He glared at her. "You have me at a disadvantage this time, but I want you to know this—you may have won this round, but you will *not* win the next. You can take that as my oath."

A tic appeared in his jaw as he looked fiercely into Lilika's eyes. "I'll allow you to accompany us, but only if you vow to stay in the back and do as you are told. If we run into any other obstacles, you're to stay out of it and let me and Torren handle it. Understood?"

Lilika tipped her head slightly in assent, canceling Keir's victory with her own triumphant smile. She winked at Deston as Keir started down the road, then fell into step next to Torren to bring up the rear.

Chapter 36

Rellik lifted his nose and sniffed the air as he stood on the grassy bank of Mirror Lake. There was no scent of the boy or the Others. Dropping his head, he released some of the tension in his shoulders and forced himself to remain calm. Maybe luck had finally turned his way. He may have let the boy slip by him once, but it would not happen again. His emotions and curiosity would not get in the way this time.

He walked up the bank toward the woods, formulating a plan of attack as a light breeze blew off the lake and circled through the trees, ruffling his fur. He lifted his face to it and breathed deeply, detecting a faint scent floating on the air. He took another whiff to confirm his suspicions, keeping his face expressionless so as not give anything away.

With an exaggerated yawn, Rellik nonchalantly walked to the edge of the trees, keeping his eyes on the ground until he came to a spot where he scratched at the dirt, pretending to prepare a place to lie. After gathering some grasses and patting them in place, he circled his makeshift bed, but instead of lying down, he launched into the air and over a rock a good ten feet away, landing next to a rabbit.

"Are you spying on me?" Rellik growled, placing a paw on top of the rabbit to keep it from running.

The rabbit, scared out of its mind, was unable to speak. Rellik picked it up by the scruff of its neck and shook it violently, which only made it tremble harder.

"Answer me! Do They know I'm here?" Rellik roared, his spittle drenching the rabbit's face.

The rabbit's eyes rolled back in its head and it went limp, but Rellik wasn't deceived by its act of fainting. His lips pulled back in a sneer and he shook it again; then realized if the rabbit truly did faint he wouldn't get the answers he so desperately wanted.

"All right ... answer me this one question and I'll not kill you," he said in his gentlest voice.

The rabbit's eyes rolled back in place and focused on Rellik. It was smart enough to know it couldn't trust the wolf, but it also knew it had no other options. Lowering its eyes, the rabbit gulped and nodded tentatively.

Rellik managed to keep a straight face in spite of his victory. "Do They know I'm here?" he asked a second time.

The rabbit shook its head no.

"So you're telling me you didn't send word to Them when I arrived?" Rellik replied, a hint of disbelief in his voice.

"There wasn't time. I just got here myself," the rabbit squeaked, hoping with all its heart Rellik couldn't tell it was lying.

Rellik's glare bored into the rabbit. "If you're lying to me, I'll not only kill you, I'll hunt down the rest of your family."

The rabbit threw a guilty glance up at Rellik and looked right back at the ground. "No, sir, I'm not lying. Pa ... pa ... please, let me go. You promised," it begged.

Rellik laughed maliciously. "Let you go? I never said I would let you go. I just said I wouldn't kill you. And I won't. But I do hope you can swim."

The rabbit's head snapped up and its eyes became enormous. It struggled harder to escape, pushing against Rellik's paw with its powerful hind legs.

Rellik was amused and let the rabbit thrash wildly about for several more minutes. But once the entertainment lost its appeal, he flicked his paw and sent the rabbit flying toward the lake. It landed with a small splash far out in the deep water. Within a few seconds, it surfaced and gasped for air, only to sink once more. For a second time, the rabbit surfaced and pawed at the water, but went right back under and did not reappear.

Rellik vacantly watched the bubbles float to the surface of the water, his mind already moving on to more important issues. If what the rabbit said was true and the fae couldn't detect his presence in Their realm, Their powers truly were getting weaker as Grossard predicted. But he wasn't fool enough to trust the rabbit's word. The wisest course of action was still to hide in the trees as he'd originally planned and once They arrived he could determine how much of their powers remained. Either way, he held the advantage.

His eyes narrowed and saliva dripped from the sides of his mouth as he stared down the road. He then ambled into the trees for cover, his chest tight with anticipation.

Chapter 37

Keir set the group's pace at a steady jog, keeping a close eye on Deston and Margaux to make sure they were able to keep up. The delay had him worried, but he didn't want the others to know that. He was also concerned over which route to take to the gateway now that Grossard knew they were on their way. The road that circled the lake had numerous places from which Grossard's men could launch an ambush. Normally, that wouldn't have worried him so much, but due to his weakening powers, he could no longer discern different energies and threats, which meant there would be no forewarning of an imminent attack.

The other option they had was to take a boat across the lake. That had its own set of risks; and for the first time in his career, Keir was unsure of the best course of action to take. While he had no doubt he and Torren could fight off Grossard's men if they kept to the road, the battle would take precious time and put Deston in danger of being captured. The advantage of keeping to the road was he would have some control over the outcome. Whereas, if they took the boat and aroused the Lady of the Lake, he'd have no control over what happened. The mist could very easily swallow them up, as it has so many others, and they could be lost forever. So the question that pressed heavy on Keir's mind was, was the faster way of taking the boat worth the risk? And with so much at stake, he knew he couldn't afford to make the wrong choice.

As his head began to throb with indecision, he finally gave up trying to figure it out and looked to the sky with a silent prayer, asking the gods for guidance.

Margaux jogged a few paces behind Deston. She was eager to talk with him, but also determined not to be the one to slow them down. Before their encounter with the Sangcou, she had come to the conclusion she had made a mistake coming on this journey and felt she was holding Deston back. But their time with the Sangcou changed all that. Now she was certain she was exactly where she was supposed to be, and she knew it as clearly as she had known the white deer was close by and watching them back at the Sangcou camp. She didn't know how she knew that, she just did.

"Don't worry about that which has passed, Margaux, for there is still much to do. Concentrate on the task at hand and the rest will take care of itself," a soft female voice suddenly broke into her head.

Margaux gave a small gasp and her eyes darted to the only other female in the group.

Lilika smiled and gave her a wink. *"You've done well, but you need to stay focused and stay at Deston's side. He's going to need your help and strength very soon."*

Oh, mon étoiles, Margaux thought. *"How—"* Before she could ask her question, a blue finger of water came into view and Keir interrupted her.

"We'll take to the trees the rest of the way. Once we get down by the lake, you can have a short rest if all is clear. Keep your eyes and ears open. I expect Grossard will have some men positioned somewhere in the vicinity of the gateway," he cautioned.

At Keir's words, Torren and Lilika drew their swords and the small group moved off the road into the trees to make their way down to the lake.

Deston dropped back beside Lilika and asked, "Will we be taking a boat across the lake?"

"Oh, no, we'll not take the boat. The Priestess governs the lake and the mist. If we get caught in it, we may never find our way out. I'm sure Keir will decide to stay to the road," she replied.

A half kilometer later, they broke free of the trees and Mirror Lake stretched out before them. Its clear teal water lapped gently at the shore and a small flock of ducks bobbed up and down with the rhythm. Deston looked across the wide expanse of the lake, unable to see the opposite shore—not because of any mist, but because of the distance.

"I don't see any mist," he stated the obvious.

"Trust me, it's there," Lilika replied and hurried forward to speak with Keir.

Deston looked up at the clear, blue sky, baffled by Lilika's remark. Either he was going crazy, or she was, because there was definitely no mist. And now that he could see the actual size of the lake, he couldn't imagine walking all the way around when there were four healthy people perfectly able to paddle a boat.

Margaux walked out of the trees directly behind Deston and stopped dead in her tracks. She looked out over the lake and suddenly felt hot and queasy as a sense of déjà vu fell upon her like a heavy blanket. *I know this place,* she thought. But how was that possible? She had never entered the high realm before today. Still, she could not deny the feeling that she had been in this place before.

Torren lightly touched her shoulder to nudge her back into motion. She flinched at his touch, but resumed walking, her eyes darting this way and that as visions of various landmarks and other anomalies floated into her head before they actually came into view. When she turned her gaze back to the lake, she saw a thick, gray fog hanging over the water. Within the fog were silhouettes of people moving about as if they were walking on water. She sucked in her breath and blinked rapidly, and just like that, the apparition was gone. But an uneasy feeling stayed with her and followed her down the grassy slope.

Deston was also distracted as he walked across the grass. He could see the nose of a boat sticking out of the tall reeds at the water's edge. It seemed ridiculous to him not to make use of it. The lake was perfectly calm and crystal clear, and there wasn't a cloud in the sky.

"Don't you think it would be faster if we ..." His words trailed off as Keir lifted his sword and whirled around with a look of pure anguish on his face.

Pushing Deston back, Kier ran up the slope toward the trees before Deston could even look over his shoulder. Margaux grabbed Deston's arm in alarm and together they turned to find Keir and Lilika battling the largest wolf Deston had ever seen.

Where's Torren? Deston thought, and almost immediately noticed a mound on the ground a few feet behind the battle.

Margaux spotted Torren at the same moment Deston did and cried out, "Mon dieu!"

An overwhelming rage consumed Deston so quickly he lost all power of reason. He started forward with every intention of joining the battle, but Margaux held his arm tight.

"Deston, you can't. You don't have a sword or anything to fight with."

Deston looked down at the empty scabbard on his belt. The Sangcou had taken their armor, his sword, and Margaux's bow. In desperation, he looked around for something he could use as a weapon—a stick, anything—but there were no trees along the shoreline. Freeing his arm from Margaux's grip, he picked up a rock and hurled it at the beast. The rock soared through the air, missing Lilika's head by inches, and hit Rellik smack between the eyes. It startled the wolf just enough to give Keir an opportunity to strike.

Rellik issued a deafening howl, as Keir's blade cut a gash along the side of his head a few inches above his eye. He swiped a giant paw at Keir, who jumped back in time to miss the force of the blow, but his claws caught in Keir's chainmail and ripped it away.

Keir yelled to Lilika, who immediately turned to Deston and Margaux.

"Quick you two—get in the boat," she ordered, running down the slope toward them.

Margaux immediately started for the boat, but Deston looked up at Keir who was now fighting the beast alone. "But what about Keir and Torren?" he yelled back.

"Don't worry about them. They'll follow when they can. Hurry, please. The boat is your only chance."

Lilika grabbed Deston's arm as she ran by. He stumbled over his feet as he was pulled backward, but then he dug in his heels, determined not to leave Keir alone.

"Deston, now is not the time. We have to go while we still have the chance. You must get through the gateway and find your mama," Lilika yelled.

The mention of Joliet instantly brought Deston around, and without further resistance he ran to the boat.

Rellik saw them heading for the lake and let out a roar of frustration. He knew if they made it too far out into the water he wouldn't be able to stop them. His nostrils flared as his anger spiked to a new high. A gruesome sound rumbled in his throat as he stared down Keir and feigned to the left. He then took a step back and launched into the air and over the top of the fae.

Keir didn't miss a beat and flipped around, jumping onto Rellik's back as Rellik's feet hit the ground.

Rellik's sights were on Deston and he didn't notice the weight on his back until Keir's sword rammed into his flesh and a blaze of pain exploded through his neck. Letting out a vociferous roar, Rellik shook to dislodge his nemesis. Keir tightened his thighs and threw his arms around the wolf's neck, squeezing with all his might to cut off Rellik's air. In retaliation, Rellik dropped to the ground and rolled to his back, crushing Keir under his immense weight. He rolled back and forth, pressing down with his full body until Keir was no longer squirming beneath him.

As soon as Rellik felt Keir go limp, he got to his feet and craned his neck to pull the sword out with his teeth. The wound was more painful than deadly, as the blade had missed the artery and only grazed the side of his neck. But the fact Keir had gotten close enough to kill him brought Rellik's rage to a whole new intensity. With a growl, he flung the sword into the trees and took hold of Keir's belt with his teeth. He twirled Keir around twice, then let go, sending the warrior flying toward the lake and raced down the bank before Keir even landed in the water.

Lilika pushed the boat away from the shore and jumped in. Deston and Margaux, already in their seats with oars in hand, waited until the boat cleared ground and frantically paddled as fast as they could.

Rellik barreled down the slope and into the lake without slowing. As his feet hit the algae-covered rocks at the water's edge, he skidded and went down hard. His bulk hit the water with such a force it created a giant swell and propelled the boat farther out into the lake. He came up sputtering and tried to regain his footing, but again he slipped on the rocks and went under. Only his nose came out of the water before he went down for a third time. When he resurfaced, he stopped struggling, for the boat was already too far out for him to catch. He paddled back to shore and pulled himself onto the grass. He had twisted his right front paw on the slippery rocks and it was already swelling and throbbing painfully. However, instead of stopping him, it fueled his anger.

Rellik looked over his shoulder and glared at the boat. Deston had the luck of his father, but his father's luck had eventually run out, and so will Deston's. He took one last look at the boat and growled under his breath. He couldn't imagine why he'd ever felt sorry for Deston, or why he had hesitated to capture him.

It was a long way around the lake and the only way to make it to the other side before the boat docked was to run like the wind, or hope for help from the mist. But he wasn't counting on that. He had already learned he couldn't depend on anyone but himself.

He turned and took off in a sprint. The weakness in his front paw slowed him a bit, but the pain from it and the wound on his neck powered him to keep going.

Chapter 38

Lilika took the oar from Margaux as soon as she was seated and used all of her strength to row in the direction where Keir had landed in the lake. Margaux moved to the front of the boat and searched the water for his body.

"There! Over there," Margaux squealed, spotting Keir bobbing face down on top of the water a few yards away.

Lilika expertly rowed to where Margaux pointed, and the three of them dragged Keir into the boat.

"Is he dead?" Margaux asked in a small voice.

The others, concentrating on Keir, didn't take the time to answer. Lilika rolled Keir to his back on the floor between the seats, letting his legs dangle over the side of the boat. As soon as he was flat, Deston tilted his head back and Lilika started mouth-to-mouth resuscitation.

Margaux sat back and held her breath as she watched the pair work on Keir's limp body. Tears gathered behind her eyes and just when she was sure he was gone, Keir coughed up some water and gasped for air. Deston sat back on the seat, worry still etched on his face, as Lilika helped Keir roll to his side. She gently supported his head in her hands as he coughed up more water. When his breathing became more regular, she helped him to a sitting position and wrapped her arms around him.

Deston, feeling like the proverbial third wheel, turned his head to give them some privacy and looked straight into a gray, swirling mass that was rolling swiftly across the surface of the lake. "What's that?" he asked.

Keir and Lilika twisted around simultaneously and scrambled to their feet. At the sight of the mist rolling toward them, they each grabbed an oar and plunged it into the water.

"Deston, Margaux, stay where you are. If the mist overtakes us, do *not* move an inch. Do you understand? Under no circumstances are you to get off that seat," Keir ordered, paddling as fast as he could. But his efforts were fruitless, as the mist sucked them in like a magnet and quickly engulfed the boat.

Deston was accustomed to fog, as it was common back home in Pennsylvania, but never had he seen a fog like this one. The air inside the mist was so thick it was like breathing through a wet towel and he couldn't even see his own hand in front of his face. It was weird the way it had come upon them at such an unnatural rate, but even eerier was the way it pressed in on him. He shifted uncomfortably in his seat, feeling more than a little claustrophobic. He knew the others were close by, but still, he felt totally isolated.

"Margaux?" he called out, telling himself he just wanted to make sure she was all right. The only sound he heard in reply was the gentle lapping of the water against the side of the boat. "Margaux … Lilika … Keir?" he yelled louder.

Again, there was only silence. An uneasy feeling crawled up his spine. No matter how thick the fog was, it should not keep them from hearing him. They were only sitting a few feet away. His need to make contact with one of the others soon became all he could think about. He squirmed on the seat and then stood, thinking if he moved to the forward bench, he'd have better luck. His movement caused the boat to rock unsteadily and with haste he sat back down. The last thing he needed at the moment was to fall overboard and be lost for good in the fog.

The heaviness of the mist grew more stifling by the minute and with each tick of the clock, Deston became more desperate. Leaning forward, he waved his arms through the air in hopes of reaching Lilika. She'd been sitting right in front of him when the mist came upon them, but now he could only feel cold air. *Okay, maybe she moved,* he thought. But where she would go and why didn't she answer him?

Deston fidgeted anxiously on the bench. Keir had told him not to move off the seat, but nothing was said about sliding across to where Margaux was sitting. He shifted his weight a few inches, then froze as the sound of muffled voices came through the mist. He tucked his hair behind his ear and turned his head in the direction of the sound. Someone was definitely talking and it sounded like more than one person.

"Hey guys, can you hear me?" he called out, thinking it was Keir and Lilika.

The voices continued without interruption, becoming more distinct as if they were moving closer. Deston squinted into the thick, gray cloud and gradually three ghostly figures took shape within the swirls. His breath caught in his throat and his eyes went wide as he realized the three were walking across the water as if it was solid ground. Two of the figures suddenly veered off and disappeared into the fog, but the third continued on alone right up to the side of the boat.

Deston timidly stared up through his eyelashes into the face of a strikingly beautiful lady. Her teal blue eyes almost matched the color of the crescent moon shaped gem embedded in her pale skin just above the bridge of her nose. She had stark, white hair that hung all the way to her feet and hid most of her translucent gown, but the small sections of gown that were visible rippled like water whenever she moved.

The lady wore no expression on her face as she stared down at Deston. Her piercing gaze locked with his and he felt an odd sensation as if she was probing his mind. He tried to look away, but she held him captive with her eyes for several seconds more before she released him and held out her hand.

"Come with me, Deston. I have something to show you." Her voice was soft and clear, and as haunting as it was beautiful.

Deston didn't know how she knew his name and he had no intention of going with her, not only because Keir had warned him not to move off the seat, but also because he knew better than to go with a stranger. However, as her eyes held his, he found he had no control over his actions. He stood, took her hand, and stepped out of the boat.

Hand-in-hand, he walked with her across the water and through the mist. The anxiety that had come over him when the fog arrived instantly dissipated with her touch, and in fact, he felt comforted and connected to this woman in a way he never had with anyone else before.

They walked a good distance before reaching solid ground. The mist wasn't as thick as it had been at the boat, but it was still enough to hide most of the surroundings. The lady stopped and turned to him.

"Deston, Prince of Tir na-nÓg, you have taken on a formidable challenge. Are you prepared for the task?" the lady questioned.

Deston hesitated, his thoughts still jumbled. "I ... I'm not sure," he replied.

The lady nodded. "Well said." She turned and led him a few more paces to a rope bridge where she faced him once again. "Very few humans have ever crossed this bridge and none have ever returned from it. But, then you are not human, are you?" As she spoke, the crescent moon shaped gem at the bridge of her nose gave off a spark. She stepped onto the bridge and continued on without waiting for his reply.

Her words snapped Deston out of his stupor and he pulled back. *What does she mean I'm not human anymore? Has something happened to me?*

The lady replied to his unspoken question without looking back or stopping, "Hmmm, I see that bothers you. After having spent the majority of your life in the lower realm, I am surprised. You are, of course, half human," she went on. "I will overlook that part, though, as I hope your fae blood will become dominant after some time and training. Although, some of your human traits will serve you well, I think."

Halfway across the bridge, the lady looked back and motioned for him to come. Even though his mind was reeling, his feet obeyed her command once again, as if they had a mind of their own. He mechanically placed one foot in front of the other until he stepped onto solid ground on the other side.

The moment his foot left the bridge the mist vanished and a scene so surreal it couldn't be of this world spread out before him. He stood frozen in his tracks and stared in awe at the exquisite, sparkling white wall with a gleaming, golden gate almost too radiant to look at. *Holy crap, this is the golden gate! I have died and gone to heaven.*

The lady didn't give him time to adjust to his new surroundings, but took his hand and guided him through the gate and across a small courtyard. They entered a building through a set of double wooden doors that were buffed and shined to such brilliance he could see his reflection in them. Carved into the molding around the doors were numerous runes and unfamiliar symbols.

Inside the large atrium, the lady stopped. "I know you have many questions, and be assured you'll have your answers. But first you need some nourishment and rest. Once you have had both, I'll talk with you again and answer your questions."

The lady moved to a door at the far end of the atrium and hesitated. "This is not the heaven you were thinking of, although it is the next best thing," she said and walked through the door.

As soon as the lady left, a group of young girls entered and surrounded Deston. They dragged him through another arched doorway into a spacious chamber with a domed ceiling and a steaming pool in the center of the room. At one end of the pool, steps led down into the water. At the other end, two marble cherubs poured water from urns into the pool. But what drew Deston's attention were the walls of the chamber, which were embellished with scenes so beautiful and vivid he wasn't sure they were walls at all. He stepped forward to examine them closer, but the girls took a firm hold of his arms and pulled him away toward the pool.

One of the girls began to untie the leather belt around his waist while two others knelt in front of him and unlaced his boots. With his attention distracted by the scenes on the walls, it took him a moment to realize the girls were undressing him.

"Hey!" he yelled, coming to his senses as one of the girls began pulling up his tunic. "What are you doing?"

"My lord, we are only helping you with your bath," the girl said demurely.

"What? Are you kidding? I'm not taking a bath ... especially not with you guys around," he shouted, a look of horror replacing the wonder on his face.

The girls recoiled at his tone, embarrassing him even more. "I'm sorry. I, um, didn't mean to yell. It's just that I … I don't need a bath," he said with as much restraint as he could muster.

Without looking up, one of the girls spoke softly, "Forgive us, my Lord, but we have been instructed by the high priestess. She requests you soak in the Spring of Eternal Life, and I'm afraid you must. But if you bid, we will leave you to your own."

Deston looked at the steam coming off the pool. "But I don't want to take a bath," he reiterated.

The girl was unruffled and unsympathetic. "I'm sorry, but it is the high priestess's request. You cannot leave here until you do as she asks. It is very nice, I assure you. You will enjoy it."

As Deston rolled his eyes, he caught sight of the ceiling and all further protests stuck in his throat. The ceiling was painted like the night sky, with all the stars and constellations in exact order—a perfect replica of the ceiling in his room at home. He dropped his eyes and looked at the girls who were huddled in a group, their eyes fixed on the floor.

"Fine. I'll sit in there for a minute, but only if you leave," he declared.

The girls bowed low, and all but one left the room. The last girl spread an oversized, woolly blanket on the marble floor and placed another folded blanket on top.

"Dry yourself with these, and when you are ready, exit through that door. Someone will be waiting for you there," she said, pointing to the arched doorway in the far corner of the room. She bowed again and left without further ado.

Deston looked around to make sure he was alone and there were no stragglers. Then, as quickly as he could, he undressed and hurried down the steps and into the water in case one of the girls decided to come back in.

As he sat on the steps and looked out over the pool, he realized it was a lot bigger than he originally thought. It even looked big enough to swim laps in if he wanted to, but he didn't. He was only there because he had no other choice, and he was determined not to enjoy it. However, as the warm, bubbly water swirled around him, his resistance began to melt. It really did feel good. He swam out to the middle of the pool and flipped over onto his back. The steam, along with the sweet smell of the flower petals floating in the water, filled his head and chased away his thoughts and worries. Somewhere off in the distance, a flute began to play, which added to the tranquility.

As he stared up at the stars on the ceiling, his eyes grew heavy and very slowly drifted shut. The second they closed, he jerked back to his senses and stood up in the water. *What am I doing? I don't have time for this.*

He knew he should get out and go find the lady, but he didn't make a move toward the steps, as the warm water was muddling his brain like a sedative. He leaned back and the water lifted his legs up to the surface again. His eyes grew heavy as he floated, but this time he reasoned it was all right. Resting them for just a minute or two wasn't going to hurt a thing.

Chapter 39

Deston's eyes shot open. Someone had called his name and it sounded like Margaux. Forgetting where he was, he sat up and promptly sank under the water. He came back to the surface sputtering and swam to the steps. He looked around for the person who had called him, but he was alone in the room. He held his breath and listened to see if he could hear it again, but the only sound was that of bubbling water. Even the flute was gone. Shrugging it off as his imagination, he waded out of the pool. He'd done what they asked, so there was nothing stopping him from going back to the boat.

A trail of water puddles followed him across the floor as he ran to the blanket and picked up the one to dry off with. As he rubbed the blanket down his legs, he noticed his feet were incredibly shriveled, as if he had spent hours, not minutes, in the water. He held out his hands and saw they too were severely pruned. His eyebrows drew together as he his flipped his hands over. He was only in the pool a few minutes, which shouldn't have been long enough to wrinkle his skin like this. He puzzled over it for a moment, then shrugged it off as being one more weird thing about the place, and went back to drying off.

Once he was completely dry, he looked down for his clothes. He had dropped them on the blanket before jumping into the pool, but they weren't where he had left them. He turned in a full circle, thinking he might have remembered wrong, but the room was empty and his clothes were nowhere to be seen.

He looked around again, slower this time. As his gaze came

to the marble statues, he noticed a chair sitting between the two cherubs—a chair that wasn't there a moment ago, he was sure of it, and no one had come or gone from the room since he stepped out of the pool. Tentatively, he walked to the chair and looked down at the pile of neatly folded clothes that were sitting on the seat and the pair of highly polished leather boots leaning up against the leg. The clothes were not the ones he had arrived in. His didn't have gold buttons, gold buckles, or an elaborate embroidered trim like these did. He lifted the sleeve of the shirt, which was silky to the touch, and looked around. Why would someone take his clothes and leave ones that were more suited to a formal affair than to a battle, like the one they knew he was about to engage in?

As the thought of the impending battle entered his head, a sense of dread filled his chest. His armor was gone, his sword was gone and now his clothes were gone. All he had left was a blanket and some fancy garments.

Hesitantly, he picked up the shirt, dropped the blanket, and quickly donned the clothes. The shirt was amazingly soft and light-weight and every piece fit like it had been custom tailored for him. Still, he felt awkward and uncomfortable in them. His other clothes were definitely not this nice, but he preferred them to these and wished he had them back.

He tugged on the cuffs of the shirt as his eyes traveled to the door in the corner. He'd been instructed to go there when finished. He hurried across the room, hoping there was someone on the other side who could retrieve his old clothes for him.

He walked through the door without knocking, and immediately came to a halt. His hand flew up to shield his eyes from an intense glare that instantly created white spots on his retinas. A few seconds later, he heard a soft thud as a screen dropped between him and the outside to dim the light.

As Deston's vision slowly returned, he saw he was standing on a balcony that overlooked a lush green landscape dotted with dozens of dazzling white buildings and small aqua ponds nestled between exotic flower beds. Beyond the buildings and stretching to the horizon were orchards of trees laden with bright red fruit.

The gothic style of the buildings and the colors of the flora created a stunning, picturesque scene, but Deston was more interested in the solitary rock formation, towering off in the distance.

The dark, barren rock was a stark contrast to the flat terrain surrounding it and looked more like a mammoth sculpture than a natural geologic formation. Its shape was that of a wedding cake, larger at the bottom and tapering in as the layers went up. The peak at the top was ringed with a jagged rim that had highs and lows as if a chunk had been broken or torn off. A slender obelisk rose from the center of the peak and extended high into the sky. On the tip was a beacon of light that twinkled like a white hot star and was too intense to look directly at, as Deston had already discovered.

Deston stepped up to the railing of the balcony to get a closer look at the rock. As he studied it, details began to stand out and he realized the layered effect was due to merlons that were cut out of a stone wall, which circled up from the base of the rock to the top. Towers were spaced at intervals in the wall, some round, some square, but all blending in so well with the rock face he'd missed them at first glance. He also spotted several carved spires and turrets rising up behind the wall, suggesting there was something beyond that which he couldn't see.

In a daze, he walked down the railing. As his viewpoint changed, he could see the top was also not what he originally thought. The section that looked broken off was actually the outline of a magnificent cathedral carved directly out of the rock. Tall turrets stood guard on each of the four corners of the structure, and stone arches connected each of those to the base of the obelisk. Grand sculptures and ornate balconies embellished the front of the cathedral, and water gushed out from beneath it and cascaded down the rock face, traveling under several intricate archways before flowing out across the flat land and dropping off the edge of the land.

What the heck? Deston thought, bending over the railing to watch the water drop off into nothingness, as if the land was floating in the sky. He stared harder at the phenomenon to make sure he wasn't seeing things. When he realized he wasn't, his breath caught in his throat.

I don't care what the lady said. This is heaven, so I must be dead.

"You're not dead, Deston," a soft voice spoke from behind him.

He whipped around and saw the lady who had come to him on the boat sitting on a crimson cushion. She moved her hand toward another cushion across from her, beckoning him to sit. As before, Deston moved forward and sat, even though he had no desire to do so.

"Welcome to Avalon," the lady said.

Deston stared wide eyed at the lady and for a second, forgot to breathe.

"You've heard of Avalon, I see," she added.

Avalon? No, it can't be. Avalon's a myth.

The lady's penetrating stare locked with Deston's and his head was suddenly flooded with visions of Avalon throughout history. As the information poured in, he frowned, but within seconds the frown was replaced with a look of awe.

"You're the Lady of the Lake?" he stammered.

The lady's face remained expressionless, but her eyes revealed she was pleased with his recognition. *"Yes, I am Evienne,"* she said, offering him a plate of fruit.

Deston graciously took an apple, but held it in his hand without taking a bite.

"When I heard of your birth, I knew we would one day meet. But I can say truthfully, I did not expect our meeting to come about so soon," Evienne continued.

Deston couldn't take his eyes off Evienne; not only because of who she was, but because she wasn't speaking with her mouth. He was reading her mind, just like she had read his. The revelation fascinated him, but was also a little disconcerting, and he hoped she couldn't read everything he was thinking. If she could, she hid it well.

"I've known your father since his birth and have watched him grow and mature into a fair and honest king. His shoes will be hard ones to fill. And from what I've seen, you're far from filling them as yet. It will be interesting to see how you progress. How you overcome your obstacles—your human side being the most prominent of those, of course. It's a double-edged sword, your human heritage, and can either be a help or a hindrance. Choosing which way to go with it will be a formidable struggle for you, I fear. But if you elect to bring only the good attributes of the human nature into this world, you could become the strongest

ruler Tir na-nÓg has ever seen.

"*Regrettably, your human side does inherently carry with it the seed of darkness, along with the other flaws of mankind—dishonesty, distrust, pettiness, greed, and arrogance. Only time will tell if you are strong enough to overcome these obstacles.*"

Evienne hesitated and her penetrating stare bored into him. Then a hint of a smile passed her lips, the first expression to cross her face. "Of course, none of this will matter if you fail in your current endeavor." she spoke out loud.

"Why did you bring me here? Are you working with Grossard?" Deston blurted out.

Evienne's expression went blank again, but her tone remained even. "You have a lot to learn. Avalon is not of this world. I do not take the side of faerie or human. I serve only the gods and the Universe. What happens is *their* will, not mine." She stood and held her hand out to him. "Come with me. I have something to show you."

Deston stood, but for the first time he didn't automatically do as she bid. He looked at her hand and then into her eyes. The information he received about Avalon, the Lady of the Lake—it was so overwhelming he didn't know what to make of it all. And the thought came to him that his mother was being held prisoner in an old monastery, while he was sitting in a magnificent palace talking to the Lady of the Lake instead of making his way to the gateway as he should. But as he looked into Evienne's eyes, his intuition told him to go with her.

Evienne didn't interfere with his decision this time, but waited silently. At last, Deston relented and took her hand. She smiled genuinely, a smile full of love and wisdom, and led him down a covered walkway to another room.

The floor of the room was a splash of color from the stained-glass windows that embellished the walls. Deston stopped just inside the door, his eyes traveling from one windowpane to the next. By the third panel, he realized the windows were depicting the story of King Arthur. Recalling the part the Lady of the Lake played in the Arthurian legends, he turned to Evienne with a flood of questions.

Evienne had moved to the center of the room and was standing beside a pedestal. The ceiling above the pedestal was open, allowing the sun to shine down and reflect brightly off whatever it was that was sitting there.

Deston walked toward her as if hypnotized. As he approached, she picked up the item and moved it out of the sunlight so he could see it. His breath caught in his throat as he looked upon the most spectacular sword he'd ever seen. The blade was polished so bright the sunlight bounced off it like a laser beam, sending a blue flash of light streaking up and down the sharpened edge. As the light traveled, strange runes were briefly visible down the center of the blade. The cross-guard was fashioned from two pieces of metal, each in the shape of a crescent moon, one pointing up and the other down. The hilt was a single smooth polished crystal quartz point that had a rod shaped piece of sapphire embedded horizontally in the crystal near the tip, its rounded ends protruding out of each side.

Evienne allowed Deston a moment to absorb the beauty of the workmanship before she spoke. "This is Caluvier, brother of Excalibur. Have you heard of Caluvier?"

Deston didn't take his eyes off the sword as he shook his head and replied, "Uh-uh."

"That is understandable, I suppose, since you have spent very little time in the high realm. The sword has an interesting story. Would you like to hear it?"

"Uh-huh," Deston nodded.

"It started a very long time ago, during a dark period in history. Things weren't going well in the lower realm and many higher beings became concerned when it seemed the darkness was on the verge of consuming the world. That's when the gods asked me to step in and help out. I am not typically asked to get involved in the ways of man, so that should tell you the scope of dishevel the world was in.

"My commission was to have two swords made, but not just ordinary swords, mind you. These were to be swords of great power and influence—swords fit for a god and ones that would help their bearer restore peace and hold the darkness at bay. I chose a blacksmith and the gods then gifted him with the wisdom and power to forge such swords. Special metal was brought in—metal unlike any found on earth—and the blacksmith worked in secret day and night.

No one was allowed near his shop until he completed the work. When he presented the swords, you could see the hand of the gods had truly been guiding him. But the blacksmith claimed it was his skills that were responsible for the creation and he gave no credit to the gods for their role. As you may imagine, that did not sit well with the higher beings.

"The day I arrived to retrieve the swords, the blacksmith bragged to me of his talents as he held the two swords tip to tip to show off his exquisite workmanship. That was, how the humans say, the last straw. The gods immediately retaliated by sending down a bolt of lightning, which struck the tips of the two swords. The energy traveled down the length of each blade into the blacksmith. Being a mere mortal, he died instantly.

"However, a moment before the lightning struck, I reached for one of the swords and my hand, as well as the blacksmith's, was clutching it. I'm sure you are aware that the first sword, Excalibur, was given to King Arthur. But the twin, Caluvier, has never been outside of Avalon. Rumors circulated for a time that Caluvier was the sword Mordred used to kill Arthur, but there is no truth to those rumors. Caluvier has been here waiting all these many centuries for the right time and the right person." Evienne hesitated and stared deeply into Deston's eyes. "That time has come ... that person has arrived."

Deston gasped and tore his gaze away from the sword to look up at Evienne. Was she talking about him, or did he misunderstand?

"When the lightning stuck, both human and immortal had a hand on this sword. Thus, the energy of both worlds was seared into it. Like Excalibur, not just anyone can claim Caluvier. It has to be the right person—someone who will use it for the greater good of both worlds. Someone who is half human and half fae."

Again, Evienne hesitated before holding the sword out for Deston to take. "This is your sword, Deston. It was made long ago for you and for this time. Take it. You're the only one who can. With Caluvier at your side, the playing field will be equal. Good will have the same advantage as evil."

Deston swayed slightly, not sure he was hearing correctly. He looked from the sword to Evienne several times; unable to grasp the reality that she was giving him something of such value.

Evienne stood like a statue, holding the sword in her out-stretched arms, waiting patiently.

Finally, with trembling hands, Deston reached out and took it from her. The moment he touched Caluvier, he felt empowered and his trembling stopped. The hilt fit his hand perfectly, as if it had indeed been specifically made for him. He stepped back and slashed the blade through the air, amazed at how light it felt. He then turned to Evienne, beaming like a little kid who had just been granted his greatest wish.

She laughed out loud. "Take good care of Caluvier and it will take good care of you," she said, taking him by the arm and guiding him out of the room and into the hall, where another woman waited. "This is Aria. She will take you back to your friends."

Turning to face him, Evienne put a hand on each of his shoulders. "Caluvier is a powerful ally. It will help you on your journey to free your father and mother. But keep in mind, the sword alone cannot defeat Grossard. You have the strength of two worlds within you—draw on that strength. Grossard may look formidable, but don't let his appearance intimidate you. His dark powers are ill-gained and he doesn't have the proper knowledge to use them well. He can be defeated. Just use your head and let your intuitions lead the way. That's how you will succeed."

Evienne leaned in and kissed Deston lightly on his forehead just above the bridge of his nose, before turning and walking away. For an instant, the skin where her lips touched burned and tingled. Deston rubbed his fingers over the spot and watched her go, her robe rippling like water as she walked. When she was out of sight, he slipped the sword into the scabbard on his belt and turned to Aria. She smiled shyly and walked out into the courtyard.

Deston followed her through the gate, but before stepping onto the bridge he looked over his shoulder one last time. His former life in Pennsylvania seemed like a distant dream and he couldn't even picture the person he had been there. So much had changed, but for the first time, he felt like he just might have a chance after all.

With a smile, he stepped onto the bridge. In the next instant he was back in the mist, sitting on the seat in the boat.

Chapter 40

The mist began to lift the second Deston sat down in the boat and it was gone even faster than it had settled on them. Relief flooded Keir's face as he turned to Deston and Margaux.

"Everyone all right?" he asked anxiously.

Margaux nodded her head and Deston answered a quiet, "Yeah." His head was still reeling from his experience in Avalon and the expression on his face showed his state of awe.

Noticing Deston's odd behavior, Keir's brow creased as he studied Deston closer.

Feeling Keir's penetrating stare snapped Deston out of his lethargy. With a jolt he looked up. A rush of heat instantly climbed up his neck at the look on Keir's face and he quickly ducked his head again. *Oh crap, Keir knows I left the boat.* Keeping his head down to hide the guilt he knew was written all over his face, he shot a glance up through his eyelashes. Keir did not look happy. *Damn,* he thought, blowing out a weary sigh.

"I know I shouldn't have left. I'm sorry. I really didn't intend to go or stay as long as I did," he mumbled to the floor of the boat.

Deston's words trailed off as Keir visibly tensed and a look of wonder replaced the warrior's scrutiny. At the same time, the oar fell from Lilika's hand. Deston's head jerked up when the oar hit the floor with a loud thud and his face turned a deep scarlet color. Sheepishly, he looked to Margaux for support, but even she was staring at him strangely.

Dropping his chin to his chest, he fidgeted uncomfortably.

He didn't think they would be this upset since he'd come back unharmed. But obviously, he had been gone too long. A new wave of guilt washed over him, adding to his discomfort.

"Look, I'm sorry if I held us up." He shot another quick glance at Keir before returning his gaze to his feet. "I know I said I wouldn't take off on my own. I didn't mean to and I won't do it again … I promise," he added.

"What are you talking about?" Margaux asked.

"I promised Torren back in the forest I wouldn't go off by myself without—"

"But you didn't go anywhere," Margaux interrupted.

Deston gave her a bewildered look. "I did so. The Lady of the Lake came and took me to Avalon."

Margaux's back stiffened and her expression clearly communicated her disbelief.

"I did! The whole time I was gone that's where I was, in Avalon," Deston fired back.

"The whole time? The mist only lasted for a minute at the most and you were sitting right here when it lifted," Margaux replied in a patronizing tone.

"What? No way," His eyes traveled from Lilika's stunned face, to Keir, and back to Margaux. "I know I was gone longer than a minute. I mean come on … I walked across the water to this bridge that took me to this cool golden gate. They had me go into this swimming pool …" He took a sharp breath and grabbed a fistful of tunic, holding it out to prove what he was saying. "Look, they took my clothes and gave me these." As he looked down at his proof, he groaned. The tunic was the same one the Elders had supplied him with back in Tir na-nÓg.

He looked up at Margaux questioningly, and then at Keir and Lilika. "I … I swear they took this one and gave me a new one to wear. It was a lot nicer than this." As he began to question his own story, he remembered Caluvier. His hand went to his belt. As his fingers closed around the hilt, his face lit up. Smugly, he pulled the sword from its sheath.

"Where did you get that?" Margaux asked as Keir slowly sank to the seat.

"Evienne gave it to me."

"Evienne, herself, gave that to you?" Lilika questioned in awe.

"Yup," Deston beamed jubilantly. Finally, someone was listening.

"Who's Evienne?" asked Margaux.

"I just told you ... she's the Lady of the Lake. And this is Caluvier, Excalibur's twin brother," Deston replied, proudly holding the sword up high so they could all clearly see it.

"Oh, pah—lease. I've read dozens of books on King Arthur and never once have I read anything about Excalibur having a twin brother sword," Margaux huffed.

"That's because it never left Avalon. So no one in the lower realm knows about it. But this is it, and it's all mine," Deston jeered.

"I'm—" Margaux started, but Lilika cut her off.

"He's right, Margaux. Two swords were made that day. Excalibur is well known because it was given to Arthur, but Caluvier remained in Avalon. Its legend has circulated throughout the high realm for centuries, but no one has ever seen it, so there was no proof the legend was true," Lilika explained. "Do you realize what this means, Deston? You've been given one of the greatest honors known to man. Very few people from the outside have ever seen Evienne. Not only that, but by presenting you with this sword, she's telling the world where her allegiance lies. She obviously sees greatness within you, and everyone who looks upon you from this time forward will know that."

Margaux looked skeptical. "But the mist was here for such a short time. How could he go to Avalon and come back? I don't understand."

"Avalon is not governed by the time of our world. The priestess knows everything, including the time constraints we're dealing with. She wouldn't take away from that or delay us." Lilika reached up and brushed the hair off Deston's forehead. Just above the bridge of his nose was a blue crescent moon tattoo. "This crescent moon is the mark of Avalon and further proof he was there."

Margaux's eyes traveled from Lilika, to Deston, to the tattoo, to the sword. All at once the pieces all fell into place. Tentatively, she reached out and ran her hand along the flat surface of the blade, but all she was able to say was, "Groovy!"

Deston touched the spot on his forehead where Evienne kissed him. He couldn't feel anything, but he had no doubt the mark was there, just like the one on Lilika's forehead.

Suddenly, the boat dipped in the water and Keir jumped up. "The priestess gave us a second gift. She put us across the lake." His relief was evident in his voice.

Deston, Margaux, and Lilika looked around in unison. The little boat was less than twenty yards from the shoreline—a feat that would have taken several hours if they had paddled it on their own.

"The gateway is on the other side of those trees," Keir stated. "Lilika, stay here in the boat with Deston and Margaux while I check to see if it's clear. Don't come into shore until I give you the signal."

Lilika nodded, but as Keir was getting ready to dive into the water, she wrapped her arms around his neck and pulled his lips to hers. They kissed and embraced, and then Keir slipped into the water. Lilika leaned over the side of the boat, holding her breath until he resurfaced a short distance away and started swimming toward the shore. Being a strong swimmer, it took him no time at all to reach the land. He then disappeared into the trees.

As Deston sat waiting, the magnitude of what he was about to do pressed down on him. He would soon be back in his world, although after everything that had happened, it didn't seem like his world anymore. His stomach twisted into knots and the palms of his hands started to sweat like they always did before a tournament. Only this was way different than a tournament. This was a matter of life or death, and he still had no idea what Grossard was like or what he was really up against.

Evienne mentioned Grossard had dark powers, but she never said what those powers were. She also didn't explain what kind of powers Caluvier had. Deston's mind wandered to the looming face-off between him and Grossard. People kept saying he could defeat the monster, but no one ever said how he was supposed to do it.

"So this guy, Grossard. What's he really like?" he asked Lilika.

Lilika flashed him a sidelong glance and returned her focus to the trees. "Grossard is a vile, despicable creature that thrives on the sorrow and destruction of anything good," she blurted out and then paused and dropped her head. Several moments passed before she looked around with sadness in her eyes. "I'm sorry. It's just … he killed my sister."

Margaux gasped in horror.

Lilika's outburst shocked Deston, but even more shocking was her revelation. "I'm so sorry. I didn't know." He folded his hands in his lap and hung his head. The weight of needing to defeat Grossard just became heavier. As he sat in his misery, two hands gently closed over his.

"You have nothing to be sorry about. Of course you didn't know. I spoke out of line. But in truth, we don't know what Grossard is like. None of us, other than your father, has seen him since he was banished. I can only tell you what the rumors say. That is, when he left Tir na-nÓg he moved into Morgane le Fae's cave. She had been training him in the dark arts since he was an adolescent. It is said he killed her so no one else could learn the magic, but no evidence has been found to support that claim. Although, no one has seen Morgane in a very long time, and after what he did to my family, I believe that could be true.

"You asked me what he's really like. That's hard to answer, because he hid his true self from the time he was very young." Her eyes turned glassy with a far-a-way look. "I can see that everything about him was just a façade all along. He secretly plotted the chaos he created in order to come in as the hero and save the day. It's so obvious now, but back then we were blinded to what he really was and to his true darkness. When Oseron put the enchantment on him and changed his appearance," she shuddered, "it was horrible and disgusting." She released Deston's hands. "Have you ever looked into the soul of someone who is pure evil?"

Deston shook his head no.

"After Grossard's real nature was exposed, he just sort of snapped. It's been said he tried to take the curse away with one of Morgane's potions, but supposedly all he did was make it worse. And he blames your father for all of his troubles."

She studied Deston for a moment, fire burning in her eyes. "You may not have wanted to hear all of what I just told you. Neverthe-less, you need to know the truth. Grossard is vicious and mean and has become even more so because of his hatred of the king and his quest for revenge. I don't know how you're going to defeat him. I really don't. But I *do know* that you will. The answers will be there when the time is at hand, for the gods are on your side—the proof is right there in that sword on your belt." Lilika squeezed his hands and gave him a halfhearted smile before turning back to keep watch.

Deston thought about what she said and knew she was right. He didn't want to hear it. At the same time, he was glad someone finally leveled with him. He still wasn't sure how he was going to defeat Grossard, but everyone said he could and he had to keep the faith that they were right.

Silence filled the small boat as the three contemplated the challenges ahead. A few minutes later, Keir ran out of the trees and waded into the water, motioning for them to come forward. Lilika and Deston picked up the oars and rowed the boat the last few feet to shore.

"The gateway is unguarded and there are no signs that anyone has been in the vicinity," Keir announced, exchanging a worried glance with Lilika. "I think it best if you waste no more time and go straight through. We know Grossard's forces are on their way. It's possible they have already set up on the other side. You'll need to be extremely cautious. Find cover as quickly as possible and try to stay out of sight."

All eyes went to Deston. "Are you ready?" Keir asked.

Deston swallowed hard as he stepped out of the boat and swung his backpack over his shoulder. "Yup."

Margaux stepped out of the boat and looped her arm through his. His head whipped around and his shock was written on his face. "Margaux, you don't—"

"Stop," Margaux held up her hand and cut him off. "We keep having this same conversation, but nothing has changed. I am going with you. You might as well accept it. I might not be of much help, but I'm not letting you go by yourself."

"You don't have to worry about that, Margaux. He's not going by himself. I'm going with him," Lilika broke in.

Keir's head snapped around. "What? You are not!" he bellowed.

Lilika's eyes narrowed as she planted her hands on her hips in defiance. "It seems we too are stuck in this same conversation. I already told you that I would go with Deston wherever he goes. Nothing you can do will stop me."

Keir grabbed Lilika by the shoulders and gave her a soft shake. "Stop and think for a moment. Once you cross through the gateway, what little power you have left will vanish. Everything you are now will be gone. You'll be left with the body of an ancient, old woman—a worthless, old woman, and you'll never be able to come back. And there's no guaranteed you'll even make it through the gateway. You could be caught in the void for the rest of time."

Lilika's resolve weakened. She shifted her weight, but continued to glare at Keir.

He ignored her look and went on, "You know how we're all struggling with our weakened powers here. What do you think it'll be like over there with no powers at all? Think ... how are you going to help Deston if you're too weak to even raise a hand?"

Lilika's bottom lip trembled, but she maintained her defiant look.

"You will stay here, guarding the gateway and wait for Deston and the king to return, as I will ... as we were ordered to." Keir's voice softened, "That's all we can do. I too wish it were more, but I am as powerless as you are."

Lilika sagged a little and Keir rushed on with a final plea. "Let's just say by some miracle you did make it through the gateway. Can you not see how you'll become one more thing Deston will have to worry about—one more burden he'll have to carry on top of everything else? Do you really want to weigh him down like that?"

Lilika dropped her eyes and Keir folded her in his arms. "I know you're bound by your oath, my sweet, but this is out of your control. The law doesn't apply in this. The queen will understand."

Lilika sniffed into his tunic and Keir gave her a squeeze before releasing her. "Deston, you need to get going. The gateway is clear, but it may not be so for long. Come with me."

As Keir headed back into the trees, Deston gave Margaux a nervous smile. Then arm-in-arm they followed, with Lilika right behind them.

Keir led them through the trees and stopped behind a large oak.

He signaled for them to halt and held a finger to his mouth, even though no one was making a sound. He listened and surveyed the area once more. When he was satisfied there were no intruders, he motioned the group to come forward.

"All is clear," he whispered. "The gateway is just past these trees. Think Leinad and walk straight through. You'll come out in your world not far from the monastery. Keep to the road along the shore cliff. You got that—the road that follows the shore cliff. It will lead you straight there. It won't be far."

His eyes revealed his worry as he put his hand on Deston's shoulder. "I don't know what you're going find on the other side. Grossard may have already posted guards—if not at the gateway, for sure at the monastery. But if you're careful, you should have no trouble getting by them. His mercenaries are mostly bulk and few brains.

"The king and queen are being held in the upper room of the tower. You must get the king and the Crystal out of the monastery and back through the gateway before the moon has fully risen. Do you understand?"

Deston gulped and nodded his head. He had come a long way—a very long way—and his mother was just on the other side of those trees. Adrenaline coursed through his veins as he took a step in the direction Keir had pointed. Before he could take another, Lilika rushed up behind him and encircled him in her arms.

"You know I'm willing to go with you. All you have to do is say the word and nothing, not even Keir, can stop me," she whispered in his ear.

Deston broke loose and turned to her. "No, it's all right ... really. Don't worry. You've already done enough and I'm grateful. I know Mom will be too. But you need to stay here with Keir and keep the way clear for us when we come back." He tried to sound confident, but he knew it didn't come across as such.

He turned to Margaux, let out a sigh and linked arms with her. "Let's roll," he said.

Chapter 41

Grossard stepped out of the tunnel into the light and a spray of salt water. Recoiling as if a herd of demons were after him, he shook wildly to dislodge the errant drops that were burning his skin. He hated water almost as much as he hated Oseron, who had forced him to live in a cave beside the sea for over sixteen years.

"You have interfered in my life for the last time, Oseron," he snarled to the wind. "It ends tonight. When the moon rises, *I* will be the one holding the Crystal and the power of Erebus will finally be *mine*. My revenge will be sweet, and you and the rest of your do-gooders will feel my wrath."

Grossard cowered in the tunnel, timing the waves. As the water pulled back, he lumbered out and scrambled over the rocks, pulling himself up the side of the cliff and away from the water as rapidly as he could go.

The climb up the sheer rock face was not an easy one, but he had to endure it even though the tunnel went all the way into the monastery. Like all faeries, he couldn't enter a holy place without losing his powers, his strength, and his life within mere minutes. Not even his dark magic could protect him inside a holy place.

At last, he pulled himself over the edge of the cliff and onto the small clearing that butted up to the outer wall of the monastery. His mood improved immensely as he moved toward the structure, but soured just as quickly as he walked through the gate and found the three korrigans he had assigned to guard Oseron gone. His eyes flew to the tower as he bellowed, "Gorm! Leevs! Nolef!"

Grossard clenched and unclenched his fists as he stomped across the yard, stopping when three small, horned men with goat legs appeared from around the corner of the tower, their heavy brows shadowing beady red eyes above abundant hawk-shaped noses.

"Where were you? Why are you not guarding the gate?" Grossard raged.

"We've been standing around here for weeks and we were bored. No one cares about this place. We haven't seen a single living being since we've gotten here. No one has even brought us food. Did you expect us to just sit around and starve to death?" Leevs bellowed back arrogantly.

Grossard cocked his head, lifted his chin, and studied the guard. "Oh, well now, how thoughtless of me. But of course you must eat," he said matter-of-factly.

He gave the korrigans what he considered to be a smile. In the next instant, a bolt of lightning streaked across the courtyard and struck Leevs in the neck. The korrigan's head rolled off his shoulders and bounced across the yard as blood spurted high into the air and quickly turned the ground red.

The other two korrigans took a step back and drew their swords, ready to defend themselves. They matched Grossard's glare eye for eye and waited for another attack.

Grossard dusted off his hands and spoke as if nothing had happened. "So, how is Oseron fairing?" he asked, turning his back and walking to the corner of the courtyard.

The korrigans kept their guard up and their swords at the ready. "He was the same the last time Leevs checked," Nolef answered.

Grossard dropped to the ground and leaned his back against the wall. He looked up at the burning ball sitting just above the horizon and a calm settled over him. It was almost over and everything was falling into place just as he planned. The only glitch was Deston's arrival, but he didn't consider that an issue any longer. It was highly unlikely the boy would make it in time to save his father—if he made it at all. Grossard yawned loudly and looked sleepily at the guards.

"Don't leave the gate again and stay alert. There may be one last attempt to free the king. Wake me when night falls," he added and closed his eyes.

The two korrigans stayed rooted to their spots with their swords drawn, until loud guttural snores drifted from the corner. As soon as they were sure Grossard was asleep, they sheathed their weapons and stood guard outside the gate, as Grossard ordered.

Chapter 42

Deston and Margaux exited the grove of trees and came to a stop in front of a massive granite mound rising out of the earth for kilometers in both directions. Deston looked right and left for the gateway, but the only thing in the vicinity was the strange rock formation.

"Do you see the gateway?" Deston whispered to Margaux.

"I don't know. What does it look like?" She had no better idea what they were looking for than he did.

"That's a good question," Deston answered.

He turned and was just about to retrace his steps when he heard Keir's voice inside his head.

"*Step through the rock,*" Keir said.

Deston started and looked back at the solid wall of stone, repeating Keir's words out loud. "Step through the rock? How am I supposed to do that?" He walked up and placed a hand on the cold surface of the granite. "It's solid. There's no way through it."

"Here—over here," Margaux declared.

Deston's gaze followed Margaux's finger to a fissure in the rock. The split was about four feet wide at the base and narrowed as it went up. Less than six feet from the ground the two sides joined together as one. "That's just a crack. It doesn't even go all the way through," Deston stated.

"I know, but Lilika just told me it's the gateway." Seeing the disbelief on Deston's face, she shrugged. "I guess there's only one way to find out," she added and without hesitating, she walked into the crack and disappeared.

Deston jumped back and his mouth fell open. A moment later, he shook his head and pushed his hair back out of his eyes. "If they wanted us to go through a big crack in a rock, why didn't they just say so instead of telling us to look for a gateway?" he grumbled to the air as he stepped forward into the crack.

A black void instantly sucked him in and propelled him forward as strobes of light flashed and wavy colored lines danced before his eyes. It felt as if he was moving in slow motion, but in less than a nanosecond he was back in the bright daylight with the sound of the surf roaring in his ears. Lightheaded and a little dizzy, he put his hand on Margaux's arm to steady himself. A white orb, sitting low on the horizon, swam before his eyes and it took several blinks before his vision cleared.

"I think we better get out of here. It looks like there was something here. It might be Grossard's guards that Keir warned us about," Margaux whispered, pointing to tracks in the dirt.

Deston picked up on her use of the word "something" and bent down to examine the prints. The mish-mash pattern of tracks crisscrossed over one another, making it impossible to tell if they'd been made by one being or several. Deston placed his hand inside one of the undisturbed imprints, and even stretching his fingers as far apart as he could, his fingers were still a good six inches short of touching the opposite side of the print. He looked up to meet Margaux's eyes with the same questioning expression she had on her face. They both turned and looked around at the same time.

The gateway consisted of three eight-foot tall gorse bushes that were covered with clumps of yellow flowers and long thorns. Behind the bushes was a weather stripped tree that was split down the middle from a lightning strike. To their left, a gravel road hugged a cliff with a sheer drop-off into the sea; to their right, scattered patches of short grass covered a flat plain. The only cover in the area was a grove of trees, but it was a good distance ahead.

"We need to get to those trees. Out here in the open we're an easy target," Deston said, remembering Keir's words.

Margaux had come to the same conclusion. With a nod of her

head, she ran to the road and headed for the trees.

The surf pounded the rocks below and the seabirds squawked their displeasure at being disrupted as Deston and Margaux ran along the cliff. The yellow, gold, and red leaves of autumn added a spark of color to the clumps of tall green grass on the bank creating a picturesque autumn setting, but Deston didn't take the time to admire it. He was only concerned with getting to cover as quickly as possible.

As he ran down the middle of the road, a cold chill that didn't come from the crisp wind blowing in off the water sent a shiver up his spine. The closer he got to the trees, the more penetrating the chill became. Unable to shake the feeling something was wrong, he grabbed Margaux by the hand and swerved into the tall grass along the cliffside of the road. The shoulder was rocky and uneven, which made it hard on the ankles, but the little bit of cover the tall grasses provided was well worth the discomfort.

Deston's nagging feeling that something was wrong continued to get stronger. He ran to a cluster of bushes and flopped down behind them.

"What's the matter?" Margaux panted as she fell beside him.

"I'm not sure, but it feels wrong," he whispered back. "I think there might be someone hiding in those trees. But I can't tell for sure from here."

Margaux blanched at his words and peeked through the limbs of the bushes at the grove not too far ahead. It looked peaceful enough and just like the one they'd left Keir and Lilika in.

"Let's stay low and keep to this tall grass," Deston muttered and darted out.

Margaux followed Deston's moves as he sprinted to the shelter of a large clump of grass, then up to a small section of stacked rocks that had once been part of a stone structure. A few yards ahead, the cliff crumbled away into the sea, taking the road with it up to the tree line. Deston cursed under his breath. They had no other option now but to go through the grove, even if some of Grossard's men were there waiting for them.

Deston squatted down behind the stones and looked through a wide crack. The grove was dark and quiet, and nothing looked out of place. Still, it felt wrong. A cold sweat ran down his back, but his chest felt like it was on fire. He placed a hand over his heart and realized it wasn't his chest that was burning. It was the leather pouch. His hand shook a little as he pulled the string over his head and dumped the contents of the pouch into his palm. The green malachite had broken into two pieces just as Torren said it would when danger was near. He shuddered as he remembered those words, but as he whipped his hand around to show Margaux, he tried to put on a brave face.

Margaux's eyes widened as she looked at the stones. When she looked back at him, he nodded his head in acknowledgement, then put his finger to his lips and turned back to peer through the crack. Slowly, his gaze moved from left to right, scrutinizing every tree and every shadow. It took him a second pass over before he finally saw them just a little ways off the road. Ogres. He'd missed them at first because their green skin was encrusted with mud, and the dirty, brown rags tied around their waist and over their shoulders acted as the perfect camouflage.

Turning back to Margaux, he pressed his finger to his lips again and pointed to the ogres. Margaux followed his finger. When she spotted them, her eyes went even wider and her face turned white, but she made no sound.

Deston looked back through the crack and counted. There were five of them, spread out amongst the trees, and all seemed to be asleep, except for one who was propped up against a trunk and was carving slices out of a large log. The ogre's back was to the road and it didn't seem to be keeping watch, which was probably because it knew Deston would have no other choice but to go through the trees and right by it.

Deston chewed on his lip and studied the layout. If they could get to the first line of trees, they could use the foliage for cover and skirt around the ogres. It was feasible as long as the other four stayed asleep and they only had to worry about the one ogre. But first they'd have to get across the road. The distance was only about fifteen feet, but if the ogre happened to look up before they made it to cover, they'd be caught out in the open with no place to hide.

Deston stared at the ogres. He had no idea how fast they could run or how keen their senses were, but he hoped they were as dumb as they looked. He whispered his plan in Margaux's ear, and though she looked as nervous as he was, she nodded her head in agreement. He checked the ogres one more time, then on his signal, Margaux bent low and dashed across to the trees. Deston held his breath and his eyes didn't move off the ogre until Margaux made it to cover.

As he hoped, the ogre continued to work on its log, clueless to what was going on around him.

Deston licked his lips and blew out his breath. "One down," he muttered softly. He wiped his sweaty palms on his tunic, pushed the hair out of his eyes and took a deep breath. He blew the air out slowly and focused on his target. He then took another big breath and started counting silently, *one ... two... three*. On three he lunged out from behind the stones, keeping his eyes locked on the tree next to the one Margaux was standing behind.

It was the longest fifteen feet of his life, but he made it to the cover of the trees and plastered his back against the trunk. His heart was pounding as if he'd run a marathon and he could taste blood from where his teeth had cut into his lip. He blew out the breath he'd been holding and cautiously looked around the tree. The ogre was still in the same spot and didn't seem to know they were there. He rolled his eyes to the sky and silently mouthed a "thank you" before turning back to Margaux and giving her a thumbs-up. They weren't out of trouble yet, but he felt a lot better now that they'd crossed the first major hurtle. He motioned to Margaux, letting her know the way to go and put his finger to his lips, emphasizing the need to be quiet. He then pushed himself off the trunk and stealthily darted from one tree to next.

Cautiously, he worked his way around the cluster of ogres with Margaux shadowing his every move. His heart pounded wildly as he eyed the last ogre and ducked behind a large tree.

Margaux waited until he was in place and then hustled to join him. She was so focused on her goal she didn't see the large dead stick lying in her path. As she stepped on it, the sound of it cracking in two was like a cannon firing through the silence.

The ogre jumped up, its bloodshot eyes roaming from tree to tree as it sniffed the air. Deston instantly dropped to the ground, but Margaux, too horrified to move, stood like a mouse caught in the hypnotic stare of a snake. Reaching up, Deston grabbed her hand and pulled her down beside him just as the ogre turned in their direction.

The ogre scanned the trees, took a couple of steps in the opposite direction and then stopped. It lifted its nose in the air again, sniffed, and turned slowly, eyeing the very tree which Deston and Margaux were crouched behind.

At that moment, a small, red fox scampered out of a hole and ran up to Deston. "Don't worry, Your Highness, I will lead them away," it stated with a salute. "Stay here until I divert them."

The fox streaked out around the tree and headed in the direction of the ogre, twitching its white-tipped tail in the air to catch the giant's attention.

The ogre's beady eyes nearly popped out of its head when it saw the flip of the tail. As the fox ran by, it lunged, but the fox was too quick, and the ogre landed in the dirt, face first. It roared in anger and reared up, waking the others.

"Whaaa?" One of the newly awakened ogres yawned. Its eyes were still half-closed, but as the fox whizzed past, it came fully awake. Quick as a cobra, which was astonishing for one so big and bulky, the ogre leapt at the fox, catching him by the tip of the tail. Fortunately for the fox, the ogre's hands were still greasy from its earlier meal and it took only a quick twist and pull to slide out of the ogre's grasp. Realizing it had only captured a handful of hairs, both ogres howled in anger and took off in pursuit, and the other three followed. The ground shook as the five ogres pounded through the trees after the fox, which stayed just far enough ahead to keep their interest.

Margaux sagged with relief as the ogres disappeared into the trees. She looked up at Deston and tried to say something, but all that came out was, "I..."

"Don't worry about it. It's over. Come on ... let's get out of here before they come back," Deston replied, more than a little shaken himself. It was way too close of a call. As he got to his feet and began darting through the trees, he said a silent prayer for the fox's escape.

Chapter 43

The road reappeared twenty yards past where it had crumbled away, but Deston decided to keep to the cover of the trees just the same. It seemed the most sensible and safest route, especially since there was no telling what other monsters Grossard might have sent. And he figured that as long as he kept the road in sight, it wouldn't be a problem.

However, he soon discovered there was a tradeoff to feeling safe. The grove, which had been abandoned decades ago, had grown wild and thick patches of bracken were everywhere. Broken limbs and fallen trees littered the ground as well. Several times he had to change their course, and even backtrack on a couple of occasions, which was costing them precious time.

Just as Deston was considering abandoning the trees and taking his chances on the road, he noticed a road cutting through the grove a short distance ahead. Thinking it was the same road they'd been following, he pointed it out to Margaux and they hurried toward it, hoping they could make up some of the time they had lost.

Twin ruts had been permanently worn down the center of the road from overloaded wagons, indicating that at one time it had been well used. That left only a narrow strip of shoulder on each side of the ruts for them to jog on. With the leather bag of stones in his hand as a precaution, Deston took the lead and they started off single file.

Deston followed the twisting road through the trees, keeping a lookout for the monastery. They were jogging at a good pace and had already gone a fair distance, but there was no sign of any kind of structure. That made him nervous and he became more anxious with each step. Finally, he pulled up to look around.

Where the heck is the freakin' monastery? We should've reached it by now. Keir said it wasn't far down the road by the cliff.

Deston's chest suddenly tightened and his stomach plummeted. There was no sound of waves hitting the shore like there had been before. He flipped around and looked back the way they'd come, wondering if it was possible that there was more than one road.

"What's the matter? Are they coming after us?" Margaux asked, looking over her shoulder to see what Deston was staring at.

"No," he replied, trying to get his bearings. "But I think we're going the wrong way."

"What?" Margaux exclaimed. "What makes you think so? Keir said to follow the road—"

"Yes, he did," Deston cut her off. "But he said the road along the *shoreline*. Do you see any shoreline around here?"

Margaux didn't have to look around to know Deston was right. They were headed away from the sea. "You don't think this road will lead to the monastery too? ... I mean, those things are back there," Margaux's voice trailed off.

Deston shook his head and looked up at the sky. It was already dusk and the light would be fading fast. "I have no idea where this road leads, but I don't think we can take the chance. We have to go back and follow the cliff like Keir said."

He didn't want to go back any more than Margaux did, but he had to get to the monastery. "Come on, it's going to be dark soon," he said and took off in a sprint to retrace his steps.

Margaux's steps weren't as light as they had been and her honey-colored eyes were so wide she could have passed for a Disney character. Picking up her speed, she fell in step beside Deston.

"So, what are you going to do once we get to the monastery?" she asked.

Deston took his time answering. "I don't know," he finally replied truthfully.

Margaux bit her lip and tried to stay calm. "What about the green box? When are you planning to use it?"

Deston winced. "I don't know. I haven't given that much thought either."

"Maybe if you used it now, we could get inside faster and bypass the ogres?" she suggested.

They ran a little farther before Deston answered. "I don't know. I don't think it works like that. Both times I've already used it—"

"Both times?" Margaux butted in.

"Yeah, on top of using it for Lilika, I used it to hide from the spriggans. There was a piece of gum inside. When I spit it out at the tree it made the hole that we hid in. But I didn't know I was *supposed* to spit it at the tree. It was just an accident that I did. And I wouldn't have known the stones were the antidote for Lilika if Torren and Keir hadn't been there."

Margaux was shocked by Deston's revelation, but it explained why the hole was so clean. "You can't worry about what it gave you the other times. What is done is done. I'm sure the next time you open it you and I will be able to figure out what to do with whatever is in there. You can still open it one more time. If Grossard is already at the monastery when we get there, I think you should use that last time to get by him and into the tower." Margaux stated her thoughts out loud.

Deston shrugged. Up until a few minutes ago, he'd been holding onto the hope they'd reach the monastery before Grossard did. When Evienne gave them the push across the lake and saved them all that time, he thought it would provide the lead he needed. But now that they had taken the wrong road, any lead he might have had was more than likely gone—if he ever had a lead to begin with. It was beginning to look as if he would have to face Grossard after all.

As he thought about the impending battle, an image of his mother flashed into his mind. He so wished he could see her again—just one more time to tell her how much he loved her. If Grossard killed him—his train of thought stalled and his heart seized. It was the first time he had thought about what would happen to his mother if he failed. As his breathing started coming in short bursts, he grabbed Margaux's arm in a near panic and pulled her to a stop.

"You know, I was thinking. Maybe I should go in there by

myself. You know, let Grossard think I'm alone." He hesitated expecting Margaux to protest, but she surprised him and remained quiet. "I mean, we don't really know much about this guy, so there's no telling what will happen. If he kills me …"

Margaux gasped out loud.

"… if he kills me," Deston continued, "you might still be able to sneak in and get Mom out. I doubt he's expecting anyone to be with me, so it might work."

Margaux's eyes became glassy and her bottom lip trembled. She looked down at her feet. Long moments passed and she didn't say anything; then she looked up and her eyes were blazing with passion. "No, that's not going to happen. We're a team and a darn good one too. Look at what we've already faced and what we've already accomplished. Neither of us would have been able to do any of that if we had tried to do it on our own. You and I are going in there together to get your mama and papa out—that's the only way it can work."

Deston's eyes went wide in disbelief.

"Don't you see? Heroes always have a sidekick and that's because they can't do it by themselves," Margaux added. "I'm your backup. I'll always be there for you. And no one is going to die, because … well, good always defeats evil. I think it's a law or something. So you see, we can't lose."

As Deston gaped at Margaux, a warm, tingling sensation blossomed out from his stomach. She was a lot stronger than he realized and pretty amazing too. What's more, she was right. They did make a great team. He wouldn't have gotten as far as he had if she hadn't been with him. He opened his mouth to tell her so, but before he could say anything, Margaux shushed him and whipped her head around. An instant later she whirled back with a look of delight.

"Do you hear that?"

Deston had not been paying attention to his surroundings, but as soon as Margaux said it, he heard it too—the sound of waves crashing on the shore. They were back on the right track. With a big whoop he took off running toward the sound.

The last hint of daylight was fading by the time the cliff came into view, but he could still see that a short distance up ahead the coverage of the trees ended and they would have to travel out in the open again. Deston slowed to a walk to ponder the risk.

"Deston!" Margaux suddenly cried out.

Deston flinched and wheeled around, expecting to find the ogres or some other monsters surrounding them, but what he saw instead was a massive dark structure about fifty yards away. The road they had taken through the trees didn't get them lost at all. It had circled them around the monastery and brought them in from behind.

"Do you think that's the monastery?" Margaux inquired.

"It has to be. Lan said there was nothing else around. But I think that's the backside." He sucked in a sharp breath. "Do you know what this means?" He didn't give Margaux a chance to respond and answered his own question. "We've totally bypassed Grossard. I'm sure he'll be expecting us to come in the front way and that's where he'll be waiting. This is genius! We can sneak in the back and get Mom and Oseron out before he even knows we're there."

He looked at Margaux with a big, goofy grin, and started running toward the monastery. "Come on, it's getting late."

Chapter 44

Rellik's foot was swollen twice the size of normal by the time he made it around the lake, though he didn't let it slow him down. As he came up the last stretch of shore and saw the small boat moored on the sand, a snarl rattled in his throat. If the boat was there, the boy had to be there as well. He pushed himself harder, his mind devoid of everything but finding Deston. Not even the possibility that Grossard was already at the monastery or the punishment he would receive when Grossard learned what he had done entered his mind, for none of it mattered anymore. The driving need to prove he hadn't lost his edge was what was pushing him on.

He was glad to see the grove of trees that surrounded the gateway come into view, as he wasn't sure how much longer his foot would hold out. He was pushing it past its limits and his sides were heaving, but he didn't stop. The second he entered the trees he could smell the scent of the Others, but he ignored it, for he knew They had accompanied Deston. It never occurred to him the fae would allow the boy to go on alone, so when Keir and Lilika dropped out of the sky as he neared the rock, he was more than a little surprised.

"Move!" Rellik roared, barreling straight at them without slowing.

The fae responded by digging their feet in and preparing for the assault. Lilika bent her knees and held a long, sharpened stick with both hands, the tip pointing straight at Rellik. She was aiming for his heart, and at the speed he was coming, she knew she would have only one chance to hit her mark. Keir stood beside her, holding Lilika's sword in his hand.

Rellik had no weapon except for his brute strength and cunning mind. He ran on, his mouth foaming, but instead of trying to ram through them, he used his powerful hind legs and propelled himself into the air and over their heads.

Keir anticipated such a move and back-flipped onto a tree branch beside the path a second before Rellik took flight. From there he pulled himself up onto another limb that extended over the path and ran down the length of it, leaping onto Rellik's back as the wolf's feet touched the ground.

Rellik felt Keir land on his back, but before he could react, Keir drove the blade of his sword into the wolf's shoulder. Rellik let out an ear-piercing howl as his front legs buckled, sending him crashing to the ground headfirst. As he tumbled head over heels, Keir was thrown off to the side. For a heartbeat everything was still. Then Rellik rolled to his feet and sprinted toward the gateway.

Lilika came running up from behind as Keir got to his feet, and in unison, they made a lunge for Rellik as he leapt into the gateway. Rellik disappeared into the crevice and Lilika and Keir fell to the ground, catching nothing but air.

Lilika's face turned into a mask of anguish and Keir was barely able to catch her around the waist as she lurched forward screaming, "Nooo!" He knew she would try to follow the wolf, and she fought him to do just that, but he held her tight and refused to let go. She pummeled his chest with her fists, then collapsed into his shoulder and sobbed.

"Ssshhh, my love. He's in the hands of the gods. It's up to them and Caluvier to protect him. They're the only ones who can help him now," Keir whispered in Lilika's ear, but his jaw was hard as he stared at the gateway. It was no easier for him to stand back and do nothing, but he knew there was no other alternative. In the lower realm they'd be more of a hindrance than a help.

Chapter 45

Rellik crashed through the gateway and took three steps before collapsing. The sword was still lodged in his back and pain was shooting down his legs. He reached behind to pull the sword out, but couldn't quite reach it. Luckily, the blade hadn't hit any vital organs or arteries and pain was something he refused to give into. But he was cognizant enough to know if he didn't take a few moments to rest, he'd be completely drained by the time he faced Grossard. And that would be certain death.

He closed his eyes and laid his head on the ground. The monastery was not much farther, but he still had to decide what to do once he got there. As his mind drifted to Deston, his thoughts became jumbled.

Suddenly, he felt the sword being pulled out of his back. He jerked his head up and shook it to clear his vision.

"Rellik, what's happened to you?" grunted one of the ogres.

Rellik turned his head and looked up at the two ogres swimming before his eyes. He shook his head again without answering, feeling no need to justify himself to these heathens.

"Where is the boy? Is he with you?" another ogre asked.

Hearing the second question, Rellik's head snapped around with renewed energy. If the ogres had been waiting there the whole time and hadn't seen Deston yet, maybe Deston did get taken by the mist after all. With a sudden lurch, he got to his feet.

The ogres hastily backed away.

"Are you saying the boy hasn't come through this way?" Rellik growled, wanting to confirm his hopes.

The ogres eyed Rellik callously, but didn't answer. They moved into a huddle and muttered to each other in guttural sounds. Even though Grossard had told them to wait for the boy, they knew he was also looking for Rellik.

"I'm asking if you've been here the entire time and if you've seen the boy?" Rellik rephrased the question, his patience waning rapidly.

The ogres finished their discussion and spread out into a circle around Rellik.

Sensing their intentions, Rellik chuckled softly despite his pain. He hated ogres, and would happily wipe the smirks off their faces if there was time. But there was still a slim chance Deston would arrive via a different route and he needed to get to the monastery.

"Iccasor, you know Grossard will not be happy if you fail to bring him the prince. Are you willing to accept the consequences of leaving your post and letting the boy get through?"

The other ogres looked at Iccasor and shuffled uncomfortably. They had all witnessed what happens when Grossard got upset.

Rellik sighed in resignation, hoping to fool the ogres. "Look, I don't know why I'm doing this, but since I'm on my way to the monastery right now to see Grossard, I'll let him know that I saw you and that you are alert and ready to take the prince as soon as he arrives. He'll be very pleased to get the report." Rellik pulled his lips back in a dastardly leer.

The four ogres waited for Iccasor to give them direction, but Rellik's patience was spent.

"Enough of this! There's still much to do. I can't stand around here any longer." Rellik took a step forward. The ogres tensed and lifted their clubs. Rellik raised an eyebrow and looked at their leader, who still appeared uncertain. "Iccasor? I'd hate to tell Grossard you're the one responsible for delaying the news I bring." He could almost see Iccasor's tiny mind reeling as the ogre shuffled his feet in indecision.

Finally, Iccasor lowered his club and grunted for the others to do the same. Rellik walked stiffly through the group, alert and ready for an attack, but once he broke free of the circle, he took off in a run and didn't look back.

The ogres, still holding up their weapons, watched him go. They stood there several minutes more before they lost interest and walked back to the trees to resume their naps.

Chapter 46

When the monastery was constructed in the thirteenth century, it was built as a fortress, as well as a sanctuary. Perched high on a cliff above the sea, it was the perfect lookout for enemy attacks. That was long ago and no one had lived in or around the ancient structure for centuries. After it was abandoned, time and weather took its toll. The small chapel and bell tower of the main structure, plus, the outer wall were all that remained intact.

Deston and Margaux stood at the base of the twenty-five foot stone wall, looking up in despair. There was only one gate on the backside, but it was completely blocked by an enormous chunk of stone and a pile of rubble.

"It's too high. I can't climb that," Margaux stated, tilting her head back to look up at the top of the wall.

Deston's eyes moved up too, as his mind traveled back to the day his friend, Mark, tried to help him get over his fear of heights by daring him to climb a rock wall at the sporting goods store. It was one of the hardest things he'd ever done. The only reason he agreed to do it was because he would be secured to a rope.

He turned back to Margaux beaming. "Ohmigod, I've got it!" he exclaimed, shrugging off the backpack. He dug through the contents until he found the rope Aren had given him. "If I can loop this over one of the battlements at the top, we can climb up," he explained, tying a knot at one end of the rope to make a loop, as Margaux watched him skeptically.

"But that rope isn't long enough to reach all the way to the top,"

she said, stating the obvious. Even after the rope returned to its
normal size, it was still less than half the length they needed.

"Yeah, but remember the Elders gave it to us, so I'm hoping it's
magical like the box," Deston replied.

He pulled on the loop to make sure the knot was tight and eyed
the battlement. All he needed to do was get it around one of the
merlons and they would be set. Backing away a few steps, he focused
on the target as he twirled the rope like a cowboy preparing to lasso
a calf. He held his breath, said a little prayer, and let the rope fly.

"Come on, come on," Deston coaxed softly as the loop soared
through the air. Just as he hoped, the rope mysteriously grew long
enough to reach to the top of the wall. However, before he could
celebrate, it fell back to the ground. Its magic allowed it to lengthen,
but there was no magic for his aim.

Again and again, Deston threw the rope up as Margaux stood
by and watched. The loop almost made it around a merlon once,
but as he pulled to tighten it, it slipped off. After the fourth miss,
Margaux reached for the rope.

"Here, let me try."

Deston held the rope away from her reach. "No, I've almost got
it. Just hold on."

"Oh, *pour l'amour du ciel!*" Margaux mumbled, rolling her eyes
and planting her hands on her hips.

Deston ignored her and tried again. As the rope fell to the
ground, she let out an exaggerated sigh. Deston pressed his lips
together to keep from responding and threw the rope up, missing a
sixth time.

"So are you done yet? Can I try it now?" Margaux asked smugly,
as he glowered at the rope as if it was at fault.

Deston glared at her, but handed her the rope just the same. He
had no doubt she would miss, but she could try all she wanted while
he thought of some other way to get in. As she practiced twirling the
rope over her head, he sat down on a rock and buried his face in his
hands, wondering whether to use the box for the last time or try to
sneak in the front way.

"Woo hoo! I got it," Margaux cried, disrupting his thoughts.

Deston jerked up. Sure enough, the rope was dangling down

the wall with the loop securely around one of the merlons. He looked at Margaux's beaming face and felt a twinge in the pit of his stomach. She had bested him again, but instead of being mad, he felt like kissing her. They could now get over the wall without having to use up the fae box.

"I'll go up first," he said, jumping to his feet. "I've done this before. Once I'm on top, I can pull you up if you need help." His voice shook just a little as his fear of heights reared its ugly head.

Margaux readily agreed and handed Deston the end of the rope. He wiped his hands on his tunic and pictured his mother's face.

I can do this. It's just a wall and I've got a rope. Nothing's going to happen.

Blowing a breath out through his mouth, he grabbed the rope and started pulling himself up hand-over-hand. He locked his eyes on the stone blocks directly in front of his face and didn't risk looking up or down. Nervous perspiration ran into his eyes, but he could tell he was making progress and that's all that really mattered.

The minute the top of the wall came into his line of sight, he grabbed the stone and pulled himself up and through the crenel. His knees wobbled as his feet touched the narrow ledge running along the inside of the wall and he hung onto the wall for support. The relief of having made it lasted only a brief moment, for he noticed a faint glow coming from the front of the monastery. They were not alone. A lump formed in his throat as he stared at the light. If they hadn't taken the wrong road, they would be facing Grossard and who knows what else at this very moment.

Deston's chest was tight as he turned back to the wall and signaled Margaux, "It's clear. Hurry up."

Margaux grabbed the end of the rope and grimaced. She'd never climbed a wall before. Mimicking Deston's moves, she jumped up and wrapped her legs around the rope. She tried using her arms to pull herself up, but her upper body was not as strong as his. After going only a quarter of the way, her muscles began to burn and she hung limply from the rope, struggling to pull herself up the rest of the way.

It never occurred to Deston that Margaux would have trouble climbing, so he kept his eyes on the courtyard instead of watching her progress. When more than enough time had passed for her to make it to the top, he looked over the side and was astounded to find she was less than halfway up the wall. He glanced up at the stars that were beginning to appear in the darkening sky and swore under his breath. They were running out of time.

"Margaux, put your feet on the wall and walk up as I pull," he called down in a loud whisper.

Margaux's arms were trembling, but she did as Deston said. Putting her feet on the wall helped some, but if Deston hadn't been pulling, she would have never made it. As soon as she got close enough, he grabbed her arm and she swung her leg over and fell onto the ledge.

Deston gave her a few seconds to recoup before he whispered nervously, "Come on. We have to go."

At the tone of his voice, Margaux sat up in alarm and looked down into the courtyard. The glow on the other side of the monastery shined like a beacon in the night sky and her heart raced even faster.

"The stairs going down are right over there, and the door into the building is straight across. See?" Deston pointed to the area he was talking about. "I don't think anyone is guarding it, but it's hard to tell from here, so be quiet and stay low."

He gave her an encouraging smile even though he wasn't feeling it and scurried silently along the walkway to the top of the stairs.

Chapter 47

As the bright white circle of the sun slid below the horizon, a small battalion of Grossard's army gathered in the courtyard to witness the final chapter of his great plan. Gorm, one of the korrigan guards, nudged Grossard to wake him as instructed. Grossard snarled, kicked out his leg, and went right back to snoring. Gorm jumped out of the way of the kick and looked warily at the sleeping giant. He still wore the scar in the center of his chest from the last time he'd awakened Grossard, and he wasn't overly eager to experience that pain again. But he knew if he let Grossard sleep, he'd be in just as much trouble, if not more. Either way, the odds of him suffering some kind of injury were high.

Mumbling under his breath, he looked around the courtyard and noticed a spriggan sitting on a rock by the fire. The spriggan's back was to him. "You!" he bellowed.

The small creature looked over his shoulder to see who Gorm was yelling at. Seeing that Gorm was staring directly at him, the spriggan tried to melt into the background and appear as small as possible.

Gorm lifted his finger and pointed at the creature. "I'm talking to *you*," he repeated.

The spriggan's pointed ears fell flat against the side of its head and it whimpered pitifully as it looked around for help, but the once crowded courtyard was now empty, except for him and Gorm. The spriggan's eyes darted to the gate and back.

"Come here," Gorm barked, pointing to the ground at his feet.

The spriggan took one tentative step toward Gorm as a fake

out, and then bolted for the gate. The deliberate defiance of an order took Gorm by surprise and he hesitated a fraction of a second too long before lunging to intercept the small creature. The spriggan scooted through the gate and disappeared into the shadows and Gorm landed in the dirt empty-handed.

He looked around and saw he was the only one left. Letting out a growl, he pounded his fists on the ground. There was no other option now but to suffer the consequences and wake Grossard himself. Grumbling loudly, he picked himself up and walked to where Grossard was lying. As he started to reach out his hand, a brilliant idea popped into his head. He smiled at his genius and picked up a round rock from the ground. Then stepped back a few paces and lobbed it at Grossard. The intended target was Grossard's chest, but the rock missed its mark and smacked the sleeping monster on the temple.

In a flash, Grossard reared up and lunged. A gigantic hand caught Gorm around his neck and lifted him off his feet before he had a chance to flee. Grossard snarled, baring a double row of serrated teeth. At the same time, Grossard caught sight of his small army reassembling in the courtyard out of the corner of his eye. It took a few more moments for the fog of sleep to clear from his mind and for him to come to his senses. His grip relaxed.

Gorm fell to the ground with a loud thud and scampered backward and out of Grossard's reach as fast as he could go.

Grossard's eyes lifted to the stars dotting the black sky and a rush of elation swept through him. It was time. All those who had doubted him, all those who had turned their backs on him would now pay the price. He walked to the fire and faced his group of supporters.

"The day we've all waited for is at hand," Grossard shouted.

An excited murmur circulated through the courtyard.

"Oseron's reign will come to an end this evening and your new king will be crowned. There'll be no more oppression for the solitaries. No more bowing down to the Others. *We* will rule the realms and take back what we deserve!"

Cheers and grunts of approval sounded from the group.

"Bring Oseron and his queen down to meet their fate," Grossard barked, his solid black eyes reflecting the dancing flames.

Two ogres immediately left the group and entered the door of the chantry, as the others moved out of the way just in case something went wrong. Grossard paced back and forth in expectation, his hand twitching on the hilt of his sword. Finally, the ogres emerged from the building, one carrying Oseron over his shoulder, the second pulling Joliet along behind. The ogres stopped in front of Grossard, dropped Oseron unceremoniously on the ground and pushed Joliet down beside him.

Joliet immediately bent over Oseron in a protective fashion, stroking his forehead and whispering soft words of comfort.

Oseron's eyes opened and he did his best to smile. "Don't worry, my love, it will be all right. I'm not going to leave you," he whispered.

Joliet choked back a sob as Grossard guffawed. "Now, isn't that sweet. Just like two little lovebirds. And I hate to be the bearer of bad news, my lovely, but your husband is lying. You see, he is going to leave you, and very soon I fear," Grossard snorted with pleasure. "But first things first."

He strutted back to the fire and faced his men. At long last he was the star of the show and the thrill was even more than he had anticipated. His eyes roamed over the small army that had congregated. The only one missing—the only disappointment was Rellik. He never for one second thought Rellik would let him down. So seldom was he wrong about those kinds of things.

Grossard turned to one of the orcs standing at the edge of the crowd. "Did you fetch the packages as I requested?"

"Yes," replied the orc, pointing into the shadows of the tower.

"Bring them here and let me see."

The orc and another walked into the shadows. The sounds of growling and chains rattling could be heard, and soon after, the two emerged into the light pulling a chain tied around two wolf pups and two female wolves. Grossard's lips pulled back over his ragged teeth in a callous snarl as he watched the wolves lunge and bite at their captors.

"At last we meet," Grossard addressed the wolves. "I don't

know how much you know or what Rellik has told you, so you may or may not be aware he was my right-hand man. He was quite good at what he did, actually—most of the time. I never imagined he would fail me." Grossard let out a heavy sigh. "But alas, he did … and with such a simple task. Tsk, tsk. Who would've thought?" Grossard tried for a look of regret, but couldn't pull it off. "All I asked of him was to bring me a boy—a small, half-human boy. Was that too much to ask?"

Joliet's hand flew to her mouth to hide her anguish, as Grossard paused and raised his eyebrows at the wolves. He turned his back and walked away as he continued, "To think a young boy such as that was able to defeat the mighty Rellik." Grossard whirled back and glared at the wolves. "It's a disgrace I tell you! But what's more, his failure almost cost me everything. There's no forgiveness for that. Someone has to pay. And since Rellik is no longer with us, you, his family, will take his place."

Grossard pointed to the smallest pup. "Bring me that one first."

The orc unlocked the chain around the pup and dragged him to Grossard. The pup growled and yipped as it tried to resist.

Grossard looked down with scorn and laughed. "You have spunk. I like that." He picked the pup up by the scruff of its neck. It immediately twisted and sank its teeth into his arm. Grossard's face lit up, but he showed no sign of distress. "Yes, it's a shame. You might have been greater than your father one day."

"I am here, Grossard. You can release my son."

All eyes flew to the oversized shadow and the single gleaming yellow eye at the gate.

Grossard leisurely turned without releasing the pup. "So Rellik … you finally decided to join us? And here I thought you were dead. So have you brought me the prince to redeem yourself then?"

Rellik stepped forward into the light and a loud murmur spread through the crowd. His left eye was swollen shut from a deep gash above it, his left leg was twice the size of the right, and the large open wounds on his neck and shoulder were oozing blood and matting his coat.

"The boy was either lost in the great lake or he has been taken to Avalon. The threat is gone and I've fulfilled your orders. So let my son go," Rellik demanded.

Grossard studied the mighty wolf for a moment. He could see Rellik's strength was failing. Silently, he instructed several of the mercenaries to circle behind the wolf to block any escape. The creatures retreated into the shadows and disappeared without being noticed.

"I'm afraid that isn't good enough. What you say may be true. The prince may be lost in the lake, but until I know for certain he is dead, he remains a threat." Grossard shook his head. "I must say, I'm deeply disappointed. You of all creatures should know someone in my position cannot let this kind of insubordination slide. Who would respect me if I did?"

Rellik lifted his head high. "I'm ready to take my punishment, but my family has nothing to do with this. Let them go."

Grossard snickered and raised the pup higher in the air. "Now there again you are wrong. Your blunder has caused me distress. But fortunately, it seems fate has taken my side, and in spite of your bungling mess, success is at my fingertips." He looked down his nose and lifted his eyebrows. "However, I cannot say the same for you. As your mistakes almost cost me everything, I will take everything from you, including the life of all whom you hold dear."

Grossard let out a menacing cackle and flicked the pup into the sky. Its legs flailed as it arced through the air and landed in the middle of the roaring blaze. The pup screamed out in pain and its mother let out a heart-wrenching howl.

Without missing a beat, Rellik lunged into the fire after the pup. The flames licked at his fur, but he was past the point of feeling pain. He grabbed his son in his teeth, the heat of the fire scorching his lungs, and jumped out of the flames a living torch. Joliet screamed and rushed to where Rellik dropped the pup on the ground, patting out the flames with her gown, as Rellik rolled in the dirt to extinguish his own flames.

Smoke rose from Rellik's seared flesh, but he managed to pull himself over to Joliet and the pup. The left side of his body was burned raw, but out of his right eye he could see his son was alive and not mortally injured. With that knowledge, he collapsed and surrendered to the darkness.

Grossard laughed. "You're pathetic, Rellik. It's not going to be any fun killing you now. Though it might be fun to let you watch the rest of your family die." Grossard's onyx eyes glowed red in the firelight. "Bring me the young female," he ordered.

The creature nodded and turned to retrieve the wolf. A mere sliver of the moon could be seen just above the horizon. "Moon," the creature grunted, pointing to the orange light.

Grossard turned and stared at the moon as if he'd never seen anything like it before. A dastardly smile spread across his face and he whipped back to face Oseron, putting Rellik and his family to the side for the moment.

"Your time has come, Oseron. Pick up your sword and defend yourself!"

Chapter 48

Deston stopped when he reached the top of the stairs. From the new vantage point he had a clear view of the door and could see for certain no one was guarding it. That was a relief, yet at the same time, it was troubling. If he were holding someone as important as the king of the fae, he would have a guard at every entrance. Was Grossard that sure of himself, or that stupid? Deston prayed it was the latter.

He took a big breath, held it in, and put his foot out to step down, but Margaux grabbed his arm and stopped him. His nerves were already on edge and the unexpected touch startled him. He jumped and reared back, bringing his fist around to strike. At the sight of her pale face, he pulled his hand back with a start.

Margaux's eyes were glassy as she opened her mouth to say something, but no words came out. He could see she was scared and he was scared too. Leaning in, he put his arm around her and gave her a quick hug, surprising himself as much as her. Then, as his face turned red, he turned back and hurried down the stairs.

Margaux shivered with trepidation and looked warily at the chapel, then followed him down the steps. At the bottom, she shadowed Deston across an open section of the courtyard to a pile of debris and crouched behind it as he assessed the entryway.

He looked over his shoulder, signaling his intentions, and darted across another wide stretch of open ground, ducking into an arched foyer. He plastered his back against the stone wall and released the breath he'd been holding. His heart was pounding wildly against his ribs. He took a couple of deep breaths to calm his nerves before motioning for Margaux to join him. At his signal, she bolted across the short distance and flattened herself against the opposite wall.

Deston caught her eye, nodded and looked down at the door latch. In a matter of minutes he was going to see his mother again. All he had to do was open the door. But his hand froze as he reached for the latch. He stared at the handle, willing his hand to move. It wouldn't.

Just open the door, he told himself and flexed his fingers. But he couldn't get the thought out of his head that Grossard was waiting for him on the other side. That was the only logical reason he could think of as to why there were no guards around. He closed his eyes as doubts infiltrated his mind. It seemed impossible just a week ago the only adversary he had to worry about was Larry, not a monster who wanted to kill him and his whole family.

What if I can't beat Grossard? Is this the end? He grimaced and pushed that thought away. *It can't be. Everyone says I can win, even the Lady of the Lake. So I might as well find out if they're right.*

Taking a long, deep breath, Deston opened his eyes and reached for the latch with a trembling hand. It slowly lifted with a soft metallic scrape and the door sagged in release, sending a barrage of crumbled mortar raining down. He pulled Caluvier from its scabbard, held it in front of him, and pushed the door in with his shoulder. The door gave a small groan and swung open to reveal a dark entryway. He squinted to see through the darkness. The walls shifted with a loud creak and another shower of mortar dust along with a few chunks of plaster came down in front of him.

"Get my pocketknife out of the backpack and turn on the light," he whispered.

He felt a tug on his back as Margaux complied. Seconds later a small stream of light burst through the darkness, illuminating the stark room.

Deston took the penlight and moved it across the walls and into all four corners. The remains of a tattered, faded tapestry hung in shreds on the wall facing the door and a large wooden beam hung down from the ceiling in the corner. Other than that, the room was empty. Cautiously, he stepped over the threshold. Margaux stepped in right behind him. Keir said his parents were being held in the upper room of the tower, but he saw no access to the upper level from where he stood. He took another few steps into the room and swung the light to the right where a door to a narrow hallway stood open. At the far end of the hall he could see a stairwell leading up.

Deston's heartbeat was echoing off his eardrums as he started toward the hall, but he still heard the soft thud behind him. He turned around with a jerk, swinging the light around with him, but there was nothing behind him—even Margaux was gone. The blood drained from his face as he gaped at the empty room.

Someone's taken Margaux!

As he took a staggering step toward the open door, his foot caught on something on the floor. He tilted the light down and saw Margaux lying in a heap at his feet. He jerked back with a gasp and the light fell from his hand, landing with a loud clank on the stone floor next to Margaux's head. He quickly snatched it up and aimed it at the entrance, expecting to see whoever had attacked her standing there. The doorway was empty, but he didn't take his eyes away from it as he squatted down and gave Margaux a gentle shake.

"What's the matter? You need to get up." When she didn't respond, his throat tightened. "Come on—this is no time to fool around."

When she still didn't respond, he rolled her onto her back. Her eyes were closed and her breathing was labored. He put two fingers on her neck. Her pulse was so weak he could barely feel it. A sharp pain gripped his heart and his throat began to close.

"Margaux, wake up. I can't do this without you," he whispered.

She laid motionless on the floor and the walls suddenly seemed to be closing in on them. He looked frantically from side to side. He needed air and he had to get Margaux out of there.

Jamming Caluvier back in its scabbard, he put the penlight between his teeth, slid his hands under Margaux's arms, and dragged her through the door and out into the courtyard. Knowing he couldn't haul her back up the stairs, he pulled her to a pile of debris and crawled under a large stone that was extending over the top of another. He pulled her in next to him, cradled her head in his lap, and absentmindedly patted her head as if she were a dog.

"Oh God, oh God, oh God," he murmured.

The thought of losing Margaux on top of everything else was more than he could bear. He was responsible for her and he had let her down. A tear leaked from his eye and traveled down his cheek. As it dropped onto Margaux's forehead, she stirred. Her movement startled Deston back to his senses and he leaned over her just as her eyes opened.

She blinked a couple of times and looked around in confusion. "What happened? Where am I?" she asked.

Deston hurriedly swiped his hand across his eyes and sniffed. "You passed out or something"

Margaux blinked again and wrinkled her nose as she tried to understand. "All I remember is stepping into a dark room. I felt really weak and lightheaded and I couldn't move or breathe. That's all I remember." She frowned and looked confused. "Where are we?"

"At the monastery. I pulled you out to the courtyard. I thought someone had hurt you, or—"

From the front of the monastery, a heart-wrenching howl split the air. Deston and Margaux both jumped. A second later, a woman screamed. Margaux sat up as Deston cried out, "Mom!"

Chapter 49

Deston bolted out from under the shelter and ran as fast as he could over the chunks of debris scattered throughout the courtyard. He was no longer worried about being seen. His only concern was getting to his mother. She was the one who screamed, he knew it without a doubt. His heart was beating in his throat as he raced along the side of the building.

Margaux lunged out after him, running frantically to catch up before he did something he would regret. He'd almost made it to the front by the time she caught up to him and grabbed him by the arm, pulling him down behind the remnants of a wall at the side of the tower. Deston reacted like a wild man, clawing at her hand to get free, but Margaux held on and wouldn't let go.

"Deston, don't be stupid. You can't help your mama if you're taken captive too," she cried out in a loud whisper.

The mention of Joliet jolted Deston back to sanity and he went still. The wild look remained in his eyes, but he took a deep breath and lifted his hand in a show of surrender.

From the other side of the wall, a booming voice yelled. "Your time has come, Oseron. Pick up your sword and defend yourself!"

Together, Deston and Margaux rose and peered over the wall. Margaux's hand flew to her mouth to keep from making a sound as she gazed upon the horrifying scene. In the middle of the court-yard, in front of a huge bonfire, was the same gigantic wolf that had attacked them at the lake. Only now, one side of the wolf's fur was burnt away and his raw skin was charred black. Next to the wolf, a beautiful woman with long black hair cradled a smaller wolf that was whimpering pitifully as she stroked its head. The woman's tear-streaked face was turned toward a monstrous creature standing over a man lying on the ground.

"Get up, Oseron," Grossard yelled, waving his sword in the air. "You have to fight me so I can claim the throne and receive the power of the Crystal."

Oseron pushed himself onto one elbow and calmly looked up at his nemesis. "I won't fight you. And you know if you kill me in cold blood, you'll never be able to hold the Crystal," he replied weakly.

As Oseron lifted up, Deston recoiled. Oseron's face was deeply wrinkled from age, and his long, straggly, gray hair fell limp about his thin shoulders. Deston blinked several times, thinking it had to be a mistake. This couldn't be his father. Oseron was the greatest warrior of all time, not an old man so frail he could barely rise up.

"So the mighty Oseron is a coward after all, just as I expected," Grossard spat.

Oseron paused to gather the strength to answer. "Your taunts don't bother me. It is you who has taken the coward's way out by imprisoning me in this monastery. What glory and respect do you think you'll receive when others learn you had to first strip my strength and powers in order to defeat me?"

"I could conquer you anytime, anywhere, and you know it," Grossard roared, his temper flaring. He planted the tip of his sword in the dirt at Oseron's feet and leaned casually on the hilt, pushing it deep into the earth. "But what do I care what others think? Once you're dead and I'm king, no one will dare say a thing against me. If they do, they'll pay for it dearly. The realms will have no choice but to respect me. So let's end this now." He yanked the sword out of the dirt and stepped back. "Stand and give me the pleasure of watching you die."

Oseron's face bore no expression as he gazed up at Grossard. "You might as well kill me where I lie, for it'll be the same whether I stand against you or not. Either way, you'll be killing me in cold blood, and the Crystal will never be yours. Do what you will, but I will not fight you."

"Oh, but I think you will. You *will* fight me or else watch as I kill your lovely queen," Grossard sneered.

Joliet screamed as one of the guards roughly pulled her to her feet, pinned her arms behind her back and gave her a hard shove forward. Grossard caught her around the waist, flipped her around and held his sword to her throat.

Oseron lurched to his feet, using all the strength he had left. However, before he could say or do anything more, a cry rang out from the side of the tower.

"Nooo!" Deston screamed and shot into the open before Margaux could stop him.

The courtyard went deathly quiet and all eyes turned to the small figure running from the shadows. Deston had taken everyone by surprise and no one was sure what to do.

As soon as Deston came into the light, a voice entered his head. *"Go back, Deston. You shouldn't be here. Run away as far as you can while you still have the chance,"* Joliet pleaded, her voice trembling with fear.

Deston came to a halt and their eyes met. "No, I won't go. Not without you," he answered out loud.

Joliet's face fell and she wilted in despair, but her eyes continued to plead with him even though she knew it hopeless. He was too much like his father.

Grossard knew Deston the minute he laid eyes on him, as the resemblance between father and son was too obvious to deny. "Well, it looks like we're going to have a little family reunion after all," he said. Letting go of Joliet, he pushed her aside and turned to face Deston.

Joliet rushed to Oseron, putting an arm around his waist to support him as she guided him to a pile of debris. She helped him down and leaned him against the stone for support and pulled the sword from his belt as she released him. With a fierce look on her face, she turned and charged at Grossard, but was instantly halted by an invisible barrier. She stumbled backward and looked confused for a moment before realizing what had happened.

"Release me!" Joliet screamed, kicking her feet and beating her fists against the invisible wall, but her efforts were fruitless. There was nothing she could do. Her gaze went to Deston and a look of pain and fear swept across her face as her knees buckled and she crumbled to the ground, choking back a sob.

Margaux, still hiding behind the wall, pressed her hand against her mouth to stifle a scream as the monster turned to face Deston. Her stomach rose into her throat and she felt as if she would gag, but she couldn't tear her eyes away. She'd heard Grossard was hideous, but the monstrous sight was even more than she expected.

Deston was also taken aback by Grossard's looks, but he didn't back down. "I'm not going to let you hurt my mom ... and dad," he stammered, trying to sound brave.

Grossard was amused. "Is that so? And you're going to stop me all by yourself?"

"No ... Caluvier is going to help me," Deston said, sliding the sword from its scabbard.

Grossard's amusement vanished in a heartbeat at the sight of the sword. The myth of Caluvier was well known throughout the high realm. No one knew for certain whether it was true or not, but his men weren't anxious to find out and hastily retreated to the wall.

Bolstered by their reaction, Deston stepped forward, artfully swinging the sword in front of him. Grossard took a step backward, then stopped.

"Hah! You expect me to believe the priestess gave you the sword that holds the power of the immortals? A mere boy who's half human?" he laughed. "I dare say, the likes of you would never be allowed to step a foot in Avalon."

Deston paused and glanced at the sword. Grossard obviously knew more about it than he did, and based on Grossard's initial reaction, he was scared of it. Deston's confidence rose. He flipped the hair off his forehead with a jerk of his head, exposing the mark Evienne had left there.

"You won't be laughing much longer if you don't let them go. Evienne gave me Caluvier so I could crush you. And you and I both know it can do the job."

Grossard's bravado dissolved again and his eyes narrowed as he ogled the sword. The stories about it were numerous, but as far as he knew that's all they were—stories.

"Caluvier is very powerful. You know that. I don't want to have to hurt you, so just let my ... let the queen and king go and no one will have to get hurt," Deston continued his bluff.

Grossard glared at Deston, then threw his head back and let out a hearty guffaw. An evil glint sparked in his eye as he lifted his sword and took a step forward.

Oseron pushed himself up from the pile of debris and stumbled forward. "Grossard, I will fight you," he yelled forcibly.

Both Grossard and Deston's heads swiveled to stare at the old man. Despite his weakness, Oseron held himself tall and proud.

A sinister leer cut across Grossard's face. "Well, isn't this a nice treat. I'm so glad you've changed your mind, Oseron. It wouldn't be a true victory without your participation."

"I'm glad to oblige. But I will only fight if you let my son go," Oseron replied.

"Tsk, tsk. You should already know I'm no fool. You should also know I can't let the prince go. If he lives, the throne will be his along with the Crystal, even after I kill you."

"You're wrong. As king, it is in my power to choose my successor. Let Deston go and I'll give you the authority and the crown."

Grossard eyed Oseron maliciously, then shook his head. "You never have understood, have you? I don't want you to give me the throne. I want to take it from you, just as much as I want to watch you suffer as you die," he sneered, and without warning he ran at Oseron.

Joliet threw Oseron his sword just as Grossard lunged. Oseron deflected the blow, but the effort robbed him of his last bit of strength and he fell to his knees.

"Run, Deston. You must go while I keep Grossard occupied. Return to our realm and prepare the others. You're their only hope now," Oseron spoke inside Deston's head.

Deston's eyes traveled from Oseron to Joliet. At that same moment, Grossard let out a blood-chilling scream, lunged forward, and drove his sword deep into Oseron's chest. Joliet screamed and ran to Oseron, catching him in her arms as he fell sideways.

The blood drained from Deston's face and he choked on his breath. In the next instant, Grossard turned and rushed at him with his sword flashing. A blue streak of light ran up Caluvier's blade, lighting up the runes and Deston instinctively reacted. He dodged to the left and leapt behind the rushing monster. Grossard flipped around in the blink of an eye and the two swords met blade to blade with a resounding clang.

The blow should have easily knocked the sword out of Deston's hand as Grossard was three times bigger, but Caluvier took the force of the strike and Deston felt little more than a quiver. He felt strangely energized with the sword's power pulsing through him and lunged and parried, blocking Grossard's thrusts and matching every move as if he had been born with a sword in his hand.

((●))

Margaux's heart nearly stopped when Grossard ran his sword through Oseron and then charged at Deston. Grossard was so much bigger and so much stronger she didn't see how Deston could survive. Not wanting to watch, she looked down and spotted the backpack lying at her feet. *Merde, the fae box!*

Grabbing up the pack, she tore the zipper apart and flipped it upside down. The items poured out on the ground and she frantically rummaged through them until she located the tiny, green box. She waited for it to return to its original size, then held her breath and prayed it would provide something to help Deston. Her chest was tight with expectation, but as she flipped the lid and looked into the empty box, her hand flew to her mouth and a sob caught in her throat.

"Oh no, please, there has to be something," she pleaded softly to the unseen forces of the box.

In stunned silence, she turned the box upside down and every which way, looking for a hidden compartment. Her shoulders began to shake and tears streamed down her cheeks. She had opened the box for the third time. Deston's last hope was ruined, and there was nothing left to help him.

The sound of the clanging blades suddenly quieted and an eerie silence filled the air. Margaux wiped her hand across her eyes and peered over the wall, expecting to find Deston dead on the ground like his father. However, to her surprise, he was still standing face-to-face with Grossard. Each held their swords high, but neither made a move.

(((●)))

"I see you are indeed in possession of Caluvier." The corners of Grossard's mouth pulled back in a fake smile. "Actually, I'm glad. Killing your father wasn't nearly as much fun as I expected it to be. It was too easy. I've always preferred a little challenge. Moreover, when I kill you in a fair fight, no one will be able to deny me the right to the Crystal or to Caluvier."

Deston was lightheaded from the battle and scarcely aware of what had happened. He glanced at Joliet, whose face was white and streaked with dirt and tears as she held Oseron in her arms. Oseron was still and his eyes were closed, but to Deston's surprise, a male voice entered his head.

"You can win this battle, my son. You have the power. All you have to do is turn his ego against him. His strength is false. Goad him into using his dark powers. That will be his undoing."

Deston could see Oseron wasn't breathing, but the voice sounded just like him, but with a strange accent. *"But I don't have any powers. I don't know what to do,"* Deston silently answered back.

"It's alright, I am here with you. I will show you the way and we'll do this together," the voice responded.

Deston's eyes moved to Grossard. He swallowed hard and opened his mouth, but from where the words came from he didn't know. "You'll never possess the Crystal. Your powers are weak. Even Morgane attested to that. She proclaimed it was pointless to try to teach you the arts as you didn't have the skills to use them. The whole realm knows that now and you're nothing but a laughingstock."

Grossard tensed, his fake smile sliding off his face. "You're too much like your father, boy. But let me remind you who is standing and who is dead. My powers are already greater than your father's ever were. And once the dark energy fills the Crystal I'll become invincible," Grossard sneered, his whole body trembling with suppressed rage.

"I doubt that. And I'm not scared of you," Deston added, understanding what the voice wanted him to do. "I know the truth. Evienne told me you're a fake, and you're too stupid to know how to use your powers, so what do I have to be scared about? You'll never gain the powers of the dark that you want, even with the Crystal. You're a freak and that's all you'll ever be."

Grossard's scream of fury pierced the night sky as he raised his arms over his head. His body began to swell in front of Deston's eyes. Deston tilted his head back and watched as the monster expanded into a giant.

"Do you doubt my powers now, boy? You're just an insignificant little bug to me and I could squash you whenever I want," he roared, snatching Deston around the waist and hoisting him into the air before Deston had time to react. "But before you die, I'll give you a small sample of the dark power you claim I do not have."

A strong smell of sulfur wafted through the air and roiling black clouds rolled in from all sides. Grossard's insane laughter blended with the roar of the wind as gigantic hunks of debris from the ruins flew across the courtyard. The ancient chapel moaned in distress and the trees were uprooted and tossed aside like matchsticks.

Deston kicked and thrashed about, trying to get free, but his arms were pinned to his side.

Grossard issued another round of gleeful cackles and his eyes sparked with malice. Then his lips slowly curled back and he raised his other arm in a theatrical show of triumph. The winds instantly stopped and an ominous quiet blanketed the courtyard as he held the pose.

Deston stopped struggling and looked up into Grossard's hideous face. A tic appeared beneath Grossard's right eye and quickly spread to the corner of his mouth. A second later, Deston could feel Grossard's hand twitching as well.

Grossard looked down at his arm in utter disbelief. His face turned a beet red and with a screech of indignation, he brought his raised arm down. A bolt of lightning streaked out of the sky straight toward Deston.

It happened so fast, Deston didn't have time to do anything more than raise Caluvier. The blade, taking the full force of the hit, became a brilliant, white light, but Deston didn't feel the electrical current at all, for the beam ricocheted off and hit Grossard in the center of his chest.

A deafening boom echoed throughout the courtyard, blowing Deston out of Grossard's grasp. He flew backward through the air and landed in a heap on the far side of the courtyard. He coughed and gasped for a breath as he rolled to his back. His head ached and there was a loud ringing in his ears as he stared up at the night sky, not knowing what he was looking at. He put his hands on either side of his head to stop the spinning and sat up with a moan. He blinked at the gaping hole on the other side of the yard and the faint wisps of smoke rising up from the dirt, but nothing registered in his brain, not even the fact that Grossard and his men were gone.

As soon as the lightning hit Grossard, the force field holding Joliet back vanished. She dashed across the yard and wrapped Deston in her arms as tears streamed down her cheeks. Deston leaned against her shoulder, but wasn't actually aware of who she was either. His mind had shut down from the shock and the only thing he was cognizant of was that someone was holding him.

Feeling Deston's limp body, Joliet pulled back and did a quick assessment. Other than a few scratches, he didn't appear to have any injuries, but it was harder to assess the emotional damage. Prying Caluvier from his grip, she flung it away and gently brushed his hair off his face.

"I had no idea the Elders would let you come by yourself," she said, tilting his face up so she could look into his blank eyes. "When I saw you run out from the shadows alone, I almost had a heart attack."

Deston looked into his mother's face with no recognition, but she knew the shock would wear off soon enough. She lifted her finger and traced the outline of the crescent moon on the bridge of his nose. As she did, he began to tremble uncontrollably. He blinked rapidly and slowly her face took form. As his eyes cleared and he realized it was her, he collapsed in her arms with a sob.

Chapter 50

Margaux stepped out from behind the debris without bothering to wipe the tears off her cheeks. She wanted to run to Deston, but held back to give him a few moments alone with his mother. She looked at the giant hole where Grossard had stood moments before and still couldn't believe Deston had managed to survive.

As she stared, a thin, dark hand reached out of the smoldering dirt. Then a small, snake-like head rose up through the smoke as well. Margaux recoiled and her heart skipped a beat. Grossard was still alive. The lightning strike had only stripped away the spell that had given him his intimidating size, leaving him a short, squatty replica of his former self. But there was no denying it was Grossard. Margaux opened her mouth to scream out a warning, but fear paralyzed her throat and only a small, weak squeak came out.

Grossard crawled out of the hole and shook his head, his black eyes glowing red from the firelight. Dazed and confused, he staggered drunkenly. When his gaze landed on Deston and Joliet embracing, it all came back to him in a flash. His face turned a peculiar shade of purple as a torrent of pure rage swept through him.

"Son of Oseron, you have not defeated me," he hissed through bared teeth.

Out of the corner of his eye, he caught the glimmer of his sword lying in the dirt at the edge of the hole. He hobbled to the weapon, picked it up and let out an ear-splitting howl.

Deston and Joliet were wrapped up in their reunion and didn't see Grossard emerge from the hole. But at the sound of Grossard's scream, they jerked around in unison.

At the same moment, Margaux's voice came back. "Nooo!" she screamed and sprinted toward the group. She knew she was too far away to get to Caluvier in time, and she had no other weapon, but she still had the green box in her hand. In desperation, she hurled the box at Grossard, hoping to distract him, but as soon as the box left her hand, she knew she had missed her mark. The box fell short and landed on the ground directly in front of Grossard. It then exploded.

The force of the blast, directed at Grossard, propelled him backward through the door of the chantry. He landed on the remnants of the altar and smoke instantly rose from the parts of his body that touched the stone. Letting out a blood-curdling scream, he twisted and squirmed in pain and blindly groped for the edge of the altar. When his fingers found it, he pulled himself over and tumbled to the floor.

Grossard could feel the life rapidly draining from his body and knew death would soon follow if he didn't get out. Gathering all his strength, he threw himself onto his stomach, reached out, digging his claws into the wood, and pulled with all his might. He moved a couple of inches forward, but then his strength gave out. Weak and dying, he lifted his head and croaked, "Help me."

Out in the courtyard, Rellik struggled to his feet and crossed the distance to the chantry door. As his shadow settled over Grossard, Grossard looked up through bloodshot eyes. "Rellik, help me," he begged.

Rellik swayed, but managed to stay on his feet. It was an effort for him to speak and his voice came out as a raspy whisper, "You want me to help you?"

"If get me out of here, I'll reward you whatever you wish."

Rellik sneered. "Yes, I'll receive my wish all right, but I doubt it's what you have in mind."

As he started forward, his legs buckled beneath him and he fell to his knees, but he pushed himself right back to his feet. His muscles were quivering, but he still lunged at the columns supporting the roof. The building was already weak due to years of neglect, and the windstorm Grossard created had added to its instability.

"No, Rellik, no!" Grossard cried out as Rellik reared back and bashed into the column a second time with his last ounce of strength.

Nothing happened for several seconds. Then the support creaked and gave way, sending plaster and timbers from the roof showering down, burying both Grossard and Rellik in a pile of debris and a large cloud of dust.

As Grossard's cry faded, Joliet put her arms protectively around Deston and Margaux and turned them away from the gruesome sight. Never in her life had she wished anyone harm, but after all the years of fear and hiding, she couldn't help but feel immensely elated that it was finally over. She raised her eyes to the sky in gratitude and her body went rigid. The moon was already more than half visible.

Deston felt his mother stiffen and pulled back anxiously. "What's the matter?"

"Your father—we have to get him back into the high realm before the moon fully rises. Come, we must hurry. Can you help me carry him?"

"There's no need for that. We'll carry him and you," said a voice from the gate of the courtyard. Joliet, Deston, and Margaux looked around to face four sets of glowing eyes. "It's the least we can do. You saved our pack. Now we will help you save yours," the voice added, as one by one the wolves moved forward into the light.

Joliet didn't flinch or take time to question the offer. She knew they'd never make it through the gateway in time if they tried to carry Oseron on their own. "Help me get your father on the back of that wolf," she called to Deston.

Deston ran to his father's side and ducked under his shoulder as Joliet took Oseron's other arm. Together they lifted Oseron onto the back of the largest wolf. When Oseron was positioned, Margaux pulled his arms around the wolf's neck and tied his wrists together with her belt to anchor him in place. As soon as he was secure Joliet climbed up behind to hold him on.

Margaux ran to the next wolf and climbed on top as Deston ran to the third. As he lifted his leg over the wolf's back, a flash of light at the side caught his eye. He looked around. The yard was empty, but Caluvier was lying in the dirt where Joliet had tossed it.

He ran to the sword and as he bent to retrieve it, he looked through the door of the chantry. There was no sign of Grossard amidst the wreckage, but the tip of Rellik's tail was sticking out from under a pile of broken beams and sagging plaster. As he stared, another section of the wall fell in and a thick cloud of dust billowed up.

"Deston, hurry, we must go," called Joliet.

Deston turned away from the scene and caught his mother's eye. She looked more frightened now than she did when she faced Grossard. He pushed Caluvier into its scabbard and ran to the wolf, jumping onto its back in one swift move. The four wolves bounded through the gate and ran like they were in a race for their lives. In no time at all they were rounding the bend, approaching the grove of trees where the ogres were waiting.

The ogres heard the pounding of feet and stepped out of the trees to see who was coming. A look of confusion flickered across their faces at the sight of the wolves with riders on their backs. The ogres stepped out of the way as the pack sped by, having no idea who it was and not interested enough to find out. It didn't concern them anyway, as the wolves were coming from the wrong direction. They were still waiting for the prince to come through from the high realm and they planned to stay put until he did, just as Grossard ordered.

Chapter 51

The wolves approached the gateway without slowing and ran straight into the space between the gorse bushes in single file, with the one carrying Deston last. Just as before, Deston felt the pull and was lightheaded as the lights flashed before his eyes. He shrugged it off and in the next instance he was back in the high realm.

As the wolves slid to a stop, Lilika and Keir appeared and rushed to Oseron. Lilika cut through Oseron's wrist bindings and Keir caught him as he slid off sideways. Together they carried him to a soft patch of grass and gently laid him on his back. Joliet and Deston knelt at his side as Lilika and Keir stepped back.

Deston's heart ached as he looked down at his father. He'd not gotten the chance to actually meet the man and now he was gone. It was so unfair. Blinking rapidly, he fought back his emotions as the last slice of the moon lifted above the horizon.

Joliet silently rose and took his arm, lifting him to his feet and away from Oseron. The mark at the bridge of his nose tingled as he lifted his eyes to the large, bright ball wavering in the sky, and tears blurred his vision. Everyone had been wrong. He wasn't good enough after all. How would he ever be able to face his grandmother and the people of Tir na-nÓg again?

The moonlight sliced a path through the trees as if there was nothing standing in its way and softly enveloped Oseron's body in a radiance that highlighted his features. The lines of worry previously etched on his face dissolved and he looked at peace, as if he were sleeping. The Crystal embedded in the medallion that was resting on the center of his chest was lifeless, black and cloudy. Even the chain looked dull and tarnished.

I'm so sorry I failed you, Deston thought and gulped in a breath as his grief threatened to consume him. He wished he had the power to go over and shake his father awake, but even if he did, it was too late for that.

A spark suddenly flicker in the center of the Crystal. A second later, a white ray shot into the night sky and shone brighter than a spotlight. The light was intense, but Deston had no trouble looking directly into its brilliance. The hairs on his arms stood on end as the air became electrified and the light surrounding Oseron began to change, turning more opaque until Deston could no longer see his father. The light then started to gyrate, shifting and sculpting and taking on the exact shape of Oseron's body.

Deston strained to see through the glow, but it was as if Oseron was gone and there was nothing left but light. The grief he'd felt moments earlier also dissipated and a sense of peace took its place. He closed his eyes, letting the serenity fill him. When he opened them again, there was a small pink ball of light levitating over Oseron's chest directly above his heart. The ball pulsed and gathered in strength and size until it covered his whole chest. It then floated up toward the heavens.

Deston's gaze followed the pink ball above the tree line and higher until it became a bright shining star in the darkness. Its points of light stretched across the sky from one end of the horizon to the other, and then began to shrink, pulling its light back into itself until it was nothing more than a small dot in the sky. Just before it completely went out, the dot burst into a blinding light, as bright as a supernova, covering the sky with trillions of small dancing specs of pink dust. The specs stayed suspended for a moment, then slowly descended like rain, covering the earth and everything on it.

As the pink dust settled over Deston, a feeling of love and joy spouted in every cell of his body. His worries and sadness evaporated and he felt more alive than he ever felt before. It was an amazing feeling and he wanted it to last forever.

He turned to his mother to see if she was experiencing the same joy, but her attention was elsewhere. Deston followed her stare and his heart skipped a beat when he saw that the old man they had brought back through the gateway was gone. Lying in his place was a handsome, young man with a strong, square jaw, wavy blonde hair, and broad shoulders. In the middle of the man's chest was a brilliant, clear crystal medallion glistening in the moonlight.

The young man opened his eyes and blinked several times. He then lifted his head and looked straight into Joliet's eyes as if he knew she was standing there. A look of love softened his features even more as he spoke, "My love, you're safe." He sat up and reached out. Joliet rushed to him and fell into his embrace.

The moment the two came together, the trees erupted in a blaze of tiny, flickering lights. Deston, too dazed to move, stood awkwardly with a silly grin plastered across his face. His father was alive. And more than that, he wasn't a weak, old man anymore. It was almost too good to be true.

Joliet pulled back and caressed Oseron's cheek, love shining in her eyes. But their intimate moment was cut short when Keir stepped in to help Oseron to his feet.

"Your Majesty, I'm sorry, but I've just received important news. I must ask for a moment of your time in private. It's urgent and cannot wait," Keir said, kneeling on one knee and bowing his head in respect.

Oseron's look turned hard and he squared his shoulders as he nodded his head. When he turned back to Joliet, the softness returned to his eyes. "Forgive me, my love, I must speak with Keir. I'll be right back," he whispered and turned to go, but Joliet stopped him before he could step away.

"Wait. There's someone you must first meet." She took Oseron's arm and turned him to face Deston.

A wave of heat rushed through Deston. He took a step back as his father looked down on him.

"My king, I would like you to meet your son," Joliet said proudly.

An array of emotions sped across Oseron's face, and uncharacteristically, he was at a loss for words. Letting out a nervous laugh, he held out his hand. "I guess I should thank you, son. You saved my life. Your mother told me you were strong, but she didn't tell me you were also brave. I am extremely proud of you."

Deston started to reach out to shake hands; then at the last second, he threw his arms around his father's waist instead.

Overcome with emotion, Oseron closed his eyes and hugged him back. Joliet joined in, wrapping them all together in her arms.

Keir held back, letting them have their moment before interrupting, "Your Majesty, if you please. This cannot wait," he repeated.

Oseron nodded in acknowledgement over Joliet's head, and then gave Deston a smile. "We'll finish this in a moment," he said, ruffling Deston's hair. As soon as he turned to Keir, the smile left his face and the two were engrossed in heavy conversation before they reached the trees.

Deston felt giddy as he watched his father walk away. He'd been waiting his whole life for this moment and a thousand questions were banging around inside his head, but he no longer felt the urgent need to get the answers. He now knew where to find them and he had all the time in the world to do so.

Joliet took both his hands in hers and bent her knees to look into his eyes. "Are you okay, sweetheart?" she questioned, brushing his hair off his forehead.

She had brushed his hair back like that a million times in the past, but this time it sparked an unexpected emotion and Deston suddenly felt like a five-year-old. His throat grew thick and he couldn't speak, which made it all the worse. Lowering his head, he put his arms around her waist and buried his face in her robe so the others wouldn't see his humiliation. Joliet smiled knowingly and wrapped her arms around him in response, resting her chin on the top of his head.

"I guess I should've told you about all this long ago," she said. Deston nodded his head against her chest. "I just didn't think Grossard would try anything so soon. I had hoped I would have a few more years to prepare you."

She took a deep breath. "You know, I saw through Grossard's façade the minute I met him. I tried to tell the fae he was evil, but they just couldn't see it until he killed that poor young man. It scared me so to see how much Grossard hated your father. Then when I learned about you, I knew he would try to use you to get back at Oseron. That's why I had to leave here. If I had stayed, you'd still be a baby and defenseless. Of course, I knew you would have to return to defend your heritage someday—it's your destiny—but I wanted you to have a chance to grow up before that time came." She hesitated and rubbed her cheek against his hair. "It was so hard to leave here, but I don't regret doing so. It was the right thing. I just wish I would have had a warning that Grossard had found us before Rellik showed up."

Her voice broke. "I'm so sorry. If I ever lost you, I ... I don't know what I would do." She squeezed him tighter, but he pushed away.

"You really should have told me, Mom. All that time in Pennsylvania I thought there was something wrong with me. I knew I was different, but I didn't know why."

She blinked back a tear. "I know, honey. It hurt me to see you struggle. But I was trying to protect you. That's one of the flaws of being a mom, I guess. We want to keep our children safe and in doing so, we sometimes try to live their lives for them. I know now I was wrong. Can you forgive me?"

Deston tried to keep a stern face, but he was too happy to make it stick. "Yeah, I guess. It's okay ... I'm okay," he said and meant it.

Joliet bent her knees and looked deep into his eyes as she nodded her head. "Yes, you are." As she pulled him back into another tight hug, Lilika stepped up behind them.

"Your Highness, the king would like you to join him for a moment."

Joliet tensed, realizing it must be important if Lilika addressed her as such. She looked down at Deston, not wanting to leave him alone. "Deston?"

"No, go ahead. Oser—I mean, Dad needs you." It felt strange calling him dad, but it also felt really good.

"We still have a lot to talk about," Joliet added.

"I know. But there's plenty of time, so go ahead. Really ... everything's cool."

She gave him a quizzical look. "Are you sure you're my son and not some imposter?"

He laughed and gave her a push toward Oseron. "Yeah, I'm sure. But I'm not so sure who you are anymore. And that's something we're *definitely* going to talk about later."

Joliet laughed in return and walked away to join Oseron and Keir. Deston watched the look of love spread across Oseron's face as Joliet put her arm around his waist and leaned into him. It was obvious they were very happy. And for the first time in a long time, so was he.

Chapter 52

With a contented sigh, Deston turned and saw Margaux sitting all alone on a rock, staring at her hands. He hurried over and deposited himself next to her. It never occurred to him she'd be anything but as elated as he was, so when she raised her head and he saw her forlorn expression and her red eyes, he was taken aback.

"What's the matter?" he asked, putting his hand over hers.

Margaux sniffed and her lip quivered. "Oh, Deston, I was so scared. I didn't know what to do. That monster killed your father and I thought he was going to kill you too. And ... and there was nothing I could do because the box didn't work for me. And when Grossard got blown up by the lightning and then came back and got buried in the chapel, and the wolves came and brought us back here, and you got your father back ... I was so happy. But now it's all over, and I ... and I don't want..." she couldn't finish as tears clogged her throat. She looked down at her lap and her tears dripped onto Deston's hand.

The air around Deston suddenly pressed in on him and he felt like he'd been put inside a box. He squirmed uncomfortably in his seat, looking around for help. But the others were all huddled in a group. Awkwardly, he put his arms around Margaux and patted her stiffly on the arm as she leaned into his shoulder and cried.

"Ssshhh, it's all right. I was scared too. But you know what? I couldn't have done it without you. I mean that. I know I can be a real jerk sometimes, but that's just because ... well, I've never really had that much to do with girls in the past. I mean ... you're different, and

I'm really glad you were there with me."

Margaux tilted her head up. "You mean it?"

"I hope I'm not interrupting anything," Lilika said, walking up to join them.

Deston flinched and quickly pushed Margaux away as he jumped to his feet in such a hurry, he stumbled backward.

Lilika put her hand out to steady him and bit her lip to keep from laughing. But her merriment came through in her voice. "I thought you'd both like to know Torren was picked up and taken to the healers. His injuries are serious, but he's alive and should completely recover in time. So that's more good news, yes?"

A small squeak escaped from Margaux and fresh tears ran down her cheek.

"I also wanted to tell you how proud I am of you—both of you. You were very courageous. Not many would have, or could have, done what you two did," Lilika continued.

Deston blushed and looked down at his feet. He had never been comfortable receiving praise, and never knew how to respond. He played with the sleeve of his tunic and finally replied. "Yeah, well, I didn't really do anything. It was all Caluvier. If Evienne hadn't given it to me, things would have been a lot different."

Lilika cocked her head to the side. "Didn't Evienne tell you about Caluvier?"

"Yeah, she did. She told me it was made at the same time as Excalibur."

"That's not what I meant. What did she tell you about its powers?" Lilika cut in.

Deston perked up. "She didn't really tell me anything about its powers."

Lilika put her hand on his shoulder. "Deston, all Caluvier does is magnify the powers, strength, and integrity of the person who wields it. That's it. You're the one who defeated Grossard—it was more you than you know."

Deston flinched and his brow furrowed. *It was me? I did that? I have powers?*

"Margaux, you were very brave too," Lilika added, turning her attention to Margaux.

Margaux's eyes filled with new tears and she looked down to hide her embarrassment. "No I wasn't. I didn't do anything. I just watched from behind a wall."

"That's not true. If it weren't for you, Grossard would've finished us all off," Deston exclaimed.

"That was just luck," she mumbled.

Lilika put her hand under Margaux's chin and lifted her face so she could look into Margaux's eyes. "It wasn't luck. There's no such thing as luck. Everything happens for a reason. You were sent on this journey the same as Deston was," Lilika corrected.

Margaux's eyes widened, but then her brow puckered again in doubt.

"Look inside your heart. I know you'll find the truth there. You're not here because of Deston. Your journey—your destiny parallels his, but you weren't brought here for the same reason."

Margaux and Deston looked questioningly at Lilika.

"Let me ask you this … do you remember your mother?" Lilika continued.

Margaux sat up a little straighter. "Of course I do. I just saw her yesterday."

"Not that woman. Your real mother."

Margaux's face turned ghostly white. "My … real mother?"

Lilika knelt down on one knee and took Margaux's hand. At that moment, Oseron and Joliet walked up. Joliet moved behind Deston and wrapped her arms around him, as Lilika looked up and locked eyes with Oseron. After a brief pause, she nodded her head and rose, letting Oseron step into her place in front of Margaux.

This was Margaux's first opportunity to see Oseron up close. She had to tilt her head way back to look into his face, and blushed at his tender look.

"I heard how brave you were back at the monastery and I wanted to thank you for all you've done for my family. I can see you are a good and loyal friend to my son. And good friends are one of the most valuable treasures on this earth, as they are very hard to find," Oseron said.

Margaux's face grew hotter, but she couldn't take her eyes away from his as he continued.

"Your bravery doesn't surprise me, though. Your mother and father were both strong, trustworthy friends of mine."

Margaux winced and the spell was broken. "No, that can't be right." She frowned. "My parents would never be friends with you. They don't believe in you ... um, I mean, they don't believe in faeries in general. They wouldn't even allow me to read or learn anything about faeries. I had to do all that in secret. So I don't see how they could be friends of yours," Margaux exclaimed.

Oseron knelt down on one knee so he was eye level with her. "The people you've been living with aren't your parents."

Margaux reared back and Deston started to reach out to her, but Joliet held him in place.

"Lilika said the same thing a minute ago. I don't understand why both of you would say such a thing. They are my parents," Margaux fired back with a slight tremor in her voice.

"Please hear me out before you jump to conclusions. Your true parents were one of us—one of the fae." Margaux swayed a little and Oseron hurried on. "It's a long story, but I'll explain it as best I can. Your mother was a beautiful young woman with the most incredible, infectious laugh. She made everyone around her feel as if they were the most important person on earth. She was truly special and deeply loved here in Tir na-nÓg."

Oseron looked away for a moment. When he looked back his eyes were glassy. "Jessenia, your mother, had such an enormous heart she even tried to help Grossard, but he abused her kindness and spoiled her good intentions as he did everything else. When he discovered we were going to send him back to his own kind, he used a dark spell on her to get her to agree to become his wife. He was so sure of himself, he never imagined the spell wouldn't work. His failure was quite a blow to his ego. He left Tir na-nÓg on the day she married your father, Jael. It was almost a year later when he reappeared on Jessenia's doorstep and tried again to lure her away with a new spell. She was pregnant with you at the time, but even if she wasn't she would never have gone with him."

Oseron's eyes hardened. "Grossard ..." He hesitated and cleared his throat. "The neighbors close by heard your mother's screams. By the time they got there, your father was dead and Jessenia was gone. Grossard had taken her. He wanted her to suffer and knew the ultimate punishment would be to lose her child right after she lost her husband. You were born the next day. He let her hold you for only a moment, then took you away."

Margaux's eyes filled with new tears. "So where's my mother now?" she asked in a voice barely louder than a sigh.

Oseron squeezed her hand before he went on. "Sadly, Grossard left her on the beach, weak and dying. She'd lost her husband and child and had little will left to live. The only thing that kept her holding on was she wanted us to know what happened so we would look for you. We did our best, but we didn't know where to start. We all assumed Grossard had thrown you into the sea."

Deston listened to the story in stunned silence, unable to imagine what it'd be like to learn your parents had been killed like that. Breaking out of Joliet's hold, he sat down next to Margaux and put his hand on her shoulder to show his support. She turned her head to him, but instead of the look of devastation he expected to see on her face, there was a look of wonder. Tears streamed down her cheeks, but there was happiness in her eyes.

"I knew it," she whispered. "I've known deep down inside for as long as I can remember. I don't look like anyone else in the Labonté family, and they always treated me differently than they did Philippe. Not exactly bad or anything, just ... distant, like they were afraid to get too close to me."

Lilika squeezed Margaux's shoulder and Margaux looked up at her.

"So does this mean I can come back here whenever I want?" Margaux asked.

Lilika knelt beside her and pulled her into her arms. "Of course it does. In fact, you don't ever have to leave if you don't want to. You belong here with us. With me actually ... I'm your aunt."

Margaux pushed back and looked in Lilika's eyes. "You're my..." Fresh tears gathered in her throat and she couldn't finish her sentence. She threw her arms around Lilika's neck and mumbled into her shoulder, "I'd like to stay very much. But I need to go back and explain to my other parents and say goodbye to Philippe."

"Of course. You're free to come and go as you like, and can stay wherever you want for as long as you want," Lilika replied, and laid her cheek on top of Margaux's head as tears pooled in her own eyes.

A loud cheer suddenly erupted and hundreds of faeries of a variety of species appeared out of nowhere to converge on the small group. Two men grabbed Oseron up and hoisted him on their shoulders. Two others lifted Joliet and Deston onto their shoulders.

Songs of jubilation rang through the air as the faeries danced around their guests of honor until a sweet trumpet interrupted the celebration. The crowd instantly quieted and split in two to make a pathway for the transport being carried by four of the Royal Guard. The transport traveled silently through the crowd and stopped in front of the men holding Oseron.

Before anyone could assist her, Titania jumped down and ran to Oseron as he was lowered to the ground. She looked lovingly into his eyes and put a hand on his cheek. They said no words, but Deston knew they were communicating silently in the way he'd come to realize was common with the fae. They stood like that for several minutes; then Titania turned to Deston. Her eyes twinkled as she smiled and held her arms out to him.

Without hesitation, Deston leaned forward and fell into his grandmother's embrace, clasping her around the neck. She hugged him back as though she would never let him go.

"You're your father's son; there's no doubt about it. I know your grand-father is as proud of you as I am," she said inside his head. She gave him another tight squeeze before setting him down and stepping back.

The crowd whistled and cheered and the sound of music rose above it all. Oseron was once again lifted onto the men's shoulders, along with Titania and Deston, and the dancers lead the procession back to Tir na-nÓg.

After traveling only a few feet, Deston looked back and cried out, "No wait."

The entire mob instantly came to a standstill and all eyes flew to him in alarm. "You forgot Margaux," he exclaimed.

Oseron looked over his shoulder at Margaux's hopeful face. "No, we didn't. We'd never forget Margaux. She's one of us," he laughed and the crowd shouted out their approval.

One of the men plucked Margaux away from Lilika and hoisted her onto his shoulder. The crowd let out another cheer and the singing and dancing resumed. Flutes supplied the tune and lead the celebration back toward to the city.

((●))

Keir stepped up behind Lilika and enfolded her in his arms. She leaned back into him and sighed contently.

"You know you're going to have to clean out all that junk in the extra room now. Margaux isn't going to want to live in your squalor," Lilika teased.

Keir frowned and pretended to be upset, but he was too relieved and happy to pull it off. He turned her around to face him and kissed her passionately. When they pulled apart, he grew serious again. "You should've told me about Deston when you first learned of him. I'm your husband and there can be no more secrets between us. I can't look out for you if you're hiding things from me."

Lilika looked up innocently. "I don't know what you're talking about. Why would I ever want to keep anything from you?" Her eyes twinkled mischievously.

Keir raised an eyebrow and studied her. "There's something else you haven't told me, isn't there?"

She played innocent and laughed; then playfully punched him in the arm before stepping into the crowd to join the procession. Keir shook his head and laughed as he ran after her. He knew when he fell in love with her that life would always be interesting.

((●))

As the procession rounded Mirror Lake, Deston looked out over the water. The moonlight reflected off the surface, turning the water into a glass mirror and for just a moment, he thought he saw Evienne's face. He lifted his hand in a wave. The reflection smiled back at him and was gone.

He looked down at Caluvier and fingered the crystal point of the hilt. He still couldn't believe he'd fought Grossard and survived. He lifted his gaze just as Evienne's voice filled his head.

"Well done, Prince Deston of Tir na-nÓg. Well done."

He let her words settle into his head. He didn't feel like a prince, or a fae, for that matter. It would take some time to get used to both, but he had nothing but time now. More importantly, he had his mother back and his father alive to teach him. At that moment, he felt like the luckiest person in the world, or perhaps the entire universe.

Suddenly, a long ago memory popped into his head. It was the ending to the stories Joliet used to tell him every night at bedtime. "And they lived happily ever after, just like us," she used to say. He always laughed when she said that, but now he realized she was serious. And for the first time, he felt like it was true—they really were going to live happily ever after just like in the stories.

Epilogue

Two dark figures wearing long black capes stealthily scaled the rocks beneath the dilapidated castle, carrying a bundle wrapped in a blanket between them. Every so often, a low moan came from the blanket as they jostled the load up and down, climbing over the wet, slippery surface of the rocks.

"Where are we?" a hoarse gravelly voice spoke from within the blanket.

"We're almost to the cave, Master," Gorm replied.

The bundle moaned again and after a moment of silence asked, "What about Oseron? The Crystal?"

Gorm gritted his teeth and looked over his shoulder at Nolef. Nolef stared back in silence, offering no help.

"What happened to Oseron?" Grossard demanded.

"He was taken back to Tir na-nÓg with the queen and the boy. He is alive and the Crystal was renewed with the light," Gorm finally answered.

A pitiful cry rose from the blanket and escalated into a howling screech. "Noo, it can't be!" Another scream of pure agony ripped through the air.

"By the dark god, Erebus, I vow I will get you, Oseron. I will see you and your precious son suffer one day just as I have. I pledge my oath on it!" Grossard's scream echoed off the walls, as the two korrigans carried him into the cave at the water's edge.

A Note From the Author

Thank you for reading the first adventure of the Chronicles of the Secret Prince. I hope you enjoyed it. It would mean a lot to me if you could take just a moment of your time to leave a quick review and let me know your thoughts. And be sure to tell your friends, for in case you didn't know, word of mouth is an author's best friend.

Follow Deston's continuing journey in:
Book II, Once Upon a Darker Time
Book III, How Dark the Light Shines
(Both available now in print and eBook)

And look for my newest science/fantasy:
Next Time I See You

To keep informed on more projects from M.J. Bell, please 'like' my Facebook page, **MJ Bell Author**, or check out my website at **http:www.mj-bell.com.**

Happy reading!

Acknowledgements

So many people have encouraged and helped me along the way to bring this trilogy to life and I would be remiss if I didn't thank them.

To my daughter Tiffany—the first to believe in me. Without you, this book would never have happened.

Aria Keehn, an amazing and incredibly talented artist who's imagination brought my books to life in spectacular color.

Brandy Bell, for all your time and effort in helping to make this book the best it can be.

Jeffrey Bell, for making the coolest website in the history of ever, and for putting up with my constant changes.

With special thanks to Janie, Charmayne, Lisa, Brenda, Laura, Lynette and Jennie, for their boundless faith in me.

And to Tim, who has always been at my side and whom I couldn't live without.

About the Author

M.J. Bell's love of reading and everything magical is what motived her to jump headfirst into a writing career. Her works include an epic fantasy trilogy, *Chronicles of the Secret Prince*, and a science fantasy, *Next Time I See You.*

Her career has also produced several awards, including: a Gold medal in Fantasy from **Mom's Choice Awards**, and the **Indie Book of the Day Award** .

M.J. grew up in Iowa, but now considers Colorado her home where she lives with her husband, Tim. Her growing family has always been her pride and joy and provides her with a great source of inspiration to write and bring a little more magic into the world.

She loves to hear from readers through her FB page at **MJ Bell Author**. Visit her website at **http:www.mj-bell.com** to keep up-to-date on M.J.'s latest project.